Look to the East

THE GREAT WAR
SERIES

Look to the East

MAUREEN LANG

Tyndale House Publishers, Inc.
Carol Stream, Illinois

Visit Tyndale's exciting Web site at www.tyndale.com

Check out the latest about Maureen Lang at www.maureenlang.com

TYNDALE and Tyndale's quill logo are registered trademarks of Tyndale House Publishers, Inc.

Look to the East

Designed by Beth Sparkman

Edited by Sarah Mason

Published in association with WordServe Literary Group, Ltd., 10152 S. Knoll Circle, Highlands Ranch, CO 80130.

Scripture quotations are taken from *The Holy Bible*, King James Version.

Library of Congress Cataloging-in-Publication Data

Lang, Maureen.
  Look to the East / Maureen Lang.
    p. cm. — (The Great War ; no. 1)
  ISBN 978-1-4143-2435-7 (pbk. : alk. paper)
    1. Vendetta—France—Fiction.   2. Villages—France—Fiction.   I. Title.

PS3612.A554L66 2009
813'.6—dc22   2009009857

Printed in the United States of America

15   14   13   12   11   10   09
 7   6   5   4   3   2   1

To my older sister *Laura*,
whose ability to recount the plot of
any book, movie, or television program
helped train me to make sure
I cover all the important parts.

Acknowledgments

I am indebted to Stephanie Broene and Sarah Mason for their talent and insight. Without them this book would be far inferior to what you see.

I would also like to thank my pastors, Scott Chapman, Jeff Griffin, and Matt Furr for not standing in the way as God uses them to teach so many people. Their understanding and ability to communicate God's wisdom has touched my life and is reflected in many of my characters.

I'd also like to thank Charlotte Cardoen-Descamps for her warm hospitality at her wonderful B&B in Poelkapelle, Belgium, and for her passion for knowledge about the First World War. Thank you, too, to Tony Novosel for pointing me to Charlotte to begin with, and to Gordon Hall from the War Research Society who advised us on so many places not to miss while researching occupied territory in Belgium and France.

Special thanks to Siri Mitchell, again, for her friendship, her encouragement, and her help with details relating to the French setting; to Tosca Lee for help with my German phrasing; and to the work of Ben Macintyre in *The Englishman's Daughter*, which first inspired this story.

And always, to my husband, Neil, and my kids, for putting up with me when deadlines loom, for celebrating book covers and boxes of books that come to the door, for making the wait until the Lord returns the best it can be.

Look to the east, where up the lucid sky
The morning climbs! The day shall yet be fair.

We're brothers all, whate'er the place,
Brothers whether in rags or lace,
Brothers all, by the good Lord's grace.

FROM *"BROTHERS ALL"* BY EDGAR A. GUEST

Once, in a little village forgotten by time, there lived two feuding families: the Toussaints and the de Colvilles. Other families inhabited Briecourt in Northern France, but their tranquil lives escape memory.

As with most enduring feuds, no one knows exactly why it began. Some say it was over *une aventure*—an indiscreet love between one man and a woman not his wife. Others insist money was the cause—a squabble between the miller and the baker over the price of flour. Still others recall it beginning with a simple difference of opinion on the faults and merits of Napoleon between two old men sharing a cup of *chocolat.* . . .

It is not, however, the origin but rather the result that matters. One hundred years later, even the purest flour made into the flakiest pastry would leave a bitter taste if made by one clan and sampled by the other.

Except for one brief moment in history, the feud rages to this day. . . .

Part One

AUGUST 1914

1

Briecourt, Northern France

Julitte Toussaint sucked in her breath and shut her eyes, as if by closing off her own vision she, too, might become invisible. Stuck high above the ground where someone so grown—just turned twenty and two—should never be caught, she shot a fervent prayer heavenward. *Please let neither one look up!* She clutched the book-size tin to her chest and went death-still in hopes of going unnoticed.

"... those days may be behind us, Anton. At least for a while." She heard his voice for the first time, the man who had come to visit the only château within walking distance of her village. The man whose blond hair had reflected the sun and nearly blinded her to the rest of his beauty. The perfect nose, the proportionate lips, the blue eyes that, with one glance, had taken her breath away.

Now he was near again, and her lungs froze. She feared the slightest motion might betray her.

She knew the other man was Anton Mantoux without looking. He was the closest thing to aristocracy the town of Briecourt knew. Though Julitte had never spoken to him, she had heard him speak many times. Whenever the mayor called a village meeting, M. Mantoux always held the floor longest.

"You'll go back, Charles? join this insanity when you could fol-low me the other way?"

Charles . . . so that was his name.

"Who would have thought I had a single noble bone in my body?"

M. Mantoux snorted. "You'll follow your foolhardy king, will you?"

"Much can be said about a man—a king, no less—who takes for himself the same risks he asks others to bear. I should never have left Belgium. I know my sister never will. How can I do less?"

"Ah, yes, your beautiful and brave little sister, Isabelle. . . . What is it you call her? Isa?"

"Careful with your thoughts, Anton," said the man—Charles— whose voice was every bit as lovely as his face. "She's little more than a child."

"A child, but not much longer. And then you may have me in the family!"

Feeling a cramp in her leg, Julitte wanted nothing more than to climb down the tree and scurry away. *Let them move on!* she silently pleaded to God. *Send a wind to blow them on their way before—*

As if in instant answer to her prayer, a gust tore through the thick leaf cover of the beech tree in which she hid. In horror she watched the tin, dampened by her perspiring hands, slip from her grasp and take the path designed by gravity. She heard a dull thud as it bounced off the perfect forehead of the taller of the two men below, grazing the blond hair that so intrigued her.

A moment later both men looked up, and she might have thought their surprised faces funny had she planned the episode and still been young enough to get away with such a prank.

"I thank You for the answered prayer of the wind, Lord," she whispered in annoyed submission, "but not for the result, as You well know."

"You there." M. Mantoux's voice was as commanding as ever, and it set her heart to fear-filled pounding. "Come down at once."

Giving up any hope of dignity, Julitte shook away the cramp in one leg, then shinnied along the thick branch until reaching the trunk that was somewhat wider than the span of her arms and legs. Her foot found the knot she knew so well, and in a moment she stood on the ground, pulling at her skirt to cover pantaloons and the single petticoat she owned, a hand-me-down from her adoptive mother. From the corner of her eye she saw the towering blond man bending to retrieve her tin, a look of curiosity on his handsome face.

M. Mantoux stepped in front of Julitte. "What were you doing up there, girl? Who—"

Enlightenment reached his eyes before his voice faded away. Of course he knew who she was; everyone in and around her village knew she was the *étrangère*, the outsider. Not only because at least half of the village wouldn't have welcomed an adopted child of Narcisse Toussaint, but because she had been born far away on the Island of Lepers, off the coast of Greece. Though Julitte had lived among the French villagers for nearly seventeen years, some still whispered of her heritage to this day, to passersby or children too young to already know.

"Come here, Julitte Toussaint." He pointed to a spot a few feet away. "Stand there, not too close."

M. Mantoux had an angry look about him, but she knew he always seemed that way from the curve of his nostrils to the arch in his brow. Even when he laughed—and she had seen him do that once—his face held the edge of ire whether with intent or not.

Intent was there now.

She obeyed his order and stopped where he'd told her, at the same time reaching for her property. The man holding the tin started to extend the item but took a moment to study it before completing the motion. His thumb traced the amateurishly tooled design, fashioned by her adoptive brother. Then he shook it and the items inside rattled. But he did not open it, for which she was silently grateful.

Both had to bend forward to pass the tin between them. He placed it, about the size of one of his hands, into both of hers.

"What were you doing on my property, and what have you there?" M. Mantoux's intimidating manner was the same he'd used when her cousin had lost one of his pigs and found it burrowing holes in the château garden. But behind his intimidation today was a tone familiarly aimed her way—distaste mixed with a hint of the fear common to those who knew only her background and not her. "And why did you accost my guest?"

Julitte wanted to raise her gaze to M. Mantoux, to stare him down as she stared down her brother when he teased her the way brothers could. But M. Mantoux was not her brother. And standing in the handsome stranger's shadow had stolen her courage.

Lowering her gaze, she mustered a respectful tone. "I was in the tree to retrieve the tin and decided to stay there until you passed by, as to escape notice. The breeze whipped the box from my hold." A quick glance at the blond cavalier revealed that his eyes stayed on her. Perhaps he was not so gallant, after all. What sort of man stared so boldly? Despite such thoughts, she knew what she must do. Keeping her eyes downcast, she turned to the handsome man she'd unwittingly troubled. "I offer you all my excuses, *monsieur*."

"Accepted."

The single word was issued softly and with a smile. Julitte let her gaze linger, welcoming his ready forgiveness. Her rapidly beating heart took a new direction.

"My friend is more magnanimous than he need be," M. Mantoux said. "You are aware, Julitte, that this tree is on my property? If you fell and hurt yourself, what should I have done?"

"I expect it would have been entirely my own fault, *monsieur*, and I would blame neither you nor the tree."

"In any case, you're far too old to be climbing like a waif. Narcisse shall hear of this."

"I'm afraid he sent me on my mission before he left once again for the sea, Monsieur Mantoux." She held up the tin. "This is my brother's, you see, and I was told to fetch it and tell him to find another favorite spot to whittle. Closer to home." She didn't mention she had been the one to introduce her brother to this particularly dense and knotty tree.

The stranger—Charles—patted M. Mantoux's shoulder. "There, you see, Anton, it's all perfectly understandable. Why berate the girl?"

Girl. But then, what else should he have called someone dallying about in a tree? Suddenly a vision of having met him under other circumstances filled her head, of her offering a brief and graceful curtsy and extending her hand for him to kiss. They would be formally introduced and have an intelligent conversation about books and history and faraway places. Oh . . .

Instead M. Mantoux dismissed her as the peasant she was, unworthy to be presented to any guest of his noble household. And the two were already walking away.

Charles Lassone glanced back at the girl from the tree, unable to resist one last look. He could tell from her dress—clean despite her foray up to the branches—that she was a peasant from the village. For a moment, he wished circumstances were different. She was lovely, peasant or not. Her hair had shades of red and gold softened by strands of bronze . . . like a sunset. And her eyes were as dark as a black ocean reflecting the night sky. He'd caught himself staring but somehow couldn't right his manners, even when she'd noted the lapse.

Charles shook the reflection away, tagging such pointless thoughts as a premature product of war. He hadn't even signed up! Yet. Now was most definitely *not* the time to become entangled with a woman, peasant or otherwise.

He was leaving France, returning to Belgium and to the side of King Albert. Rumor had it the king was leading his troops to battle. Charles just hoped he wasn't too late.

Julitte walked the half mile to the village, growing thirsty in the heat. Soon the cobbled square in the center of town came into view. Beneath the shadow of the church's tall brick bell tower sat one of the two pubs in town. It ceased to be a stark contrast to the place of worship after the proprietor had at the behest of his wife stopped partaking in spirits—and consequently stopped serving them. He'd even rolled the piano out of his door and into the church, since so many of the songs sung in the pub no longer seemed the same without the local brew or some other liquor in hand.

Those in the de Colville family had protested the loudest, since it was one less place their spirits were served, the one area to which they did not have to smuggle their goods.

Julitte was surprised to see a cluster of women and children gathered in the square. There were limited huddles Julitte could join, even among women. She was restricted to those of the same Toussaint name or to those linked in some way. Even among Toussaints, she had to be careful.

Toussaint or de Colville . . . to be born in Briecourt was to be born into loyalty to one or the other. It was a simple fact no one questioned.

Ignoring her parched throat, Julitte circled the square until she found Oriane Bouget—Ori as she was called—who was with her grandmother Didi.

"What's happened?"

"There . . . see for yourself." Ori pointed with her chin to yet another bunch off to the side. There were the men of the village, near the town hall. The grand two-story brick structure would have fit any fine town, but here it sat in Briecourt, as out of place as a gem among pebbles. It housed the mayor's office and the quarters of the *garde civique*, the jail and the postal services all in one. A table had been brought outside, and a man sat behind it taking down names, then sending the men one by one into the building.

"What is it?"

"They say we are at war," Grandmother Didi said in her loud way, "and all the men must go and fight." The tone of her voice accommodated her own lack of hearing, but just now it had quivered.

"War! With whom? Not the English again?" Julitte's father had told her about the many wars between the French and the English.

"No, the Germans, so they say."

"Again?" It wasn't all that long ago that France had feuded with their neighbors to the east, too. Julitte stared at the line of men, all of whom she knew. Including her adoptive brother.

"Pierre!" She left Ori's side to rush to his.

"Have you heard the news?" A wide smile brightened his youthful, handsome face. Brown eyes as sweet and guileless as anyone so naive might have, and here he was lining up . . . for *war?*

"What are you doing? Papa left only two days ago. Without his permission, I don't think—"

Whether it was her words or alarmed tone, Julitte caught the attention of men on both sides of Pierre. She had sat in schoolrooms with many of those in this line and knew the majority were best fit for harvesting—the sum of most dreams, the same as their fathers before them.

"Leave him be, woman!" Though his words were firm, the face of her long-ago classmate was lit with exhilaration, as if it were a holiday when anyone could be forgiven anything. "We're off to be heroes the likes of which our town has never seen. Soon this very square will be filled with statues to our bravery."

She lifted one brow. "Statues or bodies?"

"It would be a privilege to die for our country!" Pierre joined with his friend to recite the words, making Julitte believe they repeated whatever pronouncement they might have heard to form this line to begin with.

"Julitte," Pierre whispered, pulling her aside, "I must go, don't you see? Every man between the age seventeen and thirty is being called to service. I have no choice. And I *want* to go."

"Seventeen? But you're not seventeen until—"

"Tomorrow is close enough, so he said I must go."

Julitte found no words to counter such incredible information. How had this happened? Briecourt minded its own business; why couldn't the rest of the world do the same?

"I will go, Julitte." His words, soft but firm, left no room for doubt or argument.

She shook her head, wishing words to convince him otherwise would fall into place. None did. Instead of speaking, she handed him the tin she'd retrieved, full of his favorite wood carvings that were little more than toys. How could it be that he should be signing up for war when that box proved he was still a child? Such things were not the stuff of soldiers.

Turning away, she headed to her cottage, ignoring Ori's call. No one was home, with Narcisse at sea and her adoptive mother long since gone to heaven. But Julitte could go nowhere else just now. Her prayer corner was there. Her spirit, weighted with fear for her brother and all those in line, longed for the reassurance of knowing none were outside the boundaries of God's loving concern.

She needed to pray.

"Arrêtez! Arrêtez votre véhicule ici."

The French *poilu* pounded the butt of his rifle on the pristine hood of Charles Lassone's Peugeot. He had enough sense to hide his annoyance with the soldiers who'd set up this roadblock—that seemed the wisest choice when facing the barrel of a rifle. The blue and red–clad officer spoke rapid French, motioning at the same time for Charles to exit the vehicle.

He did so, skyscraping above the agitated soldier, who couldn't have been more than five feet tall. Another soldier, this one taller but still not equal to Charles's six-foot-one, came to stand before him, both of them waving their rifles in Charles's direction.

"What is this about?" Charles inquired in perfect French. Though his mother was American, his father was Belgian, and a Walloon at that, so Charles had grown up speaking at least as much French as English.

"We regret to inform you, *monsieur*, that you may go no farther in your motorcar. You may take your personal belongings and then take yourself elsewhere."

Rifles or not, Charles lost his hold on hiding annoyance. "What do you mean, take myself elsewhere? With my motor, of course?"

"No, *monsieur*. Without your motor."

"Listen here, I have dual citizenship between Belgium and America. France has no claim to me or to my possessions."

"Necessity outweighs all laws of any country, *monsieur*. Now please empty the vehicle of your belongings and then be off."

"I will not." Grabbing the handle of his motorcar door, Charles moved no farther until the tip of the soldier's rifle grazed his temple.

"All motors are being requisitioned for service, *monsieur*. If not here, then several miles down the road by your own Belgian government. We are now united against a common enemy, and whether you donate the motor here or there makes no difference. You see?"

Charles did not see at all. If his motor had to be requisitioned, he far preferred to surrender it to a Belgian soldier. But as one could not be found, there was no point in arguing.

He retrieved his bag and jacket from the rear seat, then watched with a heart nearly as heavy as the motor itself while yet another French *poilu* resumed Charles's seat behind the wheel and drove off, the crunch of crushed stones sounding beneath the little-worn tires. No doubt the 1913 blue Peugeot would be in the hands of a French officer before nightfall.

"Can you direct me to the nearest train station?" he asked of the remaining soldiers. They had regrouped into the same circle they had been in when Charles spotted them alongside the pile of logs they'd set up as a barrier on the old Roman gravel road leading to the Belgian border.

A snicker here and there gave him little hope of the easy answer he sought. One, the man who had first pounded on the hood of the motor, faced Charles.

"A station will do you no good, *monsieur*. All trains between our two countries have been requisitioned. They are now used exclusively for troops." He lifted one of his feet and tapped a dusty boot. "A hike is in store for you." Then he laughed along with the others.

Without a word, Charles started walking. At first his steps were slow, but after a moment he picked up his pace. Maybe he should be grateful only his motorcar had been impressed into duty.

2

Julitte bolted upright in the predawn darkness, jarred from slumber by noise at the door. The loft in which she slept had been partitioned into two rooms, one for her and one for Pierre. But she needn't see beyond the wall to remember the other half was now empty.

Meager gray light filtered through the single window on her side of the garret, just below the highest peak of the house.

"La, it's not even morning yet!" Julitte threw off her cover and climbed down the ladder from the loft as the pounding changed to a rattling at the door handle. The thick wooden barricade Narcisse had installed a year ago was impossible to budge from the outside but slid up easily at her touch.

And there stood Marcel Feuillet. Not quite stark naked this time, for which she sent up a quick prayer of thanksgiving. His soft belly hung over the rim of his trousers and bare toes wiggled as if waving a greeting. He'd once been a handsome, hardworking neighbor in the mines outside of town, but years of inhaling phosphate dust had ruined his lungs. To dull the pain he'd consumed far too much of the de Colville *absinthe* over the years. That had taken away the pain, and his mind along with it. Marcel was never quite sober anymore, no matter the time of day. And every once in a while he arrived at the door, forgetting that Narcisse no longer spent his winters working in the mines.

"You mustn't be up and about yet, Marcel," Julitte said as she pulled the door closed behind her and grabbed Marcel's large hand. "Come along. Aggie will be missing you soon."

"It's time to go to work. I came for Narcisse." He swayed as he spoke, as if the act of speaking shook his balance.

"No, Marcel," she said as she led him along the path to his house down the road, "no work for you today. Holiday." He'd been let go from the mines a year ago because of his unpredictable behavior, so he was forever on holiday as his wife worked her loom and did laundry and sewing for others who could afford to pay.

"Holiday? No such thing!"

He then went into a recitation from a Wagner opera. "'Hail to the day that sheds light all around us! Hail to the sun that shines upon us! Hail to the light that emerges from night!'"

Julitte tried hushing him, and not only because of the early morning hour. The song was a reminder of an indiscretion, years old but its effect felt to this day. Marcel taking Ori to the outdoor opera festival in Le Catelet had whirled the de Colville's gossip mill into grinding Ori's reputation to pieces, something Julitte—and undoubtedly Ori herself—wished everyone would forget. No one was supposed to have seen them. Who knew any of the de Colvilles would attend an opera, where none of their favorite pub songs would be sung? But the pair had been seen; it hardly mattered by which de Colville. A married man with a young temptress, as they'd called her—and she only sixteen at the time! Julitte knew Ori was no such thing. If anyone had been tempted, it had been Ori, by an older man who wanted to give her something she'd never had before: the illusion of being all grown-up, sophisticated enough to want to see an opera on the arm of a man most, once, had considered fine.

Agnès Feuillet, Marcel's wife, met them at her threshold, resigned annoyance in the dip of her brow. "Come back to bed, Marcel."

Agnès spared neither word nor glance Julitte's way, but Julitte expected nothing else.

Julitte knew her own bed was probably still warm, but a glance to the eastern horizon told her the sun would soon be shining, just as Marcel's recitation had announced. Too late to recapture sleep now.

She turned toward home, not before seeing the pull of a curtain from the other side of the street. At the window was Claudette de Colville, her dark eyes narrowing on Julitte.

She folded her arms, pretending a chill, although even in the light cotton sleep shift the air felt warm and comfortable. But she should have slipped on more than her clogs before leaving her home; she saw that now.

Just then something echoed in the valley, something Julitte rarely heard, at least within a stone's toss of her home. Only the sound of humanly powered machines landed on the ears of those living in Briecourt: the bang of weavers' looms and the whirl of spinners' wheels or the jingle of a harness on a horse pulling a wooden plow. This sounded like a motor, higher pitched than the roar of M. Mantoux's touring car that sometimes rolled through town.

With the sun just beginning to offer stingy light from behind low clouds, Julitte could see little down the road. But she was not mistaken. The motor was getting closer.

She ran home and threw off her nightgown, donned petticoat, skirt, and blouse before slipping her feet back into her wooden clogs. Rather than taking the time to brush her unruly hair, she grabbed a scarf and tied it up. Then she dashed outside.

At such an early hour few might have heard the approaching motor. But her uncle, the Toussaint baker, stood outside his shop with a broom in hand. He must have just gotten his goods into the ovens, and soon the scent of his bread would make the stomach cry out for food whether hungry or not.

But Uncle Guy was not sweeping. Instead, like Julitte, he stood facing the road leading out of town. The louder the sound of the motor, the more doors opened along the way.

A lone rider on what looked like a motorized bicycle approached, the wheels beneath him stirring up dust even as he left the dirt behind and reached the cobbled lane in town. The rider wore a leather jacket and helmet, and goggles covered half his face.

He stopped in front of Uncle Guy's bakeshop.

The man, short and sturdy of build, hopped off his seat and stood stiffly to address Julitte's uncle. "I'm here to see the mayor of this forsaken little town, if you have one." He brushed dust from his jacket as he spoke. "Can you direct me to him?"

Julitte didn't need to glance at either her uncle or the gathering neighbors to know she was the only one who understood the man's words. He spoke slowly and loudly, as if by slowing down and speaking up they might better comprehend his English.

Julitte stepped forward, pointing in the direction of the market square. She understood English better than she could speak it and awkwardly gave him the information he needed. ". . . Across from the church, yes?" she finished, pressing palm to palm and raising her hands above in the mimic of a steeple. "Big building . . . that way. The finest in town."

The man lifted his goggles and a smile sprouted on his face as he looked at Julitte. "Ah, 'tis a pity I'll be here only long enough to deliver a message. I'm following a British squadron."

He pushed his motorized cycle forward, turning back to Julitte before mounting. "May I know the name of the lady who will inhabit my dreams when I go off to war, *mademoiselle*?"

Julitte told him, and he sighed with an appreciative glance, first at her, then spreading to the other villagers, lingering on Claudette de Colville before returning to Julitte. "Surely the women here are worthy of the fight, anyway!"

Then he hopped on the seat of his motorized bike, and with an ear-ringing peal and another cloud of dust, he was gone.

"Julitte, what did that young man say to you?" Uncle Guy looked anxious and irritated at the same time. "Where is he going?"

Before she could answer, another call grabbed her attention. "Julitte!"

Ori Bouget skidded to a halt, one of her clogs sailing from her foot and landing with a thud near Uncle Guy's broom. Shaking his head at both girls now, he swept the shoe toward Ori, then waited for Julitte to answer his question.

"Did you see him?" Julitte asked Ori before getting to the business at hand. A few of the neighbors had followed the direction of the cyclist, but others who'd just emerged from their homes approached those still gathered at Uncle Guy's bakery. She didn't want to have to repeat her story a dozen times as each straggler neared.

"I did! What a loud contraption! Did you see his face? Was he handsome?"

Her uncle rapped the broom on the stoop as if it were a gavel on a judge's bench. "Julitte, enough dawdling now. What did he say? Wait—that machine of his is silent again. At the market square is my guess."

Julitte nodded. "He said he wanted to find the mayor, and then he would be following a British squadron."

"British squadron?" Uncle Guy looked skeptical. "I thought we were fighting the Germans! Is that all he said? It seemed he used more words than that."

"He said we were worth fighting for." That was near enough the truth.

"And why did you tell him your name?" This from Gustave de Colville, who stood near his niece Claudette.

Julitte folded her arms. "He asked me my name. Why should I not have told him? I'm not ashamed of it."

Gustave de Colville was one of the patriarchs of the de Colville family. Few people spoke to him the way Julitte did, but few people had as little to lose as Julitte.

Gustave took a step closer, and most, with the possible exception of Ori, might have cowered. Julitte stood still, arms clasped like a barrier in front of her.

"Everyone in this village knows a name isn't enough when it comes to you." His gaze was as cold as his tone. "Without the whole truth, a stranger knows nothing."

"It's too bad you or Claudette do not speak enough English to have enlightened him."

"This one's ashamed of nothing," Claudette said while looping her arm with her uncle's. "Not even of the way she walked down the street just this morning, wearing only a nightshift. I saw her myself."

"Tempting others, no doubt," Gustave said with a nod.

"That's enough now," said Uncle Guy as he began sweeping his stoop. Julitte welcomed his call to end the gathering. His brother, her own adoptive father, would have done so, too—but not before defending her. "Go see the mayor if you wish to know more."

The little crowd soon petered away, some in the direction of the market square, and Julitte watched them go. How strange it seemed for so many cottages to be represented by so few men. Even seeing Claudette with her uncle instead of her beau seemed odd, her beau whom she'd married just the other day before he'd marched off to war. Half the town was abuzz about the hurried wedding, until Fleur Toussaint married her beau and evened the talk.

Julitte led Ori away, stopping at her porch for the clay pot she filled with water each morning.

"Let's have tea," Julitte suggested, knowing they would both be called out to harvest the fields before long and it was never good to start the day on an empty stomach. With so many hands gone from the village, their weaving would have to wait while they did men's work as best they could.

Ori nodded. "Yes, let's hurry! Before the cyclist takes off again."

A quick trip to the water pump allowed only a wave at the departing soldier, who rode off in the direction from which he'd come.

"Look." Ori pointed toward those gathered near the town hall. "They're reading something posted on the mayor's door."

Julitte's gaze followed Ori's pointing finger. An early morning breeze rustled a paper suspended by nails at its four corners. Nearing, she saw it was already tearing in one corner.

Two paragraphs: one in English, one in French. "'To all loyal French citizens,'" she read aloud. "'In the event that any English, Belgian, Russian, or Serb refugees pass through this village, it is hereby pronounced you are to offer them aid and comfort to the best of your abilities.'"

"Refugees?" Ori's eyes rounded. Refugees meant people were leaving their homes.

Those nearby muttered. Some hurried in the direction of home. Calls rang back and forth, talk of becoming refugees themselves.

"No one will come here," Julitte said. "We're in a valley on the way to nowhere. No one *ever* comes here."

Just then there was noise behind the door. A maid stood there, the one servant in all of Briecourt. She stooped to pick up another envelope that had been slipped under the door, caught by the doorframe.

Despite a half-dozen people standing at the foot of the porch, the maid closed the door without a word. Mayor Eloi was never seen before the sun was well up in the sky, and evidently today would be no different.

"Let's have our tea," Julitte said, finishing their path to the well.

Moments later, they entered the cool darkness of Julitte's cottage. Constructed of brick like most of the homes in the village, it had a slate roof rather than thatch. Though Narcisse was gone more often than home, his was one of the most comfortable cottages in the village. The house boasted every necessity. A bed for her father in the kitchen when he was home, a table, a settle near the hearth, a sideboard along the wall full of dishes and knickknacks collected by her father from nearly every region of the world. Try though she might, Julitte couldn't quite forget the time Gustave de Colville had called her one of her father's "souvenirs." Memory of it always made her think Gustave would have liked seeing her stuck upon one of the shelves on silent display.

"So tell me the rest," Ori said. "Tell me the rest of the words that cyclist used."

"He was silly, really," Julitte said as she sliced two pieces of bread and a bit of cheese. "He asked to know the name of the woman who would be inhabiting his dreams. You see? Men are muddled when they go off to war, saying things they would otherwise be too afraid to say."

Ori sighed. "Ah! I wish I'd had a stranger say such things to me." She grinned at Julitte. "Men will always speak that way to you, though."

"Perhaps, but when they do, Gustave de Colville will be right there with the rest of my story, so the men have little to say to me after that."

"He is a fool, and so are all of the men in this village."

"You may be right, since so many were eager to run off and turn the fields red somewhere." Pain skittered across her heart at the thought of her brother. "Pierre among them."

Ori reached across the table to squeeze Julitte's hand. "He had no choice; you know that." Sitting back, the worry in her eyes dissipated. "But this war, if it comes close enough, may be exactly what we need to find husbands. Between soldiers and refugees, there may be many new choices."

At Julitte's quick glance, Ori tsked. "Oh, tell me that thought hasn't entered your mind."

Heat rose to Julitte's cheeks and she couldn't deny what her friend already knew. New people—people untouched by the tongues of this town. But she felt compelled to say, "Such thoughts may have crossed my mind, Ori, but wishing for a war to end our troubles doesn't seem very wise."

Ori took a bite of the bread and cheese, nodding slowly. "Where do you suppose they are—the men from our village?"

Pouring water from the heated kettle into cups her father had brought back from China, Julitte shrugged. To her own dismay, she found herself more often wondering where the handsome blond aristocrat she had seen with M. Mantoux might be. But she hadn't told Ori about him, although she didn't know why. She and Ori shared all their secrets. Yet this one—a man who knew the kind of life Julitte would never know, the kind of life Julitte had no right to dream of, with wealth she'd been taught would offer nothing but a challenge to her faith . . . she had no reason to think of him at all. Their paths would never cross again.

Ignoring her thoughts, she kept her words on the topic at hand. "I pray all the men of our village are on their way home already."

Ori sighed again. "I know I should too, but truly, Julitte, if they just come back after being gone a few days or weeks, what will change? Nothing. And I do want *something* to change."

Julitte nodded, remembering her adoptive father's lilting voice as he quoted from one of the books his favorite captain had loaned him. "Lepe they lyke a flounder out of a fryenge panne into the fyre," she told Ori. "If change is delivered on war coffins, we may wish we were back in the frying pan we live in now."

But neither Ori nor Julitte herself found any reason to smile over the words. "Grandmother Didi hopes you'll visit her today," Ori said. "Ever since my brothers went off, she's done little else but pray. I think she wants you to pray with her. She holds your prayers higher than anyone else's, you know."

Julitte softened the look that must have frozen her face. She knew only too well how many reasons the villagers had to look upon her as odd. From the origin of her birth to the one strange incident she couldn't hide. Some were afraid of her, while others held her in unsought awe; still others had written her off as so different she couldn't possibly be accepted as one of them.

Oh, to have the simple disdain of a fallen woman, like Ori.

Julitte stirred her tea, once again longing for change. She was twenty and two years old and called the prettiest girl in the village, but to listen to a de Colville, that was part of Satan's lure.

Maybe soldiers *would* pass through their village, ones who wouldn't listen to or care about the lies spread not only about herself but Ori as well. Perhaps one of them might be tall and blond. . . .

If at one time the life of a vagabond had appealed to Charles's sense of adventure, it was well out of his system by now. Charles had decided at age sixteen that a life of ease wasn't for him. No, he had always wanted to do things for himself and not depend upon servants. He and his sister, Isa, were the same in their thinking, and their father accused each of them of possessing a socialist streak. Something Isa ignored and Charles couldn't quite deny.

But now, after so many days of living the life of a peasant, traveling on foot and buying or begging bread, he was ready to abandon lofty dreams of a world ideally equal if it meant everyone couldn't live up to the standard to which he'd always been accustomed. Living simply for the sake of equality had lost its appeal now that his choice was no longer available.

He scoffed at himself as he removed yet another pebble from

his shoe. How foolish he'd been not to accept Anton's offer to go to Switzerland with him. Instead, Charles had imagined himself driving right up to *le Palais Royal*, walking through the gate, and past the lush gardens, a place Charles had visited before with his wealthy and well-connected parents. There he would have offered his services to Albert, king of the Belgians. Charles would have gallantly fought beside the king for their country. A country that was only half his, but that part didn't matter to Charles's naive imaginings of a glorious battle beside the king to halt the Hun.

Sitting on his suitcase for a well-deserved rest, Charles looked around the Belgian countryside, wondering if it had come to war after all. He saw no sign of fighting, although last night the sky to the east had lit up and the ground even seemed to rumble as if a rather-too-localized storm had erupted.

But this morning there was no sign of disruption to everyday, peaceful country life. Sheep grazed the meadow, warblers sang from the trees, and in the distance he saw women working in a wheat field. That was the only hint of something being wrong, that it was women instead of men in that field. But they all looked happy enough, as if their village had been afflicted by nothing more than a minor fever that touched only the men.

Fever indeed. Charles picked up his suitcase and started traveling like an unsuccessful salesman again. *War* fever. It had touched even him before those *poilus* had stolen his car.

He switched his suitcase from one hand to the other and scowled at his palm. The only time he'd had blisters before was from rowing in regattas—gondolas in Venice or pulling boats in America. Unlike this one, those blisters had been evidence of fun and usually reminders of one kind of victory or another.

Abandoning every last shred of socialism, he hoped if there was a war, little in his life would change.

Charles looked up again, noticing something down the road

headed his way. Foot travelers, like him, but scores of them. He hastened his step, eager to hear news from his destination.

He slowed as he neared. These were not just any travelers, forced to walk as he did because of commandeered trains or motorcars. No, these were different. Families carrying belongings—even the children carried suitcases nearly too heavy to manage.

Refugees.

"Ho!" he called and waved, despite a warning in his brain. Something on their faces said he might not want to hear what they would tell him. But he must know. "Good day to you all."

Some continued past, as if nothing could break the rhythm of their heavy march, certainly not a travel-worn journeyer like Charles. But one man, middle-aged and unshaven, stepped to the side with a dozen or so people behind him. In that first moment Charles noticed there were mostly women and children, save for this man and a few others—some older, but few the age of any soldier.

"You, *monsieur*, walk the wrong way."

Charles set down his suitcase, glad to take his palm from the offending handle. "And why is that?"

"The Germans have overrun us!" The cry came not from the man but from a dark-haired child next to him. His eyes, Charles noted, were wide and frightened, as if the Germans were at their heels.

"Where are they?"

"In the direction you go," the man said. "Turn with us now and find safety in numbers."

"I intend to join the fight, for king and country."

The man moved to speak, but laughter sounded from behind him. Charles caught a younger man's eye.

"Too late! I tried and was turned away. No more guns, no more uniforms."

Charles looked from him to the older man, fearing—instantly receiving—confirmation.

"He hopes to volunteer in France. If you want so much to fight, join us."

Charles eyed the group, all dressed in multiple layers despite the warm weather. No doubt the clothing was easier to carry that way or would not fit in their miserable cases.

"Are the Germans in Brussels?" Charles thought of his home, his parents and sister. Were they still there? safe?

The spokesman shrugged one shoulder and started to move forward as if Charles had wasted enough of his time. "If the Germans are not there yet, they soon will be."

Charles watched them go but did not follow, despite the invitation.

Volunteer in France?

His car had been donation enough to that army. Surely there was a better way to volunteer his services—to *Belgium*.

3

Julitte wiped her brow with the edge of the long cotton blouse that hung over her skirt. It had been a dry August so far, and hot. The sun had drawn energy from her all afternoon and wasn't letting up yet. She preferred working in the cool cellar on her loom but knew if she wanted to eat this winter, the harvesting must be done. Those left behind must bring it in—those who hadn't become refugees themselves and dispersed to the west, to Paris or beyond. As Julitte worked the field that day, she'd seen family after family departing, towing their belongings behind them.

Julitte had yet to see a single refugee from elsewhere travel through Briecourt. Much to Ori's disappointment—and to Julitte's as well.

Her clogs dragged beneath her feet as she walked from the field. Others who'd worked beside her, cousins and neighbors both young and old, walked in silence nearby. For once she guessed they weren't guarding their tongues around her, the odd one who was always speaking to God, but rather they were just too tired to talk.

She would get water at the well in the village square, eat a bit, then see if she had any vigor left to sit at the loom. Each step to the square made the sinews of her limbs shift from wobbly to stiff, and her back ached, but work waited. Water, for a start, would help.

Didi sat near the well, helping to fill the crocks for younger women after a day in the fields.

"Did you hear?"

Too tired to speak, Julitte only shook her head.

"Eloi received a proclamation for all mayors to announce. Soldiers will bring in the rest of the harvest."

Julitte raised her brows, wondering why Didi should still be frowning. Who wouldn't welcome help bringing in the harvest?

Ori came up to the well, her water pitcher in hand. "What's that, Didi? Soldiers are coming to help us?"

But Didi shook her head. "I don't think to *help*. The one who brought the proclamation said the soldiers bring in the wheat, then take it away to feed the army. That's what they did in Le Catelet."

The brief interest on Ori's face disappeared, and her frown matched her grandmother's, absent the wrinkles. "Without the harvest . . ."

"We'll starve," Didi finished.

"Will the Lord let His people starve?" Julitte asked, but she spoke too softly for Didi, who raised a cupped hand to her ear.

"Eh?"

"We won't go hungry, Didi," Julitte said. If she thought starving a possibility, she would find a way to help Didi travel, though they all knew she could barely walk without the cane her grandson had fashioned for her. "The Lord won't let us go hungry."

Claudette de Colville, just approaching them, stepped in front of Ori and brushed aside Julitte to tug the bucket up from below. "Somehow you always make it sound as though God is on your side, Julitte. If that were so, He wouldn't have given you to a family that ended up abandoning you, one way or another. Just as your *real* parents did."

Julitte pressed her lips together. How many years had Claudette taunted her this way? It shouldn't sting anymore.

But it did.

The next morning, French soldiers came for the harvest but, as Didi predicted, carried the precious grain off with them when they went. Neither Julitte nor Ori saw a soldier any closer than from the edge of town. Guards watched over the workers in the field as if protecting both the wheat and the soldiers and never let anyone approach.

That same day more families decided to leave Briecourt, and the village was quieter than ever. The noisiest shops were now silent: no more hammer and saw at the carpenter's, no clanging at the smithy or squeals of delight from the bakery. Even the two pubs were closed.

And those left behind isolated themselves. Waiting—for news or for soldiers. Neither Toussaint nor de Colville lingered on the street that day, though from her window Julitte did hear an older Toussaint tease Claudette, who had carried a broken dish to her mother's.

"So you couldn't keep your home intact for your new husband, after all," came the words from the window next to Julitte's.

Claudette hurried along, not even wiping the tear from her cheek.

Julitte lay on her mat that night, certain those who'd left had been right. Would the wind soon carry sounds of war, the boom of cannon, explosions to make her heart dart with fear?

But where else could she go?

There it was again, that rumble, those voices on the wind. Charles had heard it earlier and changed direction, away from the sound. But it hunted him.

He threw the apple core aside. The fruit had been bitter and unripe, probably barely digestible. But the taste disappeared as fear took the place where his hunger had been. That rumble was real, and it wasn't in his stomach.

He'd purposely lingered near the edge of a wood dense with underbrush. Now he scanned the countryside again.

There. Figures appeared, the first of a steady stream of men outlined against the sun setting beyond a ridge in the distance. Men on the march, rows and rows of them. None looked his way, but why should they? Here he sat benignly in the shadow of a wood, watching those he'd once wanted to join.

But they weren't Belgian soldiers. They were French—he could tell by the blue jackets and red kepi and trousers.

He marveled at their energy, the quick pace of this march. Headed west. That could mean only one thing: retreat. The threat came from the east.

Watching, he wondered what would happen if he joined them. Just fell in line alongside. French or Belgian, did it really make a difference?

Then, from the rear of the line, someone stumbled. Another fell beside him. Charles watched, intrigued, then horrified. There, from the next ridge, they came. Another row of men, these dressed in gray, with the peculiar spiked helmets worn by the Germans.

Charles snatched his suitcase, sprinting deeper into the shadows of the wood to the nearest thicket. Gunfire pierced his ears, sulfur soon reached his nose, and the ground beneath him trembled faster with what could only be artillery fire.

He should go out there. Wasn't that what he wanted? To march right up to the king of the Belgians and offer . . . what? Here he sat, unarmed, untrained, thoroughly unprepared. He watched gunfire in the distance, a volley like some deadly game of tennis. And Charles knew he'd been a fool.

They never neared the wood. The German line, advancing, ever advancing. They were magnificent. Gray and stout, strong and tireless. When they took aim, they found their mark.

And they were endless. The French were no match. They must

have known that soon after the first exchange. A ping met by a blast, a puddle of blue to an ocean of gray.

Charles clutched his suitcase to his breast as if it were a child's comforting toy and watched through cover of dark leaves. Again he told himself to break out, run across the field in between and join the melee, steal a gun from a fallen soldier no matter the origin, shout and shoot and kill.

But he knew he couldn't. None of the rifles looked like the sporting guns he owned. And what if he did figure out how to load and fire? How many Germans could he kill? He probably wouldn't even make it across the field.

That giant gray army would swoop down on him and he would be no more.

Shame outweighed all those pompous dreams of his own heroism. Charles slunk ever deeper under cover and waited. It would be over soon. It had to be.

4

Julitte woke at her loom to the roughness of half-raised heddles and a wooden shuttle beneath her cheek.

Pushing away the comb rod, she stood sluggishly. With barely enough yarn to finish the cloth she'd started, the day had been long nonetheless. She must go to bed.

Something niggled at the back of her mind. With each step from the loom, the notion of sleep began to abandon her. Something had awakened her. Was that a real noise she had heard, that pop, or only her sleepy imagination, some remnant of a dream?

She tried to ignore it as she left the cellar behind, passed the woodstove, went to the stairs up to the loft. Her mattress in sight, she took another step to her bed but her feet froze. Out of the corner of her eye she caught a flashing light from the small window at the peak of her loft.

Fatigue vanished. Julitte scrambled back down the stairs, not to the safety and quiet of the cellar but to the front door, flinging it open without thought. Only after it was done did she recognize her own foolishness. She caught her breath. Suppose the village was overrun by Germans?

But it was not, though indeed something was amiss. Off to the north, where the only road to town spread out, she saw another flash, followed fast by an echo of . . . something. Gunshot? Then another exchange, this one closest of all.

The bridge over a finger of the Somme was nearby, where for the last week a pair of men from the village had been assigned to keep watch. Though what use two graying men with hunting rifles nearly as old as themselves would be against any army, Julitte could not guess. Criers, perhaps, but she'd heard no voices. Only the pop.

She looked around. The village was quiet and dark. She had no idea what time it was, surely well into the night. Had no one else heard the sounds, or were they cowering in their cellars, as she should be doing? She was tempted to tap on her uncle Guy's door nearby or go to the church in search of the priest, but she did not.

Instead she waited. She would know what to do if she waited for direction from above.

And that direction came—sure knowledge in her heart. Breaking out in a full, instantaneous run, she sped toward and not away from the flashing lights of the night. She was needed, though by whom and for what purpose she had no idea.

The lights receded, then stopped altogether before Julitte reached the bridge. She saw no one in the trees and hills outside of town but felt rather than heard movement in the vibration beneath her feet. Soldiers? Surely not many, and they were going away.

A moan close by caught her attention.

Julitte turned to the reed bed that edged the river beneath the bridge. During the earliest morning hours this was one of her favorite spots, where she watched coots and dabchicks and listened to the music of the warblers. But now it was deathly quiet, as if even the crickets had abandoned the area.

She waited.

Another moan. There, among the flattened reeds. The foot of a man.

"Victor!"

Julitte slid to his side, seeing him facedown and nearly in the water. She pulled him away, startled not so much by the wet as the warmth of that wetness. Blood oozed from his middle.

"Victor! Can you hear me? We must get you home. . . . I . . . cannot . . . carry . . ." She tried to lift him but failed. A silent plea for help, and she entreated him again. "Victor, you must wake up."

She rose, knowing she could not do this alone. She sprinted away, only to slip out of one of her clogs.

"I—can help."

Julitte skidded on her heel, the reeds beneath her making a waxy slope. Then she saw him, farther away from the bridge. He moved toward her, barely off his knees. It was Nicholas, the man assigned with Victor to guard the road into town.

"Nicholas, I need help! Victor is hurt." She headed back to Victor, kneeling beside him, but stopped and looked up at Nicholas. "*Can* you help?"

Nicholas stumbled to his feet and Julitte winced at the blood on him, rivulets from his forehead and from his arm, another suspiciously dark stain on his thigh. Wordlessly Nicholas stumbled to Victor's side.

"Nicholas! What happened?"

"Germans . . . soldiers. Must have been a scouting party; there were only a few." He clutched at his bloody arm, sucking in air as he sank on the other side of Victor. "They must have seen our guns . . . and fired."

Despite the blood from Nicholas's arm, either of his seemed stronger than Julitte's. Together they pulled Victor from the edge of the water.

Julitte gasped. A burst of bright light shone before her, not like the rifle bursts of moments ago—no, this light was not so tangible, not so earthly, or it would have blinded her so suddenly after the darkness. And yet it didn't hurt her eyes at all.

This light was brilliant, endless. And Victor was there in the midst of it.

"It . . . it's too late." She touched Victor's mouth, feeling for breath. "He is dead."

"No . . . no . . . we'll get him home."

Julitte did not protest, though she knew it would do no good. The one physician in town had been conscripted into the war and was gone with the men who'd been ordered to fight. Even Father Barnabé, the *curé* at the church with limited knowledge of healing, could do no good now.

Together they dragged Victor's body back to town. Within a few feet of her uncle's bakeshop, Julitte called out. If they'd heard anything—and she had little doubt they had—perhaps the sound of her voice would be enough to let them know the danger was past.

Uncle Guy opened the door slowly at first, but when the door was wide enough, he dropped whatever he had in his hand—a broom held like a club—and rushed out to them.

"Ach, ach . . . this is not good."

He took Julitte's spot beside Victor, and she ran ahead to a cottage three doors down, calling out to Victor's wife, who must have been near the door because she opened it too quickly to be cautious. Like all the other cottages, this one was still dark, as if it and all its inhabitants tried to be invisible in the night.

But at the sight of Victor, his wife, Helena, fell to her knees with a cry.

Julitte pulled the older woman to her feet, away from the threshold so the others could bring Victor inside. "I will get the *curé*," she said, already turning away.

"No," Uncle Guy called from over his shoulder. Once Victor was settled on the bed near the kitchen hearth, the baker approached Julitte. Perhaps he'd guessed what she already knew. "Stay with Helena. I will go."

Nicholas stood at Victor's side as his own blood dripped near the blood of his friend. Helena broke from the moment of paralysis that seemed to have gripped her, kneeling at her husband's bed. She whispered his name again and again.

Julitte stepped nearer, but new shadows from the threshold caught her eye, de Colville and Toussaint alike.

"He . . . does not breathe," Helena said, each word choked between sobs. She looked up at last, seeing Julitte. Her eyes widened and the tears stalled. "You—you must help him."

Julitte looked toward the door again, wishing her uncle had let her go for the priest. She knew it would come to this. The only time most people wanted her around was in a crisis.

But sympathy moved her, pushing away her inadequacy. She stepped closer, touching not Victor as perhaps Helena hoped, but Helena herself. Julitte drew the woman near.

"The Lord God alone can help him, Helena. Not I."

"But you . . . you can ask Him . . . as you did before. . . ."

"My prayers are no different from yours. Can we pray . . . together?"

Helena nodded, and side by side they leaned over the fallen man. Julitte whispered quietly, imploring God's care for Victor, though she knew he was already gone. She closed her eyes, turning her hands from Victor back to Helena, asking for wisdom and knowledge of what to do, how to trust the Lord God through whatever they must face.

She waited for Helena to pray, but no words made it through her weeping.

And then gray-haired Father Barnabé, the *curé*, was there, bringing calm with the sweep of his robes, bending over Victor but shaking his head before many moments had passed. "I'm sorry, Helena. He is in God's hands now."

Julitte recalled the flash that had passed before her at the reed bed, comparing it to other times she'd seen such light. It had been more fleeting, particularly shorter than what she'd seen the first time, many years ago when she knew her birth father had died. But it had been a glimpse nonetheless. How she wanted to cry out, but not with the sorrow so evident upon Helena's face. With joy such as no one in this little village had ever seen before. Victor was with *God*.

But she couldn't show what warred inside of her—grief over Helena's loss against the utter delight of knowing Victor's eternity with God had begun. She closed her eyes so none would see that battle inside of her.

Helena's hand, still in hers, tugged at Julitte. She opened her eyes and her gaze met Helena's.

A gaze that silently accused Julitte.

She shook her head and pulled Helena close despite that wordless reproach. "He is with God, Helena. No pain, only joy. He is there, *there*. . . ."

Helena pulled back and her eyes sought Julitte's. "But you . . . you could save him, could you not? He's my husband. . . ."

Julitte received Helena's stare, her plea banishing Julitte's joy from that glimpse, that gift God's sight had given her. Such a gift helped no one. Could God not give her something that would help others, help Victor? help Helena?

"He loved God," Julitte whispered. "He is with Him now."

"But gone from me!" Helena pushed Julitte away and flung herself against her husband's body.

Julitte rose to her feet, feeling the stares of those still clustered around, knowing no one else in their village would have been thought a failure just now.

No one but her.

Charles woke with a start. Confused, he saw the rough and unfamiliar roof over his head. It was dark; he'd slept the day away.

A deep, but temporary, escape. He rubbed his face, rough and unshaven for days, wishing the memories of yesterday would go away.

He'd let himself get lost in the effort to skirt the remnants of battle and, as darkness had fallen, hadn't the faintest idea what direction to head. He only knew he'd wanted to leave all the death behind him. So he'd looked at the sky last night, remembering his childhood days with his young sister, how he'd told Isa about his dreams of navigating the seas by the stars. But he was a man now, and boyhood dreams that were never given training left Charles without talent. Oh, he could sail in a regatta; he could drive any vehicle as fast as its motor allowed; he could play golf and tennis and polo . . .

But in a war, he was worthless.

He'd stumbled upon the forester's cabin and before falling asleep spent an hour in self-imposed anguish, berating himself over what he might have done, what he perhaps should have done, what he *could* have done had he possessed an ounce of the courage that any one of the soldiers on either side possessed.

Staring at the ceiling now, Charles knew he needed a plan.

He had identification in his pocket: a Belgian *passeport* as well as an American one. Both were good for two years, listing his full name as Charles Henry Lassone, age twenty-four, occupation—and this was always the tricky part, trying to come up with a term for someone like him who only played for a living—*entrepreneur*. Travel for business purposes was always easier as far as those who checked such papers went.

Listed after the reason for his travel was his thorough personal description, since a photograph was neither required nor convenient to fit on his already visa-crowded form: height, six feet, one inch; weight, one hundred ninety pounds; hair, blond; eyes, blue; face, long; chin, square; forehead, low; nose, prominent. He used to chafe about the "prominent" nose, wondering if the clerk thought it too large for his face, but since the document rarely demanded more than a glance, he'd mostly forgotten the physical description was there. Still, it would be nice to have photographs adopted or do away with the documents altogether. His guess was a war would do more for the former idea than the latter.

If Belgium was in as much a mess as those refugees had painted and the Germans had come this far, there was little point trying to get to Brussels. His parents would have taken Isabelle to safety even if she kicked and screamed all the way to America. And based on what he'd seen, the German army could crush Belgium *and* France. He supposed he should get rid of the Belgian *passeport* and for safety keep only the neutral American one—at least he thought America was still neutral. Who knew? It had been days since he'd seen a newspaper.

Charles couldn't stay hidden forever. He must find a village and learn where he was. From there he could determine which way to head. If he could find his way out of Europe, make it to America, maybe it wasn't too late to do *something*, even from so far away.

First, he needed to hide his Belgian *passeport*.

Charles stood, foolishly tried to shake a few wrinkles from his linen pants, took up his suitcase, and headed to the door.

But as he reached for the handle, something—or someone—nudged it open before Charles ever touched it.

5

Unless more yarn could be had, Julitte would soon have nothing to do. She sat alone at her table, sipping tea she'd brewed that morning. Yarn was growing as scarce as the flour in her uncle's bakery. In the days since the harvest had been taken, no goods made outside the village could be had.

It wasn't just the shortages weighing on her mind. It was knowing that out there, somewhere, men fought for something so vital as their homeland. A sense of waiting had settled on her. Waiting for news, waiting for it to be over, for Narcisse to walk through the door, Pierre at his side. Waiting.

Shouting shattered her quiet. Julitte jumped to the door but stopped at her own threshold. Those were German shouts; she could hear that much through the open window.

Daring a peek, she pried the door just far enough to see down the cobbled street. There, a row of armed German soldiers marched forward. One in the middle, the only one with his weapon still holstered, bellowed orders.

"All men of this village will line up here. Immediately." He spoke French, and although his words were in proper order, the pronunciation was awkward.

Soldiers began beating on doors not already open, and Julitte leaned back, shutting the door and laying the barricade in place. She

41

would have hidden herself but wondered what they would do if no one answered. Go on their way? Or break down the door?

No sooner had the options come to mind than the wood beneath her hands rattled at the bang of a fist.

"Oh, God," she whispered to her Father above, "I'm in Your hands." Even as the prayer passed her lips, she wished Narcisse were here. She knew there was no kinder soul to be found, but he had the strength of a sailor and enough scars to hint he'd known his share of brawling.

"There are no men here," she called through the door. She spoke in French, although Narcisse had taught her to speak a smattering of German. Not enough to let them think she understood their language.

But the words did not send away whoever had pounded on her door, and she knew she would have to let them in or have the door torn off its frame. She lifted the lock and the door burst open.

Julitte stood immobile, staring at the rifle aimed straight at her heart, which beat so fast and hard she wondered if it alone would do the job a bullet might do: make a hole in her chest.

The soldier shoved her aside, overturning one of the chairs and bounding up to the empty garret. Bayonet pointed, he pushed past whatever was in his way, first on one side of the partition, then the other, knocking out of place the mats, a chair, an extra blanket. A moment later the tip of his bayonet pierced through a slat.

Julitte kept to the corner, where she prayed again to be invisible for her own safety's sake. When he left barely a few moments later, she ran back to the gaping door and slammed it shut. These Germans might be bullies, but single-minded at least. For now, they must only want the men. He had never even looked at her.

Julitte bolted the door, then went to the window and pulled aside the white lace curtains. She could see the street and hear the one who called orders.

"Herewith you are without rights, without property, without

liberties. Until the German Imperial Army decides what to do with you, how you may best be used for the good of our country, you will remain in your homes, in this village, answerable only to the army who has conquered your land."

From her vantage, Julitte had to lean forward to glance beyond the windowsill. There he was, not ten paces away. His back was to her, but he stood tall and stiff, a horsewhip under his arm, pistol still at his side. Shoulders made broader by his uniform, head made tall and menacing by a shiny helmet with a spike pointing straight up.

She started to retreat into the shadows of her home, but something caught her attention from down the way. A man walked with his hands on his head, elbows pointing east and west.

Julitte's heart pounded anew at the sight. It was the mayor. He stopped before the man issuing orders, wincing away from the bayonet at his back. Mayor Eloi was no match for any of these sturdy soldiers, with his slight stature and peaceful ways. She'd always thought it odd that he was a mayor rather than a priest—a mayor of a town that spatted against itself nearly every day of the year, to which he could bring no peace.

"This man—this mayor—will be held for ransom until you, his beloved citizens, prove to comply. Henceforth all men of this village are required to register with the local office of the German Imperial Army. You will provide your name, your age, your job and skill level, along with the number of your family, your livestock, and possessions of any measure. You will be available to us upon demand and be required to report to the presiding German official two times per day, at ten o'clock in the morning and at six o'clock in the evening."

He walked away then, and Julitte heard the crunch of loose gravel on the cobbles beneath his boots. There was an immediate general upheaval. Julitte was tempted to go outside too, to add her voice to the questions, the protests, the confusion. But she stayed put. In a moment the same voice rose above the others again.

"You will follow my orders in a quiet and reasonable fashion. Those who do not adhere to these rules will join your beloved mayor where he will now reside, in the confines of his jail. He is our insurance that you, his citizens, will obey lest he be made to bear the brunt of your dishonor."

The grumbling quickly disappeared altogether while the men were forced at gunpoint to form a line. Julitte leaned toward the window again, watching as the remaining men of her village—even Marcel—were marched in a single file toward the town square. And the street was quiet once more, but for the occasional, distant rumble of gunfire.

She turned from the window and her gaze fell back on the table, where she'd left her Bible. Most of the men assembled from her village had been old, too old to fight. Of the young, only a half dozen or so had remained behind after the call to arms. Her cousin Yves had been among them, Yves who'd always looked so tall and strong but had such pain in his back he'd been sent home from military duty two years ago. He wasn't much help to Uncle Guy in the bakery, because his back pained him so he could barely bend over the dough and pastries.

Then there was Bastien Toussaint, who was nearly blind, and Marcel and two de Colvilles who, like Marcel, had taken too much of their *blanche* absinthe over the years to do anyone any good. Who would put a gun into the hand of someone who shook the way they did whenever they visited sobriety?

The few others who might have gone off to fight had stayed behind because they refused to leave their families and in the chaos of mobilization had been forgotten.

But Julitte saw that all of the men, young or old, Toussaint or de Colville, had one thing in common as they walked with German guns aimed at their back.

Fear. The same fear she felt for them.

She fell to her knees to the only One who could cast away such a thing.

Charles slid silently behind the door, his back ramrod stiff against the wall. His breath caught.

Fear congealed at the sight of a gun muzzle slowly pushing the door inward. How many were there? Were the Germans searching every hiding place, ready to capture—or kill—those living in this conquered land? Even unarmed civilians like him?

Charles wanted to close his eyes, telling himself he didn't care to see the face of his executioner. But morbid curiosity wouldn't let him. If he was to die, he suddenly found he wanted to see something other than the inside of his own lids at the last moment.

And then he saw the cuff. Torn, dirty. *Blue.*

France might have built up their army in recent years to a power to be reckoned with, but they'd retained one tie to their old, antiquated ways—their colorful uniforms.

Charles waited. Even if it was an outdated rifle nothing like the ones he'd seen the Germans carrying, an old bullet could be as effective as a new one at this range. In the hands of a nervous soldier, anything could happen.

"Care to join me for some breakfast . . . Sergeant?" Charles inquired in French, stepping out from behind the door.

The man pivoted to face Charles fully in one facile movement, drawing his gun high. Reflexively Charles raised his hands to show he was unarmed. Then, since the man hadn't already shot, guessed he wouldn't.

Charles looked around. "Are you alone?"

The man seemed incapable of congenial small talk. He still pointed the gun at Charles.

Charles smiled, keeping his palms high in the air. "I am on your side, you know." For the first time in days Charles was able to issue a laugh. "Belgian by birth. A neighbor. An ally."

"You . . . have papers of some kind?"

"It's there." Charles motioned with his gaze. "See for yourself." He'd taken the Belgian *passeport* from his pocket in anticipation of burying it but had placed it atop his suitcase while waiting in silence behind the door.

The Frenchman started to move but must have realized he would have to pass too closely to Charles to grab the document. "Toss it here. One hand."

Charles did so. The man was old for a soldier, confirming what Charles knew from the uniform: he was with the cavalry. He was short and wiry, but Charles imagined he would look taller in a saddle, especially with one of those plumed hats they liked to wear, which was missing now. For controlling friendly crowds out to catch a glimpse of European nobility, this man probably looked forbidding enough.

The soldier unfolded the paper and read the description, glancing up as if to see if the words matched the way Charles looked. If he had any doubts, they disappeared with the cavalryman's tired sigh and slowly lowered rifle. He moved to the nearest chair and dropped the paper to the tabletop, brushing his face with his free hand. The other still held the gun, though it was now draped harmlessly through the crook of his arm.

He mumbled something, words Charles could not at first fathom. Something about . . . someone being dead. All of them.

Charles approached slowly, taking the remaining empty chair. "Who is dead?"

The man looked up as if startled either by Charles's nearness or that he'd heard his words.

"My regiment of dragoons. Somehow we became trapped behind

the Germans." He closed his eyes momentarily, and when he opened them again, he stared through Charles as if he weren't there. "We knew they were behind us. We thought we followed the British, but somehow we lost them. And there before us, the great gray beast—advancing." His gaze seemed to find Charles for the first time. "How did they do it? So many . . . so vigorous . . . so strong . . ."

The cavalryman sat up straighter. "But we were grand, our regiment. Our lieutenant called the charge. Lances at the ready, plumes to the wind, we galloped like . . . like . . ." Before he found the word, his shoulders sagged again. "Like little bees against a behemoth. It was suicide. My regiment . . . is gone."

"How did you get away?"

"I do not know. I charged with the rest of them, and before I knew it, with bullets whizzing and shouts ringing, I was suddenly beyond them, beyond everything and in a forest. I should have gone back for another charge. But I knew they were gone. All gone."

"If you had, you'd be dead with the rest of them," Charles said. "And the Germans not a step behind in their march."

The man's dark eyes found Charles's again. "I had the best mount. The fastest. That is the only reason I am here. The German infantry I charged—they scattered in fear of me. I was off and away before a bullet could reach me."

Charles patted the man's shoulder. "Something they won't soon forget, I'm sure."

At least this man had done something. His training had equipped him for action, even if it had been foolish. And if he had a horse . . .

"But she is gone now. I didn't know it, but she'd been shot and carried me to safety anyway. She would have lingered . . . but I put her out of her misery. She is gone; yes, gone now."

So much for thinking transportation might get easier with this newfound friend.

The soldier brushed a hand over his face, then looked around at the room again. "You live here?"

No sense lying. Even wrinkled and filthy, his clothes would never pass for a forester's. "No. I've spent the last few days or more trying to get back to Belgium to volunteer for king and country. After my motor was commandeered by . . ." He let the sentence fade so the officer wouldn't think Charles held anything against the French army. "I was forced to go by foot. Yesterday I heard the rumblings of a skirmish nearby and found my way here for cover." He raised his hands again, palms upward. "No arms to join in, not even a pistol."

Charles was relieved the soldier seemed to accept the near truth of the latter part of his story. Judgment never entered the soldier's eye.

"My name is Pepin Laroche." He tilted his capless head Charles's way, somewhat stiffly, as if he thought he still wore his tall hat.

After Charles introduced himself, he stood. Then he straightened his chair and looked down at Pepin, who appeared exhausted again. "I can vouch for the relative comfort of the cot," Charles said with a nod in that direction. "Looks to me as though you could use some rest."

The man nodded, eyeing the cot as a child might his mother's lap.

Charles took his Belgian *passeport* from the table, then turned toward his suitcase. "I will leave you to it, then, Sergeant. Although I cannot vouch for the kitchen stock. There is little food left, just a couple of unmarked tins. I wish you well wherever you go."

Pepin stood, somewhat quickly for a man about to go to bed. "You are leaving?"

"Yes, I was about to set out when you arrived."

"But—" Pepin's brows drew together—"wouldn't we be better off in number?"

Charles considered the words. One thing was obvious: whether they went separately or together, they both needed a plan.

But he wasn't sure about safety in numbers. One man alone might be suspected a spy. Two or more together, especially one dressed like Pepin, could be shot as enemy soldiers before a question was asked.

Both options came with danger, yet which yielded the least?

6

A crash at the door threatened to burst the bolt from its spot. Julitte sprang from her mat, shoving a blouse over her head and stumbling into a skirt, right on top of the shift she slept in.

German shouts, no attempt at French, commanded her to open the door. A peek out the window, the street lit only by the slimmest of dawn's rays, proved Julitte's wasn't the only house to be roused. Across the way, Gustave de Colville's threshold gaped wide, and each door down to her uncle's bakery was either ajar or being battered by the butt of a German rifle.

With another clap at her own entryway, Julitte scurried to the bolt, sliding it up and out of the way just before she jumped free of its arc and it hit the wall behind.

A pair of soldiers rushed in, speaking fast to each other and, after quickly assessing Julitte was alone, ignoring her. One went to the loft, the other to the cabinet near the stove. Julitte understood little of what they said, only an occasional word now and then. Ridicule for another town full of the French poor.

Pans clattered as the soldier nearest Julitte took the largest soup cauldron and began filling it with items from the shelf. A copper kettle, dishes her father had brought home from China, a bowl edged with gold he'd given his wife on an anniversary. From the loft above, the other soldier threw down her blanket, the pair of clogs Pierre had left behind when the army had given him a pair of boots, the tin box she'd rescued from the tree. It jarred open from the fall and Pierre's wood carvings rolled to the side, the paring knife bouncing harmlessly onto the blanket.

Julitte stood in the corner, hands clasped to her chest in the useless hope to still her trembling. Even her prayer brought no peace, not until they marched out with whatever they pleased to take.

From outside, another voice sounded above the echoing raids. In French, but awkward enough to know it was no Frenchman who spoke.

"This is a war tax; there is no need to fear. You must give the war tax freely and willingly, and no one will be harmed." The speaker walked farther down the street, repeating the label he issued to this looting. "War tax, this is a war tax, payable to the German Imperial Army under the direction of His Eminence, the German emperor, king of Prussia, Kaiser Wilhelm. Every citizen is required to pay the war tax."

At the window, Julitte saw carts being rolled along the street, soon laden with goods from the village, from homes lived in or abandoned. As far as Julitte could see, the Germans visited every home, every cellar, every outbuilding, taking what they pleased.

Julitte watched the grim faces of those with far more to lose than she: Gustave de Colville saw his silver collection carted off, his cousin Iva her coins, Uncle Guy his largest copper mixing bowls. Prized goods were loaded on one cart or another, headed out of town. No doubt going east, to Germany.

Tears sprang to her eyes. It wouldn't have been considered an impressive haul by the looks of it, but it was the best this little village had to offer. And now the shelves above her table were nearly bare of the souvenirs Narcisse had brought from his various travels. She touched what was left: an old tin cup, a chipped plate, an odd saucer. Dishes older than she was.

She remembered Claudette being teased about not keeping her home intact for her new husband. Now Julitte couldn't provide an unchanged home for those who'd marched from her home, either.

When the streets quieted, she ventured outside. The soldiers hadn't bothered to close the door on their way out, so she easily heard the voices changing from German to French.

"How are we to live?"

A morning sunray caught the moisture in Uncle Guy's eyes as his gaze followed the path the carts had taken to carry his bakeware away. Beside him, his son Yves stood with his hand on his father's shoulder.

Julitte stepped next to them. "God will provide a way, Uncle Guy. He always does." The words came from her lips, but it was as if someone else spoke, because her heart was numb. God knew, surely He knew, what it felt like to be stripped of every possession. Yet the morning's violation shriveled her insides, including that place where God's peace rested.

Though her uncle nodded, Julitte saw his doubt matched her own.

"Let's go see what they left," she invited, looping her arm through his and pulling him along.

As expected, the shelves that had once proudly displayed Uncle Guy's bread and pastries were barren. Beyond that, the kitchen was depleted of most flour and sugar and not likely to be filled again anytime soon, since regular shipments had stopped. Left behind was a mess of dishes, dishcloths, and scraps of papers that were Uncle Guy's prized recipes.

But there were a few items left.

"See, Uncle!" Julitte called, sliding a pair of dented bowls from a low shelf. "They didn't take everything."

A curse from Yves turned their attention to the huge oven set in the corner. He stood with an empty clay pot in his hands.

"Our money . . . all gone!" He pointed to the cookstove. "I put it in the pot, inside the oven under the ashes. I didn't have time to find a better spot—you know, the old—" He stopped so abruptly that Julitte wondered what he was thinking, why his gaze had gone behind the stove. Then he shook his head. "They found it and took it, those . . . those . . ." His mouth twisted and he uttered another word Julitte had never heard from her cousin's lips before. Uncle Guy went to Yves's side, searching through the ashes for something, perhaps a coin that might have been missed.

Julitte found her way out. She'd seen the Germans take her father's souvenirs; she didn't need to search her own cottage. Whatever else they'd taken didn't matter. Unless . . .

Suddenly she was running. She burst into her home and leaped up the stairs.

And there, just where she'd left it, was her Bible. Untouched.

Sinking to her cot, she laughed at her own foolishness over having feared losing the one book she never wanted to live without. A Bible was what each soldier needed most, but evidently they hadn't figured that out yet.

For days Charles and Pepin walked the countryside, foraging for food, avoiding any sounds or sign of battle.

They couldn't live this way much longer, though, wandering around in hopes of a cease-fire so everybody could just go home. Who knew when that day would come? The forest didn't provide enough food to live on long, not with such limited hunting resources, and it was already autumn. If the battles went on much longer, Charles and Pepin would have no choice but to find whatever German commander was in charge in this territory and offer themselves up. The choice was clear: live like an animal, subject to the elements that promised soon to be too harsh to withstand, or become a "guest" of the German Imperial Army.

The rabbit Pepin had snared was cooked and eaten, but Charles's stomach still ached as if empty. He knew in a while the feeling would go away, only to rear itself up again tomorrow. Hunger was new to Charles. And while he hardly welcomed it, the feeling inspired a certain kinship with an entire segment of the population he'd rarely considered before. How did those who lived in poverty manage? Surely if hunger had gnawed at his stomach on a regular basis, he'd have found a way out.

If only he'd gone with Mantoux, by now he'd no doubt be lounging in Spain or Greece or even America—anyplace safe.

Charles sat forward, brushing his fingers on the grass beside him. Walking in circles, that was what they'd been doing. Wasting time. Hiding out. Grown men, strong of mind, able of body, reduced to this. Charles turned away, as disgusted with Pepin as he was with himself.

But wait. Why hadn't he thought of it immediately? Those images of Mantoux strolling along the white beaches of America had Charles sitting up straight. Mantoux!

Charles had no idea how far it was, but surely if he could find his way back, he could find shelter at Mantoux's abandoned château.

The sun would soon set, the time they usually took to their wandering and scavenging ways, keeping low during the daylight hours and cooking before dark, when a fire would be spotted more easily.

Charles looked at Pepin. "Do you have any idea where we are?"

"A little. We've traveled south these past few days, but we're still north of Cambrai."

"And if we were to go to Le Catelet, would you know how to get there?"

"But of course. Why there? That is the direction of the fighting."

"We can skirt that, the way we've been doing. Perhaps bypass it, with any luck find a French regiment if we keep heading west. On the way, there is a village west of Le Catelet. Briecourt. Do you know it?"

"*Oui*, I'm from Perrone; of course I know of every town in that area. But surely you are not serious? Briecourt?" Pepin's mouth curled downward. "No one goes there. The people of that town are so busy fighting among themselves they've no welcome for out-siders, even if someone were to go out of the way to get there."

Charles stood, for the first time in two weeks knowing where he was going. "I know the owner of the château. He left a cellar—a big one—that holds food and wine and every luxury. Even if it's been raided, maybe they left something behind. If not . . . maybe we can still find cover there, a headquarters of our own to determine if it's possible to get past the fighting. *Comfortable* cover, at least for a while."

And there is a girl near there, or at least there used to be. . . . But Charles kept that thought to himself. She was no doubt gone. In spite of having been caught up in a tree, somehow she'd seemed the sensible kind.

Though Pepin stood too, he hardly looked convinced. "But we can find an abandoned farm closer than that here, where there hasn't been any fighting in days."

Charles knew Pepin would follow; he always did, even when he protested. "For how much longer? And eat what? We can't stay here and wait for the Germans to revisit. New waves of them are coming all the time."

"But maybe the Germans are already there."

"Then we'll find out, won't we?"

Scrambling to gather what he'd pulled from the ground that day, Pepin took a few steps, dropped a beet, picked it up, then hastened after Charles with the loot in his arms. He didn't look as hopeful as Charles suddenly felt, but there would be time to convince him.

Going *some*where was better than *any*where.

7

It took them five days to get there, when it should have taken a day or two at most. But moving German troops had once again altered, then stalled, their route, and Charles and Pepin traveled only at night. Now, just after dawn, Charles looked at the horizon, where Anton Mantoux's château lay. From this distance, it looked the same. Almost. Expansive but low-roofed, tiled in a Spanish style, with walls of a local whitish stone already blackened by coal smoke from its eight chimneys. Never before had Charles seen the estate so near dawn, at least from the outside.

But it didn't take more than a first glance to know Mantoux's home was no longer his. Charles should have known, since their night travel had taken them closer and closer to the fighting just west. The cannon boom was louder, explosions brighter. Despite that, he'd hoped the fighting had gone on to another area and left this spot unspoiled.

That hope died with what he saw now. Dotted around the grounds, on top of Mantoux's favorite gardens, were campfires and tents, horses corralled behind rope gates, even a car (no doubt commandeered) with military flags displayed on its hood.

No sanctuary to be found here.

Charles leaned against a tree, his eye caught by another tree in the distance, one that stood in a matched set like a gate to the

Mantoux Wood. That tree, on the outskirts of the farthest garden, was the one the girl had been climbing. That day seemed long ago now. What had Mantoux called her? Julitte? Thinking of her again today made him wonder where she was. No doubt following the flood of refugees that had gone ahead of the German army. Such a pretty girl wouldn't last long with this number of men billeted so close to her home.

"We cannot stay here," Pepin said, "under the eye of the German army. Where do we go now?"

"Relax, Pepin. Their eyes are to the west, not this way."

Despite his assurances, Charles knew Pepin was more right than he. The two of them couldn't stay here. He clutched his suitcase; it seemed part of him now, he'd been holding the silly thing so long. It served as a pillow during the day, when they snatched what sleep they could, hiding under bushes. It was an umbrella in the rain, a seat when no rock could be found. He'd become inordinately fond of the blasted thing. It was, practically speaking, his only possession.

Charles began walking. Anton's forest was like all of his friend's possessions: lush, well stocked, plentiful. They wouldn't be foolish enough to cook anything so close to a German billet, but there were plenty of low bushes and dense brush to offer cover, even under a bright autumn sky.

"The fight around here can't last much longer, Pepin," Charles said. "It makes sense to stay in this forest, as close to the lines as we dare, so we can break through as soon as the opportunity presents itself."

Pepin snickered. "So many Germans in one place cannot be good for us."

"Unfortunately, we've no choice but to wait for our opportunity."

"Here? And when winter sets in? I know what you have in that suitcase of yours, Charles, and all of it put together wouldn't make a coat fit for either one of us."

He was right, every word accurate. "You, Pepin, are a pessimist. The Germans will be gone before the first snowflake."

Rain spat from the sky like slender needles, poking exposed skin. Charles drew up his collar and raised his suitcase over his head. His beard itched. His clothes stank. He was hungry. The growing fury of this rain annoyed him.

"You're familiar with the town near here?" Charles said, over the wind that sharpened the rain.

"As much as any outsider could be."

"There is a church?"

"Of course. Every village has a church. Even that one."

Pepin said it as though he doubted many people from this particular village used the services a church provided. All the better.

"We'll go there as soon as the sun sets. With any luck, the rain will stay and no one will be out, not even soldiers, if there are any."

"I'm not so sure, Charles. That town . . ."

"Yes?"

"They wouldn't help a stray dog, not even before the war. Why would they help us now?"

"Surely the *curé*? A man of God?"

Pepin shrugged. "There are other rumors besides their mean-spiritedness."

"Tell me."

"About what they drink. Poison."

"What sort of drink?"

"They call it *blanche* like everyone else. Some even smuggle it outside France. But their best customers are their neighbors. To dull the pain of their lungs, from working in the mines. Listen, though—" he tapped his forehead—"it makes you crazy if you drink it more than once. Violent. Or stupid. One or the other."

"*Blanche* might kill you, Pepin, but it doesn't make people stupid. Not for long, anyway. Like someone who drinks too much wine, it wears off."

"There are more rumors, if that one is not enough for you."

Charles sighed, shifting the suitcase above his head from one hand to the other.

"There is leprosy there."

Now he laughed. "Have you forgotten I visited here—that very château? My friend would have known about these silly stories if any were true and wouldn't have lived within walking distance."

Again Pepin shrugged, but Charles could see the man believed his own tales.

"Leprosy and insanity." Charles smiled. "Let's hope the Germans hear the rumors. Maybe it'll keep them away."

Darkness would come early under such heavy cloud cover. Charles let Pepin lead the way, since he was more familiar with the area. When at last they stood on the outskirts of the far side of the wood, they stopped at the shorn wheat fields edging the most remote home and village beyond.

Charles saw the church, nestled in the middle of huddled houses. Surprisingly, its tall brick bell tower competed in grandeur with another building not so far away, just opposite in the town square. Sturdy, wide, brick, and two stories high. A town hall? In a remote, ignored village like this?

Definitely a liability. Such a building would be tempting for any army on campaign, no matter what rumors they might hear about the town. Behind every army were officers—coordinators and communication teams—and each one needed an office.

One thing was clear: he and Pepin had to end this aimless wandering. Surely if this village could feed itself, they had enough to spare for two more mouths.

It was still too early in the day to chance being caught, so they found the same kind of place they'd found countless times before: low brush, bushes in which to rest. And waited.

"No one's heard anything? anything at all?"

Julitte stood with Ori and Father Barnabé outside his church near the well in the town square. Her spirit sagged at the somber set in his old blue eyes, the shake of his head his only answer. In the past days, he'd been forced to stop traveling to other towns as he'd done for as long as she could recall, visiting the Lord's flock or to offer mass. The *Orstkommandant,* the man the Germans had left behind as the local commander, had forbidden all travel between towns. This German in charge was stocky and thick necked but wore glasses, which probably explained his assignment here rather than behind the barrel of a rifle. He'd taken up residence in one of the abandoned homes, and she saw little of him, hoping that remained true for the duration of Germany's "visit."

Father Barnabé had tried to call the village together on more than one occasion to pray, something Julitte longed for again and again, but was barred even from doing that. How much would this village bear? First most of their men marched happily off to war, eager to shed blood defending their country. Then the army had taken their wheat. And poor Victor, shot by a German scouting party. Blood touched even Briecourt, the one place Julitte thought would be safe. Already the dirt of his grave had dried, and in spring the earth would grow a grassy blanket on top.

It made no sense that the Germans had come to their little town, their town that no one visited, that kept to itself. She'd asked God more than once why the Germans had not ignored them as everyone else had before. But they hadn't been spared, and neither had their possessions.

And now . . . the Germans had taken the few remaining fit men of their village. Yves among them. Fifteen men had been marched out just after dawn two days ago.

"I thought they had separated us for some reason, the young and able from the old, that day they arrived." Father Barnabé, with his close-shorn gray hair and the many wrinkles on his face and neck, looked older still from the droop of his brows. And the vestments he wore could not hide the slope of his shoulders.

Ori looped her arm through Julitte's as if the contact would help her receive news too hard to withstand. "Why do they not tell us something? anything?"

"I'm not sure it would be the truth, whatever they say," Father Barnabé said. "I would guess they've been taken as prisoners of war."

Ah, Lord, so much heartache for those left behind.

"Maybe that's better than fighting," Ori said. "At least they won't have bullets aimed at them. And the Germans will have to feed them. More than we might be able to do soon."

"God will see us through. Somehow." Julitte said the words she most wanted to hear and to believe. Saying them helped.

"It's best if you go now, both of you. It's going to rain," Father Barnabé told them. "Stay off the street before the Germans come out again this morning. I'll be visiting homes through the day and will see you later too."

Julitte never let go of her friend's arm, all the way back to Didi's. There were fewer Germans since that first wave of them after the arrival and raid, and just now the village looked as it always had, without a uniform in sight.

But she knew they were near.

After the raid, Julitte had moved in with Ori and Didi, leaving her home when Ori had asked—pleaded—that she come and live with them. With the nights soon to be chilly, it only made sense.

There was enough wood in the forest for fuel to light their stoves, but without permission to leave the village they couldn't gather it. Best to keep just one home warm instead of two.

"These Germans have done something awful to me, Ori," Julitte whispered. "They've made me afraid of men, even though not one of them has touched me."

Ori nodded, though she said nothing.

Didi was at the table when they entered. The cottage was somewhat larger than Julitte's, with a hearth room and a separate bedroom. A loft, wider than Julitte's, had once been the sleeping rooms for Ori and four of her siblings. The hearth room was large enough for a long, polished table and a padded settle that was edged on both sides by lamp tables. A rug covered the floor, right up to the cupboard that, even after the raid, was piled with plain white dishes.

Didi had begun laying out dishes for breakfast but frowned even as Julitte delivered the water she and Ori had fetched. "I've told you before, I don't want both of you to go for water." Her voice rang out despite the early hour.

"You were sleeping, Didi," Ori said, loud enough to be heard.

"We left just as soon as we could, before anyone else would be on the street," Julitte added.

They'd been assigned hours when they could fetch water, and Didi usually insisted on accompanying only one, either Julitte or Ori, at a time. She said it would be foolish to have both young women out at the same time, together no less, and that she would deter the eyes of the soldiers as best she could by walking at their side, serving to remind them of their mothers if they spoke and answering inquiries rather than making it necessary for either Ori or Julitte to meet the eye of any German soldier parading about the village.

So far their isolation had kept them safe, even if the hours were growing long.

They shared Uncle Guy's bread, sliced as thin as Didi's knife could cut. They'd already finished the last of the cheese, had tended the last of what their gardens grew with more care than ever. For dinner they would have potatoes, at least.

It seemed all the cellars were quiet, not a loom to be heard. The three of them had sewn the last of their cotton, finishing projects only such an imposed imprisonment might leave room to do. They'd tidied every corner and taken to singing, quietly so as not to be heard outside the walls, songs from the Bible, songs from the town, songs Narcisse and his sailors had taught Julitte growing up.

Julitte wondered how long the day ahead would feel. As long as yesterday?

Rain started to pour just as the three finished their breakfast, and Julitte thought of Pierre. Outside, no doubt. Fighting in all weather. She raised another prayer for him and thought to invite Didi and Ori to pray as well.

But the door suddenly rattled more loudly than from just the wind or rain. Only the pounding of a fist or rifle butt could make such a ruckus.

"Ki! Kinn! Gehen Sie hinaus! Sortez!"

Even if he hadn't used the variety of languages, Julitte would have known the demand for a response.

Julitte approached, nearest the door, but Didi called her back.

"Get behind me, Julitte." She moved as quickly as her unsteady limbs and cane could go. "And get the scarves."

Ori was already retrieving them, the plain cotton headwear that covered their hair for church and these days, when tied loosely enough, half their foreheads in an attempt to shadow their faces. Julitte accepted hers, exchanging glances with Ori.

"God is with us," Julitte whispered.

But Ori said nothing, not even a nod of acquiescence.

The door was not locked, though its lock was modern and

sturdy, needing a key. That had been another rule the Germans demanded: there were to be no locked doors between the villagers and the soldiers of this town. Didi opened the door.

A foot soldier stepped inside, rifle across his chest. He stood aside to let an officer enter behind him. Julitte's heart pounded. They hadn't seen an officer of any rank since that first day, not since the bespectacled German had been pronounced Orstkommandant. But this was a real officer, and even one so young seemed cause for alarm. Why had he chosen to visit *their* home? And now, in this weather?

He stood in the center of the hearth room dripping water and mud on the scrubbed wooden floor amid the plain but clean furniture beside the unlit hearth.

"I am *Hauptmann* Erich Basedow. Which one of you is the adoptive daughter of Narcisse Toussaint?"

Julitte's head went light from fear. She stepped beside Didi. They knew Narcisse?

"You will return to your home and take anyone who lives here with you. This home is more suitable to provide shelter for soldiers of the German Imperial Army."

Julitte nodded, seeing the man's profile. He was arrogant; she could tell that by the angle of his nose, the height of his chin. Not handsome, but rather pleasant if only he didn't represent all he represented. When he looked at her at last, she saw his eyes were not as cold as she expected. Then he looked beyond her, at Didi, then at Ori, who pushed back her scarf as if to see the invader closer.

With a hand resting on the pistol at his side, he turned back to the door. "You have one hour to leave. After that time this home is considered free to quarter soldiers of the German army."

Then he left.

When the door banged shut behind them, Julitte exchanged stunned glances with Ori and Didi. But quick glances, because they had just an hour to pack up what they could.

8

Charles woke to more rain. Just as well. He peered outside his covering, seeing nothing out of the ordinary, hearing nothing. He went to Pepin, nearby.

"Let's go," Charles said. He pointed to the ridge that separated the harvested fields. "We'll keep to the high grass, between those two fields." They'd have to squat, maybe even crawl now and then, but if anyone happened to gaze out, if the darkness wasn't cover enough, the grass would do the rest.

Charles cautioned away images of being inside a warm church, where he might take off his wet clothes and let them dry away from his skin for once. Refused to dwell on eating real food, like bread or stew or cheese or wine. Dreams like that might distract him from this moment, when he needed to listen past his hunger, past the wakening crickets. He must be aware of each movement, each sound around him. If he wanted to live, he couldn't waste his concentration on luxuries like warmth or bread or a bed with a pillow and a blanket.

He heard nothing but the patter of rain on the hard ground around them and, once they were near enough, the ping of droplets bouncing on tile rooftops. No human sounds except his own breathing and the occasional air Pepin sucked in.

At the end of the ridge, still under cover of grass and clutching his suitcase, Charles scooted as close as he dared to the edge of the field closest to the church.

"What if the Germans are in there, too?" Pepin whispered.

There were few windows along the side of the stone sanctuary, stained glass. No light shone from inside those windows, no smoke from its chimney. But a glance at other dwellings said the same.

"It's a risk, it's true," Charles admitted. "But it's here or the forest."

After a moment, lips taut, Pepin nodded once.

"A door is on the side. Did you see it?" Charles asked.

Pepin nodded again.

"One of us should go first, alone. No sense in both of us going near if it's locked."

Charles waited, wondering if Pepin would jump to volunteer, being the elder and a soldier, but he sat motionless.

The distance between them and the church was considerable. Charles glanced between buildings, his gaze landing on what he could see of the impressive town hall. It was on the other side of the street, but would anyone inside see his sprint to the church? The risk would never be lower, between the darkness and heavy clouds.

He had no choice. Clearly Pepin wasn't willing to go first, undoubtedly counting on *noblesse oblige* to make Charles do the right thing. Blast it all.

"If the door is locked, I'll find another way in, then open it from inside if I can. I'll get a signal to you. Wait for it. Look for it."

Studying the terrain, what little he could see in the evening hour, looking again for anyone at all—civilian or soldier—he had just enough time to consider praying. Isa was always telling him to pray, but it never seemed necessary. If God was in control, which Charles had suddenly doubted since the day he'd lost his car, why would He listen to the petty fears, complaints, or suggestions Charles could make?

A burst of fire tore through his veins, and still clutching his constant companion, unwilling to leave the suitcase behind, Charles shot from the grassy cover to the darkest shadow of the church steeple. He hardly breathed until he reached the door, throwing himself silently at what he now noticed was an intricately carved entryway beneath a stone arch. Ear to wood, he listened for silence before trying the knob.

It was unlocked.

With a last glance around, Charles pushed at the door. It creaked once; he stopped. He pushed again, just far enough to allow himself entry. Best to see if he was alone before waving Pepin in.

Shadows of black and gray outlined windows, barely defining walls and floors. Charles saw he was in a plain vestibule. A hallway led straight ahead; a stairway to the left led to a cellar below. He walked as far as he dared down the hall, all the while listening for any movement. Nothing. No light, no sound at all.

Another door led to a small room, no doubt the sacristy behind the sanctuary. It, too, was empty and dark.

He turned around, descending the cellar stairway. Below stairs, it was dark and damp, with old pews shrouded in canvas, a stack of old catechisms nearby. Empty crates.

Despite the dust and mold, it was a better alternative than the forest—if they could find some help. Where was the *curé*? They had to eat.

Near one of the boxes at the foot of the stairs, Charles set aside his suitcase and found a stack of neatly folded material—old curtains or vestments for altar boys perhaps, but just what he needed if it could be used for a secular purpose. Taking a couple, he went upstairs to the door and looked outside before extending his arm in a wave to Pepin. At first Charles wasn't sure the other man saw his signal. He heard nothing, saw nothing even in the distance. Then, at last, he saw the slight, dark shadow and heard the shuffle of boots on the damp grass. Hopefully the downpour would continue, enough to flatten the rest of the old grass around their path.

Pepin slipped inside. Wordlessly Charles tossed him a scrap of white material and both of them wiped off themselves and their shoes, then rubbed away the water they'd brought in with them. Charles retraced the steps he'd taken earlier, erasing evidence of his arrival. Then, with another silent wave, he invited Pepin to follow.

"There are plenty of empty pews under these shrouds to give us cover," Charles whispered. "Find one. The *curé* is bound to come sooner or later, and we'll see if he has any food. For now . . . we'll just wait."

Pepin nodded and both headed to the canvas coverings. Charles chose the farthest and pulled it back, intent on a place for his suitcase and a spot to enjoy a real rest without rain beating his forehead.

But instantly he saw this was not to be. Someone already occupied this pew.

Squatting by her hearth, Julitte stirred the last of the embers, welcoming the little eruption of heat that came with the action. Didi smiled nearby, sitting in the chair Narcisse had once called his favorite. On its wide, sturdy seat was a cushion that Julitte herself had helped her adoptive mother weave. At least that hadn't been taken.

Where Narcisse's souvenirs once perched now stood Didi's dishware, the pieces the Germans had left her. On the other side of the hearth, Narcisse's cot was now Didi's. And in the loft, the mat Pierre once used was now Ori's.

"I believe you make the embers multiply, Julitte," Didi said in her loud way.

Julitte shook her head. "No, that's the warmth of a moment's peace you're feeling."

"I don't know how we'll keep warm this winter," Ori called from the loft above. She'd claimed she was cold and so had gone up to nestle under her blanket despite the early evening hour. They were barely settled from their harried move, with their clothes, their remaining blankets and dishes, a few books, and small family mementos, all tucked here and there in the only home Julitte had known since she was five years old.

A tap at the door startled Julitte, soft as it was.

"That's not a German knock," Didi said with a grin, letting Julitte go to the door. "I barely heard it."

"Julitte."

Before she'd even opened the door, she heard Father Barnabé's voice. She hastened to let him inside.

"It's almost dark, Father!" she scolded. Curfew was part of the new restrictions, and as far as she knew, it extended even to the town priest.

"Yes, yes," he said. "But with the rain no one is about. I'll stay but a moment."

"What's so important that you risked coming, Father?" Didi asked, rather quietly for her. Perhaps she feared the question might be heard through the walls if she could hear it herself.

"I've learned why the Germans put you all here, though they haven't billeted Didi's yet. The de Colvilles have been talking."

Julitte frowned. That was never good news, and yet Father Barnabé looked oddly pleased. He'd always been considered fair and generous of his time to both Toussaint and de Colville, but Julitte couldn't help thinking he sided with her family, if he had to choose. How could he condone the liquor the de Colvilles brewed and smuggled? Father Barnabé had long ago given up trying to change things.

"They've been talking to the *Germans*."

"To whom?" Didi asked, cupping an ear with one hand, hobbling closer with her cane in the other.

"The Germans!"

"And saying what?"

Julitte wasn't nearly as eager to hear as Didi appeared. Even Ori had crawled from the mattresses upstairs, still huddled in her blanket, to sit at the edge of the loft, where she could see what went on below the railing.

He looked at Julitte. "They told them about where you were born and embellished, shall we say. The Germans think you're a leper, and anyone who comes near you takes his life in his hands."

Didi laughed—not just a little laugh but a whoop so loud Julitte feared someone outside, if anyone were outside, could hear. Even Ori laughed from above.

"They say they're going to move Marcel to your house, Didi," Father Barnabé continued. "Only they haven't decided if his insanity is catching too, because the de Colvilles said Marcel's wife is showing signs of the disease as well. They didn't tell them about the de Colvilles who suffer the same as he does from the brew they make—and that they've smuggled it for generations."

"I wonder if the de Colvilles know they're doing us such a favor," Julitte said. "I don't care about the reason, as long as the Germans leave us alone."

Father Barnabé put a hand on the door again, but his face lost its mirth. "I wish I could say it was ignorance on the de Colvilles' part or even a hope to gain the good graces of the Germans by telling them all their gossip. But . . ."

"What, Father?"

"I believe they've decided if deportations to Germany continue, the Germans will start with those they fear. Like you. And Marcel." He sighed. "The de Colvilles only wanted the attention off of themselves."

"We'll leave it all in God's hands, then," she said, "where it belongs."

The comforting words were barely out of her mouth before she sent up a plea to trust in such things herself.

9

Charles leaned a shoulder against the thick cement wall. He could see little more than shadows through what was supposed to pass as a window hidden behind an iron grate in this hovel of a church cellar. It must be another cloudy day, at least seven in a row now. But he could smell the outside air through the crack in the painted glass. It had been a month since he and Pepin had come to this place. This prison.

He glanced back at his fellow inmates. Pepin dozed once again on one of the pews. How many hours in a single day could one man sleep? And two others they'd learned that first night had taken refuge here as well: young Dowan, a seventeen-year-old from an Irish troop fighting with the British, and Seymour, from a British squadron. Both had lost their battalions and been wandering for weeks in the forests, much the way Charles and Pepin had.

A creak from the stairs sent everyone scrambling for the nearest hiding spot. Charles slipped under a tarp hanging in the corner, the others behind crates or under pews. Pulling the tarp closer, Charles caught sight of Pepin—still sound asleep.

The man had a tendency to snore, night or day. Rather than risk the noise it would take to call out in hopes of waking him, Charles scurried to him. He shook Pepin awake before throwing a tarp over the groggy man's body. Then, with no time to get back under his own tarp, Charles flung himself beneath another pew nearby.

A tap at the bottom of the stairway calmed Charles's nerves and no doubt everyone else's. He shook his head, wondering how long it would take the *curé* to learn he should tap the signal at the top of the stairs instead of the bottom, so they wouldn't all scramble as they just had.

But Father Barnabé was old, and Charles wouldn't complain—not when the risk taken extended to the priest's life, between hiding them and somehow scrounging up enough food for all mouths to be fed. There was never quite enough, but none of them were starving. Yet.

The priest held a familiar book in his wrinkled hand, but it wasn't a book at all anymore. Rather it was a hollowed-out case that often held sausage or bread. He raised a hand for them to gather closer. "I've spoken to two families," he said as he handed out meager portions of food. "Willing to take most of you."

"Into their homes?" Charles asked. He'd once hoped for such generosity, but as the days passed, that hope had dwindled, and he began to believe Pepin's stories about the animosity in this village.

"For three of you. One must stay here, at least for the time being."

"Just as well," Charles said. He knew for them to be hidden together—three who wore soldiers' uniforms—was more dangerous than if they'd been able to separate. "When do we move?"

"Tonight. But first you must decide who stays."

Charles translated for Seymour and Dowan, both of whom spoke only English.

"Father," said Dowan, his pale ruddy skin splotching as he spoke, as it so often did beneath that bright red hair, "it's sure you are they won't be turnin' us in to the Germans?"

Charles interpreted.

"Oui."

He didn't look convinced. "But why would they be wantin' to protect us? Strangers, and all?"

The priest looked from Dowan to Charles. "Tell him they know you fought with their loved ones, for France, on French soil. That is enough."

Charles conveyed the words, knowing the sentiment didn't extend to him.

"Which one of you will stay?" Father Barnabé asked.

"Straws?" Pepin suggested.

Charles nodded, going to the broom in the corner and breaking off a strand, snapping it again four times into varying lengths. Longest would stay.

Charles found himself wishing to go even though, so far, the church had proven safe. He was sick of this damp, musty cellar, and the priest, though kind, was so old Charles feared he would be careless. Of course, who knew what kind of peasants they were entrusting themselves to?

He drew a short straw. Pepin would stay; Charles and the others would go.

"Where will we be hidden?" Seymour asked, and Charles repeated the question to the priest in French.

"One of you will go to the baker, another to a miner's home, the last to a metalworker."

Charles reached for the straws again, taking only three this time and handing them to the priest to hold. "Longest for the baker."

"No, no," Father Barnabé said. "Only two of you are possibilities for the baker, and one of those would have been Pepin. The hiding place is small, and neither you nor Dowan will fit. Too tall. You would be too uncomfortable."

Pepin handed his straw to Charles. "You stay here in the church, then. Seymour and I will draw for the baker."

Charles nodded, not missing the eagerness in Pepin's eyes. Little wonder: stay here with a doddering caretaker or in the warm kitchen of the only baker in town? For the first time in his life, Charles wished he were a shorter man.

Pepin drew the long straw; he would go to the baker.

"Settled, then?" Father Barnabé asked. He should be about to leave, business concluded, but showed no sign of going. Instead, the lines on his fair, weathered face deepened. "There is something you all must know about our little village before I send you out."

"If you're about to tell us of the rumors, there's no need, Father," Pepin said. "I already told them about what this town is famous for."

Father Barnabé raised his brows. "And what is that?"

"Why—the obvious." Now it was Pepin's turn to let his color deepen. "The fighting, long before any war started. And the men who are crazy from the *blanche* this town brews. And the—the leprosy."

Instead of holding on to the offense that had seemed so ready to appear on his face, the *curé* laughed. "I've traveled to many towns around here, Mr. Pepin, but rarely has anyone said these things to me. Where do they tell such tales?"

"Everywhere. That is, everywhere near here."

"Good, that is good. Most of us are convinced it's why so few Germans have opted to stay here. We send up thanks for whatever keeps them out."

"What were you going to tell us about the town, Father?" Charles asked.

"Some of our reputation is sadly deserving. The hostility. There are two sides to this town, the Toussaints and the de Colvilles. Each of you will be staying with families loyal to the Toussaints."

Charles couldn't squelch his scorn. "Having a common enemy like the Germans hasn't brought the town together?"

Father Barnabé lifted his hands as if in supplication to the God he served. "I pray for such a thing every day, but so far I've seen little evidence of an answer. So," he continued, "if any one of you is given the slightest liberty within the boundaries of the home you'll share, be careful to whom you speak. If you are spotted, every resident here will instantly know you are not from this town. You may risk betrayal if the wrong person sees you and knows who is helping you. That person may not be wearing a German uniform. Do you understand?"

Charles understood all too well. He may not have much freedom in the bowels of a church, but any hope of this prison widening beyond its current boundary faded.

This was just wonderful. Enemies at every turn.

10

"Your uncle was acting oddly all afternoon, don't you think?" Ori asked as they walked back to Julitte's home. "Sending us out of there without even time for a proper visit?"

Julitte cast a last look over her shoulder. Uncle Guy still stood on the stoop to his shop, watching them walk off after he'd all but shooed them out the door.

Julitte and Ori had ventured outside on such a lovely day, and since they saw only a couple of German soldiers from a distance, they'd made more than just a quick trip to the well and back. They had visited Uncle Guy, thinking he might be lonely since Yves had been sent to Germany to work. But Uncle Guy hadn't allowed them to stay through dinner, citing worries that the Germans were planning another house search any day now and telling them that they should go back to Didi's side and bury whatever remaining goods they could find.

"There's not a German to be found today," Ori said to Julitte on their way back to the cottage. "Not even the Hauptmann."

"You say that with regret."

"Well, even you must admit Hauptmann Basedow has a certain . . . look about him."

"Best to lower your voice if you're going to speak kindly of a German, Ori."

"Admit it. Even a German man is nice to look on once in a while."

"You should fear them like the rest of us."

"I do fear them," she said quickly. "But not so much that Hauptmann. It's been weeks since they came, and ever since that day . . . I told you about . . ."

Julitte remembered the afternoon Ori came home with her cheeks pink and eyes aglow. She'd been walking to the dairy to see if any milk was to be had. The Hauptmann had been approaching from the opposite side of the shop and stopped to bow and open the door for Ori to enter. Then, instead of following her inside, he'd gone on his way. That he'd stopped solely as a courtesy to Ori had impressed her far more than it should have, in Julitte's opinion.

Julitte eyed her friend. "If you so much as gaze upon that Hauptmann, who knows what he would do? And if a de Colville sees you, I hate to think what they would do. Why give them more to hold against us?"

Ori shrugged. "Why not? They'll hate us anyway."

They came to Julitte's door, where the scent of soup wafted from the open window nearby. One of the metalworkers who'd worked in the village down the road before the Germans had taken over the plant had sneaked out to the forest that morning, bringing back a cache of poached rabbits. They wouldn't have been considered poached before the Germans came, even on land once belonging to M. Mantoux. Suddenly everything belonged to Germany. Half the village, including Julitte, thought rabbits stolen from under the German hand were tastier than ever.

"I'm going to the church for a little while," Julitte said when Ori opened the door. Going back into the house after days of enforced solitude was the last thing she wanted to do. She smiled. "Save some soup for me. It smells wonderful."

It was good to be able to go to the church, if only by herself.

She missed singing with the rest of the town, missed sitting on a pew knowing everyone else was praying, Toussaint and de Colville alike, just as she was. She would take advantage of the day's freedom and imagine herself amid a roomful of worshipers, all praising and imploring God above.

Charles finished the last of his exercises—push-ups and sit-ups and knee bends he'd learned to do at one school or another while growing up. Here, these days, he had to demand some use of his limbs. Despite the lack of sufficient food, his muscles cried for activity.

And fatigue helped keep the loneliness away.

The darkened basement seemed more dank and empty since the others had gone so many days ago, despite that brief eagerness he'd felt to be on his own. How long did it take for isolation to make one mad? Charles wasn't yet talking aloud to conjured companions just so he wouldn't forget the sound of a human voice, but sometimes he imagined it wouldn't be long before he resorted even to that.

This feeling of being cut off, being entirely alone, reminded him of a game he'd once played with his sister, Isa. Their home in Brussels had a room in the cellar only he and Isa ever explored. One time they'd pretended it was a hospital, and the other had to suffer an extended quarantine. Isa had the foresight to bring a book during her turn and hadn't minded in the least being down there all alone. When he'd declared her cured, he'd nearly had to force freedom on her. By contrast Charles had lasted less than a half hour. He'd banged on the wall of that secret room, saying he was tired of the game when really it was the seclusion he hated.

He snorted at his own fears. Father Barnabé still brought him food, and even if he didn't dare stay long to visit, at least Charles had some contact with the outside world. Besides, he'd heard of incarcerated men who survived years of isolation.

But physical survival wasn't what worried him.

A noise from above caught his attention. He listened. Nothing. Maybe he was imagining things again. Until he'd figured out there was a gap in one of the window casings, he'd wondered about a certain groaning he heard now and then.

Footsteps sounded along the church floor, to the altar. There the sound stopped.

Certainly it wasn't a German; though they'd been in the church only once since Charles's arrival—fifteen minutes of time he wouldn't soon forget—their hobnail boots were unmistakable on the old wood and tiled floor.

He'd been told the church remained unlocked like every other building in the village, but few people came anymore. Services had been suspended, public gatherings forbidden. But the footsteps he heard couldn't have belonged to more than one person. Whether it was boldness or foolishness, he didn't know, but the lure of someone else so close was too much to ignore.

He crept up the stairs, knowing darkness would soon fall, bringing curfew with it. This was also the dinner hour, when everyone should be at the table and not on the street. He'd expected Father Barnabé soon, but the footsteps had been too light to be his and more like the clogs of a child than the shoes of an adult.

Charles listened at the corner between the sacristy and the sanctuary. Waited.

Nothing. Perhaps he'd been mistaken. Light through the windows barely illuminated the sanctuary, and he saw the pews and chairs were as empty as always. No candles burned, but there were none to light since the candle stand off to one side stood empty. Evidently the German requisitions hadn't spared any houses, not even God's.

Charles moved to return downstairs, angry with himself for letting his thoughts get the best of him. Isolation here was better than being a prisoner of war. He shouldn't have allowed himself above the stairs. He wouldn't have taken the risk had the others still been here.

"O Father," came a voice—a woman's, certainly a young woman. Charles stopped, still hidden in the shadows.

"So many gifts have You given me, so many reasons have I to bow to You. I can scarcely close my eyes at night for the stars You've lit for me. I cannot open my eyes in the morning without some wondrous sight You've created for me. How long have You prepared this world for me, O Lord? How long have You paved the way for my path? And yet here I am before You again, as if all You've given me isn't enough. How loving You are to me, my Father God, to listen to all of my pleas and never turn me away empty-handed.

"I ask for more of Your grace. I long for word from my brother and from my father and from Yves. We fret over them, though we know You have them under your wing, Father. We need to hear from You, if only upon our hearts. . . ."

Charles stood back, pressing himself to the wall. For a moment he knew a twinge of envy over the ease with which she prayed, as if the dialogue with the God of the universe were something she carried on with someone she knew intimately and thoroughly. Perhaps this was how an angel might pray, someone who'd been in the presence of God. The few prayers he'd prayed, even lately when desperation and fear went along with them, compared as superficial. It almost made him want to do a better job.

But he didn't pray. Instead, he listened to her. She spoke of others, and he was struck by her concern for a town that was supposed to hold only animosity toward one another. She asked for peace, for the safe return of her brother, her father, someone called Yves. Then she sang some sort of song, something he'd never heard before, about God and His creation and other wonders. Her voice was clear, not like an opera singer nor even with the richness of one of the many theaters in Brussels, but pleasant nonetheless. Like an angel might sing, such words of pure praise.

Her peace became his. How long had it been since he'd heard a woman's voice? a woman's song? Too long. It made him want to leave the shadow, to go to her side and talk to her face-to-face.

Which would, of course, be madness.

So he stayed where he was.

He had no idea how long she might have stayed. Her prayers were so easy, her songs so natural, she might have stayed all night and he wouldn't have thought it odd or grown tired of listening.

But Charles heard another noise. The door again. Someone invaded the time between God and this young woman—and, it seemed, Charles too.

"Is someone here?"

Father Barnabé. Charles stole a quick glance to see him with a candle in one hand, the familiar book in the other. Charles wanted to see the girl, but her back was to him, and it had grown too dark to see any details, anyway.

"Hello, Father Barnabé. I've been praying." She spoke without a hint of embarrassment at being interrupted from something Charles, at least, considered personal. "Will you join me?"

"I've come from Didi. She was out looking for you, worrying you might be found out of doors after dark if any Germans are out tonight."

"I'm not worried," she said, and her voice sounded light, convincing Charles she told the truth. "Remember? They think I have leprosy."

Her? He was curious to know why, if she had some facial deformity to uphold such a rumor. But he didn't dare peek, even if the priest's candle might have supplied enough light to give him a clue.

She hardly seemed worried about that ugly word, though, which indicated she was as healthy as he.

"You should go now, child," the priest said. "Didi has enough on her mind as it is."

Charles heard her shift away from the altar, loose wooden clogs on her feet clopping away. "You're right, of course. You'll carry on my prayer, won't you, Father, and with better words than mine?"

"God hears the heart."

"Yes, I'm grateful for that."

Then, moments later, he heard the door open and close again. She was gone.

Charles stepped from the shadows. "Who was that?"

Father Barnabé turned abruptly to Charles, his brows raised. "A villager," he said, "who is none of your concern."

It was the first time Charles had heard the priest use anything but the kindest tone. He was right to protect her, when to know Charles was to risk so much, but the instant reproach stung anyway. Charles had never had so many restrictions in his life. He was sick of each and every aspect of being imprisoned by the German army.

Whatever peace he'd inadvertently received from witnessing the girl's prayer was gone.

"You should not be up here."

Charles received the second admonishment without defense, although he didn't regret his boldness. Even if he'd been caught, the pleasure of hearing the girl's prayers would have been worth it.

11

January 1915

Deep into winter, Julitte's prayers held as many questions and pleas as worship and adoration. She couldn't help but worship her Creator, but seeing the German army standing in the way of peace made her wonder why God allowed the world to have gone so far off-kilter.

And now Ori was part of the insanity.

"You can't do it, Ori," Julitte said.

"It'll mean bread, enough for all of us."

"Uncle Guy does his best—"

Ori shook her head, and although Julitte looked at Didi for support, even Didi said nothing. She shook her head too, but Julitte wasn't sure at whom.

"Uncle Guy cannot produce what he does not have. The flour isn't coming in anymore, and whatever does arrive the Germans steal. Besides, what difference does it make if I clean a few offices? They'll have us all working for them if they're here much longer."

Julitte hated the boredom just as much as Ori. They'd long since run out of yarn for their looms, the only businesses in town or in the area were overseen by Germans, and to work for them was inconceivable. Something evidently Ori needed to be reminded about. "I thought the idea was to not work for them willingly."

"You cannot change my mind, and you'll thank me when we have something to eat at the end of the day."

Julitte knelt before Ori's grandmother. "You must talk to her, Didi, tell her it's more than just a mistake. It could cost her life, working so close to them. And tell her no one here in the village will ever forget. They'll never forgive her for voluntarily working for them. Never."

Didi nodded, raising a hand to pat Julitte's face. "Yes, all you say is true, *mon ange*, and I've told her so. But she's never listened to me, not even when she was a girl. What can I do?"

Ori was already at the door, scarf covering her head, jacket over her shoulders, clogs on her feet. "I will be home by five."

Julitte watched her friend leave the cottage, fighting the urge to run after her, stand in her way, demand she return and stay inside. Forced labor was one thing, if it came to that, and so was forced lethargy. Fear and boredom made a horrid mix. But willingly work for the Germans? If the de Colvilles had reason to ostracize Ori before, this would only add to it.

In the months since the Germans had first come through, they'd taken what they wanted, what they could find, but since then had left Briecourt in relative peace. Except for a few guards here and there, two at the one and only road leading into town who checked travel passes, none of which had been granted to any of the villagers, there were only two or three other German faces that had become familiar in the village so far.

But Julitte feared that would change, especially with the recent invitation for work that Ori answered now. An *affiche* had been posted offering five francs for a day's work to "make ready" the town hall. Where once the post office sorted French mail, a staff of Germans would soon sort German army mail. There was no French mail, because controlling information had been one of the first tasks accomplished by the Germans. The villagers received only one message, and that was one no one wanted to hear: the Germans were nearly to Paris, and though things were temporarily stalled, victory was at hand. What they conquered they would never give up.

Where their beloved Mayor Eloi had kept his office, one far too grand for the mayor of this humble village, a German Hauptmann would soon take up residence. That was most troubling to Julitte now. The German Ori had once noticed because of his kind manners would be the German she now cleaned up after.

Julitte turned back inside but not before catching a gaze from across the street. Gustave de Colville stared hard at her, then turned that stare on Ori's back.

Keep her close, Lord. . . . Julitte began her prayer as protection from whatever ran through Gustave's mind, but just as quickly she prayed for more than that: not only to keep her friend from harm but to keep her from temptation, too.

Charles rubbed a protesting muscle after another night on a hard wooden pew. He did his exercises regularly, adding whatever variation he could imagine within the confines of his small prison.

He also read. He'd taken one of the catechisms from the pile nearby, and the prayers made him recall the young woman he'd heard at the altar. At times the book reminded Charles he wasn't as alone as he felt. The petitions made him wonder if he might gain familiarity with God—the sort he'd heard in the woman, perhaps even similar to what his sister had. He found himself wishing he'd talked to Isa about all of this; he'd squandered too many opportunities to speak with her about something that suddenly seemed far more important than it used to.

The only other books he had with him he'd read before. But he read them again, sometimes aloud. Softly, in case anyone came in upstairs without his notice. But at least his voice was noise, and he modified the sound by reading in the three languages he knew. Sometimes he even alternated between paragraphs or sentences. One in English, then French, then German. The book he chose today was *The Barrier*, an American adventure story he'd brought back with him the last time he was in the States. He hadn't meant to pack it; he'd just forgotten to remove it the last time he'd used this suitcase. A day hadn't gone by that he wasn't grateful for it. Even so, it wasn't nearly enough to satisfy him.

He couldn't tolerate this much longer. The conflict that was supposed to be over in a matter of weeks had already outlived those optimistic predictions. Christmas had come and gone. This war could go on far longer than anyone expected. Sometimes Charles believed being a prisoner of the Germans couldn't be worse than where he was. At least he wouldn't be alone.

A tap at the head of the stairs brought him to his feet. Father Barnabé had learned to give the signal earlier rather than later, although it had taken some time for him to remember on a regular basis. Lately he'd also taken to coming into the church at the side door, almost directly above Charles's head.

Charles met him at the base of the stairs. "Good morning, Father."

The priest dipped his head in silent greeting, never taking his eyes from the book in his hand. He went to a table, opening the hollowed carrier to reveal bread, dark and therefore tasteless as ever, and this time a hunk of cheese. That was a pleasant surprise.

"There is news today," Father Barnabé said.

"From a newspaper? Or *real* news?" The saying went that anything printed by the Germans was surely a lie, since their news had an agenda far different from enlightenment.

But Father Barnabé looked too solemn to acknowledge a hint of amusement at the distinction Charles made between news sources.

"The Germans are taking over the town hall. The streets will be swarming with Germans soon."

Charles took a seat at the small table, near the food the priest offered. All such news meant to Charles was that perhaps he'd been too careful so far and should have taken advantage of streets that had *not* been swarming with Germans. As it was, what would change? Could he be more careful? No. "Is there news from any of the others? Pepin?"

"If you hear nothing, it is good," Father Barnabé said.

"I cannot stay here much longer. Especially with more Germans arriving."

The priest patted one of Charles's shoulders, then took a seat opposite Charles.

Father Barnabé had the habit of shaving at night rather than in the morning, so by the time he delivered Charles's first of two meals a day, he already had a shadow covering the lower half of his face. His gray hair was shorn so close, the shadow above his ears nearly matched the shadow below. His stark blue eyes stared at Charles just now.

"You cannot leave."

"I've stayed too long already. I should have tried breaking through the line during those first days, when everything was still chaotic. But I've decided it's not too late to go now."

The priest shook his head. He was mostly an even-tempered man, Charles had learned, but stubborn. "Even if you succeeded getting past the Germans, you might be shot by our own side. Both sides are dug in now, and nothing crosses the line. Nothing."

"I cannot stay." He knew he was repeating himself but could think of no new words to say the same thing.

"You must."

Charles's gaze went to his surroundings. Though he'd made the cellar as comfortable as he could, it was pure hell to spend his days and nights here alone. A prison of intolerable isolation.

"Then I will pretend I'm a villager, like you, and live at least with the same freedoms you have."

Father Barnabé leaned over the table. "You know we have no freedom, and less so all of the time. To walk around the church? That's all it would be. No one spends time out of doors. Your prison would be larger but still a prison. Besides, they took inventory of the workers from this town months ago, and you weren't on the list. They sent healthy men like you to German work camps. Where shall we say you came from?" He shook his head. "It's impossible."

"We could say I was overlooked. They lost the paperwork. Why would they care, if I'm another worker for them to exploit?"

"And that is what you want? To work for the Germans? That *is* what they'll make you do. Maybe here in France, but maybe not. Many have been sent to Germany to work. You might as well turn yourself in."

Charles put his elbows on the table, rubbing his face in his upturned palms. He, too, needed to shave. He didn't miss the beard he'd grown while hiding in the forest and had no desire to grow another. Never in his life had he thought shaving a luxury until he couldn't do it as he pleased.

Father Barnabé put a wrinkled hand to one of Charles's wrists. "You would never pass as one of us, Charles."

He leaned back in his chair, waiting for an explanation. But since none came, he decided to prod. "Why? I speak French as well as you. So I don't have your *patois* down, but I'm learning."

The priest was already shaking his head, staring not at Charles's face but at his hair. Though he wasn't as clean as he was used to, he knew the color hadn't changed. "There isn't a blond head to be found from one end of this village to another. And you're taller than three-quarters of those who live here. To whom shall we say you belong?"

"Father!"

The call startled Charles and also Father Barnabé, whose shoulders jumped at the sound so nearby, just at the top of the stairs. He pushed himself out of the chair, hurrying away. Charles went after him, giving him the book he'd forgotten.

Even as he recognized the voice of the one who'd called as the same who'd come to pray, Charles hid beneath the stairs. The priest climbed above, but Charles wished the woman's search for the priest would lead her down here, where Charles might see her at least. A foolish wish, but so real he was tempted to follow the father upstairs.

Father Barnabé was at the top of the stairs already, faster than he normally hobbled up, giving her no reason to search any farther. Charles moved beside the stairway, still beyond sight and then beyond hearing when the father shut the door at the top. Disappointed, Charles looked back to the table. He was hungry; he was always hungry. But just then something appealed to him even more than eating.

He eyed the stairs.

Charles didn't hesitate long enough to talk himself out of what he wanted to do. He crept up slowly, mindful of which stairs creaked, keeping close to the edges, where the wood was still straight and sturdy. From the top, Charles heard voices getting dimmer even as he pressed his ear as close as he could. The sound moved away.

Stepping down a stair to move out of the way of the door, he twisted the knob to let it open just enough to admit the dimming voices. But they were too far, the words indistinguishable. He opened the door farther and leaned past the threshold just in time to see the two figures. The woman beside Father Barnabé stood only to his shoulder, but Charles saw the back of her in the morning light shining through the clear window between the cellar door and the side of the sacristy. Her hair was instantly familiar. Like a sunset of red and gold and bronze. He should step back, out of the way, in case she turned his way. But he couldn't make himself do it.

She and the priest were in conversation, quietly now, her head bowed and his, too, as if in prayer together. He wished he could hear, not only the sound of her voice but the words she chose, recalling her prayers from when he'd heard her at the altar.

Telling himself the risk was too great already, he slipped back down the stairs, leaving the door slightly ajar. Maybe they would go into the sacristy, and he would hear her voice from there.

But they didn't.

All he heard was the sound of footsteps over the floor above as she passed outside.

But he knew her identity from the color of her hair—the girl from the tree. Somehow it came as no surprise.

12

Julitte stepped out into the cobbled street in front of the church, nearly missing the last step down. She saw nothing in front of her, only what she'd seen behind.

The door. When she and Father Barnabé had finished their prayer for Ori, something had made her look back from where the priest had emerged. It was surprising enough to find Father Barnabé coming from the cellar; she knew nothing of interest or use had been left there since the Germans had first come through, taking what they wanted.

But when she'd asked if she might help him fetch something, he shook his head and guided her away. She'd seen him close the door; she was quite sure of it.

So why, when she glanced back, had it been slightly ajar? Doors that closed with a click didn't go about opening themselves, no matter how old the knob.

Julitte slowed her steps, glancing back. She was tempted to return, but the priest stood outside the church, watching her walk off. He'd acted so strangely just now. At first she'd thought he was out of breath because of the exertion up the stairs. She'd even wondered if he was reluctant to pray for Ori, since it was her own decision to work for the Germans. But he'd prayed with as much love and concern for her as ever. Even after they'd prayed, his breathing was unsteady, his gaze hopping from Julitte to where he'd just been.

She had to admit Father Barnabé wasn't the only one acting strangely. Everyone was nervous, knowing more Germans would soon be underfoot. But it seemed they were more than just fearful of the Germans; they acted as though they were in hiding, even from one another.

Julitte came to her cottage. Curiosity was a dangerous thing these days. She should go inside, keep to herself as she'd been trying to do since the first German had marched into the village. If Father Barnabé was hiding something, she *should* let him keep his secrets. And yet . . .

❦

Late that day, later than usual, Charles watched Father Barnabé sink into one of the chairs at the small table when he returned with the second meal of the day, out of breath. The old priest often took a seat at the table, not because he planned to stay very long but because the stairs seemed to wear him out, whether he was going up or down.

All day, Charles had been unable to get the image of Julitte from his mind. *Julitte.* Even though he hadn't heard the priest talking to her, he knew her name from the day Mantoux had called her down from the tree. It was a lovely name, to match a lovely girl.

Charles knew he shouldn't reveal that he'd stolen a glimpse of her. But even if it meant the priest accused Charles of being reckless, of endangering all of them with his careless behavior, his curiosity was getting the best of him.

"I want to know why some people think Julitte has leprosy."

Father Barnabé was still. For a full second his eyes remained downcast. Slowly, he set aside the book he'd just emptied, folding his hands on top. He waited another moment, then at last looked up at Charles. "And how is it you know her name?"

"I heard you talking." The lie came too easily to him.

Father Barnabé shook his head. "I don't recall using her name, even if you could hear us. We spoke in hushed tones."

"Does it matter? I know from the time I saw her before that the Germans think her a leper. I want to know why."

"This is no concern of yours, Charles."

Charles pulled the other chair away from the table and sat with his legs stretched in front of him, folding his hands behind his head and staring up at the ceiling he knew all too well. How many beams, how many planks. He used to count spiderwebs, until one day he'd banished all of them after being tempted to talk to the creators of such lacy traps.

"If you had to spend all your time down here alone, you'd be asking harmless questions too." Good. His voice had made it seem like the topic was of little consequence. No sense letting the priest know the degree to which Julitte's face had invaded his thoughts.

The priest did not ready himself to leave, which was a good sign. Maybe he'd talk after all.

"I will tell you, but in exchange you must promise me something."

Charles lifted his brows in acquiescence.

"That you will not be so foolish as to leave this cellar, even if she comes to the church again."

He nodded. "I've no death wish."

"And you mustn't try to meet her; you mustn't even think of her."

Charles laughed. "All I have are my thoughts, Father. You cannot control them any more than I."

The priest shook his head, and Charles wondered if he would talk.

At last Father Barnabé sighed. "Julitte was adopted over fifteen years ago. Narcisse Toussaint is her adoptive father, a sailor. When he came home with a child, at first everyone suspected the worst. She has dark coloring like the rest of us, but she looks nothing like a Toussaint, so over the years even the de Colvilles believed him when he said he only adopted her when her father gave her up."

"Why did her father do that?"

"Her mother had died. He couldn't care for her."

Charles tilted his head. "So he gave her to a sailor? That makes no sense."

"Narcisse is not just any sailor." He spoke as if to doubt Narcisse was to doubt his own honor. "He's sailed between here and the Mediterranean for many years. Partly for gain, of course, for trade. But one of the stops he made was by God's design. There is a small colony of lepers on one of the Mediterranean islands, a place Narcisse stumbled on when his boat needed attention and he was forced ashore. When the captain learned what kind of island it was, he would have sailed on, but Narcisse volunteered to go ashore for the items they needed to get them safely to Greece. It's there he met Julitte's father."

"And who was that?"

"He was an American missionary. He tended the sick, prayed with them, served them. Julitte's mother had volunteered as a nurse there years before, against her family's wishes. She contracted the disease first. Eventually she died, but not before giving birth to Julitte."

"And her father?"

"He, too, succumbed to the disease. He gave her up only after he accepted that leprosy would one day take his life. By then he'd known Narcisse a number of years. After that first emergency visit, Narcisse convinced his captain to sail there regularly and bring donations to give the people there a better life. Julitte's father knew she would be in good hands when Narcisse offered to take her."

"But she's never had leprosy?"

"They have a rule—if a child born on the island shows no sign of the disease by their fifth birthday, they're allowed to be adopted away. Julitte is twenty-two now and never has shown a sign of the disease. Some believe she might still, because both of her parents had it."

Father Barnabé leaned forward in his chair, over the table toward Charles. "The Germans fear Julitte because of the leprosy and the rumors they hear about visions she receives and a miracle some think she performed. She'll be left alone by them, and she should be left alone by you, too."

The priest's warning did nothing to dispel Charles's interest. In fact, it did just the opposite. "Visions? A miracle?"

Father Barnabé lifted one hand and let it fall back to the table empty, as if he'd said too much.

"Tell me, Father."

"It's only that she seems to know when someone dies. Not medically. Spiritually. It doesn't seem to matter if the person is nearby. Narcisse told me she knew when her father died, before Narcisse was able to confirm it himself."

"How did she know?"

Father Barnabé shrugged. "I do not know."

"And the miracle?"

Now the priest stood. "I've said enough and stayed too long. I only shared this much so your imagination won't get the best of you about her."

Father Barnabé was already leaving the table, and in a moment Charles heard the priest slowly take the stairs. No more questions would be answered today. But to what end, anyway? It wasn't as if Charles could call on her right beneath the nose of the German army.

Limitations. They were the only things he'd ignored most of his life. Whim had often been the deciding factor in his adventures. Sail to the Orient? Why not! Travel north for an excursion with Eskimos and sled dogs? Why not! Head south to the equator, see how hot this earth could really get? Why not!

And now he was stuck behind the line of a war that should not be fought, forbidden by the secrecy of his being here to talk to a woman who interested him.

Maybe this was no time for anyone—priest or otherwise—to introduce a man like Charles to any woman. He deserved no more than would be allowed by this priest anyway.

And this was one host Charles couldn't afford to offend.

13

The very next day, Julitte sat beside the window in her cottage. Waiting.

And there he was, fully expected at this hour, walking down the street as he always did, Bible in hand. Father Barnabé made his rounds like a physician, but he checked both the physical and spiritual health of nearly everyone in the village. This evening he'd promised to share dinner with them, at Julitte's invitation.

"I'll be back in just a few minutes, Didi." Julitte pushed herself away from the window. "The water vessel is empty again, and we'll need more for the meal with Father Barnabé when he gets here."

"Empty already! You just filled it."

"Yes, but I tipped it over before bringing it inside earlier. So clumsy." Just as she reached for the pot beside the door, she heard Father Barnabé tap gently from the other side. "Here he is now. I'll show him in and run my errand. Welcome, Father."

She kissed his cheek, half in affection and half in the attempt to hide her gaze from him. He was uncannily good at figuring out when someone was up to something, and she didn't want to take chances by letting him look into her eyes.

"Here, Father, sit with Didi and have soup. I'm off for more water from the well."

"You invite me to share a meal, then you leave?"

"Only for a few minutes. Didi is here, and you'll keep each other company."

He frowned. "And Ori—working again today at the town hall?"

Julitte nodded, taking up her coat. "I'll be home soon."

"Yes, Julitte, be sure that you are."

His words called after her, but she didn't look back. If he were concerned only about her being out when the Germans might see her, she might have sent a smile his way. But if he was also concerned that she was curious about what he might be hiding in the church . . . she didn't want to know.

Julitte walked briskly to the town square. She passed two Germans, forever with their eye on those on the street, but kept her face down, clutching the tall vessel to her chest. She left the clay jar beside the well, walking past to the church.

"You there!"

The call came in German, but such a call in any language was enough to make her halt. She did not turn around, in case the hail was meant for someone else. But the square was empty.

"You cannot leave this vessel here unattended."

Julitte forced an even breath to her lungs, then turned back to the well. A German soldier stood nearby—one she hadn't noticed before. He'd spoken in French this time, a butchery of the language but French all the same. "I was going into the church to pray and will return in only a moment for water."

"Take it with you." He picked the jar up, handing it to her.

Julitte spared a quick glance, receiving her property. She should be glad he was not imposing a fine. It seemed that was what the Germans did best to those who didn't meet their expectations. She turned back to the church.

"What is your name?"

Still with her back to him, she told him.

"You are the one they talk about. The one they said can do a miracle."

So, even that rumor had been circulated. She glanced back and saw he was wiping his hand on his jacket, the hand he'd used to pick up her water vessel. Obviously the rumor about a miracle wasn't the only one he'd heard.

He laughed. "Go inside, *mademoiselle*. Pray for a miracle! I would like to see one while I'm here."

Then he laughed again and walked away.

Julitte took another breath, then walked quickly into the empty church, never looking back.

Charles heard the door open, followed by a light but unmistakable clog footfall moments later. He fairly jumped to the stairs. It might not be her . . . but it might.

He stopped at the base of the stairs, holding back from rushing upward. His pulse quickened, even without knowing why. He should be careful. Someone was above those stairs, and every German as well as half the town was a danger to him.

But something propelled him forward. She would go only as far as the altar, if it was who he thought. He wouldn't be able to hear her prayer from where he stood. He needed to go up.

He took the stairs two at a time. Leaning close, he hesitated. The sound of footsteps had ceased. Was she at the altar? Was it even her or someone else from the village?

He was a fool for coming up here, especially after telling the priest he would stay below stairs. A greater fool for putting his hand on the doorknob and slowly twisting. He should return downstairs and do what he always did when someone other than Father Barnabé was in the sanctuary. Hide.

Without pulling on the door, he took his hand away. He must return below, to the shadows and darkness, not only for his sake but for the father's. If Charles were to be caught, better it be somewhere else, a place no one else could be implicated.

He stepped backward down one stair, staring at the knob he'd just let go. It moved as if his hand were still there, intent on opening.

She was there, whoever had come in. Right there on the other side of the door. Indecision slowed his reaction. Should he stay, let himself be seen? or hide, stay safe?

He was tired of hiding.

And yet . . . Father Barnabé . . .

He turned and took the stairs in wide strides, vaulting the banister toward the bottom and into the dank refuge of his prison.

The door opened so slowly the creaks became more pronounced. The noise stopped, then started again. What sounded like the wood of a peasant shoe hit the wood of the stair. It, too, stopped. A stair creaked. That would be the fourth step—Charles knew the stairwell like the keys of a piano, which squeak accompanied which stair. Then silence.

Though the stairs resumed their melody, the sound of shoes had disappeared.

Whoever came down was clearly being careful not to be heard. Charles had been told the place had been ransacked before any stragglers like him had arrived. The steps were too light to belong to a soldier, because the creak at step seven sounded without the groan of step six; the person standing on it had either skipped it or didn't weigh enough for the sound of step six to register.

Then he saw her, not an arm's length away. He could stay in the corner, slip behind the tarp that had been hung over a wardrobe to give him an extra moment to hide. But he did not move. It was Julitte. He could tell by her height, by the length of her hair. She stood as if waiting until her eyes were fully adjusted to the darkness after being outside. She held her clogs to her chest, alongside what looked like a tall, slim water vessel.

"Don't be afraid."

He wasn't sure why he whispered those words, except she stood so stiffly, clutching the items close, he guessed she knew a moment's uncertainty.

"Who is there?" Her voice trembled, and he knew his guess had been correct. But she was brave; she hadn't bolted back upstairs at the sound of a man's voice.

"It's best you don't know," he said softly. "You should return upstairs and not come back."

He spoke for her own good, but his words were the ones he least wanted to utter. Maybe the way he'd said them conveyed his message, because he was glad when she didn't follow his instruction.

"I have bread in my pocket. Are you hungry?"

"We're all hungry. You too."

"I have enough to share." She set aside the items in her arms, withdrew something from the pocket of her skirt. "I can see better now." She turned slightly to face him. "I see you. Can I give this to you? hand it to you?"

Charles stepped out of the shadows that had hidden him for too short a time. He moved closer, stopped directly in front of her, and watched as recognition widened her eyes and lifted her brows.

"You—you are Monsieur Mantoux's friend."

He nodded. "And you are Julitte."

"Yes . . . but how do you remember?"

Myriad thoughts went through his mind. About how he couldn't have forgotten, even if life had gone on as before, without this insanity of war. About how her hair had etched a sunset into his memory, how he'd wanted to stay that day to meet her properly. How hers had been the last woman's voice he'd heard before his life was so changed, and the first since, when he'd overheard her prayer upstairs.

"I remember" was all he said.

She gave him the bread.

"Are you certain you have enough?"

She nodded, and he took it. The bread was wrapped in a napkin, and he put the food on the table beside him, returning the empty cloth to her.

"You shouldn't be here," he said, "and I shouldn't have let myself be caught."

She smiled. "I can be trusted."

He didn't doubt her. "It's dangerous for you to know. For all of us—not just for me, but for you and Father Barnabé."

"How long have you been here?"

"Awhile." He smiled. "And if you're about to ask how long I intend to stay, I'll tell you not long. I know I'm a danger here, to the whole town."

"But where will you go?"

"One man, alone, has a chance to get through. At least I'll try."

"Through . . . where they're fighting? Oh no. You'll be shot for certain, by one side or the other."

"Still, I'll try."

A slanted ray of light came in from the high, shrouded window and shone on her concerned face. Dust floated in the air between them. The way she looked at him made him want to turn away, she studied him so closely. Enforced isolation had made him regress to a schoolboy, afraid to be evaluated by a pretty girl. But he couldn't look away.

"Does Father Barnabé want you to go?"

"No," Charles said. "He's very brave."

"Then you should stay. It would be foolish to go."

"You sound like him."

"He's brave and wise. You should listen."

"And you should go now."

She nodded, but instead of heeding she looked at his surroundings. The old pews were still covered, the corner behind him still hidden by another tarp. Mildewed catechisms stacked to the side. A row of empty crates had been shoved to the back. He'd spent some of his day cleaning, having had nothing else to do, but suddenly saw how filthy it really was. How lacking of any comfort.

"Do you have a pillow?"

"I use a tarp, folded up."

"The pews are hard."

He didn't deny it.

"And you spend all of your time here, alone?"

He nodded.

"There are books at the pay library in town. The Germans left them alone because only a few of them were in German. I could get something for you to read."

"You shouldn't come back. It's not safe."

"I'll be careful."

She turned back to the stairway and regret filled him that she was leaving so soon, even though he knew it was best.

"Thank you," he whispered after her, "for the bread."

"You're welcome . . . Charles."

Another schoolboy reaction: his heart leaped to his throat at the sound of his name on her lips. "You know my name?"

"I heard Monsieur Mantoux speaking to you."

"And you remembered."

She looked away, stopping at the bottom stair. "I'll come back tomorrow."

He bent to pick up her things, the shoes and the water vessel, and handed them to her. Then he watched her go up, disappearing in the dim light at the top. He heard the door open, then close, and he was alone once again.

But instead of the usual gnawing hunger in his belly, he knew the first bit of hope since that day he'd lost his motorcar.

14

In the morning Julitte helped Didi clean up after breakfast, then watched Ori walk off to the town hall for yet another day. They'd heard more Germans marching in just after dawn.

Julitte did not speak of Ori's job, the job that was to last no more than a day and be over before more Germans arrived. Surely she would come to her senses now that so many of them filled the village building.

As soon as Julitte could get away that morning, she went to the pay library. M. Lemoyne still offered his books for rent, but so few people had a coin to spare for such a frivolity that he'd taken to loaning his books on credit.

Julitte scanned the familiar titles carefully. She searched for one in particular, one she feared she might not find if the German raids had been more thorough than she thought. It was a book of Northern France—not only its wildlife, lakes, rivers, and trees but its towns and roads and railways as well. If she and Father Barnabé could not convince Charles to stay, he would need to know the lay of the land. He might know some of it, but she guessed it would look different on foot than it had passing through in a motorcar on his way to M. Mantoux's.

Such a thought reminded her of the first time she saw him. She remembered her wish to have met M. Mantoux's friend as an equal, that they might have gotten to know one another despite their lives being so different. He was obviously wealthy, like M. Mantoux. And she was poor by earthly standards. But such thoughts had been wrong. Hadn't God created them equal? And now the war made their lives similar.

She snatched the book from the shelf.

She looked at other favorite titles, one of poetry, another a French translation of the tales of King Arthur and his knights. Though she'd read both, she chose instead a copy of one of Lemoyne's finest books: gilded edges, bound in dark blue leather, complete with maps and charts of Charlemagne's campaigns through France.

Finally, she chose a third book about an Antarctic expedition and all of the colorful plates that went along with that adventurous true tale.

She'd chosen not only for content but for size, and each of the three books would easily slip into the wide mouth of her water vessel. After Lemoyne logged the books, Julitte stepped out to the street. She could deliver them this very day.

Immediately she knew something was happening outside. People scurried in all directions, and then she heard why: familiar pounding at doors down the street. Already there were people out, and more soldiers were gathering groups into lines.

She rushed home to hide the books, hurrying past a startled Didi. Julitte stumbled up to her loft, and no sooner had the books been stuffed under her mattress than a soldier rapped at the door.

"What is it?" Didi called, but she spoke to Julitte and not to the caller at the door.

Julitte took a breath before speaking. No sense alarming Didi with her own worries. "I don't know. They're collecting people outside. Men, women—it looked like everyone."

"I should come too, then." When Didi struggled into her coat, Julitte helped.

Julitte opened the door, but the soldier was already on his way, pausing only long enough to direct them toward another pair of soldiers. Julitte stepped back outside, pulling Didi close beside her.

"Line up," came the order again and again as one of the Germans marched the cold, gray street.

Julitte fell into step with her neighbors, still holding one of Didi's hands to keep it warm while the old woman clutched her cane with the other.

"You—step aside. You are not needed."

A soldier pointed his finger at Didi, but Didi did not move. She looked at Julitte.

"Go home, Didi," Julitte whispered, dropping her hand. But Didi must not have heard. She stood at Julitte's side as if waiting until Julitte could accompany her.

The German put his face to Didi's. "Go! *Gehen Sie weg.*"

Didi leaned toward Julitte, who put an arm around her again, long enough to lead Didi from the line. Until the German soldier shoved Julitte's shoulder and pointed back to the spot she'd held. Julitte let Didi go, and Didi walked on legs wobblier than ever back to the cottage.

Other women were tapped out of place as well, those who were swollen with pregnancy or who held babies. Some, with older children clinging to their legs, were told their children would stay behind but those mothers would be expected to work.

"Work is a gift, a privilege," a strong new voice said from behind. Julitte looked up; it was the Hauptmann, the soldier who had been kind to Ori. "Each of you who are left in line will be assigned a task. You will do this task to the best of your ability, as befits any healthy creature. To work is to live."

Julitte glanced around, wondering if anyone else had taken the words as a threat. *Not* to work was to die? But her eye only caught Claudette's, who quickly looked away.

The Germans displayed their lack of knowledge over village politics by assigning the wrong children to be watched by the wrong women. Children were pried from their mother's arms and thrust into another's at random, Toussaint children with de Colvilles and the other way around.

No one dared to switch them back, not with armed soldiers so close at hand.

Once they were taken into various cottages and the noise in the line died away but for the gentle sobbing of those mothers still present, the Hauptmann spoke again in his tutored French. "There is no need to fear. Each of you will find purpose in your days, working for the good of all. By nightfall you will be returned to your homes, reunited with your children, your families. Again I say there is no need to fear. We are a fair people, we Germans. You will learn to admire us."

Those who were left in the line were divided yet again, men from women, older from younger, sturdy from slight. Men were marched off first.

Julitte was put next to Claudette and two other younger girls from the village. And though Julitte looked for Ori, wondering if she might be forced to join them, her friend never emerged.

One group of women was marched toward the road leading outside of town. To where, Julitte had no idea.

Julitte's group was sent to the dairy not far from the village. She glimpsed the familiar farmer at the far end of the barn, but he neither approached nor greeted them as they stepped onto the straw-laden floor. She knew his family had left the village as refugees some time ago, he alone staying behind for the good of the animals. But since the Germans had arrived, he'd had no say in where his goods were delivered.

The German soldier who'd led them from the street told them one would churn butter, another work with cheese, another with the chickens. Julitte looked around, wondering which chores might be assigned to her.

She was grateful to be working near the church, although she didn't voice any gratitude. She was still being forced to work for the Germans and doubted the villagers would see any of the fruits of this day's labor unless she could sneak something away.

A basket was thrust into her hands.

Chickens. Egg collection. Her heart skipped a beat in anticipation. Of all the tasks that might have been assigned, this was the one she would have asked for.

No sooner had the German who'd given her the basket turned his back than Claudette yanked it from Julitte's hands.

"You can do the churning, Julitte."

Julitte reached to take the basket back. "I don't think we're in the position to trade."

"They'll never know."

Julitte suspected Claudette knew what Julitte did: with the days growing shorter and the air growing colder, not only would it be warmer in the henhouse and there be fewer eggs to collect, but more importantly, some of the chickens liked to hide their eggs. If the German soldiers didn't know the habits of these free-roaming chickens and with the farmer busier than ever with other tasks, Julitte suspected the hens were hiding more eggs than ever these days. The thought gave her a moment's kinship with the feathered friends. Even they were probably hiding things from the Germans.

"Claudette," Julitte whispered, circling Claudette's elbow with her palm, "I'll trade with you only if you give me half of what you smuggle out of here."

"Poor Julitte." Claudette tsked. "I don't have to agree. We've already traded." And she held up the basket as proof.

Julitte's lips tightened. In that moment she knew exactly why the feud had lasted so many years. Her empty stomach heightened the hatred, and she lifted a quick suggestion to God that if the Germans were going to banish anyone, they would start with Claudette.

But no sooner had the irate prayer formed in her mind than another thought took hold, one she'd learned from Father Barnabé. *Just because we pray a prayer does not mean God has to answer them.*

She took a step toward the urns but was stopped when the soldier stepped in front of her. "You dismiss my orders?"

Julitte shook her head. "I—"

Claudette drew his attention with a smile. "She wanted to work with the farmer, not alone with the chickens. You know, she's the kind who likes to be around others. Do you know that kind of woman?"

He looked from Claudette back to Julitte, eyeing her from head to foot. She shrank back, folding her arms in front of her as a smile grew on his face.

"Then I will work with her." He motioned for Claudette to step closer, then took the basket from her. "You will do the churning. She will visit the henhouse. With me."

If Claudette's insinuation hadn't been so ugly, Julitte might have enjoyed seeing her smile turn to a frown, her brows draw with disappointment. But there was no time to acknowledge that Claudette's plan hadn't worked her way. The soldier was already leading Julitte to the henhouse, handing Julitte the basket along the way. Julitte took it, wishing she could feel triumphant over Claudette. But fear stood in her way.

"Your name, *mademoiselle*?"

She told him. He was like so many of the others, stalwart. Strong. He had a nearly flat nose and a wide forehead, with fair, smooth skin.

The henhouse was smaller than the first floor of Julitte's cottage, with far thicker walls to better hold the cool or the warmth and a small window at the peak, open for ventilation. Even so, the smell of ammonia assailed her. Inside, the hens roamed free, a few fluttering at the unfamiliar company.

Keeping her gaze to the straw, Julitte offered a new prayer as she started the egg hunt. *Let him be reminded women are to be treated as sisters, Lord.*

He took a step too close just as she bent to retrieve an egg. She held it up between them. "Eggs, *monsieur*. What I am hired to collect."

He shifted his rifle to hang behind him. "Ah, so you are conscientious. Work first?"

"Work and only work," she said. "As your Hauptmann said, work is a gift."

She grabbed three more eggs in plain sight from the laying box. Farther down, hens nested in a row and one pecked at her wrist when she reached for another. She hoped to find more eggs, even in unusual spots. Rolled into corners. Behind the water trough. Under straw and close to the walls. She would look everywhere and might slip one or two into her pocket, if the soldier ever took his eyes from her.

She stepped carefully, spotting more eggs nearby.

"Only work?" he asked, watching her. She spared him a glance, and disappointment creased his forehead. "You aren't so friendly as she said. Do you not like me?"

Julitte said nothing, unwilling to insult a man with a rifle on his back and a pistol at his side.

A bang at the door scattered the hens with a squawk here and there. Julitte, still bent over another set of eggs, went cold regardless of the warmth of the henhouse. Another soldier stood there, this one even bigger than the first, and he stared at Julitte from the threshold.

"You're excused from work."

She stood straight, heartbeat racing. "Pardon?"

He repeated himself. "No work for you here. Go home."

Had she really needed to hear that twice? She hurried closer to the door, but the first soldier stepped in her path with an arm outstretched like a gate.

"But—why send her from work?"

"She's the one—the leper. Do you want her touching your food?" He turned his gaze back to Julitte. "Go out from here."

She extended the basket of eggs.

"Keep them. Distribute them to the villagers, if you dare. I won't stop you."

Nearly a dozen eggs! *Lord! Such a blessing You've turned those rumors into.* She only wished she'd collected a few more.

She hurried back to the village, stopping at Uncle Guy's to give him six of the eggs to bake with for the village, then one to widow Helena since she was alone. Julitte kept four for herself: one for Didi, one for Ori, one for herself, and one for Charles.

"Have you found a way to charm the German devils into giving you food?"

Julitte stopped at her door. She knew the voice; it was Gustave de Colville, who'd been excused from the work line shortly after Didi. To the Toussaints he was known to be so cold they said snow was the last to melt from his roof every spring. She was tempted to disregard him, to go inside and pretend she hadn't heard. But she knew he would not be ignored. He watched her too closely, and soon everyone would know she had kept four eggs, not just three.

She turned to him, astounded by a thought that could only come from God. *Share, Lord? After what Claudette did? Everyone knows she is Gustave's favorite. And he's the one responsible for keeping the lies about me on everyone's tongue. Yes, so they are lies that let me keep these eggs. But still . . .*

From somewhere—surely it was heaven and not from her own scowling soul—she obeyed the urge to smile.

"No, Gustave, it wasn't my charm." She stepped closer, grabbing not one but two eggs from her cache. "It was yours. Because of you, they think I am poison and won't touch anything I've put my hands on. Surely you deserve your share."

Even as part of her hoped he would refuse the offer, his hand reached out to accept the eggs. No villager refused food, not anymore.

He stared at her, wordless, as she turned back to her home and closed the door behind her.

An hour later, carrying the books and boiled egg inside her water jar, Julitte entered the church.

Her heart struck the inside of her chest, matching the sound of her clogs on the chapel's tile floor. She glanced at the altar, sending a prayer for safety not only for herself but for the man in hiding downstairs. Then she went to the sacristy in search of the *curé*. If he was here, she would do nothing more than say hello, stop to pray, and find her way back home. She must find a way to know when he was in the church or not if she was to keep her secret to herself.

She tapped on the sacristy door, waited. Tapped again, then peeked inside. It was empty, Father Barnabé's Sunday vestments hanging neatly in the shadow of the open wardrobe door.

Readjusting the clay jar under her arm, she turned to face the door to the cellar. She repeated her prayer for safety, not for her but for Charles. For herself, she prayed that the Lord would keep her ever more tightly in His grasp. This man with a face to fascinate her made her want to do two things at once: risk staying by his side to help him in any way she could and run away, far from the images that kept coming to mind, of his smile, of his voice, conjuring hopes she knew came too quickly.

She slipped out of her shoes, once again carrying them on the stairs but not because she hoped he wouldn't hear. Only because they made so much noise, if someone came into the sanctuary they would surely hear her from one end of the chapel to the other.

She stopped halfway down the stairs. There, at the foot, stood Father Barnabé.

"Julitte? What are you doing here?"

"I—I was looking for you." That was certainly true.

"Down here? Without your shoes?"

Charles stepped behind him. "She found me here yesterday, Father."

Father Barnabé looked between the two of them as if they were errant children caught in a prank. When Julitte took the next step to descend, the priest held up a palm to stop her.

"No, no, no," he told her. "Go away, Julitte. Forget what you've seen. It's too dangerous—for all of us."

She took another step, holding out the water vessel. "But I can help. With two of us to bring him food, there will be less suspicion. And I've brought books to help him pass the time."

"This is not good," Father Barnabé told her. "Who might have seen you with this?"

"No one. I'll fetch water on my way home, so nothing will look odd. I've stopped in here before on my way to the well. Don't worry so, Father!"

She was at the bottom of the stairs by now, smiling so easily that she saw he was tempted to smile as well. She saw it in his eyes, though the smile never made it to his mouth.

Stepping past both of them, she withdrew her offerings and placed them on the table. The egg nested in bread. Three books. A candle and matches. She would have brought a pillow but didn't know how to transport it without being caught.

"Julitte is as generous and thoughtful as she is beautiful, Father. See these gifts? How could I refuse?"

"I don't expect you to." Father Barnabé stood next to Charles at the table now, looking at Julitte. "But I do expect this to be your last visit. It's far too dangerous. We're not de Colville smugglers." The *curé*, who frequently scolded those who gossiped, pressed his lips together as if he'd fallen into that trap himself.

"Smugglers?" Charles repeated the word with surprise and interest.

Father Barnabé shook his head and turned away. "I spoke hastily, often the foundation for foolishness."

"But what did you mean?" Since the priest didn't look ready to speak, Charles looked at Julitte, his brows raised expectantly.

"It isn't gossip to tell the truth of that matter," she said to Father Barnabé first. Then she looked at Charles. "The de Colvilles are smugglers, at least a good number of them. But keeping secrets to protect a life isn't the same as smuggling for gain. We've nothing to fear so long as we're trusting in the Lord. Don't you believe the Lord will protect us, Father?"

"He's given us brains to reason with and doesn't excuse us when we act foolishly."

"But I'm careful! Besides, the Germans ignore me." She didn't elaborate on why, although she'd been about to. But shyness kept her silent. Why let Charles know she was the true descendant of lepers? He might not accept her gifts . . . and he might look at her differently.

The priest was already shaking his head. "I'm afraid the longer the Germans are here, the less they'll set you apart, no matter what the rest of the village says of you."

She glanced from Father Barnabé to Charles, wondering if he was interested in the reasons behind their discussion. She wanted to change the subject. "I hope the books will ease the time."

Charles was already thumbing through the one she knew he would appreciate—the volume of Northern France topography. He looked up from the pages to catch her eye. "Thank you." His gaze lingered on her even after the words were spoken.

Blood pumped quicker from her heart even as she told herself to remember who he was. She wondered if Father Barnabé would be so protective of him if he knew Charles was wealthy. Although the priest wore the holy cloth, it didn't mean he was immune to the class animosity that had been bred among the villagers longer than hatred and mistrust between the feuding families.

"Go now, Julitte. You've done enough."

Julitte didn't move. She still looked at Charles. There was something fine about him, so fine she'd spent more time than she cared to admit thinking of him. But wondering about how Father Barnabé might react to Charles's place in society reminded her of the vast difference in their lives. Yes, the war had made them equal. But only temporarily. Soon he would go back to living like M. Mantoux, and she would stay here in the village, where she belonged. Where God had put her. She mustn't forget that he would never fit in here, and she could surely never leave.

"Julitte."

Now Father Barnabé put a hand to her elbow, and she had to look at him.

"You must go now, and you cannot come back."

"But now that I know he's here, it only makes sense for me to help you both." She knew she shouldn't argue, least of all with Father Barnabé. She looked at Charles again. "You are staying, aren't you? and not going to try breaking through the line, as you mentioned before?"

He looked down at the book in his hand. "You want me to stay even though you brought me this to help me go?"

"I brought it, but reluctantly. If I cannot change your mind— if we cannot change your mind—then you'll need to know where you're going."

"I'll stay until I have a plan." He raised the book. "And this will help me find one."

Father Barnabé raised a hand between them, as if he saw something pass that he wanted to break through. "Julitte, come upstairs with me now."

Charles frowned at Father Barnabé. "I have little enough company, Father. And long days. You'll banish the only other person I might be able to talk to?"

"I will, and I do. This is not a game. This is life. Or death." He turned away, his hand still on Julitte's arm. "Come along."

Julitte looked over her shoulder one last time, catching the gaze Charles sent her way. But when Father Barnabé thrust the empty water vessel at her, she had to look away.

Although she followed the priest upstairs and outside, she barely listened to his reproach to stay away for her own good and for everyone else's too.

She would find a way to see him again. The days were long for all of them, but how much more for him, alone? Father Barnabé himself had preached more than once about how man was not meant to live alone but rather in community one with another. It was a favorite sermon topic with the hope of mending the feud.

Well, Charles might not be part of the feud, but wasn't solitude one of the dangers Father Barnabé warned against? Surely the Lord would protect them if all she wanted to do was make the hours less lonely. And not just for Charles.

15

Julitte spent the night plotting and planning, imagining ways she might visit the church without notice, ways to easily leave the cottage. There were only so many times in a day she could go to the well. She might also check the bakery to see if any bread could be had, or the dairy for milk or gather kindling in the wood. She must devise ways to go out that wouldn't raise Didi's suspicions or offend the God of honesty that both she and Didi loved.

But by morning none of her plans made a difference. She was summoned, along with Didi, at the same time the rest of the workers were called. They were sent to the home of Evelyne de Colville to help care for the children whose parents were marched off to work.

From the start of the day through all the hours before curfew, Julitte spent her time soothing cries, feeding what little food was allotted, combing hair, cleaning faces and bottoms, playing with blocks, all the while praying for a chance to get to the church.

There was only one thing to be thankful for: Evelyne de Colville was so grateful for Didi and Julitte's help that it didn't seem to matter they were Toussaints. Evelyne did attempt to divide the children, one group from the other. A division that lasted precisely ten minutes for those children who could walk, toddle, or crawl. They had yet to care about the feud.

By early evening Julitte might have been too exhausted to plod her way to the church or the well, but the moment she stepped from Evelyne's doorstep, her pulse began to race. The curfew hour had passed, but they needed water. Surely that needed no explanation.

"Ori!" Didi called when they entered the cottage. "Come help with dinner."

But there was no answer; the cottage was still and empty.

"I'll help, Didi," Julitte said. "Just as soon as I fetch water."

Julitte did not reach for the water vessel. Instead she hurried upstairs to Pierre's side of the loft. She had one more gift for Charles, besides the bread she'd hidden in one pocket, saved from the only meal she'd eaten that day. She slipped Pierre's charcoal pencil and a couple of blank sheets of paper into the other pocket.

She came downstairs, tying her hair back with a softer scarf than the one she'd worn to Evelyne's.

"You went upstairs to change your scarf, just to go to the well?"

Julitte nodded, not daring to speak for fear of issuing a falsehood, an excuse to cover her intentions.

"I will go with you," Didi said, taking up the cane she'd set aside while she sat at the table with two potatoes to peel in front of her.

"No, Didi," Julitte said breathlessly and no doubt too quietly for Didi to have heard. She swallowed the unsteadiness away. "I'm sure you're as tired as I am. Stay here. I'll look for Ori—maybe she is on her way home already."

"I don't think you should go out after curfew."

"But it's not even dark, and we need water."

"Still, I don't want—"

Julitte hurried to Didi's side, bending to give her a kiss on the cheek. "Thank you for worrying, Didi. But I'm under God's wing, even outside this door."

Then she hurried away, water vessel in hand.

Julitte walked faster than she had ever dared before, knowing others had been stopped for running in the street, even children. There was no one out now, the dinner hour. Not even a German sentry, at least not between Julitte's cottage and the market square. A miracle in itself, since someone was nearly always at the well.

She didn't even stop there, just went straight to the church. She didn't know what she would say to Father Barnabé if he tried stopping her from going to the cellar.

But nothing stood in her way. The sanctuary was empty, and if Father Barnabé was in the sacristy, he never emerged, not even when she tiptoed past, still in her clogs.

At the top of the stairs she slipped out of those clogs. No sense having the noise echo from one end of the chapel to the other. Quietly, she descended, wondering if he could hear her approach anyway. Surely her steps to this end of the church had been loud enough. He must have known she was here.

Even though the sun had yet to set, the cellar was nearly dark. How awful it must be, stuck down here in the dim light.

"I'm here," she said quietly at the foot of the stairs.

No response at first, then a rustling off to the side. Charles emerged from the shadows, as tall and handsome as her thoughts of him remembered. The only source of light down here was from him, with his hair so blond it was almost white and his blue eyes, even barely illumined, shining.

"I'm glad. I was afraid Father Barnabé's warnings would keep you away. Or the father himself, like a gate at the top of the stairs."

"He mustn't be in the church, although I didn't look. I just came down." Then she added, "But I was careful. No one was in the square, and the sanctuary is empty. It's as if God Himself opened the way."

Charles was staring at her so intently she hardly thought it odd that he didn't respond to her words. He just looked at her much as she looked at him. Then she pulled out the pencil and paper from her pocket and the slice of bread she'd saved from her noontime meal.

She laid out her meager gifts on the table. The bread had barely dried, but that was only because of its heaviness. No one liked the taste of what Uncle Guy baked these days, least of all Uncle Guy himself. "I wish I had more for you, but the Germans haven't left us with much." She didn't bother to add that they hadn't had much to begin with. Surely Charles knew that already.

He joined her beside the table, picking up the pencil. "This is for drawing. Do you draw?"

She shook her head. "It was my brother's. I don't think he would mind your using it, under the circumstances."

"I used to like to sketch boats of all sizes. Talent, I was once told, is in the details, only I never took the time to explore many. Maybe now I might, if I can remember any."

He'd said the last words with a smile; she knew that without even looking at him. With him standing so close, just next to her, she didn't dare look at him. Suddenly she realized how careless she'd been to let herself think of him so much; her thoughts had rendered her childish. Foolish.

But surely God wanted her to help Charles, no matter how she complicated that service.

She took a step away, back toward the stairs. "I hope it helps you to pass the time. I'm sorry I don't have more paper, but my brother used all he had, except those few sheets."

"I'll be frugal and make it last."

She nodded, at the foot of the stairs now.

"You must go?" he asked.

"There is a curfew. I would have come earlier, but I've been assigned to watch over the children whose parents must work. I couldn't get away any sooner."

He reached out, brushing his hand on her shoulder. "I don't mean to add to your burdens. Father Barnabé is right. It's dangerous for you to come here. You mustn't anymore."

"The Lord commands us to proclaim liberty to the captives and the opening of the prison to those who are bound. I cannot send the Germans away, but I can, for a moment, make this prison a place to visit. And so I will."

Then, before he could study her any longer and surely guess the depth of the silly infatuation that confused a visit that should only be a ministry, she turned away and shot up the stairs.

For two weeks Julitte ended her day in exactly the same way, and somehow either the Lord blinded anyone else on the street or made certain she was the only one out. Her visits stayed the secret she meant them to be.

And though she lingered no more than a few minutes at a time, they were more than enough to feed her dreams of Charles. Maybe it was his gratitude, maybe the kindness behind his smile. Maybe it was the concern he voiced each and every time she left him with her bread, asking her how she could spare something no one else could.

Or maybe it was because no one in this village had ever looked at her in such a way.

She reminded herself this war *must* end—even though it had already lasted weeks longer than the claims of those who'd promised a quick fight to the ones who marched away—and Charles would leave. He might occasionally visit M. Mantoux, and perhaps he would remember her and Father Barnabé for their help. But he would be far too busy living the kind of life M. Mantoux lived to ever visit Briecourt once he left. Charles might be kinder than M. Mantoux and certainly more handsome, but she shouldn't want anything to do with the kind of life they lived. Hadn't her own father set an example to live a far simpler life? Hadn't Narcisse taught her riches were a burden?

Because everyone knew it was harder for a rich man to enter heaven.

16

"I thought you were imagining things," Ori said to Julitte after returning home early—the same time Julitte and Didi had arrived. The Germans had sent everyone home at noon while half of them marched away and the other half were summoned to the town hall. "But now I'm not so sure."

Julitte nearly dropped the plate in front of her friend. She turned her face away, busying herself to aid Didi, who was in the process of settling at the opposite end of the table. Julitte had never said anything to Ori or to Didi about the secret she concealed these last few weeks. She carried her guilt around like a new burden, one that hadn't yet settled into a comfortable spot in her mind.

"What do you mean?" Julitte asked, after slowing her breathing and trusting her voice again.

Ori shrugged. "When you said you thought the town hated each other more than ever. Remember? I was looking out the town hall window this morning, and when Claudette left the dairy, I saw her go to her mother's house three times within an hour. Carrying bundles each time."

With Didi settled, Julitte took her own seat. Having a secret had made her imagine suspicion in every eye aimed her way. Why had she needed to voice her fears?

"So?" Didi asked. Her tone was sharper than she would have

used a couple of months ago, before Ori had started working for the Germans. "She probably stole some eggs from the henhouse."

Ori glanced at her grandmother. "Delivering a few stolen eggs wouldn't have taken three visits. I thought it odd. She looked as though she was hiding something."

No, it's Father Barnabé who is hiding something. And me.

"I was wrong, Ori," Julitte said. "Everyone is nervous these days, with more Germans coming and going from the town hall."

"So everyone stays home when they're not forced to work. Not in and out the way Claudette was doing—unless someone was sick. But I saw her mother a little while later, and she was fine, not sick at all."

"Maybe someone else is sick. Her younger brother Benoit—or anyone else. You know half the homes on that side are connected from the smuggling they've always done."

"Not Claudette's."

"Maybe they're smuggling again," Didi said. "More food than just a few eggs."

Julitte wouldn't be surprised, even less surprised that they wouldn't share their cache with any of the Toussaints.

"Why were you able to see so much looking out the window today, Ori?" Didi's tone held something new, something Julitte was surprised to hear.

"Only that it was nice weather and . . ." Ori stopped, setting aside her fork and aiming her gaze at her grandmother. "I was thinking how peaceful the world should be under such a bright winter sky. But it's not, and I was sorry."

"The Germans—the Hauptmann you work for—he didn't tell you to look out that window, did he?" If there was any doubt about the accusation behind Didi's question before, there was none now.

Ori stood, her stew untouched. "You, too, *Grand-mère?*" She looked at Julitte then. "I suppose you thought the same? That I would spy on everyone and tell the Germans everything I see?"

"Sit down," Didi told her. "You've nothing to be angry about. You've brought this on yourself."

"I haven't! I've done nothing wrong except earn back a little of the money the Germans have stolen from us. Why is that so wrong? The vegetables in this stew are from me, the bread we have left—the cheese, too. I've shared. I brought flour to Guy, turnips to nearly every Toussaint in this village. And yet what do I get? This! Not gratitude, no. Suspicion."

She flew from the room, scrambling up the stairs and to the loft, where Julitte heard her cries and guessed Didi did too, even with her impaired hearing. But there was no compassion on Didi's face. That Ori was able to leave the table without eating meant she'd already had at least one decent meal that day. At the town hall with the Germans.

Julitte and Didi ate in silence, and Ori never returned to the table.

That afternoon Julitte sat by the window with a book—one she'd read twice before, so it was easy to pretend she was enjoying it now. She even brought up favorite segments now and then and read them aloud to Didi.

But when Father Barnabé passed by to visit various families in the village, as she hoped he would sooner or later on this particular day of the week, she let no more than a moment go by before she was on her feet.

"I'll be back in a little while," she said, going to the door.

"Where are you going?" Didi asked.

"Just down to the chapel, to pray."

"You can do that here, where no Germans will see you walking outside."

"I'll be back soon."

Then she was out the door, knowing Didi thought her behavior odd but unable to change that now. She had a book to deliver, and her pockets were full with two slices of bread, some cheese that Ori had brought home, and a wedge of raw cabbage.

Charles wished he had a ball. An American baseball. And a mitt. He'd once had a red leather baseball that belonged to his grandfather but lost it on the maiden voyage of the *Caronia* when he'd thrown it while too near the railing and missed catching it. He used to like thinking of it in the belly of a shark. It was the only thing that made him forget how his mother had glared at him for days over losing it.

Since missing that catch, he was careful where he threw balls. When he was a kid, he could lie on the floor and throw for hours. With the time he had here, he could probably hit any target on this entire ceiling and catch it back without ever missing.

But of course such a wish was ridiculous. Throwing a ball at a target would make noise, and that was one thing he couldn't dare.

So he finished the calisthenics he practiced at least twice a day. Once in the morning and once in the evening, as now. He'd learned not to breathe too heavily, because even that made noise.

And then he went to the washbowl. He still had water left and was grateful that Father Barnabé brought him what he needed at least twice a week. After freshening up for the second time that day—a luxury—he took a seat on one of the benches, examining it with a new thought just as he sat down.

Wood wasn't in short supply yet, thanks to the forest and the recent freedom to use it Father Barnabé had told Charles about. But if that were forbidden again, and if anyone recalled these pews, they might come looking for such a treasure.

Then he heard it—the soft footfall from above. Only one person's stride matched that. Julitte's. He wanted to greet her at the stairs, but at the last moment caution had its way and he slipped to the shadows.

"Charles."

He emerged from behind the tarp, glad for the candle she'd brought with her. He could easily see the smile on her face.

"You're looking well today," she said. "Like the fine gentleman I first saw with M. Mantoux."

Her voice was cheerful, a welcome sound so different from the darkness and the loneliness that were otherwise his constant companions.

She placed the candle on the table, then began emptying her pockets. She was like a young and lovely Saint Nicholas, always bringing him gifts. And he was already trained well enough to anticipate whatever she pulled out.

"I have cheese today," she said. "Courtesy of the Germans in the town hall. And another book, an adventure: *The Three Musketeers*. I chose it over *The Scarlet Pimpernel* for obvious reasons."

"Because of the revolution? Or because of the guillotine?"

"Both."

"Thank you," he said, eyeing what she'd brought. "This is all more than generous."

She turned to leave.

"Must you go so quickly this time? Father Barnabé isn't here, and it's early." He summoned his most charming smile and pulled out a chair for her. "Sit. Stay. Talk. I'm tired of listening to myself or to the birds outside."

He could see she would give in but understood her hesitation. The danger in being discovered was nothing to ignore. Still, she took the seat he offered.

"You can eat in front of me," she said. "I don't mind."

"With you here for company, my appetite is gone." He sat opposite and leaned forward, folding his arms on the table and giving her his full attention. He had many questions for her and chose the first one that came to mind. "Tell me, Julitte, why you're still here in the village. Why didn't you go before the Germans came?"

She seemed surprised by his interest. "I suppose now it must seem foolish, because even if I had no place to go, I'm sure others left without knowing where they would go. At the time I thought I was doing the right thing. I stayed because my friend stayed. Her grandmother couldn't travel, and she wouldn't leave her. And . . ."

"Yes?" He wondered what made her hesitate.

"And because I knew some people were staying behind because they wanted to keep their homes. For when our loved ones return, to be sure we'll still have a home for them, a place unchanged from what it was." She looked away. "But even if I'd been the strongest man in the village, I couldn't have stopped an army from doing as it pleases. My home is changed already, and it's been only a few months."

"Through no fault of yours. It's the Germans. I saw them when they first came through, Julitte. Like a tidal wave of gray."

"You saw them coming? I've wondered why you're here. I thought, that day I saw you last summer, you were going to Belgium."

"I was. My car was commandeered, and I never made it to Brussels. So I came back this way, to see if Anton was still here or if he'd left something behind that I might use. But the Germans were already here, too."

He tried making light of it, because maybe she hadn't considered that he should be embarrassed over being caught behind the fighting.

"You wanted to fight with your king," she said softly. "I remember your words."

He nodded but eyed their surroundings now instead of her. "Look at me now. A prisoner instead."

"It's not your fault our armies weren't able to keep the Germans back long enough to accept everyone into the army who wanted to fight."

Now he looked at her closely, and after a moment she fidgeted in her seat, folding her hands in her lap. But despite that, she returned his gaze.

"Yes," he said, "I did want to fight. But along my way to being a soldier, I learned a few things I wish I didn't know."

He should expand on that, admit he'd learned he wasn't worthy to be a soldier, but didn't. Not to this brave young woman who took the risks she did just to help keep him alive.

For a moment she remained quiet, probably waiting for him to tell her what he'd learned. Then she looked away. "They said when the men went off to fight that the women should be glorious in their suffering." She was whispering now, but in the familiar silence of the room he had no trouble hearing her. "That we should hold back our tears as we watched those men who would be soldiers march away, because it would only weaken their courage."

"Did you cry in secret, Julitte? For someone special?"

"For my brother, Pierre. My parents—my adoptive parents—always thought they could have no children. That was why my father Narcisse brought me home with him. But then Pierre was born, as if having one child in the house opened the way for more. He's like a true brother to me."

She sat up straighter and cleared her throat, as if uncomfortable—as uncomfortable as he was eager for her to continue. "I suffer his absence." Her voice wasn't so soft anymore, and she wasn't looking at him. "They said our suffering would conquer the Germans no matter what happened, because it's our way to prove loyalty to our country and way of life. But already I've seen a woman lose her husband to this war, and I'm not convinced suffering is glorious. Her husband is dead and will still be dead long after this war is forgotten."

"But how else will we stop it if we don't fight?"

She shook her head. "I don't know."

He started to smile, but a creak in the floor above made him hold his words. He lifted a finger to his lips, though he doubted Julitte would have made a sound anyway.

Nothing. No further sound at all, except for the wind that moaned at the cracked and shrouded window behind them.

"It was just the wind, I suppose, but it's good to be careful." He finished the smile he'd started before.

"I should go."

"So soon? I'm enjoying our discussion. My guess is everyone talks about the war all the time—it's all I think about. But Father Barnabé doesn't like to speak of it. He says it's because he has no news, except what the Germans tell him."

"It's true. I don't believe what the Germans tell us, though, about how they're so near victory, or the fighting would all be over by now. But I still hear the cannon in the west, and I know we're holding them back."

Charles heard the cannonfire too. Sometimes he would fall asleep counting the booms, because if he didn't mindlessly count, he would remember other details about what it was like to be out there, watching so many men die. "I should be there, with them."

"And I should say yes, and I should be brave, too, about you and my brother and the other men from the village who fight. But out there, with all of those guns, there is only death. And for what?"

She was right, of course, about the death. "Invaders are in this country and mine, ones who want to take our land—and *you*, the citizens," he said. "Protecting it is the only thing we can do."

"I know you're a wealthy and powerful man, Charles. But perhaps God has something to show you in this place that He couldn't have shown you where you lived before the Germans came."

He tilted his head and studied her. "You're a curious girl, Julitte.

Always thinking of God and how He might be involved in our lives."

"God is the only thing that matters."

He took one of her hands and heard her catch her breath at the contact. "I wish I had your faith."

"Ask God. He gave me mine."

Then she pulled her hand away and stood. He had to let her go, although part of him wanted to squash all caution and persuade her to stay even longer.

But she was already scooping up her clogs where she'd left them at the stairs.

Julitte hurried through the sanctuary, remembering only at the door to slip her feet back into her clogs. Better to flee quickly, before Charles guessed the effect his touch had on her pulse.

She stepped outside and welcomed the frigid air. It cooled her cheeks and hands but did little to cool her insides. This warmth came from within—impossible to escape.

"You certainly took your time *praying* this evening."

Julitte turned to the voice behind her. Claudette stood beside the church door, her arms folded against the wind. But neither her cheeks nor her nose was red, so she couldn't have been outside very long.

Julitte wanted to say something, but each thought that came to mind was a lie. What else could she do, if she was to protect Charles, except lie? So she said nothing. She turned back to the square and walked away.

17

Julitte and the others were summoned before dawn, given barely more than a few minutes to dress and no time to eat.

She stumbled on the road. It was still so dark she hadn't seen the dip, a dip she was sure hadn't been there when it had been only a few carts and wagons using this route. Now with more wagons and trucks going by nearly every day, it was showing wear.

She knew where the Germans were leading her—her and nearly a dozen others from the village. They headed west, closer to the sound of fighting, but between them and the blasts of light still in the distance stood the mansion once belonging to M. Mantoux. Fearful as she was to be forced to join German soldiers, she was glad she'd been summoned with so many others. And not just women.

The sun was little more than a pink promise in the sky behind her, but it provided enough light to outline the expansive walls of the Mantoux estate. Even from a distance she saw activity in spite of the early hour. Wagons marked a line from the other direction, on a road that hadn't existed before the outbreak of war. One after another, coming and going. Mostly horse-drawn wagons, but now and then a truck zoomed past, its back end covered in dark canvas.

Inside the gate, the formerly pristine gardens were not just wilted from winter. They were trampled, squashed by a graveyard of equipment and metal and tires. The door that had been painted green to complement the once-white exterior and terra-cotta tiles was now scraped and bruised and squeaked when their German escort opened it.

The smell hit her first, before any images in the dim oil light. Of vomit and excrement and decay. Death.

"You three will go there, to the laundry." The man pointed Julitte's way, along with two other women. His back was to the large hall behind him as he pointed down one of the side arteries. "A soldier will take you to the cellar. The rest of you will come with me."

Julitte wasn't the only one to walk with a hand covering her nose and mouth. At least at the laundry she could hope for the luxury of soap.

Along the way she saw what had once been a home reduced to a place no one cared about, except for whatever shelter it offered for the activity going on inside. The roof was intact, but the walls were empty and scarred, the floor layered with dirt. No furniture remained but cots standing corner to corner, and upon each lay a man, sometimes sleeping, sometimes moaning, sometimes bandaged. Always frail, a stark contrast to those Julitte saw marching every day.

One called to her as she passed—at least it seemed as though he were calling to her. But the name he used was not hers. He begged her to stop, to talk to him, to bring him something to drink. Julitte paused, but the soldier leading the way looked back and told her not to tarry.

Julitte never saw the sun that day. By the time she was marched to the village, it was nothing more than a memory in the western sky.

As she walked home, she heard nothing but the moans of those soldiers now using M. Mantoux's estate.

Throughout the next week, Julitte prayed she would never have to go back to work at the château. Far better to care for the children of Briecourt.

But she wasn't summoned at all, for which she raised a psalm of praise. She went to the church as often as she dared, each time staying longer than the last. If Charles was a prisoner, so was she, but their time together felt like freedom. Nothing else mattered, except that they took five minutes, or ten, or fifteen, getting to know one another in snippets.

She told Charles about working at M. Mantoux's, about the shambles and the misery. She hadn't wanted to talk about it because the suffering she'd seen that day confused her when all she wanted to do was hate her enemies. Yet those German soldiers mustn't be very different from her countrymen, suffering on the other side. Where Pierre was.

Most of the time they tried talking about something besides the war. She learned Charles had been born in America to a Belgian father and a wealthy American heiress. He'd gone to school in many different countries: in America and Belgium, in Switzerland and even here in France. He said he couldn't choose which country was his favorite when she asked, because there were things about them all that he liked. Neither had he a favorite food or color or book; he had a way of liking something about almost everything.

But if he had a favorite person, it was his sister, Isa. He told Julitte she would like Isa, because they both thought of God as their Father, not just as their Creator. He hoped one day they could meet.

That only reminded her that if this war ever did end, he would go back to all the countries he'd traveled, back to his sister, who no doubt lived as lavishly as he. And Julitte would stay here in Briecourt to welcome her family home. Pierre and her father and the rest of the Toussaint villagers who were scattered around France, waiting for the war to end. Waiting to come home.

She kept the topic of conversation mostly on him, which didn't seem hard to do, or else on God, which Charles didn't seem to mind. When he asked questions of her life before the war, she turned the topic away or recalled the time, always their enemy, and hurried off.

It was late in the day, later than any of her other visits. Julitte crept down the stairs, her pockets empty but her heart still light. How could it be, with the Germans dictating their comings and goings, deciding who would work and where, that she could still feel any hint of happiness inside? She would call her lightness of heart a miracle, except sometimes she wasn't sure God had as much to do with it as Charles.

She had nothing to give him today. Uncle Guy hadn't been allotted any flour in the last few days, and whatever the dairy had to spare was gone when Julitte arrived. She been there early, just after curfew lifted, but so had everyone else. She'd been squeezed to the back of the line the moment the dairyman opened his door.

"Charles," she whispered, and a moment later he appeared.

"You're here," he said with a smile. "I'm glad."

"I came only with apologies."

"Apologies! Why? You've been nothing but generous."

She pulled her empty pockets inside out. "I've brought nothing. I'm sorry. I was unable to get anything at the dairy today, and there is no bread. Maybe this afternoon, the Germans said."

He pulled a chair away from the small table. "Then we'll be hungry together and keep our minds from it for a little while by talking. Can you stay?"

How easily she took the seat, as if there were no reason at all not to spend her time exactly as she pleased, with whomever she pleased.

"I wish that you could have tasted Uncle Guy's bread before the Germans took away his flour. Everyone loved his bread, even the de Colvilles, although none would admit such a thing."

"Why do the Toussaints and the de Colvilles hate each other as they do?"

Such an easy question to ask, so impossible to answer. "I'm not sure anyone knows anymore. It's just our way of life, something everyone is taught as they learn to walk or to talk. I suppose you must think us odd, with our fighting even now, when we have a common enemy."

He shrugged. "My father is Belgian, Julitte. The land of the Walloons and the Flemings, one side with one way and language, the other side different. And my mother, American. The North and the South went to war over their differences."

Julitte contemplated his words, something inside stirring. He made her feel as though she wasn't different at all. Of course, he didn't know all there was to know.

She couldn't help admiring him, and sometimes, because he was always happy to see her, she wondered if he might hold her in special esteem, too. But on her mat at night she cautioned those kinds of thoughts. Of course he welcomed her company. Would a starving man not welcome the hand that brought bread? The man lonely for company, companionship?

Still, the feelings persisted, especially at moments like this when she was in his presence.

Her heart strengthened its beat to pounding. She hadn't wanted to, but suddenly it became clear: she must tell him more about herself. Maybe he would prove to be just like everyone else and put her at a safer distance if he knew. If her constant but unspoken reminders of the differences in their lifestyles weren't enough to stop her from dreaming about him, perhaps she should see if another avenue would cool her interest in him. If he pushed her away, she would have no choice but to tame her own wayward thoughts of him.

She needed to speak now, immediately, before she changed her mind. "I need to tell you, Charles—something about me that you should know."

He smiled so easily she wondered what he could be thinking. "I already know you, Julitte. That you're beautiful and brave and belong to God in a way no one I've known does. Do you know, when I first heard you praying upstairs, I wondered if you might be an angel?"

She wanted to laugh but could barely smile. Would he still think that if he knew her heritage?

So she shook her head and pressed on. "I need to tell you about where I came from—"

He held up a hand and she stilled, waiting for what he would say. "I know, Julitte. About the silly rumors. I don't care."

"The rumors—about me? That I am from the . . . island . . . the Greek island of . . ." Why was it so hard to say? It was where she came from, and in her mind it wasn't hard to remember the place she'd last seen her father.

"Lepers, Julitte. Your mother went there to serve, your father to minister. How could I not admire someone whose parents were so selfless?"

Everything inside her seemed to melt in relief, even the part of her that was ready to act like steel against anyone who called her a leper. "You know? But how?"

"Father Barnabé told me, when I asked about you. I heard your prayer, and I was curious to know everything about you."

"And you're not afraid I might have the disease that claimed my parents?"

He shook his head. "I'm not a physician, but I've known enough people who are afraid of unfounded things to not fall prey to that sort of thinking myself. Besides, Father Barnabé told me of the rule they had, about letting children leave the island if they show no signs of the disease by the time they're five. You've been gone all these years and are still healthy. Why should you or I or anyone else be afraid?"

"I'm not afraid," she admitted. "Not even if I were to get the disease. God made me; He'll take me by whatever method He designs."

Charles's gaze bored into hers. "There is no one else like you, Julitte. Your faith is in every breath."

"The war makes everyone think of faith," she said. "Death and faith. Do you fear death, Charles?"

He tilted his head as if pondering his response. "If I want to be a war hero, I should say no. But I'm finding it hard to lie to you. So yes, I will admit it. I do fear death. There's only one thing, at this moment, I fear more."

"And what's that?"

"Your thinking I'm a coward."

That he should consider at all what she thought made her want to smile, but she wouldn't dwell on that now. "It's natural to fear death if your faith isn't clear. In our hearts, I think all of us know of a judgment that comes after we die, when we finally face the God who made everything."

"How could my heart know something that my mind doesn't?"

"God puts knowledge in all of us, even before we learn anything else. Like instinct in animals—how birds know to build a nest or mothers to take care of their young. He whispers knowledge every time we see something He made."

"I believe a God who is capable of making this earth must be perfect," Charles said. "But He made us with a choice. He must have known we'd choose our own way sooner or later."

"So He chose to come to earth as one of us. In Jesus. To help us become more like Him."

Charles reached across the table to stroke the side of her face gently. "You've thought all of this through. Your faith seems very much like Isa's, but then I've never wanted to talk to her about it, so I don't really know."

"My faith is no different from any else's who knows God." But Julitte knew there was more to tell him, something that might indeed make her different from this sister he spoke of. She doubted Father Barnabé had told him everything. "Here in the village, some people think I'm odd. Not only because of where I'm from but because I talk to God more often than most. It isn't that I try to be different. Perhaps if everyone in the village talked to me, I wouldn't need to find company in God as much as I do."

"I think you talk to God so much because it comes easily for you. I've heard you." He paused, catching her gaze again. "Father Barnabé said you knew when your father died."

Her breath caught. "What did Father Barnabé say?"

"He said you knew before Narcisse ever came home to tell you that your father was dead."

Julitte neither denied nor confirmed the statement.

"How did you know, Julitte?"

She'd known the question would come and wondered at her own willingness to speak. Never before had she wanted to talk about this bond between her and God. It was a bond that seemed unusual, and yet she knew it must be available to everyone. Now she wanted to share everything with this man who knew so little of God and so much of the world He made.

And yet she wondered if the way he looked at her would change.

"I don't like to talk about these things because it reminds me how others think of me. As different. But if I'm different at all, it's only because of what God does; it's nothing I've done. Do you believe me?" When he nodded, she took in a breath, surprised to feel her hands shaking. "The first time it happened, I was at my loom. It was like any other day and I was thinking of nothing in particular. I was young, nine years old at the time, and the loom felt too big, but my adoptive mother had always shown patience with me, and so I worked hard but maybe not effectively." She let her mind drift to the image of Narcisse's wife and smiled. Then Julitte glanced back at Charles. "The day it first happened was sunny, not unlike today was. I felt nothing strange, perhaps a bit of boredom as I worked on a large piece of material."

She swallowed. "And then suddenly all the emotion I'd felt in my life was gone. No boredom, no frustration, not even the longing to finish the task at hand. I closed my eyes, wondering at the strange freedom from what I'd felt a moment ago. When I did, I was paralyzed with new emotion . . . except . . ." She paused, unsure what word to use, she'd so rarely described the day. "*Emotion* isn't the right word. I have no word for what I felt. Peace, of course, but more than that. Joy, indescribable. Relief and love and as if the heaviest burden had been lifted. And then I saw my father. He stood before a bright light . . . not blindingly bright, not the kind that hurts your eyes. It was a light that illumined as no other. It shone directly on his face—on his perfect, wonderful face."

Julitte opened her eyes, feeling her own hand on her smooth cheek, a cheek that looked so much like her father's, at least as it had before he'd succumbed to the disease. "In that moment I knew that only God could heal my father's face in such a way, and he had been healed. The joy he felt after a lifetime of seeing such suffering—and to see my mother suffer and then suffer so himself—is not something I can tell you in words. I can only recall and long for it myself someday. Since then, if I'm near someone who dies, I get a much briefer glimpse. Maybe it isn't so much a vision as a memory of that one moment God gave me, when He let me see my father's entry to heaven. I don't know."

Charles pulled her hand away from her face and held it inside the palm of his. "No wonder your faith is so strong."

"I've read too much of the Bible to think miracles keep faith strong. Look at the things people saw from the beginning, and still they ended up doubting. I think it's talking to God every day and reading the Bible that feed my faith. It's so full of wisdom I can't doubt it."

"Would you think me silly if I said I think God directed you to me, to tell me about Him?"

"I believe it too." She looked down at their hands, still entwined, then gently pulled away. "I must go. Didi will be expecting me. I haven't been home yet. I'm sorry I didn't bring you anything today."

He smiled. "Your company is always enough."

She couldn't hide her returning smile, but his words only made her rush away more quickly. She knew such words—and having him hold her hand—would play over and again in her mind, until all of it meant more than it should.

18

In the morning there was a tap at the door, even before Ori had gone off to her job. It was early enough for another raid, being just after dawn, when most people like Julitte, Ori, and Didi were still at breakfast, such as it was. But it was far too civil a knock to be a soldier. Julitte answered.

Father Barnabé stood there, a frown on his wrinkled face. Julitte swallowed the last bit of bread, but it barely went down beside the lump that formed at the priest's solemn look.

"Is . . . everything all right?" she asked.

He stepped past her.

"Didi." He nodded his head respectfully, ignoring Ori and keeping his back to Julitte. She closed the door and stepped around him to see his profile, but he didn't look her way.

Was he angry that she continued to visit Charles despite his warning for her to stay away? He must know, despite her effort to keep her visits a secret, even from him. Perhaps he'd come to tell Didi everything so between the two of them her whereabouts could be accounted for. Father Barnabé was good at confronting those who strayed, and she was fully prepared to receive his lecture now.

"Didi, I know it's early, but I'm here to collect you. Ask no questions, because I have no answers, except that you and I, as elders in the village, are required."

"By the Germans?" Didi asked. Julitte noted her tone held no fear, just curiosity.

"No."

The priest assisted Didi to her feet, then took her red cloak from its hook and draped it around her stooped shoulders.

Ori stood too. "But where are you taking her?"

"Just for a little walk across the street." His voice was calm enough, but Father Barnabé chose not to make eye contact, convincing Julitte something was amiss.

"Care if I come along?" Julitte asked. How calm her voice sounded, when that lump in her throat had grown so large each word pained her to utter.

"Are you an elder in this village?" Didi asked, her tone sharper now. Maybe she was just a little fearful, after all. "He said this is for the older people. You stay. Clean the dishes."

Julitte glanced at Ori, who appeared every bit as worried as Julitte felt. Father Barnabé took Didi's arm, but the door was barely closed behind them before Julitte sprang to the window to see where they went. She looked first one way, then the other, but saw no one—until turning forward. There, directly across the street, they stood at the open door to Gustave de Colville's home. In a moment they disappeared behind it.

"They really did go across the street! Not down the street to Uncle Guy's but to Gustave's."

"No!"

Ori crossed to the window and peered out as well, but Julitte knew she couldn't see any more than Julitte did: Didi's red cloak disappearing through a doorway that hadn't been darkened by a Toussaint in all the days of either Ori's or Julitte's life.

Ori closed the shutter and fell against it, hands behind her. "Do you think they're talking about me? about punishing me for working for the Germans?"

Ah, Lord, here I've been frantic and selfish in my worries when Ori is worried too!

Julitte shook her head, pulling Ori to the table. "There is enough punishment doled out by the Germans. Even the de Colvilles aren't that cruel."

"Didi must be angrier than I thought, to talk to a de Colville about me. Why else would she go there? You saw her accuse me of spying not long ago. But truly, Julitte, I wasn't doing that the day I looked out the town hall window. I wouldn't!"

Julitte tried to smile. They'd spent little time together since Ori had started her job, and Julitte couldn't deny a growing hardness in her heart over Ori's choosing to work with the Germans instead of staying united against them. They could get by without the food she earned, even though Julitte had to admit she welcomed anything extra now with a secret mouth to feed.

Julitte forced her own worries away and focused on Ori instead.

"Tell me what you do at that job, Ori, so I might understand why you still go."

Ori looked away, but not before Julitte saw the hint of a sparkle. "I just clean, and sometimes I deliver things from one office to another. I do what they tell me to do."

"And that Hauptmann? Are you working for him or for someone else?"

"For him." Eyes still hidden by her lids.

Julitte reached to Ori's lap and pressed her hand on one of Ori's. "You aren't . . . This Hauptmann—he isn't becoming something more to you, is he?"

Ori stood, and the chair scraped against the wooden floor. "It's hard not to get to know someone you spend all day with. And he isn't like the others—with guns and helmets and ugly voices. He's kind to me."

Julitte didn't need to see her friend's eyes anymore. Her tone admitted all. "Oh, Ori."

Ori sat down again, this time grabbing both of Julitte's hands. "You should understand, Julitte, of all the people in this horrid little village. You know what it's like to be ignored, disregarded. But he's not like that. He sees me; he talks to me and asks me questions and listens to what I say. He makes me feel—"

She stopped then, and Julitte guessed it was because Ori thought she disapproved. Certainly she did understand what it was like to be ignored, particularly by the men of their village. And maybe Julitte shouldn't cast a stone at Ori while she had her own secret. Was it any less dangerous to want the company of a would-be soldier in hiding than it was to want the company of a German? Either man could bring danger to everyone in the village.

Except there was one difference. Dangerous men, both of them. But Charles was not their enemy.

Julitte tried to pull away but Ori clutched her tighter. "You do understand, don't you?"

"I want to, Ori. God loves us all, German or otherwise. But . . ."

Ori let out a little cry, freeing her hands to put her arms around Julitte. "You do understand! Just as I hoped you would."

Julitte knew to be most honest was to correct Ori, to tell her she didn't think it wise to befriend an officer in an army who did the things they did. But Julitte couldn't. She could only avoid looking her friend in the eye. "I won't judge you, Ori. It's not my place but God's."

Ori let Julitte go, and Julitte stood. She returned to the window, but there was no sign of activity across the street.

"I want to stay, to wait for Didi," Ori said even as she went to the peg where her coat hung. "But I cannot be late. I'll come home at noon."

With Ori gone, the time Julitte spent staring at the doorway across the street seemed to go on forever. Curiosity about the unprecedented meeting soon gave way to tension, and Julitte forced herself to leave the vigil at the window. Only to pace.

"Be still, and know that I am God." "Lean not unto thine own understanding." "Perfect love casteth out fear." All of her favorite verses came to mind, but whatever peace the Lord sought to offer through such words was quickly tamped by Julitte's fear.

Had this meeting something to do with Claudette seeing Julitte at the church not so long ago? True, Claudette was forever unfriendly to Julitte, but Julitte had never been able to forget that encounter. She'd felt as though Claudette had caught her in some sin or bested her in some way. Accusatory or triumphant—Julitte had never decided which look had been in Claudette's eye that day.

Between her worries, Julitte was tempted to go to the church, knowing Father Barnabé would not find her there while he was busy at this mysterious meeting. But she'd never visited Charles at such an early hour and feared he might still be sleeping. What else was there to do in that awful cellar?

Besides, she wanted to be here when Didi returned.

Julitte's heart ticked away the seconds while she grew sick in the stomach for wanting news, waiting alone despite the comfort God's Holy Spirit offered.

Finally the door opened, and Didi came in with Father Barnabé behind her. Julitte rushed expectantly to them.

Father Barnabé helped Didi out of her cloak, then hung it on the hook near the door. Without a word, he put his hand back on the doorknob.

"You're leaving?" Julitte asked. "Without telling me where you've had Didi this past hour or more?"

"I must go," he said. "I have things to take care of."

"At—the church?"

Father Barnabé glanced at Julitte, then at Didi, pausing as if to speak. But instead he shook his head and went out the door.

Julitte faced Didi, who went to sit in her chair by the warm hearth stove.

"I saw you go into Gustave's."

"Sit down, Julitte."

She pulled a chair from the table closer to Didi, who now only looked at her hands, as if studying the pattern of wrinkles made deeper by rubbing a finger over the top of one.

At last she looked around, to the kitchen corner, then up toward the loft. "Where is Ori?"

"Gone. To the town hall. To work."

"Just as well. She isn't thinking clearly lately."

"I don't think she's done anything she regrets." *Yet.*

"I will tell you about this meeting, Julitte, because we've agreed that everyone—yes, de Colville and Toussaint and nearly every French citizen who remains in this village—must know. Except for Ori. None of us could decide what to tell her, so for now she will be told nothing. It's too great a test—of her loyalty to me, to everyone she knows, including you."

"Ori loves us, Didi. She would sooner die than hurt us."

Didi threw up her hands. "I hope you are right, because I don't know how to keep from her what everyone else will soon know."

"And what is that?" She knew she was acting dense but was too afraid to speak freely. Surely this meeting *had* been about Charles.

"About who is hiding."

"Hiding?"

Didi offered a tired half smile. "You would try to act as though you know nothing, even now? Claudette heard you talking to a man in the church cellar."

Julitte raised chilly fingers to her suddenly heated cheeks. "Am I to blame, then, for giving his presence away?"

"It was only a matter of time before someone saw something. It just happened to be you, by a de Colville."

"Oh! Father Barnabé was right. I've been a danger, not a help at all."

"Shh, now. Do you think you're the only one who was seen? Gustave saw Guy talking to his stove. I myself saw a shadow in the window of Claudette's mother's, a tall shadow that did not belong to a de Colville. And let us not forget Ori and what she saw from the window! There have been many sightings, not just yours."

"You mean—Charles was in those places? away from the church?"

"Oh, child, think! There are seven men in this village who never stepped foot here before the Germans came. Seven soldiers, stragglers in hiding. One by Father Barnabé, another by your uncle Guy. An Irishman hides at the metalworker's home, and an Englishman is at your uncle Xavier's. Three more hidden by the de Colvilles, one of them by Marie-Hermine, Claudette's own mother."

Everything deflated inside Julitte, including the worries and guilt she'd clung to instead of the comfort her Father God offered. But only for a moment. New concern rose.

"Seven? We must hide *seven* men from the Germans?"

Didi nodded. "And so we have, but at least not from each other anymore." She squeezed Julitte's hands in hers. "For the first time in my life, Julitte—and that is a long life, to be sure—I am on the same side as the de Colvilles. United against the Germans."

"United," Julitte echoed softly. "Toussaint with de Colville."

She never would have imagined it possible.

But with God? All things were possible.

19

For a full day and part of another, Julitte stayed inside her cottage. Everyone did. Perhaps, like her, the others needed time to absorb what such a secret might mean. If any one of them was caught helping a straggler, the *affiches* hung on the wall of town hall said they would be subject to severe penalty, even death. Julitte didn't doubt the Germans capable of carrying out their threats. Somehow, in a war, life became expendable. Even that of a civilian.

The next afternoon Julitte lingered by the chapel on her way to the well, watching the door, wishing she might go in. But Father Barnabé was inside; she'd spoken to him on the stoop just minutes ago. He'd come to her only long enough to say that although she was no longer the only one who knew his secret, he still forbade her to see Charles. It was no less dangerous than it had been before.

He was like a bulldog, with his shorn hair and the wrinkles on his chin. She'd never noticed such a resemblance before. She turned away, intent on getting water anyway, but her gaze was caught by something else. A wagon pulled into town by a pair of mud-spattered military horses.

She cast aside her water vessel, first walking, then running toward the cart to see if her eyes were mistaken. They were not. The dirty wagon held familiar cargo. She ran back to the church, rushing inside.

"Father! Father! Come outside!"

The clopping of her shoes made more noise than her voice, but soon the priest came from his sacristy.

"What is it?"

"The Germans! They've brought our men home. Come!"

The sight was more horrible than she'd first thought. Men—or what was left of them—who'd been among those taken from the village all those months ago. How could they have shrunk in size in so short a time? Emaciated, putrid, bearded, and filthy, every last one of them.

Her cries had summoned not only Father Barnabé but others from the houses nearby as well. Word spread quicker than fire from one cottage to another, and as the men hobbled from the wagon, villagers came from every direction. Germans, too, but they lingered on the outskirts of the square, rifles resting across their chests.

Uncle Guy had once been tall and lithe, but age and so little food lately had slowed his step. Just now something must have made him forget his limitations, because Julitte saw him emerge from his bakery, curious at first, then hasten awkwardly toward the foul wagon.

She watched the hope and eagerness on her uncle's face turn to horror at something still in the wagon. She stepped closer. And there was Yves—or was it? He wore rags on his feet, not the fine shoes he'd worn the day he'd been taken. No coat. His clothes were as filthy as the animal cart, his light brown hair and beard long and matted. He was the tallest of her cousins and had once been the most handsome. Now his bones jutted around his eyes and along his jaw and chin, and though his eyes were still blue, they were set in red.

He tried to move but fell back on the straw. Uncle Guy climbed in and Julitte scrambled to follow. Yves was thin but still heavy for her, yet she pulled him gently up and helped him struggle to his feet. Uncle Guy carried most of his weight; she acted only as a buffer between him and falling if he leaned too far to her side.

All the way to his home, she prayed he would survive the next step. At last in the bakery, they took him to the room her uncle used, behind the kitchen. Father Barnabé, the village healer, had followed. There were other patients for him today, some Toussaint and some de Colville, but Julitte knew the feud had nothing to do with having chosen to follow them here. Yves was the weakest.

"Water," Father Barnabé requested even as he reached for a towel that lay on Uncle Guy's table.

Julitte found her uncle's water jar, poured some in a bowl, some in a cup. Though she held the cup to Yves's mouth and he opened it to receive the water, he coughed and most of it rolled down his face. He closed his eyes, refusing more.

Uncle Guy took his hand from the other side of the cot.

"I—I'm glad I am home," Yves whispered. "But for too short a time."

"Non, non." The smile on Uncle Guy's face was there but uncertain. "We'll take care of you, and you'll be well."

Yves opened his eyes again, moved his free hand toward his father's face, but it dropped to his side, limp, before reaching his target. "Father."

Then his eyes closed.

"Yves!"

Julitte was barely aware the call came from her own lips, because she saw him not here, but there, in the light, as if he were walking away—away from her and away from her uncle. The image was fleeting, no more than a moment, but as real as any other time it had happened. Her call for him to come back was left unheeded.

Uncle Guy put his hand on his son's face, to his mouth as if to feel for breath. Then he looked from his son to Julitte, and whatever he saw there could not have given him hope.

"You . . . you can do nothing?"

That he asked Julitte such a thing rather than Father Barnabé, the town *curé*, came as no surprise to Julitte. Nor to Father Barnabé, who looked at her too, with the same feeble hope.

O Lord, if ever there was a time I would ask for a real miracle . . .

But she knew the request was too late. Yves would never want to come back now, even if he were allowed, no matter how much he loved his earthly father.

Charles sat in the pew beneath the high, opaque window. He knew something had happened the day before but had no idea what. Two days ago Father Barnabé had told him Julitte had been seen coming from the church too often and had even been heard talking to him by one of the villagers. At the time Charles received the scolding without defense. He knew he'd grown lax. Never seeing a German soldier, wanting company so desperately, had made him weak. And Julitte's company was especially hard to resist.

But as no real harm had been done, he'd let go of his guilt.

Until yesterday afternoon, when he'd heard the frantic footsteps and Julitte's voice calling for the priest. Charles had waited at the stairs, hoping it wouldn't be long before one or the other came down to tell him what had occurred.

But no one came.

What if there were more ramifications than just the rest of the villagers knowing about him? What if that feud Pepin talked about—and Father Barnabé confirmed—had inspired someone to turn Julitte over to the Germans?

He'd tried to pray but found his attempt so far short of what real prayer should be, or at least what he thought it should be based on the way Julitte prayed, that he'd stopped. Instead, he'd spent the day and the night imagining himself and Julitte before a German firing squad.

The town was quiet even now, keeping the worst of his imaginings at bay. How long before he could venture out, be sure the entire town hadn't been evacuated? He might be the only one left. He and the Germans.

He cursed his own powerlessness, his own foolishness for having been caught behind the German line to begin with and for staying so long. Too long. Was he a man or a child, waiting and cowering like this? What good was he to anyone? What good had his entire life been? None.

To end this way . . .

Such thoughts were bitter company. He wished, if he were to die, he might have at least known a sliver of the faith Julitte knew.

God, O God . . . I haven't done much to improve myself all these years. I've done nothing to make my life matter, and now, if death is near, my life seems pointless. If . . . if I can know what I'm coming to in death after I've wasted this life . . . help me to learn what You want me to know. Give me the faith Julitte told me You would give, if only I asked.

A feeble prayer, it hardly made sense. But if God was really God, a God who made Charles, then He would know the truth and the meaning behind those words.

Then Charles heard the sound of footsteps. Clogs.

"Charles? It's me. Julitte."

He met her at the foot of the stairs, taking her hands in his. He realized he was touching her only after feeling the smoothness of her skin, the slenderness of her hands. Suddenly he knew why he'd hated himself so much lately, not only because he was worthless in this war, but because he had nothing to offer her but his cowardice.

"I'm sorry I couldn't come here sooner."

Her face was lovelier than he remembered, even from the day before, making his realization sharper, the pain of disappointment in himself deeper. Her eyes, darker than her hair, were wide and full of concern for him. Her cheeks smooth, her mouth so perfect he wanted to kiss her but didn't, because she was speaking and everything in her tone said she'd worried for him.

"I thought you might have heard my footsteps yesterday and how frantic I was when I called Father Barnabé."

"What happened? Is he well?"

"Yes. I've been with him through the night, seeing to men who were brought home. They were taken before, to Germany, but some have been sent back home—they were of no more use to the Germans. One of them died during the night, and another . . . I don't know."

Charles knew he should breathe easier, be pleased that the entire town wasn't under suspicion of hiding him and the others. But the long, anxious hours convinced him of what he must do. And quickly.

For the moment he set aside his resolution and squeezed her hands. "I'm sorry. Were you close to the man who died?"

"He was my cousin."

One side of her mouth curled downward, and her lips trembled as if she held back a sob. Charles gazed at her face, seeing her grief, wanting to fix it, but still touched with relief that none of the fears he'd harbored overnight would come true. And so he said nothing, only looked at her.

He stared at a lovely indentation she had above the right corner of her mouth, wondering why he'd never noticed such a detail before this moment. He wanted to see it again, to know if it would appear only with that expression or if he could get it to show with other emotions as well. A smile? Laughter? Some other emotion that had nothing to do with grief or sadness or anger or fear.

Such a silly thought. He must be giddy for not being at death's door after all. She needed his comfort right now, not an infatuation.

Charles rubbed his thumbs over the top of her hands, knowing he must let her go even though part of him wanted to hold on longer. He noted she hadn't pulled away. But he couldn't give in to this nearly overwhelming interest he had in her, the urge to feel her hands in his longer, to know each emotion behind that indentation. He turned away, reminding himself of his uselessness and the reason for it. "I'm sorry for the loss of your cousin. This war."

He spoke the two short words not with compassion but with all the hatred and scorn and shame he felt inside. Stepping away, he sensed rather than saw her follow, felt the hand she put on his shoulder. He wanted to enjoy the concern behind her touch, to pull her near, and feel her closeness, but didn't. Yet he couldn't stop himself from looking at her. His eyes wouldn't deny him that. She leaned toward him with sympathy when it should have been the other way around, him offering sympathy for her loss. How did she know? Could she read his thoughts, or was his self-loathing that obvious—or deserved?

He had to do *something*, starting with telling her what he'd decided. "I'm going to break through the lines, Julitte. I'm leaving. Today."

Her dark eyes widened farther; then her brows drew together and she shook her head. "It's too dangerous, Charles. It must be so hard for you to stay here, cooped up like a prisoner, but you're alive. Out there—"

"Out there would be better than here, even in a shallow grave on a battlefield—if I can take just one German with me."

She shook her head. "War heroes aren't always made on battlefields."

He stepped back, because her words were too tempting. "I know one thing: heroes aren't made in cellars."

She looked ready to speak again, but something stopped her. A noise—upstairs? It startled him too, because the sound was closer than he expected. At the top of the stairs. Had someone come in the back door? Surely they would have heard someone walk through the sanctuary.

Charles, used to the habit of slinking to the corner under the tarp, pulled Julitte along. He slipped the tarp around them both, putting her to the wall, and himself just beneath the covering. And waited.

No voices, but steps. Descending the stairs.

He should be frightened, if not for himself at least for Julitte. But she was so close, here nearly within his arms, and his mind went soft, too soft to control. He smelled the scent of her hair, like raspberries. For a moment it was dizzying. She was near, yet he wanted to pull her closer. One arm was there already, shielding her from the roughness of the wall. If she looked up at him, he could not tell because of the darkness.

There was more than one set of footsteps on the stairs. Father Barnabé only came alone. Charles hovered over Julitte, knowing if it was Germans, he would have to kill them or die protecting her.

"Charles? It's Father Barnabé. I've brought someone."

He heard Julitte take a breath even as his brain first registered how fast his heart was beating. For a moment he considered stepping outside the tarp and keeping her behind him, since the priest would undoubtedly disapprove of her here and at such an hour. But it was too late. She was already pushing aside the tarp.

"Julitte!"

"She only just arrived," Charles said. "To tell me what happened yesterday."

Julitte approached Father Barnabé. "I wondered if he thought the worst, the way I burst in here for you."

Their explanations were met by a glare, but Julitte moved past

Father Barnabé toward another man Charles didn't recognize. He was tall—every bit as tall as Charles himself. Younger than Father Barnabé but topped by gray hair nonetheless.

"This is Guy Toussaint," Father Barnabé said.

Charles shook his hand; he recognized the name as not only the baker but another host. Pepin's.

"We've come to a decision regarding you," Father Barnabé said. Evidently whatever he'd come to say held off his annoyance over Julitte being here. "Has Julitte told you that five of the men the Germans sent off to work have returned to us? Guy's son among them?"

He nodded. "Yes, though she also told me not all of them survived."

Father Barnabé frowned. "Guy's son has died."

Charles let his gaze return to the stoic man. "I'm sorry to hear of your loss, *monsieur*."

The baker bowed his head in acknowledgment but said nothing. Charles looked at him, so solemn and yet here. He wondered what could be so important to bring him away from his son's barely cooled deathbed.

"Guy has agreed that this is an opportunity. One man has died; another may too. That will be two fewer mouths the Germans think they must feed. Two men whose identities, right now, are barely known, at least by those Germans who oversee this village."

Charles could scarcely believe what he thought he was hearing. "What are you offering, exactly?"

"We have little time to lose," Father Barnabé said. "You shall take the identity of Yves Toussaint."

Charles still looked at Guy. "You—you would do this for me? On the heel of your loss?"

Guy cleared his throat. "It is a practical solution. We can barely feed ourselves, and if they learn there are fewer mouths to feed, they'll barely increase our rations from what they are now."

"Guy will bury Yves in the woods behind the bakery—though digging in frozen ground will require a miracle. It was decided that Dowan would come here from hiding in the metalworker's house and take your place. You will go home with Guy now and take Yves's place."

"But what about Pepin? Or Dowan and Seymour—they will still be in hiding while I'm free?" Charles's objection surprised even him. He should be jumping at this chance, limited as it was, and not let anything stand in his way.

"Pepin is too old and too small to be believed a son of Guy. Dowan speaks no French, and even if we could hide that, we couldn't cover his red hair and freckles. You're the only one who might be believed one of us." He looked above Charles's gaze, at the top of his head. "As it is, we'll have to dirty your hair to dull the color. Or shave it off, perhaps. Cover it with a cap."

Julitte took a step closer to Charles. She looked so hopeful he automatically wanted to smile, especially when one corner of her mouth dipped, making the indentation he'd seen earlier momentarily reappear. "When I was little, my mother once used something to cover the gray that started to show while Narcisse was away so long at sea. If her concoction was able to hide gray hair, shouldn't it work on any light color?"

"It's certainly worth a try," Father Barnabé said. "What will you need?"

"Only what I have, thanks be to God." Her eyes fairly beamed, she looked so pleased. "The Germans didn't take our spices. Rosemary. Sage. Water to boil it down."

"Go, then, and come back as quickly as you can. We've no time to lose."

She shot a smile at Charles, then slipped into her clogs where they'd been forgotten under the table.

Freedom—such as it was, living in a town occupied by the German

Imperial Army. Freedom to see Julitte as often as he could, under the circumstances. Certainly more freedom to do that than he currently had, with a protective priest standing in the way.

Too bad he couldn't accept such a generous offer.

20

"Wait, Julitte."

She heard her name and the surprisingly solemn tone. "Yes?"

The frown on Charles's face didn't dissipate even when he looked from her to her uncle. "This is an extraordinary gift, more extraordinary than letting me hide here." His glance swept to Father Barnabé. "And feeding me."

Father Barnabé waved his words away. "It's no more than anyone would do, anyone who cares about another human being."

"It's more—much more. How many others would risk their lives as you have? But I cannot accept. If I do, I can never escape. I'll be counted among you, and if I escape, my absence will be noted. All of you would be in more danger then."

Julitte's heart hit the bottom of her stomach. So, he'd meant it when he said he was leaving. She felt Charles's gaze on her, as if he waited for her response rather than either of the others'. "You cannot leave," she told him. "It's too dangerous."

"It is dangerous," Barnabé echoed. "I've said so all along."

"So is keeping me here." He faced Father Barnabé, placing a hand on one of his shoulders. "You once said there are those in this town who used to smuggle before the war. Could you not at least ask them about the smuggling route? A route to smuggle *me* . . . out of France."

Father Barnabé looked from Charles to Julitte, but she couldn't pull her eyes from Charles. She'd known all along it was foolish to imagine Charles as anything more than someone who needed her help, the recipient of a mission from God. Why had she allowed herself to wonder if he was growing to care for her?

"It could work," Uncle Guy was saying slowly. "Certainly the de Colvilles have been smuggling for generations. Successfully."

"We don't know anything about their routes," Father Barnabé said. "And they've never smuggled people, only their *blanche*."

"Who knows if the routes are even still intact?" Julitte demanded, ignoring the confusion in her mind, her racing pulse, the heat of fear mustering inside. "Everything is changed now, no matter what direction they smuggled from."

Father Barnabé nodded and opened his mouth, but Charles held up a hand to stop the *curé* before he could echo Julitte's words. "My mind is made up, with or without a smuggling route. But right now, this offer you've made must be acted upon. You must offer the freedom of taking Yves's place to another."

Father Barnabé rubbed his hands together. "Yes, of course we shall." But he continued to eye Charles. "I wish you would not ignore our counsel, though, Charles."

Julitte caught and held Charles's gaze. "You could stay, Charles. Safely, at least as safe as the rest of us."

She stood closer now, easily within reach when he put a hand over one of hers. He smiled, but it wasn't the smile of a man accepting a safer freedom. It was the smile of man who'd made up his mind. "I'll go, Julitte."

"Then we must leave now and speak to Gustave de Colville," Uncle Guy said, "to ask him about the smuggling route, if we are to bring you useful information. And if one of the men they're hiding might be suitable to take Yves's place instead of you."

Uncle Guy led the way to the stairs, Father Barnabé following.

But the priest stopped with one foot on the bottom stair. "Julitte? You are coming?"

She shook her head even before she knew what words she could use. "I'm staying for a little while, Father." She wanted to say more, something reasonable and innocent, about hoping to help Charles with such a dangerous plan, but the truth was all of that would be an excuse. She wanted to stay for far more complicated reasons.

"For a little while, then." He followed Uncle Guy up the stairs.

They were alone. None of Julitte's other visits had contained even a hint of awkwardness; each visit left her feeling it was too short.

But now . . . everything was different. As if all the moments she hoped to share with him must be stuffed into this one, however long it lasted.

"Is there anything I can say to change your mind?" Let him think she was only concerned about his safety, because that was certainly true. Only all of a sudden she knew it was much more. Ever since learning he was here—no, even before that; since the moment he'd caught her in that tree—his face had been engraved in her mind. She'd never dared entertain thoughts of the men from her village, knowing neither they nor their family would accept her, the *étrangère* from the Island of Lepers. But this man . . . he knew; he'd known all along and still welcomed her. Somehow she believed he would have welcomed her company even if she hadn't been one of only two people in town who knew he was here.

He stepped closer—as close as he'd been when he stood with her beneath the tarp, when she'd wondered if he could hear the pounding of her heart as surely as she heard it herself.

"Do you know, Julitte," he whispered, "that you are part of the reason I must go?"

She could barely think with him in such proximity. "Me?" It wasn't until she spoke that she truly felt the question. If she were in the equation at all, he should stay!

"Yes." But he offered no explanation. She wanted one, and to express a counteropinion, too, but here he was, so close, his eyes staring into hers, and she had only one thought: he would kiss her. She'd never been given a kiss except the chaste kind from a parent or Pierre or another relative, and just now her head was so light her vision nearly blurred around the edges. All she could see was Charles.

His mouth felt wonderfully smooth against hers, his arms around her strong. So this was what it was like to long to be so close to another human being that if there were a way to become one person together instead of two, she would choose it. To have her mind joined with his, so they would be together in experience and thought and emotion.

He lifted his mouth from hers but not for long, only looked down at her to smile, to lift a hand from her back to her hair, to wind his fingers in it, to kiss her again.

"I think the moment I first saw you near that tree, with your hair in the sunlight and your eyes so dark, I wanted to kiss you."

"I shouldn't admit I would have let you," she whispered. Then, because she knew whatever time they had left together was limited, she had to ask another question. "Charles, you said I was part of the reason you need to go. What did you mean?"

"Don't you know?"

She shook her head.

"I thought my kisses made it clear. I wish there were no war. It's complicating everything I feel—about you, about me. I'd call on you properly, take you with me to my home, where you could meet my family, my sister. We could know each other under normal circumstances."

Her heart pounded as it had so many times in the weeks and months past, only from a far different cause than fear. "But if there were no war, we wouldn't know each other now."

"Of course we would. Do you think, having met you, I would have forgotten you? That day under the tree was enough for me never to forget you, Julitte."

She wanted to smile but didn't. "I want very much to believe you, but I don't." She didn't let him interrupt, though she saw he wanted to. "You would have forgotten me with the next fancy party at M. Mantoux's."

"You have no appreciation for the impression you left on me. I would have come here for you."

"And then, even if the rumors about me didn't send you on your way, you would have eventually gone back to your life, and I would stay here, where I belong."

"Why do either one of us belong anywhere? You weren't born here any more than I was."

"Not born, but placed." Her parents had lived lives as simple as could be, both sets, natural and adoptive. Their faith had always been strong, their choices pure. Perhaps because a life of comfort and ease allowed less room for God. She shouldn't want anything else but the example they'd set. No matter what her dreams might hold.

He pulled himself to arm's length, and she felt a slight rigidness spread through his touch. "So if I were to ask you to marry me, right here, right now, if there were no war going on and our future clear, you would say no? Because you think your home is here and mine somewhere else?"

"I—I don't know what I would have said."

He laughed and held her close again. "Then maybe I was wrong before. I may be the only one in the world who should be grateful for this wretched war, if only to bring us together."

He kissed her again, although she wasn't sure she had her answer.

"But why am I part of the reason you must go? It should be the opposite."

He shook his head slowly, looking away from her. "I'm not worthy of anyone right now, Julitte, least of all you. Here I am, hiding away in a cellar, useless to you or to anyone in my country or yours. How can I hope to convince you I could take care of you or even convince myself that I'm capable? I could no sooner spend the rest of this war—no matter how long it lasts—in hiding and call myself a man than I could expect anyone to marry me, especially someone whose respect I hope to earn. So I'll go and I'll fight, and then I'll come back to you, just as I would have after that day I met you under the tree. I'll prove it to you."

"Is it only your pride standing in the way of marrying me? Not your lifestyle or mine or the difference in our faith?"

"What is the difference in our faith? You once told me all I had to do was ask for faith, and God would give it to me. Well, I've asked. And He's proven His faithfulness already through you, explaining to me exactly what I need to believe. And our lifestyles? That's something we can work out, even if it's a happy medium between yours and mine. Even if it requires me to give away half of my inheritance. You must admit I've survived rather humbly these last months, and other than wanting to shave my whiskers on a regular basis, I haven't missed much. I can live any way you like. But it's not my pride, Julitte. It's my self-respect. There is a difference—a large difference."

"And if you get shot in this quest for self-respect while escaping to freedom? Or if you make it and die on the battlefield?"

He moved his hands to her shoulders, where he held her firmly. "Then, my dearest Julitte, I will know that moment of joy you tried to describe to me, when I go to meet our Savior, and I will be waiting there for you where our lifestyles will no doubt become identical. For all eternity."

And then he kissed her again.

21

It was several hours before Father Barnabé returned, alone. Julitte saw from his frown that he'd expected her to be gone long ago, but she neither apologized nor explained. No wonder there had been two weddings before the men marched off to battle so many months ago. There was something about the possibility of never seeing someone again that lent boldness, even to her.

Explaining her absence all day to Didi might be difficult in a far different way, but she would face that later.

"There is a man—his name is Serge de Colville—who is coming tonight for you, Charles," Father Barnabé explained. "He knows the route and will go with you."

Charles's brows rose. "Go with me?"

"Yes." Though it might have been good news, it was hard to tell how Father Barnabé viewed it. He was still frowning.

"How is it possible that Serge could go, Father?" Julitte asked. "He's counted; he's on the list the Orstkommandant keeps."

"Yes, yes, I know. But he has wanted to leave since the day the Germans took up residence here. He thinks one of the men the de Colvilles are hiding is similar enough to him to take his place."

"And what of Sandre's son? Is he still . . .alive?"

"He may recover. We don't yet know. But I do know we cannot take too many chances, having someone taking another man's place. As it is, we've decided it's best to let the Germans know of Yves's death. We cannot dig a grave; the ground is too hard without a sturdy shovel left to us. And we want to bury him properly."

Charles took Julitte's hand. "There, you see? God means for me to go. I have nothing to worry about. I have my own guide to see me to safety. How much more proof do either one of us need that this must be what God wants me to do?"

Julitte tried to smile, even though her heart was heavy at the thought of him sneaking through German-held territory. Could peace about such a decision, even the kind of peace God had given to Charles and perhaps wanted to give her, be felt through her own worry?

"You will leave at midnight, so I suggest you get some rest." Father Barnabé turned once again to the stairs. "And the belongings you brought will have to be disposed of without a trace. You cannot carry them and you cannot leave them to be found. Do you understand?"

Charles nodded.

"Julitte, come along with me now."

She knew she couldn't ignore Father Barnabé's command, much as she wanted to. She'd spent so little time with Charles. Too little. Now she must say good-bye—but with a priest watching?

"I will, Father Barnabé."

He moved no further. "Now, Julitte."

She nodded, frowning just the same. "Yes, I just want to say good-bye. Will you let me? Please?"

"I will be upstairs in the sacristy, then, with both doors open. Make sure if the Lord Himself were to interrupt, you needn't be ashamed. And, Julitte," he said, already on the bottom stair, "Didi has been waiting for you all day; she asked me about you. You mustn't tarry too long, if only for her sake."

Julitte nodded again, then waited until Father Barnabé disappeared up the stairs, all the time both anticipating and dreading the next moments. How could she let pass something she didn't want to end, knowing it must?

"Charles."

She said his name without knowing it, was ushered into his arms with an urgency that matched her own. He kissed her, not as he had before—deeply yet somehow still gently—but this time desperately, nearly harsh in the whirlwind that must be inside of him, too. This wanting and fear and hope all swirling inside. She never wanted to let him go.

"He thinks I can rest," Charles said, his cheek to hers. "He thinks I want to waste these last couple of hours that I could be with you. Here. Alone."

"I mustn't stay," she said, "no matter that it's what we both want."

Charles put both hands to the sides of her face. "Do you, Julitte? Do you want to stay with me?"

She kept his gaze and repeated the words he'd used earlier. "I thought my feelings were clear from my kiss."

He pulled her close again and she heard the laugh originate from his chest. "If ever I would like to see a miracle, it's now. A miracle of time, so we might have all of it we wanted, without any dangers around or ahead."

She let him hold her and kiss her again, even though the use of that word—*miracle*—always made her cool inside.

"What is it?" he asked.

"What?"

"You retreated from me for a moment; I felt the difference just now in the way you kissed me. Why?"

She tried to pull away. "I—I didn't."

"We haven't all the time we need, Julitte, so we should use what little time we do have in the best way we can. With only honesty between us." He led her back to the table where they'd spent so much time talking, today and other days. "Do you know, in all the times we've talked, you never told me about the miracle some people whisper of when you're around?"

"So, Father Barnabé told you even about that."

Charles shook his head. "No, he didn't, although I've asked him more than once. Will you tell me so when I leave here, that will be one fewer question I have? We're already being cheated out of time, Julitte. Don't be afraid for me to know of you everything I can in the short time we have."

"But it wasn't a miracle at all, and I hate that people think it was. When they speak of it, they don't even mention God. And if it were a real miracle, it would be because of Him, not me. So I never speak of it."

"I already believe your faith is strong, and that if He were to use anyone to work a miracle, it would be someone like you. But I don't believe you, by yourself, can perform a miracle. Unless of course it's to turn me into a complete fool around you, doting on your word or smile."

Warmth rushed through her at his playful teasing, making her less uncomfortable about the topic he was so eager to pursue. "That would be a miracle, since I'm the daughter of a sailor and the daughter of a missionary both, while you are no less than—"

But he was already shaking his head. "No, you're the daughter of the Most High God, as a prayer says in one of those catechisms over there. So if you were about to mention a contrast in our parentage, it ends there. If God chose to use you for a miracle, it's nothing for you to be embarrassed about."

"All right. I will tell you, because maybe too little knowledge of it is just as bad as the wrong knowledge of it." She sat in the chair he offered, folding her hands in her lap. "When I was eight and my brother Pierre only three, he wandered off when my mother and I were working in the garden. We don't know how long he was gone, only that he must have fallen into the river. When we found him . . ."

She fought the swelling in her throat, surprised at its presence after so many years; having had little time to practice telling it without such emotion challenged her control. "He was floating with his face in the water. I ran to him and pulled him onto the embankment. I could hear my mother's cry, like mine, for the Lord to save him. Her cries were so loud, others heard and came. My brother's little body was so still, I could tell he wasn't breathing. My mother tried to revive him, but nothing happened. And then, the only thought in my head was how the Lord had breathed life into Adam, that first day of Adam's life. And so that's what I did. I put my mouth on my brother's and . . . I didn't know what I was doing, except mimicking what I'd imagined God doing. I breathed, and in a moment, so did Pierre. He coughed and coughed and water came out, but he was alive after all."

Julitte passed her hand across her forehead. "Didi was there, and some others. They thought Pierre was dead and that I brought him back to life. That's when all the talk started, and some people believed it." She sighed. "I suppose it didn't help to quell the rumors when I knew my father had died before Narcisse could tell me. And later, when I knew others were dead . . . people kept whispering about me. That *I'd* saved Pierre, when it was God all along. He breathed His life into my brother, or maybe Pierre had been breathing the whole time, only we were so distraught we couldn't see it. I don't know. I only know it was God who answered our cries to save my brother. Not I. Some people think I chose that miracle, as if I've purposely refrained from doing such a thing again."

Charles took one of her hands in his. "You are extraordinary, Julitte. I've believed that from the moment I met you. But I know it was God, not you." He kissed her hand. "I might have been afraid to love you if I thought otherwise."

"Afraid? To love me?"

He still held her hand. "Yes. You mentioned the differences in our parentage, but it's I who would have far more cause to feel unworthy of you than the other way around. I did nothing but inherit my family's wealth. You, on the other hand, have lived a faithful life. I can only pray God uses me as much."

"He will, Charles." She put her hand over his. "But you have to be alive to let Him. Are you sure you must go?"

"Don't you see, Julitte? If God can use you for a miracle, He can keep me alive long enough to let me be of some use to Him. Everything you've told me convinces me I'm doing the right thing."

Sounds at the stairway called their attention. "Come along then, Julitte," Father Barnabé said. "Do not make me use the stairs again. It's time for you to go home."

This time Julitte knew she had no choice but to follow Father Barnabé's order. Both of them stood, and Charles embraced her, kissed her. But too soon she left the warmth and comfort and strength of his arms and went to the stairs, where she stopped to look at him. This, she knew, was a moment she would never forget. She looked at him, letting the image imprint itself on her mind. His light hair, the width of his shoulders, the length of his legs, the curve of his brows, and the look of his smile.

She moved toward the first step up, but her feet would not take her. "Will you contact me? somehow find a way to let me know you've made it through?"

"I will."

After one last glance, she joined Father Barnabé at the top of the stairs.

22

Faith. Trust. Self-respect. Become worthy of Julitte.

Such words played in Charles's mind over and again. Through the boom of cannonfire in the distance, beneath the flare of rockets brightening the night sky, under the flutter of planes both German and English. Crawling through drainage ditches, swimming through canals, under bushes when a hailstorm assaulted him like bullets.

When Charles suggested to Serge they might both pray, Serge made a show of shaking his fist at a God who would allow such weather when all they were trying to do was escape to freedom. Something France said was the right of every man.

But the hail hadn't made Charles doubt God.

Nor the mud in the drainage ditches and canals.

Not even the youth of the boy who'd met them here, in Belgium, a boy who couldn't be more than eleven. A boy Serge didn't know, and he'd known every guide so far along this harrowing smugglers' route. The route Serge trusted had ended, and a new, supposedly quicker route had been established through Brussels. That had taken some trust, but somewhere between the outer circle of town and the hospital where they'd taken refuge, even Serge had shed his doubts. Survival through an occupied city had a way of bolstering confidence.

Charles and Serge were two of seven men hiding in yet another cellar, this one beneath the hospital. The food was certainly more plentiful, for which they were grateful. And the company more varied. English, Canadian, Belgian of course. All ministered to by a woman who reminded him of someone that at first he couldn't place. Maybe it was just being here, in Brussels, where his family had spent so much time, he expected everyone to remind him of someone.

Then it occurred to him. She was probably old enough to be his mother, and lovely like her. As lovely as yet another mother figure, not in his life but in his sister Isa's. Growing up, Isa had spent more time with an English innkeeper's family than she had with her own. Maybe it was because both women were English and their voices so strikingly similar. This nurse, Nurse Cavell as she was called, was tall and thin and regal. And brave.

"It will be your turn next, young man," Nurse Cavell said to Charles from the door. The opening led to the street but was hidden from the rest of the cellar, as was the room in which they'd been stowed. Behind a wardrobe in the corner, where no one would think to look if they all remained quiet.

Charles withdrew the folded notes from his pocket. He'd been given paper and a pencil in this very cellar but didn't have any envelopes.

"Nurse Cavell," he said, "you've been more than kind already, and I shouldn't ask for more but . . . could you manage to have these letters delivered for me? One to a family home here in Brussels. Another to someone in France. Occupied France."

Charles had already read the note he'd penned to Julitte so many times that he could've recited its contents by heart.

J—I write to you from a safe place, although not yet my destination. Know that I think of you with every waking moment and in my dreams as well. I cannot say how long it will be before I can write to you again, but I love you now and will love you until my last breath. Never doubt that. Until I see you again, C.

Nurse Cavell automatically reached out her hand when he'd extended the papers to her, but now she hesitated. "Notes can be dangerous for those who receive such things without permission from the Germans. The person holding such a letter might be treated as a spy if caught with it, whether here in Brussels or in France. Perhaps, if either of these letters is to thank someone for helping you, such a thing is best left to wait for a safer day."

He shook his head. "My family is here in Brussels. Or they were. Even if only a servant remains, they can go to the embassy with word that I'm all right. And this one . . . it's for someone who's worried about me. A woman. To let her know I'm all right."

Nurse Cavell smiled and accepted the notes. "I can only try." She slipped the papers into the pocket of her white apron. "Go now. The guide will take you to the canal."

He started to leave, but whether it was from the stark resemblance he'd noted or the safety and hope she'd offered since he'd arrived just a day ago, he felt the urge to draw her close, as he might have his own mother.

He settled for taking one of her hands in his. "Thank you, Nurse Cavell. And may God continue to protect you."

She patted the top of his hand. "And you. Now go."

The boy who'd brought him and Serge to this hospital refuge stood there again, dressed in a dark jacket and a cap that covered down to his eyebrows. Charles followed him into the night.

Less than an hour later, Charles cowered inside a barrel, wishing he'd never left that cellar.

German voices lingered not more than a foot away. Then he heard a hand come to rest on the top of the barrel in which Charles hid. *Bang!* That hand, now a fist, rattled the wood, accompanied by such anger-filled commands that the tone alone might have made Charles's ears ring, if the rap so near his head hadn't been enough.

Then a call, and the voices followed that command. Reprieve. So, God would see him through this, too. The inkling of doubt that had been ready to show itself left only shame alongside his renewed hope.

Forgive me for being afraid.

Charles hated fear, because with it came the vivid image of himself cowering under a bush while those far braver battled for life, for country, for victory. He supposed it was only natural to feel fear; how could a human being live without it, at least under such circumstances? Perhaps it wasn't the fear itself for which he should feel shame. Perhaps it was what the fear made him do or not do.

Perhaps even the Lord Himself had felt fear, praying in the garden before He was crucified. Hadn't Charles read in one of those catechisms that He'd asked to have the cup removed, knowing what was ahead?

Yet Christ hadn't let His fears stop him—the way Charles had when he might have picked up a fallen gun and joined that battle so many months ago. Then, fear had paralyzed him. This time, Charles would prove he could be stronger than his fears—if he ever made it beyond the iron fist of the German soldiers.

It was a good thing the docks hosted a variety of stenches. This pickle barrel smelled more like the last man who'd been hidden inside than it did of vinegar or brine.

"They are gone," came the voice of the boy. "I will be back. You wait."

Charles knew there was little else he could do. Serge mustn't have been squashed into a barrel the way Charles had. He doubted he could emerge without breaking the slats unless he had help.

Part of him longed to burst free of this rancid barrel and run to Quarter Leopold, where his family had lived off and on for as long as Charles could remember. But the boy had said all the fine homes along there had been closed or were billeted with Germans. Surely his father would have left long before any real trouble came to their door.

"One hour." The boy's voice again. "There was a raid, but you're safe."

And then silence.

He should have been relieved. No doubt it was lucky to be sitting here on the dock instead of inside a boat ransacked by German soldiers. And yet, wasn't it likely that goods stored on the dock would be searched as well?

With each strike of boot against dock, Charles held his breath, waiting for the barrel top to be pried loose or the bayonet on the end of a German rifle to penetrate the slats and cut him through.

So he prayed, wishing he had the power to stop thinking, to simply sit and have his brain fall into slumber while the rest of him remained alert. But still the thoughts invaded his mind without relenting.

For this moment, there was nothing Charles could do except wait. Only with freedom could he do something—something to make a difference in this war. Or somehow smuggle Julitte out too.

The barrel was tilted to one side, and Charles braced himself for movement. Then they came, the French—not German—voices. Not pallbearers come to transport his body in the coffin of a barrel, but sailors to let him finish his journey.

To freedom.

Part Two

JUNE 1916

23

Julitte saw the birds first: every color imaginable, every wing boasting a different curve or size. Where did they come from? A garden—no, an orchard, of oranges and apples and pears and . . . what was that? A coconut, Narcisse had once called such a thing. Her mouth moistened in anticipation. She remembered someone cracking one open with a mallet, then gently pulling apart the two sides so as not to lose the milk inside. And the white meat inside! Like a nut, crisp and filling.

Looking past the bounty now, she searched for someone she couldn't find. Where was he? Beyond the garden? Beyond the light?

Nowhere.

Julitte woke, something beside the heaviness of hunger weighing her insides this morning. Charles was not here. He was nowhere to be found.

She hadn't seen him in the light, and she took comfort from that. But she was never sure anymore.

"You were crying out again."

Julitte heard Ori's voice from her mat on the other side of the half wall Narcisse had built to separate Julitte from Pierre so many years ago.

"What did I say?"

"I don't know. I couldn't understand more than a groan."

Julitte sat up, brushing her hair away from her face. She looked at the little window at the peak, seeing gray light. It would be dawn soon.

"When did you come home?" Julitte asked curiously, having stumbled up to the loft before Ori had returned. Unfortunately, not an uncommon occurrence, neither her own fatigue nor Ori's absence.

"Late."

Nor an uncommon answer, not even the curt tone.

Julitte stood, having nothing more to say. More than Narcisse's wall stood between Ori and Julitte now; there was no talking through the wedge that had grown between them. A wedge in the form of a man, a German Hauptmann.

She dressed and the silence settled between them again, the way it had so often lately. Then she went to the stairs.

"Julitte."

Julitte glanced at Ori but did not turn back. She was sitting up, a light blanket still covering her knees.

"There is something I wanted to talk to you about. Or someone, I should say."

Julitte's heart thudded. She'd never told Ori of Charles, though Ori had learned about at least a couple of the men hiding in the village, those who'd taken on false public identities.

"Yes?"

"There is an officer who noticed you at the well recently. He would like to meet you properly."

Julitte did not move; she only wondered what sort of madness had affected her oldest friend to think she would want to be *properly* introduced to any of their barbarian occupiers. "I would say no, thank you, as has been taught to me, but instead I just say no and leave it at that."

Downstairs, Julitte heard Didi's even breathing, accompanied by a snort now and then. She slept more than ever these days, with so little to eat, fatigue had set in and moving her old muscles became harder. Even Julitte's youth hadn't protected her from the exhaustion that came with so little sustenance these last few months. Those days the Germans summoned her to work were more difficult than ever.

On the table she found a hunk of cheese and new loaf of bread. No doubt Ori had brought it back with her whenever she'd returned last night . . . or early this morning.

To her own shame, Julitte eagerly reached for a knife from the cupboard. Even as she cut a slice from each, she hated herself for needing the food for which Ori paid so high a price. But the gnawing inside Julitte wouldn't let her cling to her pride enough to refuse it.

She would, however, refuse to her dying breath even a single step in the direction of Ori's downfall.

The cheese was so good, and the bread—such bread! Reminiscent of the kind Uncle Guy used to bake before the Germans came. Far better than anything he could make now, with ingredients that could barely be digested. Even better than the charity bread that came on occasion, when trucks marked *Relief* too rarely rolled into town.

It would have been easy to keep eating this bread until the last crumb. But even though Ori seldom shared their meager meals with them anymore, allowing them to use what they were officially rationed by the Germans, Didi still needed to eat. It was almost all Didi could do—she never left the cottage anymore.

Another day. Another month. How many had it been since the Germans had come?

Since Charles had gone?

Julitte started this early summer day as she did every other, praying for his safety and for Pierre and her father and Ori's siblings and cousins. For Didi's strength to carry her through another day. For Ori to come to her senses. And for herself, a purely selfish prayer that today would be the day, at last, that she would receive word that Charles had made it beyond the line. Or even that Claudette would tell her that her brother Serge had made it to safety, along with the straggler he'd guided.

But she'd prayed that prayer for so many months now it seemed more from habit than from faith. Charles had promised to send word to her, and she'd believed only one thing would have gotten in his way—that his body was surely buried in one of those hills growing between here and the German front. She'd seen the determination in his eyes when he'd said, "I will," and believed nothing less than death could have stopped him.

Yet no tears came; even that had grown to be too much for her. She felt as old as Didi sometimes.

"You should reconsider meeting Hauptmann Brecht," Ori said from the bottom of the stairs. "He is a nice man, not like the others."

Julitte looked at her with a touch of surprise. Lately she'd taken to sleeping through much of the morning, ever since her hours at the town hall had changed. She went there only when the Hauptmann asked for her.

"Nice like your Hauptmann Basedow, who has you without benefit of marriage?"

Ori joined Julitte at the table but did not sit down. "You judge me without knowing what it's like." Her tone was as harsh as the look on her face. "Without knowing what it is to have a man look at you as if you are all he needs, as if nothing else exists except you. One who would jeopardize everything for you, just to be with you."

Julitte folded the rest of the bread inside a cloth, trying with every bit of her strength to ignore Ori.

Ori sat and Julitte felt her stare. "You have no knowledge of what it is to be loved, Julitte. If you knew, you would understand."

If Julitte would denounce what Ori believed, she had no choice but to speak, at least a little, about her own secrets.

"I do know. But you've chosen a man over what you believe about God. Over any loyalty you once had to your family. I wouldn't want to live here, in this town, and suffer the looks you suffer. Is it worth it, to walk down the street to him, past the stares of de Colville and Toussaint alike? to know they cannot trust you—or me, anymore, living here with you—because you're a willing partner to one of them? Do you love him so much that you threw away what you value and your self-respect?"

"What self-respect did I have here, an outcast? Just because of going to the opera with a drunkard."

"This war would have been—could have been—the chance to redeem yourself in this village, if you'd held fast to what all of our men are fighting for. But you threw it away because you wanted a man. Any man. Even a German, one responsible for shooting at our brothers and cousins and fathers and uncles."

"He isn't! He's as much trapped in this as the rest of us. He only does as he's told."

"And obeys, even when following those orders means death to our men and hunger in our bellies. Have you forgotten, Ori? The peal from the west isn't thunder—it's cannonfire. It's men being blown to pieces, men like my brother and yours, too. Because of the Germans!"

"No! Not because of Erich. It isn't him who decided to wage war. He's as much a victim as the rest of us."

Ah, Lord, teach me how a kind word can turn away wrath. Bind my judgmental tongue against my friend. Let me love her the way You love her.

But even as the prayer ended, Julitte could only despair that a German bullet had taken Charles's life. A German bullet from some unknown German—it didn't matter anymore which one had pulled the trigger. They were all responsible. All to blame.

She looked at her lap, at the same clothes she'd washed a thousand times that had somehow held strong, despite fraying edges and color long ago faded. She'd once wanted to call even her clothes a miracle, but lately, without word from Charles, with Ori so far from being the friend she once was, with Didi so ill, the loneliness seemed to be pulling her from God just as surely as the Hauptmann had pulled Ori from her own faith.

Julitte stood, wishing she could go outside to walk the fields or the forest, but such freedom was a luxury long since denied. At least she might escape to the well for a few minutes. She only wanted to be away from Ori and from this conversation.

"Why did you say you knew about a man's love?"

Ori's soft inquiry stopped Julitte's eager steps to take her away.

How she wanted to talk of Charles, if only to say his name aloud after so many months of keeping him on her heart. Say it aloud so her ears could hear it. She longed to share something with Ori again, to make alive their friendship that had withered. But she couldn't.

"He is dead." She started to move again, leaving it at that.

Ori touched her arm to make her stop. "But who was he?"

"It makes no difference now."

"Wait," Ori whispered. "I'm sorry, Julitte. I'm sorry you haven't been able to trust me or talk to me. I'm sorry I've made it impossible for you."

Julitte glanced at her friend, wishing again things might be fixed between them. But the Hauptmann still stood in the way.

Julitte turned away.

"Öffnen Sie die Tür! Öffnen Sie die Tür!"

Shouts and a bang and a rattle; then the door burst open and suddenly German soldiers stood in the middle of the cottage. Fearful fire in Julitte's blood gave her energy, fueled by the food she'd eaten a little while ago. She scrambled toward Didi, who was just stirring from the loud noise, eyes open but unfocused and disoriented.

"What is the meaning of this?" Ori demanded in a voice Julitte had never heard her use before. "Hauptmann Basedow has given orders . . ."

But the soldier spoke only in German, as if he didn't understand Ori's French. Neither he nor the two others beside him looked at her. Holding aside rifles, they spread out to the cupboards, the wooden chest next to the door, up the stairs. One stomped on floorboards to see if any were loose. It was a typical raid, one every house in the village had suffered before. But not this house for some time.

There was something different, though. They weren't taking anything, perhaps only because there was so little left. Instead, they pounded on walls, bayoneted between floorboards.

Julitte's pulse, still quick from their sudden entrance, thudded harder. They were looking for someone. Did they somehow suspect that certain houses had secret guests? She shut her eyes against the invasion and held Didi close. Julitte could withstand such a raid because she had nothing to hide. But if she were one of those who did . . . *God, O Father God, be with them now!*

The tumult stopped when one German called to another, and Julitte opened her eyes. All three of them clustered around the woodstove. It had been shiny and clean only moments ago, but now it was spattered with wood shavings and ash.

Whatever they were looking at hadn't come from the oven. Instead, a brick from behind the flue was missing, leaving a black hole in the wall. Julitte watched, wondering about the damage. How would she fix it? There was no mortar to be found these days, at least not for villagers.

They stepped away, but instead of holding just the brick now missing from her wall, they held a box as well. No larger than the span of a man's hand, similar to the one she'd once known Pierre to possess. Where had it come from? If it had been behind the brick, Julitte never knew it was there.

Ori, who had stood by silently since her protests went unheeded, closed the door firmly behind them once they left, taking the box with them. She walked to the stove. The hole did not penetrate the wall, but it revealed the backside of the brick that lined the outermost wall.

"Do you know what they took?" she asked.

Julitte, putting the blanket over Didi's shoulders, stood. "Rest, Didi. I will get your breakfast in just a moment." She joined Ori. "I have no idea. I didn't know a brick from here was even loose."

"It must have been a hiding place that Narcisse used," Didi said from the cot. "We all have one of some kind or another."

"But he never told me," Julitte said. "I wonder what was in that box."

"Money, no doubt," Didi said.

Ori nodded. "I'll see if I can get it back for you."

"Yes," said Didi as she reached for her cane and struggled to her feet. "If anyone can, it's you. To my shame."

Ori's cheeks filled with color and she opened her mouth as if to speak, but instead she walked back to the stairs and went up to the loft.

And Julitte cut bread and cheese for Didi's breakfast.

24

"It cannot be done without jeopardizing everything we've set in place already."

Charles had heard that before, but he'd come this far and wasn't about to change his mind now. "Why not? We follow the underground mail routes already established. But *out*."

"After you drop inside. Just like that." Major Liam Parker let a report fall from his hand and slouched in his desk chair.

"Drops are made behind the line all the time."

"With carrier pigeons, Charles."

"But men have been dropped." He didn't really know, since he was hardly privy to all of the underground work that was ordered from this office and others, but he wasn't afraid to bluff.

Major Parker shook his head before Charles had even finished. "I know you're concerned about this village, but you know the countryside has access to food that isn't available in the cities. Apart from that, the CRB distributes food, kilos and kilos of it, all over Northern France."

"*Phff.* How much of it do you think is actually reaching the people who need it most? We have not one shred of evidence that any of the efforts we've made in the last few months have actually gotten to the places I'm most concerned about."

"This town is too close to the front, Charles. And it's isolated.

Obviously anyone who doesn't belong there would stand out in an instant." The major leaned forward, folding his hands on the desk in front of him. "We could never achieve what you propose, and to jeopardize lines we already have in place for something so risky is out of the question."

They sat in an office—a nice, tidy, safe office in Folkestone, England, well beyond the reach of the battle guns raging from Belgium down through France and all the way to the border of neutral Switzerland. Even the occasional German bomber that flew overhead didn't count for much danger here. Charles was far safer than anywhere he'd been since August of 1914, nearly two years ago.

The safety Charles enjoyed chafed at him even as he thanked God for it. He was free while Julitte was still there, within the echo range of the big guns.

"I advise you to wait," Parker said. "Wait until we receive our next report—"

"You've said that before, and nothing changed." Frustration sent Charles past caring that he sounded every bit as annoying as his own father had once accused. He'd waited long enough for this meeting, and before that he'd waited to work his way into a position of requesting such a meeting to begin with.

Charles should be used to waiting by now. That was all he'd done in Briecourt: wait for meals, wait for someone to talk to. Wait for the war to end. When he'd followed the smuggling route with Serge de Colville, Charles had practiced waiting again. Waiting for the sun to go down so they could travel after curfew when fewer sentries were about. Waiting for word that it was safe to go on to the next rendezvous, new places that weren't part of Serge's network. And when they'd found abandoned farmhouses to hide in, it reminded him of the days he'd first roamed undercover with Pepin, waiting for troops to move so they could travel in relative safety.

In Brussels, where he and Serge had been ushered to the back door of the Belgian hospital, they had waited some more. He had little hope the two letters he'd left in the care of Nurse Cavell had been successfully delivered. Shortly after his escape through the route she'd set up through Antwerp and on to the Netherlands, he learned she'd been arrested by the Germans. His letters had most likely been confiscated as evidence or hastily burned if the nurse had time. He prayed the latter was true, that his letters couldn't have been used in the German tribunal's guilty verdict.

Just over two months after she'd been arrested, all of the headlines declared Nurse Edith Cavell had been shot by firing squad, having confessed she'd helped some two hundred young men escape to freedom.

Men just like Charles.

Charles carried his guilt to this day. How was it that the Lord had let her die for Charles and others like him but spared him?

It was one of the many questions he had, even though upon gaining his freedom, he'd immediately acquired a Bible. He'd been eager to read the words Julitte had once called priceless. He hadn't read far to know Nurse Cavell was in a better place. Hadn't the papers reported her saying that she would face God and eternity with more than patriotism? She would face God without bitterness or hatred for anyone. He wished he could feel the same. But thinking of her sacrifice, knowing that Julitte was still there, living under a regime capable of such a heinous act, no doubt suffering at the very least hunger week after week . . . His love for God, the love he'd learned through Julitte, sometimes wasn't enough to rid him of the hatred that grew against the Germans.

His wait in the Netherlands had seemed to go on forever. First at the American embassy, where he and Serge had established their identities. Then they'd been ferried across the English Channel and directed to a British Military Intelligence office here in southeastern England, to Folkestone, where he'd once visited a seaside resort in a world that seemed far different and so long ago. Now the town hosted soldiers in every direction—those about to embark for battle or those coming home on leave—while civilians cowered in fear of planes dropping bombs.

He'd quickly telegrammed his parents, making sure they were in their American home with Isa safe at their side. Their response had been brief but welcome, how they'd done everything but bind and gag Isa to get her out of Brussels. But they were safe, and Charles was relieved they'd gotten away in advance of the throng of refugees who were left in far worse conditions.

Even now, people were still escaping. Charles had been told he was one of many escaped Belgian refugees who'd been interviewed since the beginning of the war. He gave the British all the information he could about troop movements he'd noticed, railroad activity, even what he saw of the morale behind the lines, only too eager to share what he knew if it would help. He immediately volunteered his services to do anything he could to alleviate the suffering of those still caught behind the lines—particularly in Northern France.

And while the British seemed eager enough to have his help, he'd never been able to direct his own efforts. So far he'd supplied the intelligence department with little more than clerical duties: his knowledge of Belgian railroads came in handy, as did his knowledge of French, English, and German. On paper, he knew the major was right about the CRB, the Committee for Relief in Belgium, sending literally tons of food for those caught behind the lines in both Belgium and Northern France. But how much of it went past the Germans? Those in Briecourt were too hungry to have received much help. From what he'd gleaned so far, no one had ever heard of Briecourt until he mentioned the name.

Only one thing made all of this waiting tolerable. He wasn't about to give up on his plan to get Julitte safely out of occupied France.

"You do understand, Charles," Major Parker said as he walked

Charles to the door of his office, meeting adjourned, "that if I'm ever to be of any help to you and this little town, it must serve us both—your concerns and the war effort?"

Charles caught Parker's eye. He was a middle-aged man, shorter than Charles, whose eyes were set inside a flare of wrinkles from each outer corner, adding a look of permanent concern. Charles knew the officer couldn't provide a network of links inside occupied territory just to bring out Julitte. There must be more—and he'd rehearsed this more than once. Now was his opportunity to convince the major, before he was rushed out the door.

"What about setting up a radio? There are people there—good, honest people who've already risked their lives to help others. They'll agree to send messages on troop movement, supplies, activities behind the line; I'm sure of it."

But Major Parker was already shaking his head. "You've shown me the location of this town, Charles. It's out of the way, inconvenient. How much would anyone see from such a location, even if they had a radio and were willing to risk communication? They could only provide the minimum help, and therefore hardly worth the effort and certainly not the risk."

The argument was everything Charles had feared, exactly the same he would have offered had he been in the major's place. And yet it had been his only hope.

The weight he'd been carrying in his chest since leaving Julitte settled firmly back into place. Was there no hope then?

Charles refused to imagine it. The very Bible Julitte believed, the same Charles himself was studying and found no fault with, told him with God all things were possible. All things.

Even convincing a cautious, sensible British major that it would be worth the risk to go into this village.

25

With the sun nearly gone for the day, Julitte longed for only one thing: her bed. She'd worked through the daylight hours, having been marched off with others to a textile factory some miles away, one that had been converted to a laundry facility. She'd scrubbed, sewn, pressed, and folded all manner of clothing, both military and civilian. By the end of the day the only dirty clothes nearby were her own, wilted from perspiration or speckled with dirt from those she'd washed.

And now she was back in the village, once again at the well. Didi no longer went out on her own, nor did she do any of the cooking. She'd taken to her bed most of the time, to her admitted shame too weak, too stiff, too old to be of much help to anyone anymore.

Then Julitte heard the rumble of a motor followed soon by the whine of a missile. She'd heard it before, but never so close. She looked to the sky, expecting to see an aeroplane do what they always did: drop their lethal cargo somewhere to the west, then turn around and do it again.

But this motor grew louder. Closer.

Julitte stood, transfixed by the flying machine, knowing its sting was far more deadly than things God had made to fly. Then, just beyond the village, something fell from its belly. A shower of golden rain sputtered alight, then burned itself out, not entirely unlike the fireworks she remembered from a Bastille Day celebration she'd seen one July when Narcisse had taken her and Pierre to Paris.

Then something else fell, dark, crashing into the ground, sending at once another shower, this one upward, of sparks and earth and light, along with a ripple that touched the ground all the way to Julitte's feet.

Suddenly she was aware of not one plane but many—three, four, six . . . The noise was deafening but now all around her. Voices, German and French, people calling and running in every direction.

"To the cellars!"

"Run!"

"Take cover!"

Julitte had little awareness of anyone speaking to her, she was so dazed by the sound and tumult. Then someone shoved past her on the way to the church, and she nearly followed to keep him out. Charles hid there!

But he was long gone.

Clarity returned and her mind filled with Didi. Julitte must get her to the cellar.

No sooner had Julitte taken a step than someone grabbed her arm. Father Barnabé, pulling her toward the church.

"But Didi! I must get her—"

"You go to the church cellar, Julitte; it's closer. I'll go to Didi."

Julitte nearly refused, knowing her effort to bring Didi to safety would be faster than the father's, with his bad knees.

But in the chaos someone shoved a baby into her arms; it was Evelyne de Colville, whom Julitte had worked with taking care of the children. She knew she must fall in line with those clamoring to be inside, and so she did.

In the sanctuary, everyone headed the same direction: to the stairs. The stairs she'd used so many times before to see Charles.

There was no quiet to be found now. People cried around her;

some still yelled, giving orders to stop crying or talking or to help someone along on the stairs, repeating demands to hurry. Outside, the boom of war seemed at their doorstep, still accompanied by the rattle of planes.

Julitte glanced down for the first time at the child in her arms. A de Colville, but he didn't seem to mind being carried through the rush by a Toussaint. He clung to her and looked as if he might add his own tears to those around him, only was too confused just yet. Julitte patted his back in an attempt to give comfort she didn't feel.

The cellar brimmed with activity. Civilian and soldier, de Colville and Toussaint. German and French. She didn't know if the planes overhead were German or French, though she supposed the latter. *These bombs are meant for you, not us,* she wanted to say. But one of the soldiers, surely no older than Pierre, looked as fearful as she, and so she said nothing.

She found the corner where she'd once hidden with Charles and stared at the familiar tarp, seeing Charles, knowing his image was nothing more than a figment of her imagination but for one moment calmed by such a vivid recollection of his smile.

It was then the child in her arms burst into tears.

She soothed him, holding her free arm out to another child nearby, an older boy who'd come in with Evelyne. The three of them clung to one another, and the thick walls of the church cellar quaked along with them.

She had no idea how long they waited; certainly long after the air outside quieted. One of the German soldiers spoke first and went up the stairs. Other Germans followed, but villagers like Julitte were hesitant. She waited.

At last someone hailed them from the top of the stairs, and even in German she knew it was a call that all was clear. The evening skies must be empty once again and familiar blasts relegated to the west.

Along with Evelyne, Julitte helped the children up the stairs, back through the sanctuary, and out into the streets. No sooner had she stepped outside than another de Colville came to her, pulling the child away. His cries started anew.

Julitte did not offer help, knowing she would be rebuffed, even now.

Instead she stepped past the well, intending to retrieve her water vessel and then hurry home to see if Father Barnabé had comforted Didi through the bombing.

But she never bent to pick up the vessel. There, not three doors down from the edge of the square, lay a figure in long, dark robes. The vestments of Father Barnabé.

"Father!"

She was not the only one to run toward him but the first to reach him. He lay there, untouched by any of the bombs that had fallen, as if he'd chosen to take a nap right there in the gutter.

No light, no glimpse of heaven, was greater or more lovely than just then, as Father Barnabé opened his eyes only for a moment, then closed them once and for all with a smile touching his wizened face.

A crate of food. A few leaflets. Emergency supplies to be dropped every six weeks in various spots around Picardy. That was all Charles could get them to look into, all Charles could hope would happen for now. For the first time in his life, his father's connections hadn't awarded the kind of response he'd hoped for, even after all these months.

Not that he knew for what he should have hoped. That somehow his father's wealth and connections could get the entire front line to shut down just long enough to get Julitte out? No, war was one thing that might demand all the money his father had, but it wouldn't make a dent in the outcome.

The supply drops were something anyway. The best news was that Briecourt was on the British intelligence map. They knew how dire the conditions were, and more than that, they knew they had a ready operative in Charles to open communication between free France and that area.

Charles reminded himself every day that he had another Father now, one with far more power than all the gold in his father's American bank accounts. It was to this Father Charles increasingly appealed.

Another wait, seeming the longest of all.

26

Julitte stared at the letter in her hand, at the careful writing beneath the gold-etched monogram centered at the top. *ANC.*

She hadn't known it before this moment, but those were her grandfather's initials. Her mother's father once held this very page in his hand, had written the words she stared at now.

> *Kind regards to Captain Jean-Antoine Rivollet from*
> *Agapios Nestor Constantinos*
> *It is with great happiness I have recently learned of the*
> *existence of my granddaughter Julia Kaligenia, daughter to*
> *my beloved Anatolia Constantinos. I am eager to bring Julia*
> *Kaligenia home and in that regard am prepared to compensate*
> *you generously for her safe return.*

The letter went on with instructions, and if the quality of the paper wasn't enough to convey the wealth of the writer, the directions to the Greek estate atop a hill banished any doubt.

Her mother's family—one of wealth?

"Well?"

Didi's voice, always a little too loud for pleasant conversation, was no different now. Julitte looked from Didi to Ori, who surely knew what the letter contained. It had been given to Ori from her Hauptmann after the soldier who took it had turned it over.

"It's from my mother's father," Julitte said, too softly at first, and had to repeat herself so Didi could hear.

"On such fancy paper? I thought your mother was a missionary."

"That was her father," Ori said.

"Well then, who was her mother?"

"She was a nurse."

Julitte was glad Ori filled in details Julitte had shared long ago, the only details Julitte herself had known until this day.

Over the years she had wondered if her parents had any family but had long since given up thinking about them. If they had cared about either her mother or her father, they, not Narcisse, would have adopted her. As far as she knew, nary a word had been exchanged on either side of her family. She'd always told herself she was relieved. Anyway, she couldn't imagine being part of another family, nor did she want to.

"What does it say?" Didi asked.

Julitte wanted to answer, but the words blurred in front of her and she no longer trusted her voice. Were they fighting in Greece? Would she have been spared knowing of this war if she'd been taken into the care of this unknown grandfather years before?

But then she wouldn't have known Narcisse or her adoptive mother or Pierre. Ori, Didi.

Charles.

How could she wish, even for a moment, for things to have been different?

"Her grandfather wants her to come back to Greece," Ori said.

Julitte lifted her gaze to Ori, who had the grace to look embarrassed over revealing the details.

"Ha," said Didi, settling back in her chair. "Let them come for you here. There are a few of us who would volunteer to stow away and go with you."

"He may not be looking for me anymore," Julitte said. "There is no date."

"But the paper," Ori said, pointing to the sheet. "It doesn't look old—look how white it is. Surely it can't have been hidden for long."

Julitte shrugged, setting the letter aside. It made no difference now. They could no more come to her than she could go to them, even if she wanted to. Still, she wondered how long ago Narcisse had hidden the letter. And why. He'd once called riches a burden. Had he wanted to spare her that?

She stood and walked to the door, pausing only long enough to grab the water jar. She walked slowly toward the town center, hugging the clay vessel close, taking it with her past the well and inside the church.

She missed Father Barnabé. His heart must have simply stopped beating, so they said of that day. Julitte preferred to believe the Lord had taken Father Barnabé to spare him from any more of the ravages of war.

Two homes had been damaged that day: a missile fell through the roof of one empty house, leaving a hole right down to the cellar. Another lost its chimney. Julitte's home, and thankfully Didi, had been untouched. Didi had barely been aware of the ruckus.

But now the church was empty.

She longed to revisit memories of Charles, those favorite and familiar images of him, but today she just needed to pray.

The sanctuary was quiet, for which she was grateful. She hadn't been inside since the bombing, since lately a surplus of German soldiers used it for a dry place to spend the nights. She'd seen them march out that morning.

Inside, the light was dim and the sound of her clogs loud. After only a few steps closer to the altar, she stopped. Someone was already there.

At the sound of her approach, he moved to a standing position. For one giddy moment Julitte thought it was Charles. He was tall, like Charles, and even in the pale light she saw the lightness of his hair. But no—this man held a helmet beneath his arm, and he was already turning to her and bowing in that stiff German way. Bowing, but it occurred to her that when she'd come in, he'd hastened to his feet. Had he been at the kneeler before this same altar where she worshiped?

"Fräulein," he said. Then he passed her without another word.

Julitte approached the altar, kneeling where she always did, noting that the leather covering was still warm. He must have been here for some time. A kneeling German . . . something she couldn't have imagined before this moment.

Then she bowed her head, knowing her heart needed softening and her Creator was the only one who could do that for her.

Charles walked toward the building that housed Major Parker's office, starting this day as he had countless others: leaving the hotel room in which he lived to check in with the major, where he was often put to work on what he considered some mundane task, usually one of several civilian translators who checked and rechecked documents received. Nothing privileged, nothing of any importance so far as he could tell. Safe work in a relatively safe place.

There had been a time when he would have wanted such a job, far from the bombs and the bullets. Even now, part of him knew if he stayed where he was, if one of the German bombers that occasionally flew over Folkestone didn't hit the buildings in which he worked or lived, he would survive the war. Certainly he had a far better chance of doing that with a desk job.

But it chafed him. So he'd put Briecourt on the intelligence map.

So what? Did that guarantee Julitte safety? or Father Barnabé, Pepin, or Didi? He knew how little food they'd had when he left; it must be far worse by now.

"Just the bloke I was looking for this morning," Major Parker greeted from within his office. He stood as Charles neared the threshold.

Charles's pulse quickened. "News?"

"Of a sort. Have a seat. Tea?"

Sitting down for a cup was the last thing Charles wanted to do, but he collected his scattering thoughts and sat anyway, shaking his head at the beverage offer.

"Evidently there is a captain of a French sailing ship who's visited the airfields in Calais on a regular basis since the outbreak of hostilities. Because of his continued interest in a particular area, rumors reached him about the drops we've made around Briecourt. One of our men is seeking him out for further interrogation."

"What is the man's name?"

"Captain Jean-Antoine Rivollet. Is that a familiar name in the little town where you stayed?"

Charles shook his head. Toussaint, de Colville. Not Rivollet. "Why is he interested in Briecourt?"

"Evidently a man connected to the Greek royal family is seeking someone behind the lines. In Briecourt."

"And you believe it? Isn't the king of Greece married to the Kaiser's sister?"

"Precisely why the matter came to my attention. Ripe for intrigue, wouldn't you say? Greece may be persuaded to fight with us against the Turks, but everyone knows the king sympathizes with the Kaiser. Question is, what could possibly be of interest in this little French village? from where you came, of all places?"

The quietly uttered inquiry made Charles's gaze rise to meet the other man's. Trust was a highly priced commodity these days.

"I cannot imagine what they could be interested in. Other than the town hall, Briecourt is just like any other village in the Picardy region. But," he added, keeping his gaze level, "if you'd like to drop me in, I would do all I could to learn the truth."

"Yes, I expected you to say as much. For now, we wait. I'd like to hear what this French captain has to say first. Then we'll decide."

Wait. Why was he not surprised?

27

"Julitte. *Julitte.*"

Julitte stopped, turned her head to one side. She'd heard her name whispered but didn't see anyone. The street was empty, as usual at this hour.

But there—the door to the bakery was cracked. Her uncle Guy peeked out into the early morning darkness.

She'd been on her way to the dairy to see if she might bring Didi some milk. Julitte approached Uncle Guy, who opened the door wide enough to allow her entrance. He hobbled out of the way, still weak from the day of the bombing. The bakery had been spared any damage, but Uncle Guy had been on the street when the first bomb fell and was nearly trampled getting back to his bakeshop.

"There'll be no bread in the bakery today. But I have something for you just the same. Come in. Close the door."

She noticed how thin he'd become since the Germans had arrived, how heavily he leaned on his cane. It made her wonder how gaunt she must be, too.

"Jeanne-Marie Toussaint has been finding things in the wood and we've been dispensing them, one to each house."

"What is it?"

"A miracle," he said, and in those two words his voice reminded her of Yves, once so young and cheerful. "Tins of food, of sweet jam and meat. And this." He held up a paper. "Real news. It's what I've been saying all along—if the Germans were as victorious as they want us to believe, why isn't the fighting over? They're not so victorious; they're not even winning. See for yourself."

Julitte wanted to read the paper, but more than that she wanted to see the food. Smell it, taste it. Devour it.

Her hands shook as she received the package: a loaf of bread wrapped in cloth, a tin of jam, another of meat, so she was told— they were both unmarked.

"Bury the tins when you're done," he cautioned. "If we're caught, they'll demand to know where it came from and raid us looking for more."

Julitte saw the box, formerly hidden in the back of the cupboard. It was empty. "Is it all dispensed, then?"

He nodded. "You were the last."

"And you don't know where it came from?"

"Jeanne-Marie found two crates in the forest when she was looking for firewood. It couldn't have been there long because the flyer is dated—only a month old."

"And the bread? After a month . . ."

Uncle Guy shook his head. "It came as flour and salt and oil. I made the bread secretly when the Germans gave me their castoffs to bake. They never knew how many loaves were really baked the other day."

Tears tickled her eyes at the thought of such treasure. "Thank you," she whispered. She slipped the tins into her skirt pockets, removed the scarf from her head, and wrapped the bread inside. She would have to hurry home if she was to escape notice with such a bounty, before many Germans were out on the street.

"Did you ever hear from him?"

She stopped at the door, hearing the gentle inquiry. She knew to whom Uncle Guy referred.

"No." Then, turning back to the door, she added, "I fear the worst has happened."

Because voicing the words seemed to make them true, she slipped outside, away from talking further about her fear of what might have happened to Charles, away from her tears so ready to fall.

She stumbled from Uncle Guy's, not looking where she was going. Barely five paces away she was halted by the chest of a German soldier.

"I beg pardon—," she started, but then one of the tins, not pushed deeply enough into her pocket, fell to the cobblestone with a thud. She scrambled on her knees after it.

But the tin had rolled toward the boot on the soldier, and he bent to pick it up. Julitte did not move, cowering at his feet. Her breath stopped. She didn't want to, but she knew she must look up at the face of the soldier who could as easily hold her hostage for possessing such a tin as have her sent to Germany to work.

There stood the soldier she'd seen in church. He looked down at her, placing a hand beneath her arm to aid her to her feet. He held the tin, offering it back to her.

She accepted with a nod.

He spoke in German, and she nodded once more although she wasn't sure what he'd said, her knowledge of German was so limited. Surely something about hunger and maybe hiding something? Had he just counseled her to hide this?

She wanted to run away and do just that before he came to his senses and remembered what every other German soldier evidently knew about domination and punishment. But there was something about him that went against her fear of his uniform and language. Maybe nothing more than the memory of how warm had been the kneeler he'd used at the altar.

Still, there was no reason to keep standing here. She took a step away.

"Sprechen Sie Deutsch?"

His words stopped her. She shook her head.

"Sprechen Sie Englisch?"

"Yes, a little."

"Gut. Das ist gut. Für mich auch, ein bißchen." He laughed. "Good. That is good. Me too. A little, too."

She nearly wanted to return his smile, he was so friendly, his voice so kind. But she couldn't. Even if God wanted her to—and she supposed He might—she couldn't do it.

"Are you called Julitte?"

She nodded.

"My name is Christophe Brecht." He clicked his heels, bowing formally.

Though she recognized the name of the German who'd told Ori he wanted to meet her, Julitte had no idea how to respond. She did know one thing: for her to be seen by a villager conversing with a German might exact a higher price than if he had her sent to prison for hoarding secret food.

She acknowledged his introduction with a nod, then started to walk away again.

He followed. "I saw you in the church that day, yes?"

She nodded.

"I have a question."

She kept her gaze ahead, dreading what he might say. If he thought because she shared a roof with Ori she, too, might give him favors . . .

"God gives you miracles. Is true?"

His words surprised her into quickening her step. "No."

"People say—"

"Fables. Stories."

"Even stories have some truth. A little, yes?"

"They do not like me, so they talk."

"They do not like you; they say, 'She not so pretty.' They do not say you do miracles."

"What have they said to you?"

"Your brother was dead. You make him live."

She shook her head; it was the same story, so contorted from the truth. "Not me. God."

He trotted ahead of her, turning to face her fully. "Yes. God. I agree."

She stopped, folding her arms in front of her. "God can do this with anyone. Not me alone."

His blue eyes, like the color of a bright morning sky beneath the blond wheat of his hair, stared into her. "With me? That is my question."

She wanted to tell him no German who could march into another country and do what they'd done could ever be used by God. But she knew that was not the answer God would give. "Yes. You must ask Him."

Now he was shaking his head. "But I want no miracle. I want . . . I want no more death. Why does He not stop it? The death? I want to know why."

Now he was not so happy. In fact his blue eyes looked ready to shed tears.

"I have no answer," she whispered. Then she turned away.

The saddest part was that she'd told him the truth.

Charles looked through the spyglass he'd borrowed from the sailor nearby. The tool was fifty years old if it was a day, but it still worked. He'd never seen such a sight as what he looked at now. Only war could bring this much activity, so many English boats along the shore of France. Like pups all trying to get to the motherland, squeezing in here and there.

He itched to be ashore but knew his wait wasn't quite over. Soon, though, he would meet with two men. One a British operative. The other a French sailor under the direction of the captain who was so interested in Briecourt.

It was nearly sunset by the time Charles set foot on land. No complaints, though. He would have paid his own way across the channel, but Major Parker had arranged for him to go by military boat. Faster, such as it was.

Along with transportation, he'd been given directions to a coastal pub where the major's contact person was to introduce Charles to the French sailor. He'd be late because the boat had been delayed docking, but he assumed those in the business of intelligence or espionage were accustomed to waiting. Certainly Charles was, and he hardly counted himself in this business.

The pub was crowded with soldiers, French and British alike. All they had in common, evidently, was thirst and a taste for beer, although many of the French soldiers drank wine. Charles made several passes of the place before finding three men at a small table along the bar. He'd expected only two, but since all wore civilian clothes, it might be a sign they were the ones Charles sought.

"Mr. Gloster?"

The men stood, as if they'd anticipated his arrival. One wore a French sailor's beret and double-breasted coat; another, a cutaway jacket over a striped waistcoat and high, impeccably white wing-collared shirt and ascot tie—the jacket of tailored cut and costly vicuña entirely out of place in this kind of a pub; the last wore a plain but well-made tweed jacket above creased brown trousers.

The man in tweed waved Charles away from the empty seat nearby. "Let's leave here, shall we?"

Charles barely heard him above the male din, nodding and leading back along the path he'd just followed from the door.

Outside, the street was busy and noisy with sounds from the shipyard: sailors shouting orders one to another, water splashing against the base of the dockmaster's office not far away. People walked here and there, soldiers and sailors and a few civilians like themselves, and somewhere a dog barked while a motorcar idled nearby. The man who'd spoken took the lead, and while Charles followed, he eyed the men beside him.

Charles instantly passed over the Englishman with his clipped British tongue—obviously Mr. Gloster, who Major Parker had told him was one of his men. The expensively attired man appeared wary, more wary than Charles felt. It was he Charles hadn't expected. His gaze shifted here and there too quickly. Not that a dock in the middle of a country at war wasn't a good place to be nervous, especially for someone dressed so expensively. If not for that, he'd probably at least heard the same rumors Charles had, about German U-boats lurking along the coast.

But the other man, the older one, didn't look nervous at all. No doubt the French captain's man. He fit right in with his sailor's cap of white with a red pom-pom stuck in the middle, a black scarf tucked inside his collar, white trousers, and strapped shoes. He glanced at Charles a few times too, as if equally curious. The sailor had a tugboat way about him. He was sturdy rather than tall, arms nearly bursting the seams of his coat, with a face as rough as a mast, capped by gray hair so thick it took nothing from the aura of health and strength in his wide shoulders and sure step.

They walked back toward the very dock Charles had just left, farther down where the activity waned. The sun was setting over the water, but with all of the ships crowding the port, Charles could barely see any of the light reflected on the channel.

Gloster took a turn away from the dock and into a gangway

between warehouses, prematurely dark but with no chance of being overheard or interrupted. "Mr. Lassone, I assume."

Charles nodded.

"We understand you're the one responsible for requesting supplies be dropped specifically in the Briecourt area."

"That's right."

"And that you yourself took cover there when you were caught behind the line in '14."

Charles glanced from Gloster to the sailor, who looked as if he wanted to speak but waited for Charles. "Yes, that's right. I could go through the entire timeline of events, but then I thought it was the captain's man who was prepared to supply information to me."

The sailor stepped closer, grabbing the lapels of Charles's jacket. "You were in Briecourt, then?"

Charles nodded, at the same time prying the man's grip away.

"You must forgive me," the sailor said and looked down at his own hands as if surprised at their actions.

Gloster patted one of the sailor's broad shoulders. "We will get to all of that in a moment. This gentleman—" he referred with his hand to the nervous one in the suit—"is Titos Tsakolos. He represents an opportunity to provide an act of goodwill, so to speak, which might just help persuade the king of Greece to side with his own prime minister and join this war as our ally. *If* we can bring someone out from Briecourt and safely home."

"And who from Briecourt could be known by the king of Greece?"

"Her name is Julia Kaligenia Constantinos," said Titos. He spoke flawless English, though the Greek name seemed more comfortable from his tongue than it would from most others, including Charles's. "Her birth name, that is. But she is no longer called that."

Charles's heart picked up its rhythm. *Julia.* Who would deviate from a birth name? He suddenly felt dense, as if he'd been missing something too long. Greece . . . and here before him a sailor interested in none other than Briecourt. Yet he forced caution. "A woman, then? Do you mean she has a different surname now? Because . . . of marriage?"

"No," he began. "By adoption—"

The sailor shoved himself between Charles and the Greek man and grabbed Charles by the lapels again. "You were there not so many months ago. You must tell me if she is all right, my daughter. Julitte."

28

"But, Didi, you ate hardly anything!"

"I ate enough. So there's more for you. Now eat before Ori comes home."

Julitte could remind her that Ori hadn't come home before midnight in quite some time, but she didn't.

Instead, she watched Didi push the last of the bread at her, and her stomach grumbled for want of what was before her. Although they rationed themselves, this was the last of the food they'd been receiving from Uncle Guy. After today it would be back to the dark bread, when they could get even that.

She knew the portions had been unequally sized to begin with; Didi had made sure of that. Even as she swallowed, knowing Didi wouldn't let the bread pass her lips, Julitte still had a heavy heart resting on her near-empty stomach.

They'd taken part in something else Julitte wasn't particularly proud of: they had concealed the *manna-food*, as she called anything that was said to appear from the skies, from Ori.

Julitte hated keeping it from her, but Ori spent far too much time with her Hauptmann and, when home, spoke of him far too well. It was enough to fill Julitte's stomach with something else—disgust.

She was barely finished when the door opened and Ori entered.

Julitte folded the empty napkin that had held the bread and placed it in the middle of the table with the others.

"You're home early today," Didi said.

Ori never looked their way. Her shoulders drooped, as if she was tired. That was odd, since she'd become accustomed to staying out all hours and sleeping during the day. "I'll be staying home the next few days. Erich is going away for a little while. He's going . . . going to fight."

Then she went to the loft, but Julitte could hear her crying even if Didi couldn't. Part of her wanted to go upstairs, comfort the friend she once had.

But instead she exchanged glances with Didi. Having Ori home meant she would need to eat with them. And all the manna-food was gone.

※

Charles looked at the landscape before him—at least what he could see of it in this fog: a flat field of biplanes manned by the British Royal Flying Corps. In the last two days he'd seen a stream of pilots coming and going every few hours, particularly around dawn or dusk, ready to fly reconnaissance missions—sometimes four a day—when the weather cooperated.

Most of the pilots were younger than him, even the so-called seasoned ones. Charles had been told it didn't take long to earn that distinction. Surviving training and more than a few months of flying commanded respect from everyone.

As soon as the weather cleared, he would go up in one of those planes—ships, as the pilots called them. It hardly seemed possible that these things could fly, made of plywood and canvas with a few bars and wires holding it all together.

There had been a time Charles wanted to fly, when he was eighteen some few years ago. He'd asked his father about it, who'd agreed to buy a plane if Charles did the research as to where the money would be best spent.

But no sooner had Charles found a pilot to take him on his first flight—the older brother of a college schoolmate—than the young man had been killed in the very plane he'd recommended for purchase. That had ever after soured the idea of flying.

There wasn't much to convince Charles that getting over the enemy line was going to be either safe or easy, even if they did plan to send a squadron. After arriving in Clermont-Ferrand in central France the day before yesterday, before the fog had set in, Charles had met the colonel. He was so far the oldest man around—and he perhaps forty at most. Competent, no doubt, and certainly knowledgeable about aircraft. He'd spoken easily of the commitment to the mission, including precautions taken to prevent any accident. However, after hearing about the likelihood of fire or simple mechanical failure, the chance of being struck by bullets from German antiaircraft guns, or the possibility of being shot by a friendly barrage, Charles found his brief education of the flying fleet brooked more worries than he'd naively imagined before.

Which was perhaps why he found himself here, alone rather than lingering in the mess hut with everyone else. He needed time with God.

Lord, if ever I could use some extra protection, it's now. Instill in me a trust so sure I won't feel anything else.

Charles's prayer reminded him of who was in control. He already knew this mission was the right thing to do, no matter the danger. Besides that, here was his chance, at last, to quiet the memory of his own cowardice, to cancel it forever.

And it was the only way to Julitte.

Julitte watched Ori brood around the cottage for three days. The only welcome part of her behavior was that she didn't want to eat, so the meager rations they were allowed seemed to go further.

Perhaps because Didi was eating less as well. And Julitte didn't know why.

"You should talk to Didi," Julitte said to Ori, who'd come down from the loft for the first time that entire day. It was evening, just after the sun would have set had it shown itself that day. Instead, between rain and fog, the out-of-doors was as dreary as it was inside with Ori's endless tears.

"Talk to Didi about what?"

They spoke in conversational tones even though Didi was on her cot, awake. But she wasn't looking their way, and Julitte knew she wouldn't be able to hear them.

"About why she eats so little. I thought it was bad enough that she never leaves the cottage anymore, but now she won't rise. She hasn't left her cot in two days, even to sit at the table."

Ori looked at her grandmother. "Is she sick?"

"Maybe if you came down and spent time with her instead of crying all day, you would know." Julitte's tone made Ori look at her in surprise. Maybe Ori thought she had enough heartache, having watched the man she loved march off to war, without withstanding abuse from Julitte, too. Maybe Julitte *should* be more compassionate, since she knew what it was like to miss someone she loved. But the words were out and she had yet to regret them. "She says she isn't sick, only tired."

"Everyone is tired," Ori said. "It's the war. No food. The sound of guns in the distance, the death. The war."

Julitte nodded. That was all true. Still, there was something more, something different about Didi recently. For her, even talking seemed too much of an effort. True, she nearly had to yell to hear her own words, and that was certainly harder, but Didi had always loved talking before. Why, at least, wouldn't she leave her bed?

Without warning the door burst open. There, with the dim light of evening behind him, stood a German soldier. Not tall, but rather square, from the width of his forehead to his trunklike limbs and booted feet.

"Ori!" The name came with a moan, and whether he was happy or sad was impossible to tell. His gaze searched the room, but by the time he spotted her, he was teetering.

Julitte popped from her seat and hurried to Didi, who labored to a sitting position.

"Alfred, go away," Ori said, still sitting at the table. She sounded weary rather than annoyed. "*Gehweg.* You're drunk."

Despite Ori's apparent lack of concern, Julitte noted that her foot tapped a quickened beat on the floor beneath the table. Was that an annoyed beat or a nervous one?

"No! I come for you." His French was barely discernible. He went on, mumbling that Hauptmann Basedow had left Ori as spoils.

Didi struggled to her feet, using Julitte's shoulder as a crutch. "Leave here! Out! Out with you!"

With those few words, her voice sounded like the old Didi, full of fire. How many times had she used that tone on Ori when she was a little girl? For a moment Julitte was glad to see the old Didi back. But a drunken soldier still staggered into their cottage.

Retrieving Didi's cane from the floor beside the cot, Julitte handed it to her. No sooner had Didi taken a single step than the German soldier stumbled forward, knocking into Didi. If he'd meant to hit her, he didn't raise his hand nearly far or fast enough but did succeed in jostling her enough to send her sprawling backward into Julitte's ready hold. The soldier himself went down in the other direction.

Ori hovered over them, hands on her hips. "Go now! You cannot hurt an old woman. Now get out!"

Ori's shrill voice must have been loud enough to reach beyond the threshold, because Julitte saw the de Colville door open across the street—only to quickly shut.

Who wanted to get involved in a dispute with a German soldier, even a drunk one? Especially on behalf of anyone from this household?

Julitte guided Didi back to the cot, where she slumped against the wall, letting her feet still dangle to the floor.

"Ori, we'll have to get him out of here," Julitte called, hurrying her words in the hope the soldier wouldn't understand. "Together."

The man had barely regained his unsteady footing. Julitte knew they could overcome him in his present state.

But Ori didn't move. "We can't assault a German soldier," she whispered. "Do you know what they'll do to us?"

"So *you'd* rather be assaulted?"

"No—of course not!"

"He probably won't remember what happened anyway, if we just push him out the door. Think of how it is with Marcel. You know he never remembers one day to the next. This soldier won't either."

"This one will remember he didn't get what he wanted," Ori said grimly. "That'll be enough." On her face was something Julitte hoped never to see, particularly on a friend—fear mixed with acceptance.

"No! You—"

The German regained his stature, such as it was, and headed toward Ori, who stood with the table between them. He spoke, once again in German, his words stuttered and slurred. Though Julitte understood none of it, his intentions were clear.

"Alfred, you cannot do this." Ori gripped the back of a chair. "Erich will return soon, and if he learns about this, he'll have you before a tribunal in no time. Think of Erich, Alfred. Your friend. Erich."

Even if his French wasn't very good, at least he must have recognized his friend's name. Alfred mumbled something in German again but Julitte knew only one thing: reminding him of his friend had been a good try on Ori's part, but a useless one. The soldier was still advancing.

"I say it again, enough talking!" He stumbled around the table even as Ori retreated closer to Julitte and Didi. Around the table they went, in a full circle, until the soldier stood directly in front of the cot.

Didi raised the cane, still clutched in one hand, to the height of the soldier's knees, holding it there until he took the next fateful step. And landed sprawled at their feet.

"*Leutnant!* Leutnant Kemnitz!"

There stood yet another soldier, taller, fair-haired. Orders followed: loud, sharp, unavoidable. From Hauptmann Brecht.

Even for someone so deep in his cups, the commanding tone couldn't be ignored—at least by a trained German soldier. Alfred was back on his feet and out the door in less time than it took Ori to collect herself and come to Julitte and Didi's side.

Then the Hauptmann bowed their way. "This will not happen again, I assure you."

Ori followed Hauptmann Brecht to the door. "Please, Christophe, may I lock the door? Alfred is . . . persistent."

"He'll be spending the night in a safe place; you have my word. No need to fear."

Another bow, a glance to Julitte, and then Hauptmann Brecht was gone.

Despite his assurance and Ori's nod of acceptance, Julitte still wished he'd agreed to the locked door.

Lord, help me to trust Your Spirit to be a barrier instead.

Even with her prayer, Julitte struggled to close her eyes that night and heard Ori stir as often as herself.

29

The fog and rain lifted after a third long day of waiting. Now, with the sun sinking low in a clear evening sky, Charles knew that his wait was over.

It exhilarated and nearly paralyzed him all at once.

"You there!"

Charles turned at the call. The pilot he'd met two days ago, Jimmy Cripps, motioned Charles to join him on his path to the planes. He looked to be all of eighteen or perhaps nineteen years of age, but Charles had been told he was seasoned. He wore a leather jacket and white silk scarf, leather headgear and goggles. On his arm hung another set of goggles and a parachute.

"For you."

Charles accepted the items. "Where's your chute? Just in case, I mean?"

Cripps laughed and turned to him, swinging open his jacket only long enough for Charles to glimpse a pistol tucked into the other man's belt. "This is my safety. If we catch fire—*ping!*" He pressed a finger to his temple and cocked his thumb, then laughed again. "Better than falling to the earth in a crate of flames."

Cripps led him to one of the larger two-seater planes, this one with two engines, each in its own gondola complete with a wooden propeller.

"You'll sit where the bomber usually sits." Cripps pointed to the cockpit between the engines. "There, just inside the nose."

The other seat hung out beyond the cover of the upper wing, suspended just above a few bars and wires connecting the cockpit to the rear rudders.

"Once we're at the spot, you'll have to slip out beneath the wing. Here." He pointed to the side of the cockpit, a narrow escape route at best. "Try not to stand on the bars; they're not built for this."

Charles nodded, wondering if an airplane existed for what he was about to do. When he'd asked the colonel earlier why they didn't drop soldiers inside enemy territory more often—huge numbers of them if necessary—Charles had been told they didn't think the human body could tolerate the change in altitude, withstand a jump, and be any good as a soldier anytime soon afterward. Unwelcome news if ever he heard any.

"Let me help you with that," Cripps said as Charles fumbled into the leg loops of his parachute. "They told you how to do this, right? The chute will do all the work. Best to make sure it's on right—don't want a tangle of the cords, now do we? Free it like so, and make sure this hasn't loosened around the waist." He motioned to the sturdy rope holding the bulk of silk material and lighter cords in place. "Don't want the ropes to end up round the neck."

Before long the entire field teemed with personnel—other pilots, wing men, propeller men.

"So, this is your plane?" Charles asked.

"Actually, no, I'm just flying it this time to get you over the line. My plane is over there."

He nodded to a row of sleeker, smaller planes that seated only one. "If we were closer, you could see the blood on the wing from my last kill." He grinned. "I was that close to the dirty Hun."

Charles wasn't eager to see such memorabilia, although he had to admit he was grateful for Cripps's experience. But was flying one machine much like flying another?

"Have you flown this one before, then?"

Cripps laughed yet again, obviously detecting Charles's wariness. "Sure, with an observer instead of the likes of you. You know—a gunner. Hop in now."

Charles refused to acknowledge the slight nausea in his stomach or the light-headedness blurring the edges of his vision. He could do this. He would do this.

And he would see Julitte soon.

"You can sit back and enjoy the ride for a while," Cripps said as he adjusted his goggles. "It'll take an hour or so to get up to ten thousand feet, where we'll meet the others in our flight pattern. There."

He pointed to a row of other planes, single seaters, also swarming with activity.

"Once we're up, look for the one with the streamers. That'll be our leader."

Charles nodded. He'd been given explicit details about the number of planes assigned to the mission, a rendezvous spot, expected departure and travel times. Mainly what he remembered was the drop location and which direction to head from there. Not for the first time, he silently thanked Julitte for the book of French geography he'd studied.

Someone provided a ladder, and he climbed to the front of the plane. It seemed a while before Cripps joined him, evidently checking one thing or another. When he finally boarded and started the engine, he did more checking. Wing movement, rudder response.

Then, with a heightened roar to the engines on each side of them, the plane rolled forward. How did they do it? How did these fliers go out day after day, in this contraption that rattled like an empty tin can blowing in the wind, that buzzed so loudly it nearly deafened the ear? And into the midst of nothing less than enemy fire?

Maybe pilots had to love what they do or they wouldn't do it. How else to tolerate the noise, the choppy ride, the danger?

Lord, if ever I needed Your help . . . For Julitte, Lord, whom You love. Let me bring her out.

The moment the wheels left the field, one wing tipped to the side, only to right itself. And then—sailing. Charles had expected the ride to be smoother, like gliding on a bird's wing, but it was loud and bumpy. Who knew air was not as smooth as it looked in calm weather like this?

So this was what a bird saw. Squares of farmland, hills, trees, a lake here and there. Narrow roads and canals.

"See that straight line—there?" Cripps yelled over the engine noise and wind. "The road home, Mr. Lassone." He laughed. "If ever I get separated from my squadron, that's what I look for first. The Roman Road."

Charles found his hands gripping the rope around his waist. Praying again.

He forced his mind on their destination rather than the journey. On their freedom, his and Julittte's, rather than what lay before him now: a jump from a rattletrap with Germans in between here and there.

This was the quickest way in, the fastest way to Julitte. Once he secreted her away from that village, he had all the necessary papers allowing them passage right through Northern France and eastern Belgium, through Liège and on to Maastricht in the Netherlands. To freedom. Charles was confident they'd have little to worry about with the kind of documents he'd been provided. Stamped, signed, and so close to a real German pass that Charles was sure it would survive any scrutiny, just as he'd been told such things had worked for others.

Time went by and Charles tried to do as the pilot suggested: enjoy the ride. They had joined the rest of the squadron—five other planes, each in their place, the one with the streamers at the fore cutting through the wind. But with the sun sitting low on the horizon, Charles couldn't see much of the countryside anymore. And he was chilly, his body jostled so thoroughly he felt every bone, big and small. Still, there was something amazing about doing what man ought not do: fly.

"We have company," Cripps called from behind.

Charles looked from left to right, seeing only dark outlines of the other planes they flew with. This plane was slightly behind and above the rest of the formation. He could hear nothing over the din of the engines beside him—but there, off to the far left, a black shadow floated against the purple sky. There wasn't enough cloud cover to hide in for long.

And then Charles saw it. The iron cross emblazoned on its side.

Images of pilots shooting at one another, of the kind of blood Cripps had mentioned staining his wing, of loops and fire and a quick, crashing death played in Charles's mind. Would the others engage, letting Charles and Cripps go on? Or would this mission be deemed more important than a sole German plane and this enemy allowed to go on his way?

Cripps was yelling again, and Charles had made out no more than a few words about an observer and information when one of the other planes left the formation and dipped its wing.

"Watch!"

Before Charles unfolded the fight he'd prayed would be avoided. The one plane soaring toward the other, a flash of machine-gun fire from above the cockpit, the other plane turning fast, one wing slanted in the turn. The other flew around, then above, outmaneuvering the German like a sleeker, faster bird of prey after a slower, larger one.

It was over before Charles knew it. The iron cross fell in a dive to the unrelenting surface of the earth. The craft was no longer either pilot and plane or captain and ship but in an instant a single heap of crumpled wood, followed immediately by flame.

It wasn't until it was over that Charles realized the German plane had never even shot back.

"Why didn't he defend himself?" Charles called to Cripps. "Not even a shot fired!"

"No. Reconnaissance. German, though. He'd report our position quicker than we'd have reached our destination."

From the periphery of his vision, Charles saw Cripps salute the other pilot. The formation had split up but now regained their places.

"Not long now," Cripps yelled some time later. "When the captain fires white smoke, that'll be your signal to jump and for the rest of us to head home. Got it? Don't want to be off course now. Get ready. Maintain steady."

Charles had no idea how to follow such an instruction. How could he ready himself for a jump from a plane, trusting his life to the flimsy material strapped to his back?

Maybe it was the altitude—it was hard to breathe, to think. Although, Charles had felt the descent in the last little while and the air wasn't as cold. Best not to feel anything at all. Just go by instinct.

"Get ready," Cripps barked again.

Charles stood from his seat, where the wind nearly whipped the goggles from his head. He pressed them back into place.

He lost any sensible thought except what needed to be done. He could no longer tell if the shudder of his body originated from the plane or inside himself. But he *must* do this; he had no choice.

He must first slip one leg over the edge. Then the other. Slide out from beneath the wing.

And so he did.

"Tallyho!"

Charles heard Cripps call out, his voice holding all that Charles could not feel in that moment of sailing through nothing but choppy air. Confidence, exhilaration.

He was well clear of the plane now, with the ground so far beneath him, nothing but stars up above. The air assaulted him, pummeling his skin so that he feared the goggles would be permanently embedded in his face. His brain told his arm to move to the rope, releasing its precarious hold on the silk and cords behind him. But his arm did not move against the wind.

With effort but no more than the slightest adjustment, the rope came free at last and Charles heard a ripple behind and above. Then, with a startling jerk, his body was wrenched from a flat position to an upright one, jarring muscle and bone to the marrow. Suddenly he was no longer falling; he floated, his body adjusting to the sudden shift, the wind no longer the enemy.

And in the distance the buzz of the airships disappeared.

30

Through the night Julitte and Ori took turns at Didi's bedside, which had turned to a sickbed—and now, Julitte feared, a deathbed.

Didi, resting against the pillow, turned her face away from Julitte and closed her eyes.

Julitte leaned down, and placed her head on Didi's shoulder. "Please, Didi, don't give up. You must be hungry. You must eat."

But despite the words and the tears that dampened the shoulder of Didi's gown, she did not turn back to Julitte.

"Why won't you eat, even a little?"

One of Didi's hands rose as if to pat the top of Julitte's head but never made it before it fell back to the bed, even that too much an effort.

"Forgive me, Julitte," Didi said. The words were spoken so softly Julitte was sure Didi couldn't hear her own voice. Perhaps even Ori couldn't hear, seated as she was beside the table behind them. "I don't want to be here anymore. I want to go to heaven."

"But we need you here. Ori needs you more than ever."

Didi's brows drew together and Julitte knew she'd said the wrong thing. Perhaps it was partly because of Ori that Didi no longer wanted to live in a village that ostracized her and anyone under the same roof. Even though for the first time in Didi's life the rest of the village was united against a common foe.

"You eat the food," Didi told Julitte. "There will be more for you, at least for a while."

"But I need you, too." Julitte's face was only inches from Didi's. "Don't leave me here alone."

Didi did not speak. She turned away again, closing her eyes.

Her breathing was steady, but no matter how Julitte tried, she could not get Didi to eat. This, the third day.

How long, she wondered, did it take the body to give up its soul?

She turned, seeing Ori at the table. Her face was splotched and wet. As Julitte's gaze fell on her, Ori pushed herself away, running to the stairs and up to the loft.

Julitte folded her hands, resting her forehead on the tent she made of her arms and hands. *Why do I feel so alone, Lord? As if even You have abandoned me? I will tell You now that I love You, though I feel no love. I will praise You, though I feel no joy. I will wait, but I ask Your comfort for us all, especially for Didi. Let us find hope again, even for the sake of Your servant Didi.*

Julitte stayed beside Didi, praying quietly, knowing Didi prayed too. Even if she didn't hear all of Julitte's words, Julitte knew Didi was comforted knowing she prayed over her, the same way she always had.

At last Didi fell back asleep, breathing quietly. Julitte remained on the chair nearby, still praying. She watched, a small part of her envying the older woman, that she had such a strong will to die and that her body would obey. Soon, sooner than Julitte wanted, Didi would be at their Savior's side.

A place Julitte wanted to be. But did she? If Charles was there already . . .

She hadn't allowed herself to think of him as she used to, though the calendar neared the completion of yet another month since she'd seen his face. Yet she recalled each detail, from the inviting blue of his eyes to the shape of his brow, to the feel of his lips on hers. When she did let her mind go to him, one moment she convinced herself he was alive, and the next she despaired, sure only death would have kept him from getting word to her. But he must be alive; it was impossible to think someone her own age, stronger than her, with just the start of faith to help him through this life, could have been taken to heaven so soon.

She wondered what he was doing, if he thought of her at all, if he wondered about her welfare.

But nearly as quickly other thoughts plagued her. Once again she sent a plea to God to let her know if Charles was in heaven with Him, if he waited for her there as he said he would. God could so easily spare her such uncertainties, and yet He didn't.

And so she couldn't think of Charles because the not knowing made her wonder if God still loved her as much as she'd always believed He did. The way her own father had taught her, the way Narcisse had taught her, too.

Yet she worshiped, she praised, because that was what both her fathers had taught her. Even her American father, in pain, dying a slow death, had done so. How could she do less?

Julitte didn't know what time she fell asleep, there in the chair beside Didi's cot. She woke on the floor, her head on Didi's bedside.

With a glance at the window, she knew dawn was not far off. So started another day.

After checking Didi, Julitte went to the well, walking slowly, glad the street was deserted. She was growing used to the sound of cannonfire in the distance, something she never thought would happen. How could she forget what such a sound represented? Death. And yet she barely took note of it as she poured water into her jar, even though the battle drum seemed steadier—and louder—than ever.

Then, because the street was vacant, not even a soldier to be found, she sat on the stone bench nearby, water jar in her lap. She closed her eyes, remembering how the square used to be before the war. She remembered singing and laughing, and even with the underlying animosity so rampant in this village, it was a good memory.

She'd learned to sing from her adoptive parents; all of the Toussaints had been blessed with heavenly voices. When the Toussaints gathered in this very square to sing, it was said they could be joined by angels, but the de Colvilles would never know it, since they refused to be an audience to any Toussaint. They even shut their windows against the sound. It all seemed so silly now, the feud that no one understood any more than they understood why all of their men had to go off and fight this war.

When she opened her eyes, she saw the church, absent its bell, which the Germans had stolen. Automatically her gaze fell downward to one of the cellar windows, the one with a crack in it. Charles had told her it was his only source of fresh air. She remembered his smile, marveling now that he could have smiled at all while so long a prisoner in the dank, dark basement, death always so close at hand. *Man wasn't created to be alone,* she'd once told him. Little wonder he'd chafed against the solitude.

She wanted to go there, to that spot he used to occupy, imagine again being there with him, talking to him, sharing stories and hopes and questions about faith. Kissing him.

She stood, setting aside the water jug. She'd been in the church many times since Charles had gone but never alone to the cellar.

Stepping inside the church, the sound of her clogs echoed only once before she slipped out of them and clutched them to her chest, preferring instead to feel the quiet. She passed the altar, resisting the urge to stop. She could take advantage of the solitude, and would, after she visited the cellar. It wasn't often she went to the altar anymore, since Father Barnabé was no longer here. Thinking of him reminded her that soon—too soon—Didi would see him again.

At the back of the church, the stairs creaked beneath her step in their once-familiar fashion. She remembered the days when such a sound had been a prelude to her visits with Charles. How light her heart had been back then.

She descended, arriving at the base and looking around. The crates and the last of the pews were now gone, long since used for fuel or commandeered by the German army. All that was left was the old tarp that once hung by the stairs, the one she and Charles had hidden behind so long ago. She wanted to touch it, to remember.

But there—in the dim light—she'd missed the figure at first. On the ground, the dark outline of someone asleep on the floor.

Charles? Had she somehow been transported back, and he was here as before?

She rushed to his side, stooping beside him. "Charles!"

His shoulders twitched as if he'd been startled awake, but no sooner had she touched him than she realized her mistake. It wasn't Charles at all. The man's back hadn't revealed the soldier's jacket he wore, but now as he turned, the metal buttons winked at her in a moment of reflected light.

"Wer ist das?"

He pulled himself upward and Julitte jumped to her feet, backing away, recognizing the face of the German Leutnant Alfred Kemnitz, who'd come for Ori.

His eyes, groggy, stayed unsteadily upon her and something else reflected in the light: a look in his eye. The same look he'd directed at Ori last night.

Julitte dropped her shoes and took flight toward the stairs—only to have him grab her from behind, a fistful of her hair. She fell to her knees, and the sudden stop had him pitching over her, freeing her hair from his grip. She crawled around him, hampered by her skirt caught under her limbs. Regaining her feet, she stumbled to the stairs, topping only a few before he clutched at her again. She heard the cotton of her skirt tear as he pulled one way and she the other. She smelled the foulness of old liquor on him but knew enough of it had worn away to give him more strength than he'd had the night before. He stood, one hand on her shoulder, the other still on her skirt.

Then, from where she had no idea, a shadow fell over them both from a stair above. She had no time to look up before something— or someone—kicked the soldier away, landing a solid boot against the man's shoulder. The Leutnant was just unsteady enough to fall back, down the pair of stairs he'd already crawled behind Julitte, and roll into an unmoving heap on the cement cellar floor.

Julitte pulled her skirt out of the way, scrambling upward, intent on one thing: getting out of the cellar. And though the darkly clad chest of a figure stood in her way, it was only for a moment. He put an arm to her back and gently nudged her forward. Up past the cellar door.

She never stopped, not even to look at the face of her rescuer.

Outside, the sun was high. She wanted nothing more than to run all the way home, but as soon as Julitte stepped outside, she realized she'd lost her shoes. She'd shut the door behind her, and whoever had saved her hadn't followed her out, even this far.

But she wasn't going back. She would rather face the rest of this war barefoot than go back in there.

Charles chased Julitte up the stairs, but no sooner had he reached the top than the soldier on the cellar floor stirred. Charles stopped. He could either kill the man, or let him live.

For one rash moment killing was the best option. But how could he? How would Julitte explain such a thing? Who would take the blame for his death? Her? Besides that, Charles had never killed before, and it wasn't something he wanted to do now. If he were found, a firing squad would be the end of him—along with his mission to get Julitte to freedom.

So he slipped into the sacristy at the top of the stairs, waiting by the door to assure himself the soldier wasn't resuming his pursuit of Julitte. He heard her run through the sanctuary and burst through the door, shutting it solidly behind her.

The soldier never bothered to come up the stairs.

Charles knew he would have to find a different hiding place. He had no idea where Father Barnabé was. Charles had hidden in the woods the night before, keeping an eye out for the familiar priest, but there had been nary a sign of him.

There was only one place Charles could think of that had once been willing to harbor a straggler. The bakery. If the baker was still there, Charles could at least find help in contacting Julitte.

And be one step closer to getting her out.

31

Julitte had barely regained her breath by the time she reached her home, water jar in her arms, feet dusty from the road. She slipped inside, eager to close the door, wishing she could lock it but knowing such a thing would only bring a fine she couldn't pay if any German found out.

Setting the water aside, she leaned against the closed door, waiting until her pulse quieted. Never, never again could she go in that church.

"How long, Lord? How much, Lord? How much will You let them take from us? Do You mean to keep me from church anymore? Do You mean to keep me from visiting Your altar? Even that!"

"Julitte?"

Ori's voice from the loft stopped Julitte's rant. She'd been aware of only one thing: anger taking the place of fear of the Leutnant—anger not just toward the Leutnant. Also at herself for going there to begin with. And at God for letting it all happen.

Ori came down from the loft, sparing a glance to her grandmother, who was still sleeping. "What's wrong? What happened?"

Julitte didn't want to say but knew Ori wouldn't give up asking until she learned something.

"Your Leutnant was at the church just now."

"Oh . . . Oh!" She stepped closer to Julitte, arms outstretched as if to draw her close. "Did he—"

Julitte stepped away, wanting no human contact, not even Ori's. "No."

"No?" She didn't sound convinced. She looked at Julitte from head to toe, as if assigning her unkempt appearance and bare feet to only one cause.

"No," Julitte said, more firmly now. "But he would have if someone hadn't stopped him." It was then she realized she had no idea who. Except . . . she did have one idea.

"Who?"

"It must have been Hauptmann Brecht. All I saw was a boot over my head, pushing the Leutnant away."

Ori smiled. "You see? I told you he was different. Thank God for him, Julitte!"

There was no room in Julitte's mind for gratitude. The Leutnant's hands' latching on to her was too fresh; thinking of it felt as if it were happening again. She sucked in a breath, closing her eyes from the memory. "It was dreadful, the way that Leutnant grabbed at me—as if . . ."

She couldn't finish. Suddenly the spectrum of emotion overwhelmed her, from one moment of joy thinking she'd seen Charles to the next moment of horror. A torrent of tears gushed from her eyes, sobs wracked her shoulders, all strength abandoned her limbs, and she sank to the floor. Being attacked so personally was too intimate a thing; it hardly mattered that it was not likely *her* he wanted, individually, but Ori or maybe even any woman. He'd had access to Julitte herself, and his strength versus her own weakness made it all too clear just how vulnerable she really was.

Ori gathered her up in her arms, rocking her, hushing her, soon crying with her. And Julitte remembered why she loved Ori and mourned their estrangement. She'd been her friend, her one true friend in this village.

Not long after Charles slipped into the back door of the bakery, he learned he could fold his six-foot-one frame as if he were a circus contortionist. And share the tight confines with Pepin. Though he could barely breathe and doubted Pepin had it any easier.

They stayed that way for what seemed hours, until at last with a tap, the false wall fell away. Without the wood holding them in place, first Pepin and then Charles fell to the floor, just behind the baker's oven.

"La!" said Pepin. "And I thought I was crowded in there before!"

But he laughed a moment later, stretching to his meager height.

Charles stood as well. He'd barely revealed himself at the back door before he was rushed into hiding, the wall tacked into place. And there they had remained, while German voices not far away laughed and joked and passed the time as if all of life were peaceful and good.

Charles had thought they would never leave.

"What are you doing here, my friend?" Pepin asked, reaching up to pat both of Charles's arms. "They told me you escaped long ago!"

He nodded. "I did. I'm back." He turned to Guy. "I need to get a message to Julitte Toussaint. Immediately. This very night I'll be taking her to the frontier with me."

"You came for Julitte?" Guy asked.

"Yes." He was prepared to explain how her natural mother had a connection to the household of no less than the king of Greece, although what sort of connection he would likely leave out. Her grandfather was neither servant nor sailor, but a weathly industrialist with more money than this bakery had ever seen. But he had more news before getting into that.

He tapped his belt where he'd hidden the pass for Pepin. "And papers for you, and Dowan and Seymour too. The only ones I knew well enough for descriptions on the passes."

Pepin's eyes seemed bigger now than when Charles had first met him because his face was narrower, but they momentarily grew even larger. "You did this for me?"

"I've done nothing yet. You can thank me when you're on the other side of the German line. In the Netherlands."

Pepin threw himself at Charles more closely than they'd been forced to endure a few moments ago. Charles pried himself away.

"I cannot believe it!"

Perhaps Charles should not have been made uncomfortable by the tears in Pepin's eyes. He could guess, from just that brief time hiding behind the oven, how hard it must have been for Pepin for nearly two years. Day and night, whenever a German was about, to be thrust into what felt like a coffin? And if caught—face a real coffin?

Yet he didn't want to accept the gratitude. Not until the mission was complete.

"Will you go to Julitte now, Guy? bring her back here? Don't tell her, though. If she's too eager to get here, she may attract attention."

"Yes, I'll go," Guy said. "How is it you singled her out, that you risked your life to come back to her?"

"I've been in contact with her father. Narcisse."

Now it was Guy who neared Charles, putting a hand on his shoulder. He hadn't remembered the lanky Guy looking anything like the stout sailor he'd met at the shipyard; but now, seeing Guy's face again, Charles saw the resemblance in his bright blue eyes. "My brother? You've seen him?"

Charles nodded. "Yes. He's well but anxious about Julitte. Her family—her Greek family—wants her safe."

He didn't elaborate, leaving out entirely just how important and influential her family was.

"Her Greek family! But we thought they didn't want her, all these years."

"They've changed their minds. Go now," he said as he nudged the older man forward. He noted the man now used a cane, something new since the last time Charles had seen him, so he prodded gently. "Bring her here."

Guy nodded, picking up his pace to the door, but there he slowed his step as he slipped outside—only to steal back inside and shoo them off, into the kitchen. Charles saw little more than the dark shadow of a spiked helmet before he rushed back to the oven with Pepin.

"We cannot do this," Julitte insisted. She directed her gaze to Didi in the corner, inviting Ori to do the same. "Not with Didi . . . being so ill."

Dying.

Ori's eye, too, fell on her grandmother. She frowned, settling back in her chair. "We mustn't pass up this opportunity. It will have to be at the town hall, where I used to share meals with Erich."

Julitte shook her head. "To thank him with his own rations?"

"Of course. It isn't about the dinner, Julitte. It is about company. And the sooner, the better. Tonight."

Julitte shook her head again. "I want to thank him, but I don't want him to assume something—anything. I'm not willing to . . . be friendly with him."

"You must pay him a little attention, show your gratitude, which is nothing less than honest and sincere. He deserves as much. And if he responds in the way a gentleman would, as I'm sure he will, then maybe we'll regain the kind of protection we had when Erich was here. This time through you."

Ori's words sent a freezing chill down Julitte's spine. Perhaps they did have a certain amount of protection from the Germans. Certainly more food. But what of the villagers? They hadn't welcomed the idea of anyone fraternizing with the enemy.

Ori must have seen Julitte's doubts, since she shook her head as if Julitte had spoken. "We'll be spared more raids, be given better work opportunities. Because of your friendship with him. That's all I suggest."

They could spend the rest of the war, however long that might be, confined to their cottage, nearly starving and cleaning billets, or Julitte could be civil to the one German officer who might be able to offer them some special favor. If being civil was all it would take.

Dinner. One meal.

A meal. Food.

One slight nod from Julitte was all it took to have Ori fly from the cottage. She didn't even take her scarf.

Alone with Didi, Julitte went to her side. Lately Ori's grandmother drifted between sleep and near wakefulness, but Julitte liked to speak to her as if she were as healthy as ever, loud enough to be sure Didi heard.

"I don't know if this is a good idea," Julitte told Didi. "I do think I should thank him; that would only be right. But for us to share a meal with him? Willingly? Have him think it was my idea? He's a German, is he not?"

She paused as if Didi might say something, but of course she was silent.

"All right, so he is created by God," Julitte went on. "But how can I forget, even for a little while, what his army has done? How do I put it from my mind? If I felt safe, perhaps I could remember he spoke of God to me, that he might even have faith in the same God I love. But I don't feel safe, not anymore. I cannot."

Another pause.

"I want to trust in our Father. I do. But I've seen things happen that God would never condone; I know evil can touch even God's children. It's the way of life, good and evil side by side. Sometimes someone else's choice for evil touches even those who choose good."

She rubbed her eyes, as tired as ever. "But I'm so hungry, Didi. . . ."

And so she went on, talking to Didi, talking to God, at times offering Didi water or what little bit of the bread was left, which Didi could not—or would not—take. Soon Ori was back, a smile on her face—something Julitte hadn't seen on her friend since Hauptmann Basedow had been sent away.

"Hauptmann Brecht is arranging for your dinner tonight. You're to be there at nine."

"Me?" Her heart rate sped. "Just me?"

"Of course. I thought that was understood."

"But not alone! I thought you would be there too."

Ori shook her head. "I told him you were grateful to him and would be agreeable to sharing dinner. I was never part of the invitation."

Julitte stood and paced, then stopped in front of Ori. "I won't go there by myself. I'll be a lamb to slaughter!"

Ori shook her head. "No, no, Julitte. Hauptmann Brecht isn't like that at all. He's really quite shy, you'll learn."

"Shyness doesn't come with such a uniform."

"It does with him. You've spoken to him."

"But you're grateful to him too, Ori. He saved you as sure as he saved me. We should both go."

"I expressed my gratitude. It's you he wants to share dinner with."

Julitte turned away, one hand grabbing the other, squeezing so tight her fingers turned white and red and ached after only a moment. "I don't think I can do this." She aimed her gaze at Ori. "I'm afraid."

Ori pulled her close. "Not of him, Julitte. He's a good man. Like Erich."

Julitte pulled away. If he was anything like Erich Basedow, she wanted no part of him.

32

Julitte sat beside Didi, who was barely conscious. Taking a spoonful of water, she placed it between Didi's lips. If any went in, it was by accident. Most of it rolled down the side of Didi's face, and if she swallowed, Julitte couldn't tell.

"*Grand-mère* Didi," Ori said, sitting beside Julitte, "you must be so hungry. You must eat something. For us?"

Didi closed her eyes, not bothering to wipe away the bead of moisture that had rolled from the corner of her mouth down the side of her face and to her neck.

Julitte took the napkin and wiped it for her. "Perhaps I shouldn't leave this evening. I can go another time, can't I? With Didi so weak—"

But Ori was already shaking her head. "It would be an insult not to go. You must go. I'll be here with her."

Julitte sighed. She knew that; she'd been willing to grasp at any excuse, and being with Didi seemed the best one of all.

Ori patted Julitte's hand, but she took no comfort in it.

"It'll be fine, Julitte. Once you know Christophe, you'll like him. Everyone does. Well, almost everyone."

"And those who don't?"

"I heard Christophe say to Erich that he wasn't popular with the *Kommandantur*."

"Why?"

"I don't know, but I think because he would order things differently than the way they have."

"Differently . . . how?"

Ori shrugged. "Erich once said of Christophe that he holds too high a standard for this world."

"And what would he do with those who don't measure up?"

Another shrug.

The information was hardly welcome. "If I don't . . . become friendly with him, might it make everything worse? You know I won't."

Ori's lips tightened. "I know; I know. You've always been stronger than me. But if you grow to care for him? What then?"

"I won't."

"You might."

"I won't."

A tap at the door ended their discussion, and Julitte, for once, was glad to know someone was at the door. They had no visitors anymore except unwanted German ones. Only they never knocked.

At the door was her uncle Guy.

"Uncle! Come in off the street."

He did so, with a glance over his shoulder as if he, too, wanted to avoid being seen by patrolling Germans.

"You must come and sit with Didi, Uncle. She's so much weaker than she's been in the past. Will you tell her you've come to see her?"

For a moment he looked surprised, as if he'd forgotten his cousin was ill. Then he nodded, going to Didi's side and taking the seat Julitte had vacated.

But Didi did not stir, even when Guy took her hand and told her he hoped she would be well.

He stood too soon, facing Julitte. "I need you to come to the bakery."

"Well—of course. Do you need help with something?" Hope rose. "Do you have flour?"

But he shook his head. He glanced from Julitte to Ori, then back again, as if searching and failing to find more words.

"Why do you want her to come with you?" Ori asked. "Is there anything I can help with too?"

He shook his head again, still wordless.

"You should stay here with Didi anyway," Julitte said, taking her scarf from the hook on the wall.

"How long will you be gone? You know you must be back soon."

"Why must she be back?" Uncle Guy asked.

Julitte exchanged glances with Ori, not wanting to say why. The longer she could keep her dinner plans to herself, the better. "To help with Didi," Julitte said. That was certainly true. What was the measure by which something less than the complete truth became an untruth?

Then she followed Uncle Guy, stopping beside the door only long enough to slip into Ori's clogs.

The late June air was uncommonly cool, and Julitte wished she'd taken her shawl. But Uncle Guy walked rather quickly, surprisingly so since patrol guards frowned on anyone hurrying, even for so short a distance. As usual, the shades were pulled on the two windows that used to display Uncle Guy's pastries, such a time long gone. Somehow the bakery still smelled inviting, though, even two years after its ovens had baked anything worthy of pride. Maybe the smell was nothing more than a memory, indelible because of the wants of her almost-constantly empty stomach.

Inside, instead of leading the way past the empty shop tables, back to the kitchen, Uncle Guy stopped. He waited, as if listening, but there was nothing to hear. The bakery was empty. Then he turned to Julitte. "You mustn't make a sound, no matter what you see. German guards patrol along the street at all hours and come in over the slightest noise. Do you understand?"

"Yes, but, Uncle, you're so mysterious today. What is it you need my help with?"

Instead of answering, he turned away, leading the rest of the way to the kitchen. The room was dimly lit with only high windows here, but those too were shrouded. There was nothing on the tables, the shelves nearly bare. No work to be done; no flour or butter.

"Julitte."

In the corner, where the oven shadowed the wall, Julitte saw two silhouettes—one tall, the other small. It was from that corner her name had been issued. And by a voice that struck joy and pain straight to her heart, all at once.

He stepped out from the shadow and she heard her name again, saw his face for the first time in so many months. Whether it was the emotion or her lack of nourishment making worse her weakness, she did not know. She wasn't even sure it was joy or sadness that he was here, in danger after all, that overwhelmed her. But overwhelmed she was, from her brain to her knees, which buckled so unexpectedly she would have landed on the floor except that Charles caught her in his arms.

"You—you're here! But how? For how long? I didn't know. . . ." Even as she spoke, she knew he surely hadn't been here in hiding all this time, because the sharpness of his jaw, the gauntness of his cheek, had disappeared. He was in full health and vigor; she could see that even at this first moment.

But he would neither hear nor answer any more questions. Instead he kissed her, and she hadn't the strength to resist even if she should have found the will.

From somewhere, the smaller shadow gave a little laugh. "So he has come not just for the Greek family's interest or for me, after all.

Not even because of your brother's worries about his daughter. We should have known, Guy."

With Charles's hands on each side of her face, steadying her, Julitte found the strength to stand on her own, to look at him. There it was, that love she'd first seen in his eyes in the cellar, not diminished, only grown. Like her own.

"Are you well?" he asked with some urgency. "Are you all right?"

She nodded. "Yes—yes."

But now the love wasn't alone in his eyes; next to it was concern, even fear. "I mean—this morning—has that sort of thing happened before? If only God would have let me come back sooner."

She tilted her head. "This morning?"

"Yes, at the church. I was there."

"No—no, it couldn't have been you! I wouldn't have run from you. I thought it *was* you when I first came to the tarp. But then I saw his face, that German Leutnant. I wanted it to be you, but it wasn't. Oh, Charles!"

"I came from above. I shoved him away, and you disappeared just as he was rousing from the fall. I couldn't let myself be caught or you be attacked again either."

"What's all this?" Uncle Guy said, standing nearby. "Someone attacked you, Julitte?"

She nodded, then shook her head, still clinging to Charles because she knew if she let go, her limbs wouldn't hold her. "I went to the church cellar because that was the last place—" She glanced at Charles, suddenly embarrassed to admit in front of her uncle that she'd gone to the church from missing this man. "I wanted to remember. For a moment, I thought it was you asleep on that tarp. But then he came at me, and I was so frightened. I tried to get away."

Charles nodded, his hold on her not one bit loosened. "Then God did bring me back in time. Only just. Praise Him for that."

She raised her hand to his cheek. "You speak of God as if you know Him now."

"How could I not, after such an introduction from you?"

Then she was awash in love, not only from Charles but from God, too, because He loved her even now, when she'd felt so far away from Him and for so long.

"I'm here to bring you home, Julitte," Charles was saying, stomping out her thoughts. "I brought passes so we can travel relatively freely. Once we get you out of Picardy, that is. Your father is waiting for you in England."

"Narcisse? You've met him?"

"He came to me when he learned someone had convinced the British to drop food packages to this region."

"So that was you too."

He shook his head. "That was the flying corps. All I had to do was tell them how dire things are around here."

"But now you're here. Back here." She said the words with awe and sorrow, gratitude. Guilt. "Because of me? You've endangered your life again?"

"Sit down, Julitte. I have something to tell you."

Guy was closest to the table, and he pulled out a chair. They all took seats, Charles nearest, never letting go of her hand.

"There is a family in Greece who contacted Narcisse," Charles said softly. "Your family, Julitte. They're so worried about you, they've sent men to find you. Through Narcisse and now through me."

"Agapios Nestor Constantinos. My grandfather."

Julitte hadn't seen a look of surprise so apparent on his face since that first day she'd met him, when the tin dropped from above and bounced off his forehead. But she couldn't smile over it. Her grandfather. The man who must have disowned her mother or she might not have had to die with only Julitte and her father by her side.

"You know?"

"My father—Narcisse—left a letter behind from Agapios. It said he wanted to meet me."

"And he does. More than that, he wants you brought to safety."

"Who is this Agapios?" Guy asked. "Narcisse told me your father was an American missionary, your mother a nurse on a Greek island."

"All of that is true," Julitte said.

"But her mother was the daughter of a wealthy Greek shipping industrialist, a man with close connections to the king. Perhaps you don't know this, that the king of Greece is married to the Kaiser's sister. Because of his connections to Germany, King Constantine of Greece doesn't want to join forces with the British even though his prime minister has made it clear ours is the side Greece should ally with. Julitte—" he leaned even closer—"do you realize what an opportunity this is?"

She shook her head, hardly able to keep up with the information.

"That you—if we bring you safely out—can influence a country, an army. If your grandfather uses his influence, expresses his gratitude to the British for bringing you to safety, we may make a difference far beyond any one of our lives here in this room. You can make a difference in this war, Julitte."

"But how can I leave? The Germans won't just let me walk away."

"There is a route waiting for us, from north of here all the way to freedom in the Netherlands. All we have to do is follow it—out. Tonight, as soon as darkness falls."

She wanted to stand, to think while moving, which had once been her habit. But months of fatigue wouldn't let her obey. Her limbs were too heavy, though they'd never been so slight. "But I cannot leave Didi. . . ."

And had he said *tonight*? Suddenly the truth sorted in her mind. If it was Charles who'd saved her from the attack, what must Hauptmann Brecht be thinking she wanted to thank him for? An awkward misunderstanding had nothing to do with it; outright fear of being questioned over the matter—interrogated—was something else altogether. Tonight, at dinner.

How could she leave, with a German Hauptmann expecting her company this very night? *Oh, Lord, what a fool I was to agree to such a thing when I knew in my heart it was never the right thing to do!*

But she couldn't bring herself to admit her mistake—not now, with three pairs of eyes staring at her, one of them Charles's.

"Didi is dying," Guy said, and the statement startled her. Julitte might have thought the same, but never once had she voiced that word about Didi. Her uncle's tone left no room for doubt, not even much for compassion, it seemed. Perhaps death had become too commonplace lately.

Julitte looked at Guy. "How can I leave her?" And how could she admit aloud that she knew she, Julitte herself, was the only comfort Didi had just now? Ori brought too many worries. Julitte knew she wasn't enough to make Didi want to live, but how could she let her die without being at her side, praying over her? If Didi could speak, Julitte knew what she would say: *Stay by my side until the Lord calls for me.*

"Julitte, you must come with me," Charles said. "For the sake of many, not just for one. I don't know what is going on with the Allied forces, but I do know I need to get you out as soon as possible. They're planning something—I don't know what—but it's my guess it has something to do with this area."

His hand held fast to hers, and she clung to him, wanting to agree. And yet . . .

"I cannot go tonight. I cannot."

"She's not thinking clearly," Uncle Guy said.

"It's the hunger," Pepin said. He raised a fingertip to his temple. "It makes you slow after a while."

Julitte shook her head, knowing she must tell them the truth. "I cannot go because I'm expected at the town hall this very evening."

She couldn't raise her gaze; she stared at the small patch of floor she could see between her lap and Charles.

"Why?"

How innocently he asked that question, and how innocent should have been the answer. Why, why had she agreed to go? And how could she admit it all?

Gently, she pulled her hand from Charles's and lifted both hands to the table, where she rested her forehead on her palms. "It's all so foolish now," she said, so low she wondered if anyone but the Lord could hear her.

"What is it, Julitte? Why are you going to the town hall—where the Germans are headquartered?"

She sat up straight, letting her hands drop to her lap. She stared ahead at the wall on the opposite side of the table, unable to look at Charles just yet. "Because I'm to dine with Hauptmann Christophe Brecht. Tonight." Then she found a sad smile. "To express my gratitude to him for something he didn't even do."

She glanced at Charles just long enough to notice one small twitch appear then disappear at the corner of his mouth. "What is it he thinks he did?"

"Saved me from the Leutnant. This morning."

Charles stood, rounding his chair, leaning over its back as if to say something, but he didn't. He ran fingers through his hair before sitting again, reaching for her hands. "All the more reason for you to come away with me. As soon as the sun sets."

"And have the Hauptmann hunting her down?" Guy neared them, palms up and waving. "No, no, she'll have to go. Once she's finished, then you take her away."

Charles went nearly nose to nose with Guy. "Finished? Don't you mean, once he's finished with her?"

"No, not at all," Guy said, backing away although he was nearly as tall as Charles. "It is only dinner, after all."

"You've lived under the Germans all this time and don't know what could happen, Guy?" Pepin asked quietly. "Even I am not so naive."

"Yes, yes I know. But there are two things to consider. One, she has already agreed to go." Guy looked at Julitte. "Did you not?"

She nodded, miserably.

"And two, if she does not appear, it isn't only Julitte who will suffer. This village has been fined, citizens jailed or deported, and our rations reduced for insults less consequential. She must go."

"Why, Julitte?" asked Charles, leaning closer. "Why did you agree to go?"

Somehow she found the strength to gain her feet, turning her back to him. "I do not know! I shouldn't have. I thought it was he who helped me, and when Ori said I should thank him, I had no idea it would mean even a moment alone with him. And I was hungry."

"Ah, Ori," Guy said. "So being out of the frying pan since her Hauptmann left, she wants to throw you in to take her place?"

Julitte didn't look up. She would cast no blame in Ori's direction. Julitte was the one who had agreed to go.

Charles came up behind her, putting gentle hands on her shoulders. "I would give anything to spare you this, Julitte. Even risk what little comfort this village knows for some supposed insult. I'll take you away right now if you will come with me."

Julitte looked up, but not at Charles. She looked at Guy, who would no doubt suffer, and thought of Ori, too. Could Julitte flee and leave them to suffer on her account?

"I cannot. And there's Didi. . . . I cannot leave her. Not until she doesn't need me anymore."

Charles squeezed her shoulders, turning her to him. "The longer we stay—and the longer I stay here—the more dangerous it'll be to bring you out."

"Didi will not last," Guy said solemnly. "Perhaps not even the night."

33

Julitte stood at the door of their cottage. Although she knew it was time for her to leave, it seemed nothing would get her feet to move.

Ori, next to her, reached out and pinched Julitte on the cheeks. "To give you some pink," she defended, when Julitte winced. "Your shadow has more color than you today."

"Is there nothing I can say to convince you to come with me?"

Ori smiled, shaking her head. "You'll be much more relaxed once you're there. He's not an ogre, and there will be food. Real food. Bring something for me."

As empty as her stomach was and as alluring as it had sounded earlier, even that didn't get her feet to move. How awful to suddenly have the idea of food make her stomach recoil. It was her stomach she blamed for agreeing to go, and now it rebelled.

Ori opened the door and stood with it wide beside her. Julitte knew she would have to go. Even the sure knowledge that Charles was here, that he'd come for her, that he loved her and loved God, did not give her the courage she needed to face what lay ahead. She wanted to turn the other way, to the bakery, instead of the direction of the town hall.

But she knew she couldn't.

And so with each step she raised a word of prayer.

Charles wanted nothing more than to go to one of the windows, to peer outside and wait, watch for Julitte and see if she would truly go through with it. She would be leaving about now, walking the street to the town hall, where everyone, German and villager alike, would see her go. Willingly.

And then what? He cared nothing for what the villagers would think. But what would happen when she stood in the same room, alone and unprotected, with a German Hauptmann?

Images threatened to drive him mad or compel him to do something that would endanger not only his own life but hers as well. And so he paced.

Waited.

And prayed.

God's sovereignty was his only hope.

Julitte did not even have to tap on the door of the upstairs room. It opened the moment she stood before it, as if someone had stood just inside, waiting for the floor to creak or a footfall to sound.

A man stood there, not the Hauptmann. He had on a servant's jacket, white, neatly pressed. He said something in German, something Julitte assumed was an invitation to enter. Her feet took her inside.

When he closed the door behind her, she turned around to stare at it rather than the room in front of her. Solid wood, paneled. Polished, with a shiny brass knob.

"Ah, Julitte!"

She had to turn again at the sound of the Hauptmann's voice. He was only a man, she told herself . . . created by the same God she worshiped.

"Come in, come in." He smiled broadly. "I have been practicing my English for you. You will see."

Then he turned briefly to the servant beside them, speaking in low and quick German, something about serving dinner right away.

"You are hungry?" he said as he led her farther into the room. It was a fine room, with wood paneling on the lower half of the walls the same shade as the door, and furniture she didn't recognize. She'd half expected to find odds and ends from the village being used by the Germans so close at hand. "For your hunger, I must apologize. This war . . . it is not so efficient as it could be. The Allied blockade does not help. If they knew their own people suffer by not letting supply ships through, I wonder, would they do something differently too?"

There was a pair of plush chairs, so deeply cushioned Julitte gave a fleeting thought to what it would feel like to sit in them. But he led her past, under a wide, wood-trimmed archway into another part of the expansive room. A table had been set for two, although the length could have allowed a half-dozen more guests. Candles darted light on the crystal glasses and silver cutlery, and bread—real bread, not dark—already awaited them on their plates. Just one roll apiece, but the sight of it made her want to bypass the Hauptmann altogether and stuff the bread into her mouth before she was even seated. Her mouth watered at the thought, despite the tempest still in her stomach.

"Wine?"

She shook her head. "No. Do you have milk?" Something she hadn't tasted in weeks, despite two cows in the village now owned by the Germans.

He looked from Julitte to the servant, who gave a slight nod. He disappeared into another room, through a door Julitte hadn't noticed before.

He was back in a moment with a narrow glass, full to the brim with the white, frothy liquid.

She sipped at it, eager to receive the sustenance, wondering if her stomach would tolerate it after so long without and under such turmoil within.

"Now you must tell me," the Hauptmann said when the servant disappeared again, "why I receive your favor. Ori said you are grateful."

She nodded; she'd rehearsed this since coming from Charles's side. "Yes, for saving us. The other night, in our cottage."

"And that is all? the only time?"

Why must lies always prove fruitless? "Yes . . ."

But he was looking behind her, at something on the floor she hadn't seen when she'd passed under the arch. A pair of clogs. Hers.

"Oh . . ."

"Tonight, this meal, is to amend your suffering the Leutnant's hand. I found him senseless at the foot of the stairs. Your clogs—he said they were yours, the woman living with Ori—and I thought the worst."

Julitte stared at the bread on her plate, unable to speak, unable even to lift that piece of food that so tempted her, to swallow past her closed throat. The servant returned with a platter of more food: vegetables and chicken, potatoes and cheese. She nearly fainted.

She said nothing until the servant placed the platter between them, leaving them alone once again.

"He did try the worst," she whispered at last. "But I was spared, thank the Lord."

The Hauptmann, seated at the head of the table to her left, was close enough to touch her. He placed a hand on her arm.

"Yes. That is why I wanted to speak with you, Julitte. Leutnant Kemnitz . . . he was . . ." He pointed a finger toward his own head, spinning the tip around and tilting his head as if dizzy. "He was *betrunken.* Do you know the word?"

She nodded. She didn't need to know the German word for someone who'd drunk too much.

"Still, he told me he was pushed. It wasn't you, could not be you." His words were stalled but he mimed the push and she knew what he meant. "Too strong to be you, *Fräulein. Sehr stark.* Julitte, do you know who it was?"

She could not speak; her throat sealed so tight she felt strangled, and the sight of food was almost too much to bear.

"Ich habe eine Idee wer dies getan hat," he continued, low. He glanced at the door the servant had used, as if to make sure it was closed. "I have an idea, and I believe you will agree. Was it an angel, sent from above to protect you? *Die einzige Person in diesem Dorf die Gott benutzt hat, um ein Leben zu retten?* the only person in this village God used to save a life?"

She breathed once, then again, until she realized she was breathing steadily. An angel? Perhaps so . . . directing the boots Charles wore.

Hauptmann Brecht withdrew his hand from her arm and began serving the food from the platter. More food than Julitte had seen in well over a year.

"Do you think me foolish?" he asked. "Or has God abandoned us for the killing?"

She shook her head. "He is here, in our midst. Brokenhearted with us. Waiting until our leaders stop all of this."

"But why does He wait? Why doesn't He stop it? He's God; He can."

"How would He do such a thing? What would become of faith? And which side would He want to win? Isn't there good to be found on both sides?"

"And evil."

She nodded because she knew it was the polite thing to do, though she'd only seen German evil. But maybe that blockade he'd mentioned, the one that might even be playing a part in her hunger, also touched German civilians. Surely the God she loved would think that evil too.

The Hauptmann chatted on, telling her about the church he'd attended back home, about his parents and brother and sister, whom he heard from regularly. His words, though halting, became easier to understand once any new topic became clear. He told her his family was nearly as hungry as those here in Briecourt, that it was only the army Germany could afford to feed. He admitted he shouldn't be telling her this, that it was never sound policy to let the enemy know of any weakness, but that he couldn't consider her an enemy because he was convinced she loved God.

And soon, because he was friendly and smiled so often, because he spoke of God and church and family, Julitte's stomach eased its tension. She ate slowly, beginning to taste the chicken, the vegetables, the bread. The chicken was fragrant white meat that fell from the bone in each moist bite. The vegetables were crisp and green, like life itself. The bread, warm and light like air except with sustenance and taste, and though there was no butter, she didn't care. Each bite was a memory of life as it used to be.

But she found herself full long before she expected.

"You cannot be finished."

She nodded. "My stomach isn't accustomed to . . ." She let the sentence linger, wondering if he would feel the blame for what his army had done—shrink her stomach so that it couldn't tolerate even what it wanted, or at least very much.

He wiped his mouth with his napkin, setting it aside although his plate wasn't empty either. Pushing away from the table, he took her hand and led her to the sitting area, stopping to pick up her clogs. He set them near the door.

Julitte's heart lightened. This was it? He was letting her go?

But instead of leading her to the door as well, he took her to one of the chairs she'd noticed earlier. He invited her to sit but she remained standing.

"I should not stay long," she said, finding the courage to speak but not to look at him. She prayed he wouldn't take offense. "My friend's grandmother, with whom I share a cottage, is ill. I need to be by her side."

"Yes, I understand," he said but still did not move. He'd stopped close in front of her so that when she looked down at the floor, it was his boots she saw rather than the clogs she'd borrowed from Ori. "Do you know, Julitte, you are beautiful?"

She kept her eyes fixed downward. Her heart plummeted even as her pulse raced with panic. So, after all, had it come to what she feared?

"It is not easy for soldiers," he whispered. "Each day—is it our last? Even in villages, away from the fighting, we are hated. Women would see a bullet in our back if they had a gun. And the children. They smile, but only when we go away. Do you see that?"

She said nothing, not even when he took one of her hands in his. She knew he wanted her to look at him, but she did not.

"I'm grateful to you, Julitte. You come here tonight because you love God, and He makes you to see past my uniform. I want that we might be friends."

If by *friends* he meant what Ori had been to the other Hauptmann, the one she called Erich, then Julitte should flee this very moment. Although this Hauptmann spoke of God, although he'd been nothing but a gentleman each and every time she'd seen him, Julitte knew what she saw in him, no matter what he believed.

She pulled her hand from his.

"Has my eagerness to enjoy your company made me see something that isn't there?" he asked.

"If we share a love for God, then we are friends—in faith. But I will not lie. I do not see past your uniform. I cannot."

"You don't see a man? one who desires your company?"

She shook her head, risking the insult such a reaction would bring. She glanced up to see if an offense was taken but was unable to read his perfect facade. "To the women of your country you would be brave and handsome, a hero." She looked down again. "But not to the women of mine."

Julitte wasn't sure what she'd expected, risking the wrath of no less than a German officer. But what else could she do? Let him think she would be like Ori?

He laughed, and in that, she found her fear start to dissipate.

"You are honest, as I fully expected." Placing her hand on his arm, he led her toward the door. "There is only one remedy for this. Since I believe the future of France belongs to *Deutschland*, then we take time. I ask only that you might find a smile for me now and then. A smile at my approach, that is, not my retreat."

She wanted to smile now; was he really walking her to the door, handing her the clogs, letting her go?

"If I smile now," she said, "would it be the kind you don't want to see? the kind with a good-bye?"

"But this isn't good-bye, Julitte." He kissed her hand. "I am here to stay."

Then, clinging now to the clogs in her hands, Julitte passed through the door he opened, walking away with relief and something she had certainly not expected. Tentative affection for a brother in faith.

34

It was past dark and therefore past curfew, but Julitte couldn't help herself. Instead of stopping at her cottage, she passed her own door and went to the bakery. Looking both ways before slipping inside, she saw the street was empty, the bakery quiet.

But she assumed too much. There, in the kitchen, she found neither Charles nor the little man called Pepin. She found Uncle Guy and a pair of German soldiers seated at the table with coffee cups before them.

"Uncle," she greeted.

He stood, nearly knocking over the chair he'd sat in. "It's late, Julitte. What is it?"

She held out the clogs, and a lie came far too easily. "I came to borrow your shoe brush. To clean my shoes."

One German at the table laughed, then translated for the other, who laughed as well.

"I have a brush, *Fräulein*," said the German who spoke French. "But you must come to my billet to get it."

"Do not trouble yourself." Uncle Guy went to a low cabinet across the room. He took out a small horsehair brush and handed it to Julitte. "You can use this." Then he turned to the soldiers. "I would like to accompany my niece back to her cottage, if that is all right?"

They both stood. "It's time for us to go too. Come on, Helmut, on your feet."

The other soldier took a last sip of whatever was in his cup—surely not real coffee; that hadn't been seen in any village kitchen for months—then hurried after.

Julitte walked stiffly, glad the soldiers allowed her uncle to come as well. But at her door they ordered him home, in deference to the curfew law. Julitte slipped inside, hoping her appearance, however brief but certainly not disheveled or distraught, was enough to soothe any worries Charles might have had over this night. Uncle Guy would tell him not to worry.

She went to Didi's side, where she found Ori.

"And so? How did it go?" Ori asked. Two simple sentences, spoken with more wariness than curiosity.

"Did you expect me to be later?" Julitte asked, but the words were lighthearted instead of bitter. How could she be anything but happy, having escaped the night so easily?

"I wasn't sure what to expect. I told you he is a gentleman."

"Yes, he was polite." She didn't mention that if she had been willing to stay, she might still be there—certainly Hauptmann Brecht wouldn't have sent her away.

"Did you bring me anything to eat?"

Julitte wanted to slap her own forehead for being such a dunce. All that food, and she'd had access to it! What had she done? Squandered the opportunity because of her fears. Ori had never forgotten; she'd always brought food home when the roles were reversed. "I'm sorry. I could hardly eat a thing myself, I was so nervous. I forgot."

Ori shrugged, although her gaze didn't meet Julitte's.

"I'm going to sleep now," Ori said, standing. She went to the stairs but turned back. "Will you visit him again?"

"I don't know," she said, looking at Didi.

It all depended on how long she would be in the village—and when God called Didi to His side.

Julitte woke with a start. The light—unlike any other—was there on the horizon, so plain, so vivid, and yet her eyes took it in without squinting.

She realized she'd fallen asleep by Didi's side again and fumbled closer to reach for Didi's hand. Had Didi's passing been the source of the light? But she was warm and supple, and in that first moment of cognizance Julitte realized Didi still breathed. Labored, but audible.

Julitte looked around the cottage, orienting herself. Surely it was near morning. What an odd dream. As real as other moments when she'd seen the light of heaven, but this had been so different. There was no sense of heaven opening for someone, for her or even for Didi.

She stiffened. For Charles?

Her heart knocked into her chest wall, but she shook her head. This had been different. She didn't understand.

She must wait for curfew to lift; then she would go to the bakery.

"Didi?"

The older woman did not stir.

Julitte took a cloth, wet it, and brushed it on the older woman's drying lips. Reflexively her lips moved, but she never opened her eyes. So Julitte set about her routine, praying, speaking words from the Bible over Didi.

"'Even I will carry, and will deliver you.' . . . 'Thou hast taught me from my youth. . . . Now also when I am old and greyheaded, O God, forsake me not; until I have shewed thy strength unto this generation, and thy power to every one that is to come. . . .'"

Julitte whispered the words she knew Didi would welcome,

praying silently that she would hear and take comfort in the words God had provided. Even as Julitte spoke, her heart and mind returned to Charles, praying safety upon the bakery, upon him, as he waited for her to come to him.

The sun was shrouded behind clouds today, with a warm wind blowing from the south. She heard the wind on the roof, the tap of the tree that had grown too close to the back of the cottage. Curfew would lift soon.

But no sooner did it than a tap of another kind sounded. At the door.

She rushed to answer it with a glance toward the quiet loft. Ori was still asleep.

"How is she today?"

Julitte let her uncle Guy inside, but he didn't go farther than the threshold. She knew it wasn't only concern for Didi that had brought him here so early; he wanted to know when she would be ready to go.

"The same. Weak. She won't wake, won't eat."

Her uncle's dark eyes leveled on her. "You mustn't wait. Tonight, Julitte."

Then, with barely more than a glance in Didi's direction, he placed a hand back on the door, as if to close it once he left. "Do not come to the bakery. The soldiers come every morning, and I expect them soon."

He closed the door behind him, but a moment later she heard someone speaking. German-accented voices asking Uncle Guy what he was doing about so early. She heard him answer that his cousin was ill, dying, and soon the voices disappeared.

Julitte returned to Didi's bedside.

How much longer, Lord? I don't know how to pray today . . . except that Didi might not suffer.

Ori came downstairs sooner than expected, and they shared the same nearly inedible brown bread they'd had for breakfast the day before. Neither spoke. Julitte wanted to think it was sadness over her grandmother's condition keeping Ori quiet, but with her lack of eye contact Julitte wasn't sure. There seemed a new barrier between them, this one erected by Ori—after Julitte came home too early last night.

Another knock at the door came later that morning, but this one was decidedly German in its volume. The handle rattled from the pounding.

Then, before either Julitte or Ori could reach the door, it opened.

"Oriane Bouget."

Ori stepped forward.

"You will follow me."

She had only long enough to grab her scarf and slip into her clogs before chasing after the soldier, who was already two steps out the door.

"You don't have to wait, you know," Charles said to Pepin. For the moment he sat comfortably at the table, his limbs spread out before him. But the wall was open in the event they would both have to jump back into the unyielding hiding place in which they'd spent entirely too much time already. "You could go on your own. I'll give you explicit directions, and you already have the pass."

Pepin nodded, although by the draw of his brows he didn't seem to like the idea. "I will wait one more night." He pulled the pass from beneath his shirt. "Here. It's safest with you anyway."

Charles hesitated but took it, slipping the folded sheet back into the flat compartment on the underside of his belt. He didn't like the wait, nor did he welcome Pepin's waiting as well. He, at least, had a choice.

"You must speak to her as soon as I can bring her here," Guy said. "Convince her to go."

"She'll listen to you, my friend," Pepin said with a new sparkle in his eye. He exchanged glances with Guy. "Did you see the way she looked at him?"

But Charles shook his head. "Julitte takes direction from God, not from me."

"If you plan to wed, all you need tell her is that God placed you in authority over her. You tell her what to do, that she must go."

"Submission for her is no less important than submission for me, Pepin. Both of us to God. If God wishes her to stay by Didi, then it's my job to trust He'll still see us through."

Pepin raised his palms as if to argue but must have changed his mind, because no words accompanied the gesture.

But Charles couldn't help asking God to increase the faith Charles held in his heart. They would need no less than divine intervention to get them safely out, especially if the people waiting to aid their transport gave up on them too soon.

Ori did not return to the cottage all that day. Julitte looked for her twice, going only as far as the well in front of the town hall. But Ori was not to be seen.

Gustave de Colville, however, came out of his cottage just as Julitte returned home. "I saw you go there. Last night."

Julitte did not turn; she kept her hand on her door handle. The tone of his voice was painfully familiar, as if nothing had united this town, as if no Germans existed as the common enemy, as if they had no shared secret of men still living and hiding under various roofs.

"Yes, I went there for a short while."

"To . . . dine?"

His tone revealed that was the last thing he believed she'd done. Or perhaps only the first, among other less savory things.

Julitte didn't defend herself; no words could convince someone who didn't want to believe the truth.

"And now she is there. Do you know why?"

Julitte shook her head, though she still had her back to him.

"Because he's returned. Her German lover. I saw him. This morning."

Julitte looked sharply down the street, instantly wishing she might go back to the town hall and drag Ori home. But she never moved. If he was here, there would be no bringing Ori home now.

"It means trouble; you know that. He was sent away for a reason, and for these last few weeks there have been fewer inspections, less trouble. He won't let the Orstkommandant continue to be so lenient."

Julitte went inside her cottage, wondering if what Gustave said could be true. Was Ori's Hauptmann here to stay? And if he was, what had happened to Hauptmann Brecht?

Julitte longed to go to the bakery, knowing Charles was so close at hand, but knew she couldn't leave Didi for any length of time while Ori wasn't here to stand by. He would have to wait, and all Julitte could do was pray continued safety for him. For all of them.

35

Didi's body seemed to be caving in on itself, from her eyes into their sockets to her toes curling down and inward from lack of use. Her hands, once so strong and competent, were now shriveled and stiff. Sometimes when she slept, her mouth would fall open, and Julitte would be convinced she'd passed on. But Julitte saw no light for her, and she continued to breathe.

Decay was a hard thing to watch, though Julitte knew it was the way of this world; nothing escaped it.

Ori did not return until the following afternoon, and if Gustave hadn't already told Julitte that Hauptmann Erich Basedow had returned, Julitte would have guessed it the moment she saw Ori's face. Alight, in love amid the ruins of this town, even with battle rumbles that seemed increasingly loud by day and night, increasing in dosage.

"Erich is back!" Ori said, grabbing Julitte's hands and pulling her from the chair she occupied near Didi. She hugged Julitte. "He came back for me. He truly loves me, Julitte."

"The German army lets their soldiers go where they wish?"

She laughed. "Of course not! But Erich found a way to come back to me. Because of his love for me."

If Ori wanted Julitte to share her happiness, Julitte knew she let her down. She turned away, sitting again by Didi's side.

"How is she today?"

"The same."

Ori pulled something from her pockets: bread and a pouch of tea. "Give her some of this tea. It's rose hip. It'll make her feel better."

It was far too late for that; surely Didi felt no pain in her peaceful sleep. Julitte had taken to silently calling it Didi's waiting sleep, as she waited in sleep for the Lord to come for her. "The last time I tried having her swallow something, she nearly choked. She can't take it."

Even so, Ori steeped some water with the tea and Julitte rubbed it on Didi's lips in the hope that some might make it in.

"Have you been here all day and last night too?" Ori asked, once they both sat by Didi's side again.

"Where else would I go? I went only to the well. I didn't want to leave her."

"You didn't see Uncle Guy today?"

Although her voice sounded as casual as ever, merely curious, Julitte raised her gaze to study her friend. Why had she asked about Uncle Guy in particular?

"No, not today. Yesterday he stopped in for only a moment to see how Didi was doing."

Ori nodded. "Yes, I thought I heard his voice." Then she stood again. "I'm going back to the town hall. I only came to give you a little respite from Didi. I know the hours are long."

"Must you go, Ori?"

Ori smiled. "If I thought you wanted my company, I might stay. Or if you needed my help with Didi. But I know more than either of that, you want me to stay because you don't want me with Erich. That's no reason for me to stay."

Julitte denied nothing. "Will you be married, under God, if he loves you so much?"

"Of course. Eventually."

Julitte stood as well. "If you've come to give me respite, would you stay just a little longer?"

"Yes. Why?"

Julitte looked away. "I would like to go outside. I won't be gone long."

Then, before Ori could ask more questions, she slipped into her clogs and hurried out the door.

Having Charles so close and yet unable to see him or talk to him, unable to simply be with him, had made the hours lag even longer. She wanted to throw off all caution and rush to his side, but fear kept her immobile.

The street was quiet but for the typical German soldiers. She was tempted to walk past the bakery for fear of being seen going inside but called her fears overdone. The man named Pepin had been hiding here for nearly two years, and never once had she hesitated to go inside before now. She must pretend all was the same.

The bakery was quiet, the same empty shelves, no sound of work coming from the kitchen. She called out her uncle's name.

He emerged from the kitchen before she could reach it.

"You mustn't stay, Julitte. We're being watched more closely than ever. Did you see the sentry?"

She glanced back at the door. "I saw a soldier outside. I thought he was doing his rounds, same as always."

Uncle Guy shook his head. "He's been up and down this street a dozen times in the last hour and always stops at the same spot, directly in front. You must go tonight, Julitte, the moment the sentries let up their watch. Whether or not Didi is still with us."

Julitte wanted to argue but saw in her uncle's eyes that she ought not. She nodded, though she remained still even when her uncle took her elbow to direct her away.

"But can I not see him, just for a moment?"

"He is safe. Don't jeopardize that for a moment. Go home

now." But no sooner had she turned, willing to go, than Uncle Guy grabbed her wrist. "Be ready when the sun sets, all through the night. I will come to your door the moment it's safe to pass."

She nodded, then went on her way, sparing no more than a quick glance at the German soldier who watched her leave.

Julitte shut the door of her cottage soundly, leaning against it just inside.

"What is it?" Ori asked. "You look as if someone is chasing you."

Julitte shook her head. "No. Only there are more soldiers in town today. And that battle thunder! It feels closer and more constant than ever. The streets shake from it."

How easy it was to blame her agitation on the war, even though she should be used to it by now. But how could she, really, ever become accustomed to such a thing?

Ori went to the stove and poured Julitte a cup of the rose hip tea. "Here. Drink some."

Julitte accepted the cup, taking her familiar seat near Didi. With her free hand, she took Didi's old and frail one, at once accosted with a prayer she never thought she would pray. *Lord, I know You're coming for her, but I beg You to make it soon. She cannot live like this, and I cannot wait much longer.* Even as such words formed in her mind, she asked forgiveness for her impatience, especially over something so firmly in God's hands.

"You're good to her, Julitte," Ori whispered. "More so than I."

Ori did not sit. Instead, she went to the door. Undoubtedly back to her Hauptmann.

Julitte stroked Didi's hand. Her mind was full of what would happen this very night. How did one prepare to sneak out into the night? Certainly she could bring nothing with her, not that she had anything to bring. She glanced to the table nearby, at the Bible awaiting her touch. No, even that must stay. She had few extra clothes and no satchel to put them in anyway.

Even as she had such thoughts, she could not help but lift a word of praise.

"Do you know how the Lord has provided for us, Didi?" she said, as she so often did. "Look at my skirt. You cannot see it has only the slightest wear inside the pocket, though I've washed it, worn it again and again. And the manna-food, those baskets that came from above. I know now how they came to arrive, but isn't it still the Lord's provision, no matter how it came about?"

She sat back in her chair with a sigh. "I think of the people of Israel and the forty years. Oh! Please, God, I beg You not to let this war last so long. But isn't it similar? I dreamed about that the other night when I saw a bright light in the distance. Do you remember the story, Didi? Of how the Israelites saw the pillar burning in the distance to light the way? That was what I saw in my dream; I see it now. Do you think the dream meant something, Didi?"

Her breath quickened when Didi's grip on her hand tightened. It had been many days since she had reacted to any of Julitte's words. Had she imagined it? What had she just said that might have made Didi respond?

"Do you think about our Promised Land, Didi? of heaven?"

But there was no response. Not even a finger moved within Julitte's hold.

Had she dreamed the light for Didi, then? A reminder that heaven was surely on the horizon? Better that, because Didi's passing was expected, than another thought Julitte had. That the light had been there for her and Charles, to show them the way. To heaven.

As the day wore on, Julitte read to Didi from the Bible, as she did every day. She drank more tea, rubbed more on Didi's lips; she ate the bread Ori had brought. Like Didi, Julitte waited, through the evening and into the night.

She woke with a start, by habit reaching for Didi's hand. She felt cool to the touch, but not cold. Her fingernails, once so white at the tip and so pink beneath, were vivid purple, the way her feet were turning. Julitte waited for Didi to take her next breath and for a moment half-feared it wouldn't come. But then it did, haltingly, and Julitte pulled the blanket over Didi's arms, covering her hands against any chill.

Then Julitte realized there was enough light to notice such things. She looked to the window. How could it be? She'd listened last night as the birds quieted and the crickets took up the song of creation—a song that went on despite the battle cacophony not so very far away. But now the birds were stirring again. She'd prayed through the night.

She must have slept but couldn't recall the moment she'd dozed. Had something awakened her? Standing, Julitte went to the door. If Uncle Guy had come for her, surely she wouldn't have slept through the slightest sound. But even if she had, he could easily have come inside and shaken her awake, with the door always unlocked.

She looked down the street. Curfew hadn't yet lifted, so the street was empty. Nearly. Her gaze caught a pair of sentries who fairly strolled down the cobbled way, as if they had nothing more to do than enjoy the birds waking to an early morning mist and the never-ending cannonade.

She returned to Didi's side. Ori hadn't returned, either, but there was no surprise over that.

Julitte wanted to do nothing more than hurry down to the bakery, no matter what warnings her uncle might give. But she must wait, at least until morning curfew ended. She sat beside Didi again.

"Another day, Didi." She'd meant for the words to bring cheer, but Julitte found no cheer to boost them. "Didi?"

She leaned closer.

Julitte put her hand on Didi's arm. "Didi?"

She listened for Didi's next breath, watched to see if her lungs moved to accept any air. Yes . . . or was it only Julitte's imagination?

Julitte called her name again, squeezing her hand once more. There was nothing, no response from Didi and no light from above, either. Surely she still lived? Yet . . .

"Didi!" Tears ran warm down Julitte's cheeks, but she didn't bother with them. "I know where you go is a far better place, where no guns need be, nor wars, nor even a single tear. But I can't see you."

Didi had breathed her last. Without a light, without allowing Julitte any vision of her passing. Left in its place was only the sting of death and separation.

Julitte wept; even the sure knowledge that Didi was at the Savior's side offered little comfort now.

36

Charles did not dare breathe. Not that he could expand his chest for such a luxury anyway, wedged as he was like a stowaway in steerage. He was folded next to Pepin, whom Charles could tell dared not breathe either.

All night they'd been like this, with one sentry or another parading in front of the bakery, often stepping inside.

Then it started, the sound Charles had dreaded most of all. Pounding. Not the kind of a fist at the door or even the butt of a rifle. Nor even the kind from bombs crossing over the not-so-distant no-man's-land to hit the ground nearby. This was much closer, nearly intimate, and far more deadly to Charles and to Pepin.

The walls just outside beat to the sound, and Charles's heart along with it, mixing with a twinge of nausea at what surely must be to come. Discovery.

Though he tried, he could decipher no words from the shouting on the other side of the wall. German voices to be sure, and on occasion perhaps Guy, but not a word could Charles understand.

The voices barely faded and suddenly the wall fell away. Charles prepared for the worst, tempted to shut his eyes. And he did momentarily, if only in deference to the light contrasting with the darkness in which he'd hidden all night long.

"Come! Quickly!"

Guy's voice.

Pepin was out before Charles, and he followed their shadows from the kitchen and to the back of the bakery.

"Go two doors—the first will do you no good. Two! Go now, and quickly."

Charles skidded past Pepin, who stumbled on the wet ground, and it occurred to him that the other man probably hadn't seen the out of doors in well over a year, not since the sky had been their roof. But there was no time to enjoy such a moment now. He pulled Pepin to his feet and dragged him along. Two doors.

Charles didn't even knock. He slipped inside, and there stood an older man, stocky of build, gray headed.

For an old man, he had power behind his shove. He thrust Charles to a sea chest at the corner. "Inside, both of you!"

Such a feat should have been impossible—the spot looked even smaller than the one they'd just vacated. But Pepin jumped in and disappeared. Charles peered inside to see that the bottom dropped away, revealing an opening just below and to the side. It took less than a moment to follow the way Pepin had gone.

"If my door opens, use that hatch to go to the next house."

No sooner had the words been uttered than the pounding sounded at the parlor door.

"Yes!" the man called in answer to the noise. He closed the chest above Charles. "Yes, I am—"

But the sound of a door bursting open finished the man's statement.

Charles didn't stay long enough to hear any more. He made his way through the passage, Pepin just ahead, and they were ushered out again, this time by a woman no less than sixty years old. She held open another door, this one to a closet with yet another door at its rear. Through another parlor Charles fled on Pepin's heel, past scant furniture and dark wood and dimly lit rooms, just ahead of pounding and more pounding.

Until the last door, where a boy hastily thrust aside a rug to reveal a portal in the floor. Charles nearly fell down the hole, skipping the top three stairs as Pepin fell in. Charles narrowly missed him, landing in a heap on a hard earth bottom.

And there, darkness. Dank. But no silence. A darkly clad shadow hovered in the corner.

"Keep your mouths shut," hissed the shape that blended into the wall.

Charles had no argument with that command.

Ruckus from outside drew Julitte from Didi's side. Julitte had been waiting for the light, expecting it, longing for it, praying for it despite knowing where Didi was. But the light never came.

Instead, pounding, battering. Then cracking wood. Julitte ran to the door. Outside, the mist thickened, dampening and chilling everything it touched.

There, across the street, at the very place she prayed would be covered in safety, were not just a few but a multitude of soldiers. They scurried around the bakery, fanning out down the street; one slipped on moist pavement, only to right himself. Shouting, rifles in hand. One called for a torch, and another ran off to comply.

Julitte ran too—not away from the noise and the wet, as anyone else might have. She ran toward the bakery.

"Julitte!"

She heard Ori's voice but ignored it. There was only one reason for such a ferocious search: the Germans suspected the truth.

Someone grabbed her from behind, and for the shortest moment she thought Ori had caught up to her. But the grip was too firm, the outline behind her too tall. She writhed against the grasp and he doubled his hold until her back was pressed to him, a sturdy arm around her neck.

Another soldier came upon her, but his back was to her. He spoke in German, and she caught only a few words: *Feuer*—fire. *Bäckerei*—bakery. Then he turned a glare on Julitte and she saw he was none other than Ori's Hauptmann Basedow. The drizzle made his helmet glisten, and raindrops began to bead on his wide, decorated shoulders.

Whatever he'd said made the soldier behind her tighten his grip. Turning, he issued more orders, and the soldiers nearby started scurrying again—all but the one holding Julitte, who only tightened his hold when she tried to move.

Doors previously busted wide and shut again now crept open once more, all the way down the line on the de Colville side of the street. People came out, slowly, timidly with gazes cast nervously about, hands held high, some to show compliance, others protecting themselves from the rain.

Julitte, forced immobile by the iron grip encasing her, saw Ori, who wore a look of such horror-filled tears that Julitte knew immediately she was stricken not with worry over Julitte's sudden detainment but with guilt.

Another command from the Hauptmann. Erich, as Ori so lovingly called him.

A soldier counted those present, and Hauptmann Basedow paced up, then down the line of people, his back stiff, a pistol still holstered at one side, his riding whip hanging from the other. Julitte saw all of the remaining de Colvilles, from the youngest to the oldest. Only Guy was among them, the sole Toussaint represented. The rest must still be hidden; never had the divide in the town been more apparent.

"You are hiding something; this I know to be a fact," the Hauptmann said in French as he walked the length of them. "If we must set fire to this entire village, we will find your secret."

Then he spoke again, this time in German, and soldiers went along the other side of the street. More pounding, more smashed doors, what few windows remained unbroken now threatened anew. Within moments the rest of the villagers had joined those already on the street, Toussaint and de Colville alike. The light rain seemed to turn to a vapor, as if they stood inside a cloud.

Julitte tried to free herself, if only to join the others, but was given no such liberty.

A call came from a soldier in front of Julitte's cottage. *"Eine tote."* Someone missing?

"Sie ist tot," another soldier called, emerging from her home. Dead.

Julitte's eyes shot to Ori, who looked from the cottage to Julitte, then back again. She might have tried moving toward the cottage— Julitte saw her feet turn in that direction—but a soldier pushed the villagers into a single file line with the barrel of his rifle, Ori among them.

Two soldiers, torches held high against the cloud around them, trotted closer.

Another order, and Julitte heard the word again. *Bäckerei.*

"No!"

Julitte's cry went unheeded as the soldiers pranced by; they never even looked her way. She fought but with little success, helpless to free herself from the grip of someone so much bigger and stronger.

What little strength she had gave out too quickly, and she gave up when she saw Uncle Guy staring her down, shaking his head nearly imperceptibly. Why was he not protesting the loudest? It was his bakery, his livelihood, his home. Uncle Guy was the one who should try stopping them.

Flames did not take hold as quickly as the soldiers must have expected, as they stood back with the flames licking the front corners. When one sputtered out, a soldier went inside, no doubt in hopes the flame would have better success with dry contents.

Charles!

Julitte struggled again and failed but looked back at Uncle Guy for assurance. He was far too calm to be imagining what Julitte imagined.

Since the bakery stood by itself and because of the spewing mist, the buildings nearby—and those not far off started an entire row of de Colville housing—were in relatively little danger. For the moment.

"Which will be next?" Hauptmann Basedow called with a half smile, as if calling for a game. "Come now. Confess your secrets and the rest will be spared."

Julitte searched the faces. No one spoke; no one looked from the ground up to the soldiers or even to their neighbor. *Give us strength, Lord. Give each of us the will to be silent, no matter what. If there is any hope at all . . .*

"Next!"

The soldiers stood ready at the Hauptmann's bidding, torches still lit despite the cloud. They were at the end of the de Colville row, before the door kept in the care of Claudette for her soldier husband.

"No!" She fell forward out of the line and to her knees. "You mustn't burn my home. I beg you!"

Gustave de Colville stood behind her, pulling her back to her feet, drawing her close, too close, so that her face became hidden in his shirt. She squirmed away, and his grip, softened no doubt by age and lack of nutrition, couldn't hold her.

The Hauptmann, only a few paces away, stared at her. "Burn it."

"No!"

"Claudette!" Gustave tried holding her back, but she rushed to the Hauptmann as if she had no fear of his uniform or his power or his deadly intentions. She grabbed at his arm, and Julitte knew the other girl had lost all capacities but one: the capacity to talk.

"I'll tell you, only don't burn my house! Not my house!"

"What have you to tell me?" said the Hauptmann, standing so much taller and stronger, peeling her hands from him as if she were a dirty child and he didn't want his clothes soiled.

"They're hiding—there, down the line. Burn that one if you must, but not mine."

The Hauptmann said something in quick, low German to another soldier, who grabbed Claudette's arm and pulled her along. The three of them walked the street to the fourth house in the de Colville row. The door was already askew, hanging on one hinge. The Hauptmann went inside first, followed by Claudette still in the grip of the soldier from behind.

Julitte searched the row of her neighbors and relatives, a sad collection of the bent and broken. Like her. She sagged against the arms still clutching her; she couldn't see his face and didn't want to. Instead she looked for the one source of help she might be able to count on.

But Hauptmann Brecht was nowhere to be seen. She wasn't sure if she was relieved or disappointed. Surely if he were here, he could make Hauptmann Basedow stop.

A shouted order had several more soldiers jog inside, guns at the ready. Julitte heard little, only the dim sound of a commotion, more shouting. And then they marched out. Claudette and the soldier escorting her, her arm twisted behind her, followed the Hauptmann.

He stopped and turned and Claudette nearly bumped into him.

He called to the soldiers down the way, those who still held torches, and pointed down the street, issuing more orders in German.

Julitte watched Claudette's face go from exhausted dejection to incredulity. "They are to burn . . . which?"

The Hauptmann turned back to her and leaned closer. "Yours, of course. For knowing about these men and not coming to me sooner." He called again to the soldiers. "Carry on."

And then they went, torches high once again.

"No! No!" Claudette cried and took no more than two steps forward before she was caught back again by another soldier, kicking as ineffectually as Julitte had a moment ago. "But I told you about the men! You said—"

"Take her to the town hall." He had to shout over her protests, but the one holding her readily obeyed.

Then more shadows emerged from the de Colville house. The first was someone Julitte had never seen before. Somewhat taller than herself, thin and dark, shabbily dressed. No shoes.

Her heart swirled in confusion. The next shadow was short— one she wasn't sure she welcomed: the little man called Pepin. Surely if he . . . ?

And there he was, hands atop his head like the others before him. Charles. Tall, strong, only the slightest hint of a beard's shadow growing on his face.

Alive.

But captive.

37

Julitte watched the Hauptmann walk dispassionately along the street despite the growing heat from the flames behind them. The rain did what the soldiers could not, containing the fire to just one of the connected de Colville houses. They kept their torches from the outer wall, feeding the flames with the contents of Claudette's home. In spite of their efforts, the roof of both the bakery and Claudette's house remained intact, even when the walls beneath went alight.

The Hauptmann stared at the downcast faces of the villagers. All still refused to look at him except Julitte. The only face he did not study was Ori's, who stood off to the side, behind the others, just within Julitte's line of vision.

The Hauptmann paced along the line. "Him." He pointed to Gustave de Colville. "And him." Uncle Guy.

Then he came to Benoit, one of the youngest in their village, a de Colville.

"You live in the house where we found the men. Who are your parents?"

"My father is off to war."

"And your mother?"

The boy hung his head, hands behind his back.

The Hauptmann laughed. "So you'll protect her, will you?" He patted the boy's head. "Good boy."

No sooner had the compliment been paid than the Hauptmann grabbed a handful of Benoit's hair, which was far too long for a boy his age. Benoit cried out when he was dragged down the way.

"Who will claim this boy? If no one stands forward, I will have him shot in your place."

Uncle Guy, having been marched only a few paces away, stopped short despite the gun at his back. "He's my grandson. His mother is dead."

Julitte wanted to shake her head but stayed as still as everyone else who heard the lie. A Toussaint . . . protecting a de Colville?

Hauptmann Basedow stepped closer to Uncle Guy until they stood face-to-face. "You work in the bakery. I've not seen this boy there. I think you are lying."

"He's done nothing—"

But Uncle Guy did not finish his statement, could not. Before another word was uttered, the Hauptmann turned and drew his pistol. With the handle turned round, he struck the side of Uncle Guy's head. The older man went down, bright red blood staining the pure white of his hair. He lay unmoving even as Julitte tried to wrench free but was held fast in place yet again.

She stared, willing her uncle to move, to show some sign of life. But he did not.

Yet there was no light, no glimpse into heaven the way Julitte had seen in the past. Because he still lived? She couldn't tell any more, since she'd seen no light when Didi entered heaven. Perhaps she could no longer tell.

"Come now, who will claim this boy?" The Hauptmann resumed his unhurried pace, his voice as calm and friendly as if he were the referee calling a village tournament to continue. He grabbed the boy again, and with his pistol still in his hand, the Hauptmann appeared deadlier than ever. "Who will allow him to be shot in your place?"

"No! He is mine!"

Marie-Hermine de Colville fell from the lines and clutched her son to her, crying, smoothing his hair where the Hauptmann had released his grip at last.

"Take her," the Hauptmann ordered. "Leave the boy."

Marie-Hermine was led away, following the others who'd been taken to the town hall. They stepped around Uncle Guy, who'd been left alone by the soldier nearby. He lay there, as still as death.

Two steps from Julitte, Hauptmann Basedow stopped. He studied her and she knew she should look away, bow her head, cast her gaze to the ground as the others had. But she did not. She looked in the face of evil and wondered how God could love even him.

"And her."

Julitte had seen the basement of the town hall only once in her life, when she was fourteen years old. She'd followed Narcisse there secretly, when he went to claim one of the sailors he brought home. The young man had been wild and handsome and nothing at all like Narcisse, and she'd wondered why her father had invited him home at all. He'd brought with him a drink surely as strong as anything the de Colvilles had brewed, and the more he drank the louder he became, until he'd gotten into a fight with a de Colville and the mayor had ordered him locked up for the night.

But in the morning, when Narcisse had come for him, Julitte listened as he asked to pray for him and then gave him counsel. He'd spoken of God's love and healing, of forgiveness and mercy, of the gifts God had given him to be a good sailor and that he would find another woman. But when Narcisse's prayer ended, all the man had said was that he would go back to sea. Julitte had never seen him again, had never even thought of him until this moment.

There were two iron cells in the basement, and she was thrust into one already holding Claudette and Marie-Hermine. She'd barely tumbled inside the bars before her gaze sought the other cell across from them, where the men had been placed. Charles was there, gripping two bars and watching her silently.

I'm sorry, she wanted to say, but she feared speaking at all, especially in front of the soldiers who lingered. If she'd gone with Charles when he'd asked, they would be free right now. She told herself to look away, to deny herself the luxury of seeing his face, even now, even here. She should give in to her shame and turn away but couldn't. She mirrored his stance, gripping the cell confines and staring at him across the bars and aisle that separated them.

It seemed none of them wanted to talk, other than the Germans, who spoke freely, laughing at something one of them said, holding their guns so comfortably it was obvious they knew how to use them. Claudette and Marie-Hermine cowered together in the corner, crying gently. Gustave de Colville, Pepin, and the other man stood behind Charles, all solemn, stiff. Silent.

Eventually the soldiers dwindled in number, so that only two guards remained, one at either end of the cellar. They occasionally called back and forth to each other, and Julitte understood a word now and then. They spoke of the two soldiers with torches, laughing over the trouble they had carrying out their orders to set the bakery afire.

Hours went by without a word uttered but for the two Germans, who eventually grew quiet as well. Julitte watched Charles, having longed so many months for him. But not like this.

The astonishment of the morning soon wore off, and in its place the grim truth took hold. Seeing the innocent deported to Germany had taught Julitte that German justice was as far from mercy as the east was from the west. Slowly, deep within Julitte's stomach, the nausea began. Everyone knew the sentence assigned to stragglers. She'd heard rumors early in the war of those apprehended being sent to Germany as prisoners of war.

But then there had been the later ones. There were plenty of rumors about the German punishment for any Allied soldiers caught behind the lines.

Death.

Julitte had never known such fear, so strong that for the first time in her life her faith seemed a pale answer.

"What are you going to do, Julitte?"

For a moment Julitte wondered from where the question had come. Was God speaking audibly to her now, verbalizing the one question she knew she was asking but shouldn't? What was *she* going to do? She should ask only what God would do, since surely her life, and especially Charles's, was in His hands. If she couldn't trust God now, then her faith meant nothing.

But Claudette was behind her, looking as if she'd just spoken.

"Did you speak to me?"

It wasn't the question of a Toussaint to a de Colville. It was from one prisoner to another.

Claudette's face had long since dried of tears, but her eyes, so wide and dark, were full of the fear that reflected Julitte's. "You'll do something, won't you?"

Now Marie-Hermine neared as well, as if catching whatever vision Claudette suffered. "Yes. You being here with us is a sign. That God hasn't abandoned us. What will you do?"

Julitte shook her head, raised both palms. "I can do nothing! I'm a prisoner just like you."

"But . . . you saved Pierre. We haven't forgotten. You brought him back to life."

Claudette took yet another step closer. "And you knew Victor was dead even before the *curé*. His wife said you saw heaven; she knew it from the look on your face. You'll save us, won't you?"

Julitte pressed away from them but the bars held her in place. "I did nothing," she whispered. "God saved Pierre, not me."

Marie-Hermine stepped closer than Claudette, laying a hand on

Julitte's arm. "When you pray, God listens. Now is the time for you to ask for another miracle. For us. For yourself."

Julitte shook her head. Had she not this very moment known what a failure she was, that she'd let her fear grow larger than her faith? How could anyone believe her prayers were any different?

"He listens when you pray, too." She could barely hear her own breathless words. "I'm not any different!"

"You are, Julitte." Gustave de Colville's voice rang out from the other side of the aisle, and she wondered how he'd heard her. "You must pray for us all now. And save us."

"I can do nothing!" She turned and grabbed the bars again, her fear mixed with anger. "It isn't me; it was never me."

"God chose to use you; that is enough."

His words were calm but did nothing to soothe Julitte. She looked at Charles again, who said nothing, but his frown had deepened. Because he knew the foolishness of their request or because of her refusal?

One of the Germans walked the aisle, strumming the butt of his rifle along the bars before Julitte. *"Klappe halten. . . . Kein Wort!"* His face, hard and angry, left little doubt as to the command for quiet. *"Keine Unterhaltung."*

There was a single bench in each cell, no cots, not even a blanket. She took a seat with the others on the bench against the cement wall, but all she could see was the others, staring back at her. It wasn't just Charles who looked at her now; the others watched her as well.

I can do nothing, Lord, she cried inside. *Only You. Show them, Lord. Not me, but You. Help us!*

Then, gaze downcast, her prayer deepened. *Help me to trust You, even to death. My death . . . or Charles's or both.*

Exhaustion weighted Julitte's body. She'd learned in her vigil over Didi how to sleep on a chair and this bench was little different. Sleep, just now, would be a heady escape, away from those who looked to her for something she couldn't possibly give.

But sleep did not come.

Charles could not take his eyes from Julitte, no matter how harshly he judged himself over her. He'd failed her. He'd come here with one mission: to get her out. He shouldn't have allowed her to stay, not one more night. And yet he had.

And failed her.

He'd already asked forgiveness of God and felt no condemnation there. Nor did he feel such from Julitte herself. He'd seen her whisper she was sorry as clearly as if she'd said it aloud, but that made no sense. Didn't she see it was his duty to get her to freedom, and it was he who failed?

Not even Pepin shot him a gaze of condemnation. Charles hadn't blamed the man for wanting to travel in number. He'd been that way since the day Charles had met him.

Nor did the de Colville and the man they'd hidden seem to blame him. He wondered how long it would be before they realized the same thing Charles had: if it hadn't been for his return, perhaps none of this would have happened. Instead the de Colville seemed as eager to believe in salvation through Julitte as the man's family members across the way.

But lack of condemnation from the others didn't help his guilt.

No one spoke, except for the two Germans on either end of the cellblock. Charles was left to his thoughts, which he raised to heaven in prayer. To his own amazement it was his failure that bothered him most, not the possibility of his impending death. Failure to bring Julitte to safety, to help the Allied cause gain the good graces of someone in the circle of the king of Greece. He'd be a hero to neither Julitte nor the Allies.

Such a thought left him at the mercy of his own condemnation, contrasting what he'd expected and what had become reality. So stark a difference. Pride again, his constant enemy, more intimate to him than the Germans because they weren't inside his heart.

Some time later the clank of boots sounded on the stairs to the cellar, followed by German voices and the rattle of guns held ready by the soldiers accompanying them.

Three soldiers stood before them, all with their spiked helmets in place, uniforms crisp, collars laced with the insignia that went with officers. Boots polished and spotless, even so close to the front. A Leutnant and another beside him, with one pip of an *Oberleutnant*. And the Hauptmann.

"So your secrets have come to an end. An end of secrets, the beginning of a trial. Tomorrow."

The Hauptmann spoke in competent but awkward French, and what his tone lacked in lilt he made up for in rigid volume.

"My Oberleutnant will represent all of you for your defense. All as one." He faced the cell holding Charles and the other men. "It is my understanding two of you are Allied soldiers." The Hauptmann's gaze lingered on Charles. "And one of you a spy."

"That is not true." Charles stood and met the man from the other side of the bars.

"It cannot matter." The Oberleutnant's French was more halting than the Hauptmann's. "You are guilty. Enemies behind the line long after the deadline by which you should have turned yourselves in."

Charles aimed his gaze at the shorter of the two men, who even with the spike on his helmet barely reached Charles's shoulder. "And you are to *defend* us? How?"

"The truth is your only friend."

"Truth? Whose?"

The man bowed and offered a confident smile. "The only one that matters, of course. German truth."

Charles looked past the soldier to Julitte on the other side. She looked every bit as sullen as Charles felt. She must have understood enough to know what Charles knew: a German defense was no defense at all.

38

The night passed slowly. Julitte listened to Claudette and Marie-Hermine softly cry, holding one another, and for a moment she wished she could join them, cling to them, feel the humanness of someone beside her. More than that she wished she could reach Charles, if only to clutch his hand, touch his face. But he was too far.

Eventually her cellmates' tears faded; they might have slept, but Julitte doubted that. Even she, as tired as she was, found sleep too elusive. And so she continued to pray.

A window, high on the wall at ground level, had been opened by one of the soldiers, and birds announced the sun before it even appeared. The harsh yak of the magpies overpowered the high-pitched *b-r-r-r-r* of the warbler. And still, in the distance, the boom of cannonfire sounded, ever present and constant—louder, if that was possible, but perhaps it was just the beat of Julitte's heart.

They were each allowed use of the lavatory, marched outside one by one from the cells under the sights of a rifle. Julitte had been marched before at gunpoint, with others off to work, but would never get used to a gun pointed at her so personally; she closed the door eagerly against it.

It must have been hours later when Julitte and the other two women were led up the stairs inside the town hall first, to a room offering a row of long tables at the head, with a dozen chairs facing it. Whatever adornments the room might have known were gone; the walls, once painted a light shade of gold, were dull, leaving only squares of dust where paintings must once have hung. There was no need for the oil lamps to be lit on the long, barren tables; the sun shone through the tall, unveiled windows, lower halves opened wide to catch the breeze of summer on this last day of June. A day like this, with birds and sun and breeze, was a day to celebrate creation, except for the bombardment off in the distance.

Then she saw Eloi, the mayor, and Léon, the *garde champêtre*, both in the corner, both bound at the wrist and guarded by a pair of German soldiers. She'd nearly forgotten they, too, had been the "guests" of the German military off and on since the Germans had first marched in. Ori had told her they'd been housed in one of the upstairs rooms and for the most part had been comfortable, as she'd put it. From their position so far from the front of the room, it seemed they were no more than witnesses today.

Julitte followed Claudette and Marie-Hermine, while a German soldier pointed to the row of chairs facing a judge's bench of sorts, the long table set up opposite the row of wooden chairs upon which the prisoners were to sit.

In the center of the makeshift judge's bench sat a man in the dark robe of a judge, someone Julitte had never seen before. He was a large man who seemed to be well fed considering the times. He looked as if someone had blown air through his ear to puff out his cheeks, making the collar pinch into the skin beneath his round, fair face. Instead of looking at her or any of the other prisoners, he studied papers before him.

Julitte's heart had settled in her hollow stomach. How was it that she could walk, breathe, function, amid such fear? She looked at the women beside her, then shifted enough to see Charles down the way. She had no doubt they all shared some measure of fear, and yet here they were, their feet still holding them, their legs still strong enough to support them before what might well be the stiffest of punishments.

Then soldiers marched in with all the pomp of any ceremony; swords bounced light from the window and their boots echoed off the floorboards. A single command gave direction to make way for those they escorted: the Hauptmann and his officers and, on the other side, the Orstkommandant, who was no more than a figure-head beside Basedow. They took seats to the left of the row in which Julitte and the others sat, and she could only stare at the men who held their lives in their hands.

With little fanfare and without prelude or introduction, the Hauptmann stood. He didn't bother with his clumsy French. Though he spoke only to the Germans in their now-familiar lan-guage, his gaze landed one by one on those beside Julitte and at last upon her. Whatever he said was not likely to be benevolent, but Julitte knew one thing: it was truth. German truth, anyway.

And though her heart continued to beat, her lungs to take air in and then out, some of her senses seemed to fail. She stopped registering what she heard immediately around her. She no lon-ger attended to the German words that came too fast to decipher. Instead she listened for the birds again, just outside in the tree that grew not so far from the confines of the building. And her nose sensed a faint trace of lemon wax—had Ori once cleaned this room? Then Julitte smelled the outside, not the hint of distant gunpowder floating on the breeze but the grass that someone must be cutting even now, because it was sharp and fresh.

Her gaze refused to dwell on the soldiers who decided her fate and the others', though they had no God-given right to do so. She imagined instead the ocean Narcisse had taught her to love, the wheat fields her brother had worked and which her mother had taught her to pray over. The red poppies of spring to the golden harvests of fall. And she thought of Charles when he smiled at her as if no one but her existed.

God granted her peace.

Charles listened to the trial that had no right to be called such a thing. The Hauptmann himself laid out their crimes—beginning with the clothing they wore, from the remnants of a French uniform on Pepin and the man from the de Colville cellar to the Indian leather boots Charles wore, strikingly similar to those used by the British army. Which was, of course, untrue. Major Parker had gone to great lengths to procure for Charles black ankle boots of German issue rather than English. If the Hauptmann fooled the others, it could only be due to the fine condition of the boots, something Charles had worried about when guessing anyone caught behind the blockade would likely have trouble finding shoes in good shape. But he'd worried more about the jump from the airplane and accepted the sturdy boots anyway. Blast his worries.

The Hauptmann reported more ridiculously bloated suspicions that couldn't possibly be proven, of sending carrier pigeons over the line with secret information about troop movements, train routes, even information about casualties and supplies. If any of them had been able to do even a portion of what they were accused of, they could all die heroes.

When at last their "defender" took the floor, he wasted no time on formalities. "Guilty?" He spoke with the expected lack of zeal. "Surely so. Our orders for all enemy combatants caught behind the line to turn themselves in was blatantly ignored. Yet you can hardly blame them for trying to aid their losing countrymen. I beg pity of the court, since each of them cannot help what they are. Send them to Germany, where their hands can be put to good use."

No questions followed, from either the accusors or the judge himself.

The unnamed, silent judge took up the pen that rested on the table before him. He wrote on the tablet nearby, tearing off one sheet, scribbling again, tearing off another. A Leutnant who had arrived with the other officers approached the table, standing at attention until the judge handed the stack of papers to him. He clicked his heels and turned to the row of defendants, holding the papers before him. Then, still standing at attention, he waited.

Charles looked down the row; the number of papers in that stack matched the number of those who suffered under this farce of a trial. Their verdicts, perhaps even their sentences.

The Leutnant seemed to be awaiting orders, but rather than utter them, the judge's gaze fell on each of the defendants. Charles sat numb, wishing he might at least have been able to sit beside Julitte so he could hold her hand and gain some comfort. But he dared not even look at her, knowing whatever sentence they received would feel all the harsher because of his failure to protect her.

No sooner had the judge commanded them to stand than a commotion sounded behind them. Charles, along with everyone else whose back was to the door, turned to see what caused the disruption.

A man boasting the two pips of a Hauptmann on his shoulder boards strode past the soldiers standing guard at the door. He marched forward, scanning the room, and rather than going to the presiding judge, he stopped before the Hauptmann who'd prosecuted the case.

"Back so soon, Christophe?" the seated Hauptmann asked before the one standing in front of him could speak.

"Evidently not soon enough. What have you here?"

"Exactly what it looks like. A trial."

The Hauptmann named Christophe sent a glance from the man

opposite him to the judge—a disparaging look, confirming what Charles suspected. This was more of a sham than it appeared. "So I was told by half the villagers outside. But with him as the judge? He's barely a lawyer."

"I expect the villagers want news," said the Hauptmann. "We were just about to read the verdict and sentencing, if you'd like to stay."

"A word with you in private first?"

"*Nein.*" He turned to the Leutnant. "Proceed."

"Erich, this is not the time—"

"Step aside, Christophe," the Hauptmann said. "And then you may have your word with me."

"My news is more urgent than you—"

The Hauptmann sprang to his feet. "We have spies in our midst. Wait with your news."

Then he eyed the Leutnant again, who still held the papers. The Leutnant approached the women on the other end of the row, where he stopped, standing at attention again. Waiting again.

Charles watched, his gaze snapping between the Leutnant and this newly arrived Hautpmann, whose eye sockets nearly doubled when his gaze fell on one of them—Julitte. Recognition?

Was this the Hauptmann, then, who had received Julitte's gratitude for saving her from the drunken Leutnant?

"There must be some mistake," he said, going to the Leutnant with outstretched hand, as if to take the verdicts away. When the soldier held the papers closer, refusing to hand them over, Christophe turned again to the other Hauptmann, continuing to ignore the one in judge's robe, who remained docile and quiet despite the interruption. "I beg a word now, Erich. Before these verdicts can be read."

No impact but a lofty smile. "I say again, Christophe, *nein*. And if you speak again—" these words spoken minus the man's smile—

"I will have you reported to the Generalmajor before these sentences are even carried out."

Rather than argue, Christophe's gaze fell back on Julitte, who looked at him with deflating hope. He stepped aside, one hand on his sword.

The Leutnant raised the papers in his hands, those sheets that contained the future of each person sitting before this mockery of a trial. He folded them to his chest and stood stiffly by, as if waiting for further orders. The Hauptmann in control nodded to the judge, then took his seat, while the officer who knew Julitte took a seat off to the side.

The judge, or the lawyer acting as a judge, cleared his throat and glanced at the Hauptmann before proceeding. "Each of you here today is charged with crimes against the German Imperial Army. Because of your guilt, you will be punished accordingly. But your town, for their silence and compliance, will not be spared. It is hereby declared that a fine of ten thousand Marks must be paid as penalty for what this town has done. So that you will know you are not alone in the punishment."

Charles knew such a fine must be in theory only, since he was sure the village would not be able to pay. The Germans had already taken everything.

The judge looked again as if for direction and the Hauptmann nodded, setting off a nod from the judge toward the Leutnant, who faced Marie-Hermine once again. He did not even speak her name; perhaps he didn't know it.

"You, as an enemy of the German Imperial Army during this time of strife, are found guilty of aiding and abetting an enemy combatant. For such crime you will be sent to Germany, assigned to a labor camp for not less than fifteen years."

He clicked his heels, bowed slightly, then moved on to Claudette, who stared up at him with wide, dark eyes even as Marie-Hermine clung to her. His words were a repetition of those he used for her mother.

Then he came to Julitte. What had Charles expected? What had any of them expected? That between God and this new Hauptmann who came charging in, she, at least, would be spared?

But he repeated the verdict, repeated the sentence.

Fifteen years.

Not death. That, at least, was something. But fifteen years . . . the same years in which he'd envisioned her being his wife, perhaps carrying his child, traveling between Belgium and America, Greece and France. . . . The best years of her life and of his.

God, O God, how can this be? Must my inadequacies make her suffer?

Gustave de Colville was the first of the men to be pronounced guilty. His sentence: identical to the women. Fifteen years of labor in Germany. Still, he'd been spared a death sentence, and that brought some comfort, though such an assignment might mean death just the same for someone of Gustave's age.

Pepin was the first of the men viewed as enemy combatants to have the Leutnant stand before him. Charles eyed him; Pepin did not look up, either at his compatriots or at the soldier before him. He stared straight ahead, as if blind.

Charles closed his eyes in prayer. *Fifteen years, Lord, or even twenty, twenty-five . . . Let it be years of life, and not—*

The Leutnant went through the charges of being an enemy soldier, of being a spy, of being in contact with the enemy, of intentionally staying behind this side of the battle line in order to do harm to members of the German Imperial Army.

"Your sentence . . ."

Charles, along with Pepin he was sure, could not breathe.

"*Tod durch das Executionskommando.* Death by firing squad, to be carried out twenty-four hours hence."

The one word that mattered more than any other: *Tod*. Death. A cry came from the other end of the row, from Julitte, he was sure, though she didn't know Pepin. But she must know what a different sentence meant. Words that had nothing to do with work camps or Germany but with death. And so it was, one by one, until he came to Charles, the verdict pronounced, the death sentence proclaimed.

Death by firing squad for the three of them. Within twenty-four hours.

Hadn't he once consoled Julitte that if he didn't make it beyond the occupied territory, if he died fighting for his freedom or that of another, he would wait at the gates of heaven to greet her, where they would spend eternity together?

Yes, such words should console him. He knew she believed them too. But to be cut off from the hopes and the dreams he'd had since knowing her . . . even heaven seemed little consolation.

His insides went dull and heavy, and Charles knew he wouldn't be able to walk because he couldn't lift his feet. But he was not required to move forward yet. Instead, he watched the Hauptmann, the one called Christophe, step briskly forward.

"This sentence is not final," the man said, not to the judge or any German because he spoke in English. He addressed the defendants, specifically Julitte. "There is a *real* military council at Saint-Quentin. Each trial held in this province must be approved. They will review—"

"I will have that word with you now, Christophe," the other Hauptmann said in German.

But Christophe did not approach him. He turned, standing stiffly in attendance. "*Nein*, Erich. I will go to Saint-Quentin myself, with news of what you've done. For their sake as well as yours."

Then he saluted once and strode from the room.

39

Whatever peace Julitte had been given during the trial abandoned her the moment Charles's sentence was pronounced. Nor was it to be found in the confines of her cell. The rest of the morning came and went in silence, then the afternoon and evening. All without a hint of any peace, in her nor on the face of anyone in this cell or the one opposite. Maybe Julitte would never know peace again. How could she, without Charles? Even now, her spirit railed in anger. God, Sovereign, Creator, Almighty, had abandoned her.

How could she not have realized it, even before the trial? She'd been at Didi's side when she died, Didi whom Julitte had loved. But at the moment when Didi's spirit separated from her body, had Julitte been given even the slimmest glimpse into Didi's path to heaven? When Julitte had seen the paths of others—Victor, whom she'd liked well enough but had never loved? Yves, another who had never known her love the way she'd loved Didi?

When had God removed His blessing from her? And why?

Words of Job's wife came to mind, temptingly so, in Julitte's anger. *"Curse God and die,"* the woman had said so bitterly to her husband.

And yet if he had, he would have missed the truth: that God had many more blessings in store for him if only he made it through the test.

"I cannot do it," she whimpered, knowing she would fail the test of letting Charles go. *To a firing squad, Lord? And why? Because of me!* No, this was one test she could not pass. "I cannot."

"You must," came the whisper. It was Marie-Hermine, huddled nearby. No one slept, this the second night in the cell. And squander these last moments outside a work camp for some, these last moments of life for the rest? "Do you struggle with what God wants of you? You must do whatever He asks—to free us!"

Julitte wanted to scream, to lunge at the other woman in anger and frustration. She wanted her to know—wanted everyone to know—she was no different, her faith no different, and that she, like everyone, had failed God more than once in her life.

But she did nothing. Yes, she'd failed. But the cross . . . The image played in her mind, reminding her it made no sense for God to remove His blessing because of something she'd done or not done. The price for her mistakes had already been paid.

Then why? Why had God removed His blessing?

Even now, Marie-Hermine would not quiet herself. She pressed words into Julitte's ears, telling her God would save them because of Julitte, if only she would ask Him, if she would do as He told her to do.

The guard hovering in the dark corner called for quiet, pointing at a watch hooked around his wrist as if to remind them of the late hour.

"Let her keep praying," said Marie-Hermine, low.

"Yes," Gustave called across the way. "What will they do, give us another trial? Pray so we can hear you."

Surely they did not want to hear her prayers, so full of confusion and anger and fear. Never in her life had she refused to pray with someone. But now, de Colvilles asked and she must let them down. Better to refuse than to be a hypocrite and pray words she could not share and still claim to be a loving follower of God.

And yet words came to mind, verses she loved most, Jesus' words when He began His ministry, about those who were blessed, about faith that pleased God, about suffering and grace and God's strength. Words of psalms that spoke of God's wonders and power, of His worthiness to be praised. They came from her mouth as if independent of her faltering spirit and rebellious mind. Her heart, at least, was obedient.

At last she asked Claudette and Marie-Hermine to pray with her and she taught them the words from psalms.

"'For who is God save the Lord? or who is a rock save our God? It is God that girdeth me with strength, and maketh my way perfect.'" And then, "'They go from strength to strength, every one of them in Zion appeareth before God.'"

Soon the men joined in as Julitte spoke a phrase and the others echoed, Charles's voice among them, so deep and comforting. "'Hear me, O Lord; for thy lovingkindness is good. . . . Turn unto me according to the multitude of thy tender mercies. . . . And hide not thy face from thy servant; . . . for I am in trouble: hear me speedily. . . . Draw nigh unto my soul, and redeem it. . . . Deliver me because of mine enemies.'"

As she went on leading them, words from psalms she hadn't recalled memorizing came to her with ease. "'Make haste, O God, to deliver me; make haste to help me, O Lord . . . Deliver me.'"

As the night went on, she half expected the German guard to call for quiet. Surely if he understood half of the words—prayers to deliver them from their enemies—he'd have done so. But the hours went on and their prayers did too. When her voice tired, someone else took the lead, each in their turn, each resting, then praying, then praying together again.

Clatter on the stairs brought the guards to their feet, stopping the procession of prayer. It was late, no doubt past midnight, but not nearly dawn yet. A change of guards? One who would stop even their prayers?

An exchange of salutes; the oil lamp turned up. Everyone stood—the three women in one cell and the four men in the other.

With the wick turned higher, the flicker of light spilled onto the new arrival's face. Hauptmann Christophe Brecht. Julitte jumped toward the bars holding her in, her heart batting with hope.

He met her at the bars, but the look upon his illumined face cautioned her. His eyes were wider than usual but somber, his lips taut.

"I'm sorry. A . . . wrong . . . A tragedy of *Gerechtigkeit* . . . of justice." His English seemed more uncertain than ever. Then he grabbed one of the bars as if to steady himself, breathing once deeply. "I waited the afternoon for the military council but would not be heard. So I chased them—on the way from the door. For nothing! Something is happening—I cannot tell what—but I fear this war will swallow every injustice. Including this."

Julitte leaned in on the iron so her cheeks touched the cold bars near his hand between them. "But to be shot! They did nothing, nothing at all to deserve such a punishment. They must not be shot!"

Hauptmann Brecht was already shaking his head, withdrawing. "I can do nothing. The council refused to take the time."

"But such an injustice can't be undone when the war ends and reason returns—"

The Hauptmann stiffened to a familiar soldier's stance. "I will appeal your sentences again." Then he slumped forward and grabbed the bars yet again. "I will beg your years of servitude be shortened."

"But, Christophe! That does nothing for the others."

He stepped back once more, turned on his heel, and saluted the men in the cell opposite. "My apologies."

"Christophe!" Julitte shouted after him, but he didn't turn back.

Julitte sank to the floor, sobs wracking her shoulders. Had her prayers made her hope, after all, that God hadn't abandoned her?

But He had.

40

Soon it would be dawn. This, the first day of July, the last day of life for Charles. The thought threatened to banish whatever prayers had kept such images from Julitte's mind through the darkest hours of the night.

A new guard arrived before even a hint of light reached the window, a soldier Julitte had not seen before. With one hand he held a shining lamp; with the other he strummed his rifle along the bars of the cell holding the women. But he looked at the men. His lips curled into a smile that oddly matched the cruelty in his eyes.

"Do you sleep away the last hours of your lives?" His French, flawless. He laughed and lit another lamp. "If you listen hard enough, in between the cannonfire you will hear the sound of a saw. It is wood they cut. For your coffins."

Julitte's gaze found Charles, who stood at the sound of the soldier's arrival but did not approach the bars. She saw placid compliance on his face. Did he really accept his coming death? Could he stand before her and trust that he would wait for her in heaven, the way he'd once told her he might?

A call from the top of the stairs sent the soldiers scrambling in response, even the one who'd kept watch through the night. They trounced up, boots clattering all the way, leaving them without a guard at all.

"Getting the firing squad together, no doubt," said the man Julitte didn't know, the one who'd been hidden by the de Colvilles. Suddenly she wanted to know his name, since he was about to die. She wanted to know at whose side Charles's body would fall.

"Who are you?" she asked.

He bowed as if he hadn't a care in the world. "Maréchal La Mare. A deserter of the French army." He grinned. "If only the Germans knew, they would have thanked me for my lack of patriotism these past two years."

Gustave de Colville turned to the man. "A deserter? But you told us you were caught behind the lines, separated from your unit while fighting."

He bowed again. "A confession, even a deathbed confession, surely might help get me into heaven, do you not think so?"

Gustave turned to Pepin and Charles. "And you? You?"

"Pepin was a soldier, you can see from his uniform," Charles said. "And I . . . was on my way to become one."

"Come now," said Maréchal, "no confessions from either of you? I alone will die today with a cleared conscience?"

"I was a soldier," Pepin insisted. "My horse died beneath me!"

"I can vouch for him," Charles said. "We met not long after the Germans came through. He smelled of gunpowder from battle."

"Ah, so we have one hero among us, anyway, who will be shot for what the Germans call truth. What about you? They made something of your boots during the trial. Are you a spy?"

Julitte watched Charles's face go grim. "If it's truth you want, I'm not at all sure I would have made it into the army. I am not a soldier."

"But you came back," Pepin said. "After you were free."

"What is this he says?" Gustave asked. "You were free?"

Charles turned from them. "It doesn't matter now."

"But it does, if you want to be remembered."

Charles did not look at Gustave; instead his gaze returned to Julitte, who held it steady.

"He came back to bring me to safety," she told them because he would not. "So he is a hero."

Charles shook his head, turning away even from her.

Silence followed. Gustave found a seat on the bench. Pepin paced. Maréchal put two hands on the bars, staring ahead. Charles leaned along the side bars. Waiting.

He did not meet Julitte's gaze.

So this was it? The end of his life?

Charles regretted how many years he'd squandered, knowing his new goals would be left unmet. He could have used his resources for good, made a difference. Perhaps. If he'd lived, at least he would have done what he could to help end this war. God knew his help would have been puny in comparison to the need, but might his effort—if only he'd been successful—have been something?

He stole a quick glance at Julitte. Bringing her to safety so the king of Greece might change his mind and join with the Allies wouldn't have been puny.

God, O God . . .

Words failed him, even after hours of prayer. He wished he knew the Bible the way Julitte did. Her prayers earlier were ones that had been echoed in heaven for centuries. He wished he'd been given more time to learn, to grow, to prove this change the Creator God had begun in him not so long ago. This renewal that had come through His Son . . . and Julitte.

He didn't want to die a failure, but there was nothing he could do to change that now. Perhaps Christophe, the Hauptmann, would be

Julitte's hero, after all, if he could rescue her from the sentence she'd been given. At least then he would have earned her gratitude.

"Did they push back the time to torture us through the morning?" Pepin asked awhile later, his tone high, agitated. He never broke his pace. "Well, it is working! I would rather get this over with than dwell on it any longer."

Maréchal laughed. "Breathe in, then out, my friend. It is life, while we have it."

"How can you speak so casually?" Gustave said from the bench. "Aren't you afraid to die?"

Maréchal turned to face Gustave. "No. I am afraid only that the bullet will not hit me in the right spot, and I will die slowly. That is all."

Charles looked again at the window. He'd had a wristwatch, but one of the guards had taken it from him soon after he'd been shoved into the cell. With a grim sort of satisfaction he realized he still had his belt and would no doubt be buried with the evidence that he really was a spy, there to take others out to safety.

Still, he guessed the sun had risen more than a half hour ago. An execution within twenty-four hours of the trial meant it would have to be sometime this morning. Surely the German army would be late for nothing.

He couldn't help but agree with both Pepin and Maréchal: if heaven awaited—and he couldn't doubt it, especially now—then waiting was surely harder than being dead. But the process of dying? Maréchal had a point.

Still, he wished they would keep their thoughts to themselves. He wanted to keep his mind on what awaited him—an eternity with his Creator—not on the present circumstances.

A scuffle at the stairs drew everyone, including Charles, to face that way. He stole a quick glance at Julitte, who stopped not at the far end of the opposite cell, closest to the stairs but to this side, where she could best see him. He nodded once her way, conjuring a solemn smile. It was all he could do just now, about to be led to a firing squad.

But it wasn't the stomp of German boots on those stairs. It was the rattle of clogs and the whisper of leather softened by wear.

Benoit de Colville reached them first, throwing himself at the bars, skinny arms stretching through to his mother. "Mama!"

They clutched each other through the bars. A moment later another man reached the bottom of the stairs, obviously a villager, and behind him was none other than Dowan, who'd been hidden every bit as long as Pepin had before these last few days.

Confusion set in at the sight of him. What was this? A moment of pity to let their loved ones see them before they were marched off to carry out the sentences? But who had they claimed Dowan to be? How was it he walked the street just now to get here?

"What is it?" Charles demanded. "What's happened?"

"There's no time; we must hurry." Dowan ran from one end of the cellar to the other, as if looking for something. He searched high and low but kept shaking his head, hands empty. "I don't know how much time we have, and I see no key. Grab those benches."

He thrust one at the other man who'd arrived with him.

"But what's happened?" Charles demanded.

"They're gone—all of them. Every single German. We saw them march out—didn't leave a single one behind. The villagers searched, but not one soldier is to be found, even here in the town hall. I am free and so, very soon, are you."

"What?" Gustave de Colville's eyes rounded, and Charles watched his gaze travel from Dowan to Julitte, but he said nothing.

Nor did Charles. If they were gone, who knew for how long?

"Maybe it's the end of the war!" Pepin said. "Maybe they're turning tail and running back home."

Charles didn't take time to contemplate such a heady thought, although he could scarcely believe such a thing. From what he'd heard when he was with the Allied officers, they'd have counted themselves fortunate to add Greece to their numbers. That hardly made sense if the Allies had been on the verge of winning.

Charles grabbed the bench in his cell and, like the two on the other side, started battering the bars, to bend them out of the way in hopes of slipping out. If the shellfire pelting the village made this building quake, bludgeoning the bars sent waves to meet those rumbling from cannonfire.

Life itself was on the other side.

"This will take too long!" Dowan yelled. "We need that key."

"Here! I have it here!"

Julitte, who'd tried with little success at Claudette's side to maul the bars with the bench that had been in their cell, looked with wonder at the new voice amid more clatter on the wooden steps.

Ori.

Behind her was Eloi, the mayor.

"The men first!" Julitte called when Ori came to Julitte's cell with key at the ready.

"There is time," Ori said at the lock on Julitte's cell. "The Germans have been called to the front—every last one of them. Even the Orstkommandant was called to the mending station. You can hear the barrage. It's worse than ever."

"All of the soldiers have been called to fight?"

Ori nodded and Julitte saw the worry flicker over her face, but before another moment passed, she swung the door wide. Claudette and Marie-Hermine rushed out, each to the arms of those who waited.

Julitte raced to the cell opposite, pulling Ori along. "Free them!"

"Maybe it really is the end of the war," Gustave said on the other side of the lock. "We've all heard the guns—closer and louder than ever."

"But who knows who will win?" Pepin said.

Then their door, too, was open, and Gustave was the first out, Pepin behind him.

Julitte staggered into Charles's arms, overcome with relief. "God be praised!"

She barely knew the words had come from her own mouth, but suddenly, from behind her, Marie-Hermine de Colville put a hand on her shoulder.

"You saved us, Julitte. We are in your debt." Then Marie-Hermine pulled Claudette closer, pushing her at Julitte. "You must thank her too, Claudette."

Julitte could see a private war raging behind Claudette's eyes, but before she could obey the older woman's command, Julitte shook her head. "No! No—it was God alone. Not me."

Marie-Hermine laughed. "Who but God could make every German disappear? But it was because of you."

"No—"

Claudette pulled her arm from her mother's grip, still staring at Julitte. "I thought we've hated each other too long to forget, but my mother is right. I don't believe we would be free right now if it weren't for your faith."

Julitte couldn't refuse their gratitude, however misplaced. She was sure of only one thing: a feud so lasting could be resumed far more easily than it could be laid aside.

"It doesn't matter now," Charles said. "We must be out of here—all of us. If the Germans return, they'll carry out their sentences."

"Wait!"

It was Gustave, nearest the stairs, but his eye was aimed where the soldiers had been posted.

They'd left behind their uneaten breakfasts. Bread, more than Julitte had seen on one small table in many months. Two hefty loaves.

Gustave took the bread, then followed them out of the town hall.

The town was in chaos, the sound of cannon closer than ever and not a single soldier in sight. Villagers were already walking down the road, satchels on their backs. To where, Julitte could only guess. Away.

The earth beneath Julitte's feet seemed to tremble in a fear that matched her own. She clutched Charles's hand, who seemed intent on the same path others took: the only road out of town. Pepin and Dowan were on either side, along with another man they'd called Seymour.

But she pulled back. "I must see to Uncle Guy."

"Julitte—"

Dowan touched her arm, a grim set to his face. He shook his head and spoke English so fast Charles had to translate. "He's seen everything from an attic window where he was hiding—everything that went on in the streets of this village for over a year now. He saw what happened that day, too. Guy revived from the blow to his head, but when a soldier bent over him to see if he breathed, Guy reached for the soldier's pistol, and there was a scuffle. Another soldier shot your uncle, Julitte. He's dead."

Julitte's gaze flew back to the spot she'd seen him last, but there wasn't a trace left behind—of him or even a struggle. She wanted to find him, his body, to see for herself, but knew there wasn't time. Another death . . . another one she loved, but no light to let her know of his passing.

She caught sight of Ori, standing in the distance. "Was it . . . Hauptmann Basedow?" Julitte asked Dowan. "His gun? The man who gave the orders?" For some reason it made a difference.

Dowan shook his head.

Julitte looked at Ori again. She'd stopped at the last house on the edge of town.

"Will you come with us?" Julitte called, even as the pace Charles set barely slowed.

Ori shook her head. "He'll come back to me, and I'll be here."

Julitte peered over her friend's shoulder. Half the town was scattering under the peal of cannons, some leaving but others running to the church or into their homes, no doubt to their own cellars.

Just then the whistle of firepower sounded closer than ever and Charles pulled Julitte close. One—two—each boom exploding inside her heart. Then, ears ringing, insides quaking, she let Charles pull her forward again. All Julitte could do was look back at Ori, who stood as if oblivious to the clamor around her.

And behind her, the town hall smoldered. The one building that had never belonged in this remote, humble town now appeared a better fit. The roof had caved in on itself under the crash of cannon-fire, rendering it somewhat less than a one-story building.

"Ori," Charles called.

She turned toward them, a hand over her brow to shield her face from the sun.

"If you want to protect yourself, set the town hall ablaze. If your Hauptmann returns, tell him the prisoners are all dead."

Then he turned, taking Julitte's hand back in his. "They'll believe it for a little while, anyway."

Julitte nodded, eagerly matching the quick pace Charles set. "For Ori's sake, I hope she never sees that Hauptmann again."

41

Julitte watched as below her countless people roamed in the shadow of a basilica in the market square of Maastricht in the Netherlands. Everyone free to do as they pleased, choosing items of more variety than she'd seen in almost two years: food, scarves, lace—even something as unnecessary but lovely as flowers. And not a German soldier in sight.

Only hours before she'd been brought here by vegetable cart, sitting beside a woman who smuggled as many civilians out of occupied Belgium as her route allowed. That wasn't the first cart Julitte had sat upon between here and Northern France, with the help of French and Belgians brave or desperate enough to do what they could for the money the Allies paid. In Cambrai, Charles had swapped his newer, sturdy clothes for those of a beggar, torn and tattered. Those boots the Germans had noticed he traded for a pair barely intact around holes on top and bottom. He became not only a pauper but a crippled one at that, a patch over one eye and legs that needed the help of a walking stick to hold him upright when he made to step down from the wagon they were given.

Then, with that battered wagon full of goods for sale—obvious castoffs few would take note of—and Pepin, Dowan, and Seymour concealed underneath, Charles had played the head of an impoverished family who'd lost their home to the war. Julitte his wife; her sister Claudette; their mother Marie-Hermine and brother Benoit, grandfather Gustave. Few of the sentries studied their papers beyond the seal. They were of no interest, although Charles, even with the acquired disguise, had raised a brow or two.

At Liège, where they'd waited a day to arrange passage out, Charles had taken them to a woman who was known at the border to barter in trade between there and free Maastricht. She'd suggested for them to split into groups, even allowing for some to be smuggled.

But the old feud erupted once again when Charles insisted he take Julitte out first, and so the woman had agreed to take them all, so long as the men, even Benoit and Gustave, be hidden in the bowels of the false bottom beneath the vegetables. Including Charles.

Despite Julitte having to sit on her hands to keep secret her trembling, the revised papers Charles provided succeeded yet again. Four women and a vegetable cart were waved through at the border as easy as that.

After their arrival in Maastricht, Charles met his contact, who arranged accommodations and care for his unexpected companions. Then, allowing only a swift farewell, he'd whisked Julitte to a different hotel altogether, here on the square.

She'd barely had a moment to look back at the men who had hidden with Charles and at the de Colvilles she'd known most of her life. Their freedom was intact, their lives their own and no longer the property of the German Imperial Army. Perhaps the feud no longer mattered outside of Briecourt; at that moment of good-bye, few would guess their smiles were anything but those of good friends.

To her surprise a variety of fine clothing awaited her at the hotel on the square. Charles said she had only two hours to freshen up before his British contact would come for them. After that, they would start their journey to Folkestone, where they would meet Narcisse and Titos Tsakolos. The man who would take Julitte to

Greece. No time for rest, he told her, because they were already days late. Julitte didn't complain; she was eager to go to Narcisse at last.

Julitte had taken a warm bath with water that came right out of the wall. She'd flushed the toilet three times just because it was there. Then she'd dressed slowly, in silk stockings and underthings and a petticoat so fine and thin it barely existed, topped by a dress with a skirt that hung above her ankles and completed with a jacket of powdery blue. The skirt wrinkled when she sat and clung to her when she walked, but the blended silk shimmered ever so slightly when she'd neared the light streaming in from the window. It was a shame it was too short.

She had only to hook the laces on her new shoes and slide her hands into new gloves. Her hands, so calloused and rough, didn't belong next to such luxurious material. And the shoes were stiff, made of shiny black leather rather than wood carved to match the shape of her feet. Not nearly as easy to slip in and out of, and she couldn't feel the air the way her clogs had allowed. The laces, impossible.

And she was afraid of the hat that matched her jacket; it had long pins sticking out of it and she had no idea how to wear such a thing.

A tap at the door drew her attention from the window, and in her haste to answer, she fell out of one of her unlaced shoes. Picking it up, she called, "Come in."

There was Charles, as fresh as she, wearing clothes that exceeded in splendor those she'd first seen him in under M. Mantoux's tree. Gray linen trousers and high-collared jacket over a vest of somewhat deeper blue than Julitte herself wore. His shoes were every bit as shiny as her own, though they had an inset of canvas at the sides, and beneath his arm he held a straw hat trimmed with a ribbon that matched his vest.

But he did not go farther than the threshold. He stood there, staring at Julitte.

"You're lovely." His voice seemed strained, as if the bow tie he wore was tied too tight.

She held out one ankle, clearly visible beyond the hem of her skirt. "Who can button such laces? Not I."

At last he stepped into the room, keeping the door ajar. "Is there no hook?"

"Hook?"

"Yes. For the laces."

"Do you mean those nasty-looking things sticking out of the hat? I was afraid to touch them."

He laughed, going to the table at the end of the settee. "Here. Sit."

She did so and he knelt before her. One of his hands held her ankle, and though he did so gently, she nearly started at the contact. No one had ever touched her there before.

In a moment the shoes were laced, having been secured with a hook she hadn't even noticed.

"The pins," he said as he stood and reached for the hat, "are to hold this in place." He pulled her to her feet.

She twisted her face. "But how? Without pain?"

He raised one hand above his head. "They go into your hair. . . ." Now he swirled a finger around once. "If you pile your hair up on top of your head, you can stick the pins into that. I can ask someone to come and help, if you like."

"Must I wear it at all? It seems so silly." She looked down at what she wore, holding out her skirt. "And this is lovely. But you can see it's too short."

He laughed again, pulling her close. "It's the way women wear dresses in the city now, since the start of the war. Just one of many things you'll have to get used to, Julitte, if your grandfather has any impact on your life. Or me."

She glanced over his shoulder toward the little closet that housed the bath. "Not all of it unpleasant, I suppose. I won't miss going to the well for water." She didn't mention her other wonderful discovery, about the toilet.

"We're to meet my British contact downstairs now. Are you ready?"

She nodded and would have led the way to the door, but Charles withdrew a piece of paper that had been hidden by the shadow of his hat.

"What is that?" Julitte asked.

"A telegram from my sister. Looks as if it's been transferred from one office to another in search of me." From the grim set of Charles's mouth, whatever words the telegram held could hardly be happy. "She's asking for my help—to come here, of all places."

"To the Netherlands?"

"No. She wants to go home—to our home, in Belgium."

Julitte put a hand on his forearm. "You'll tell her to stay in America, though, won't you? She mustn't know how it is over here."

"Yes. . . . Yes, I'll send word for her to stay put." But he raised troubled eyes to Julitte. "The problem is, once Isa has it in her mind to do something, she never listens to anyone."

Julitte pressed her fingers to his arm, surprised at her own concern for someone she didn't yet know. "You must *make* her listen, Charles."

She gave him a hopeful smile. Charles could be very persuasive; all he had to do was tell his sister everything they'd been through.

He nodded, and though his smile was slow to return, there it was emerging again. Throwing aside the hat and the telegram, he pulled her back into his embrace. "This may be the last time we're alone for quite some time, Julitte, with you on your way to Greece soon. So with your permission, I'll kiss you now."

She'd felt like frowning about leaving for Greece until hearing those last few words. "Consider permission granted."

Then his lips were on hers, smooth and warm and wonderful.

Afterward he studied her face. "You started to frown just a moment ago. Why?"

She tried to smile now but knew the effort hardly produced results.

"Don't you want to go to Greece?"

"Part of me wants to go, since my grandfather wants to meet me. I'd like to meet him, too. But none of me wants to leave you behind."

His brows gathered. "I would go with you. Except . . . the war . . . When I thought I'd have to face a firing squad, all I could think was that I wanted more time to make a difference. Major Parker is bound to trust my help now. This war could go on much longer. How could I not want to do something to help, knowing people who once were free aren't anymore?"

She looked away, unable to make eye contact. Working for the war effort, no matter in what capacity, seemed far too dangerous to Julitte. Hadn't he already made the difference he'd hoped?

"I suppose it's best that we don't marry too quickly anyway," he said slowly. "We should take time to get to know one another. Although . . ."

"Yes?"

He took both her hands in his. "I feel as though I know you better than anyone I've ever known. Maybe what we went through took the place of years of acquaintanceship."

She nodded, her heart skittering.

"Then perhaps you might consider going to Greece as my fiancée. And while you're gone, while I wait for you, we can expect to be married when you return."

She knew her hands would be shaking were it not for the steadiness of his. If he thought she might need time to consider such a proposal, he was wrong. "Yes, Charles, I'll marry you."

His arms slipped around her waist. "As easy as that? And what will help Narcisse give his permission for us to marry? I had the impression he wants to be more protective of you."

"Perhaps you should ask me."

Julitte looked with surprise to the open doorway. And there stood one of the men she'd prayed over, missed, and longed for since the day he'd left just before the outbreak of war.

"Papa!"

This time her shoes held secure as she hastened to the doorway and was swept up into his arms. He kissed her cheek soundly, then held her at arm's length. "Well, you're too thin, but that can be changed. You're all right, child?"

She threw herself at him again. "Yes, Papa. Thanks to Charles."

With an arm still around Julitte, Narcisse held out a hand to Charles, who approached.

"We expected to see you in Folkestone, sir," Charles said.

Narcisse put a momentarily fierce look on his face, which, combined with the strength he always exuded, might have worked to frighten a child if not for the twinkle in his eye. "Yes, I supposed you didn't expect me just now. It is fortunate for you, young man, that you left the door to this suite open."

"I believe you must have heard my intentions are honorable."

Narcisse patted his shoulder. "That I did. And I'm grateful to you for bringing my Julitte out. But I'm glad I won't have to give her away until after we've spent some time together."

"I have much to tell you, Papa, and much to ask. Have you heard from Pierre?"

He nodded. "Still fighting, but recently assigned to a communications tent well behind the lines, thanks be to God for that. And what of those left in Briecourt?"

She told him about Father Barnabé and Didi and Uncle Guy, Narcisse's brother. "I'm sorry, Papa. He awaits us in heaven now."

Narcisse dabbed a tear on her cheek. "Yes, and you no doubt saw a glimpse of that yourself."

Now more tears replaced the one he'd wiped away. "Oh, Papa, I didn't! Only for Father Barnabé. I don't doubt they're there, but . . . perhaps there is too much death. I thought God had turned from me, yet He mustn't have because He sent Charles to bring me to safety. But I no longer see what I once saw."

Narcisse drew her back. "He's withdrawn nothing, child. Nothing can separate us from His love. Neither death nor life nor angels nor spirits, nothing now or in the future, below or in the whole world could ever separate us from His love. Remember that? Be grateful for the sight He gave you, for how long it lasted. The Bible says secret things belong to the Lord, but the things He reveals to us belong to us forever."

"I know you're right, Papa. I won't ever forget the gift He gave."

Narcisse's gaze went from Julitte to Charles before settling again on Julitte. "He was with you when you needed Him most, but never doubt there is another test ahead of you. It was easy to lean on God when you had nothing else. But now, with a new life ahead, perhaps God will choose another way to keep you near."

Julitte nodded, and her gaze took in Charles now. "I've learned my doubts don't keep God from working."

Charles took one of her hands. "We can only be stronger together, with your faith and mine. When one of us doubts, the other can help."

A tap sounded at the door.

"Pardon me, sir."

Julitte looked to see a British soldier at the door, and for a moment her heart thudded in her breast. This would take some getting used to, seeing soldiers who weren't the enemy.

"It's time to meet the train, if we expect to catch the ferry to Folkestone tonight."

Charles retrieved her hat and carried it with his; then they followed the soldier from the suite. Julitte realized it might not be too difficult to grow accustomed to a soldier nearby, one like this one who fought for freedom.

Julitte looped her arm with Charles. She was grateful to him most of all, even as she mourned those who'd died without the freedom he and this soldier wanted to fight for. She mourned those whose lives had been cut short, whose eternities had begun far too early. She didn't doubt eternity, even though God had removed His gift of seeing a glimpse into heaven. With or without that gift there would be more tests ahead.

But she had a very long memory.

Author's Note

On July 1, 1916, the Battle of the Somme officially began, after over a week of increased bombardment. This "Big Push," as the first Battle of the Somme was called, cost between fifty-seven and sixty thousand British soldiers dead or wounded *on the very first day*. By the time this particular battle was called off that autumn, the casualties were staggering—400,000 British, 200,000 French, 500,000 German. Gains on the Allied side for such a phenomenal loss were limited to twelve kilometers of land (about seven and a half miles).

In February of 1917 the Germans made a strategic withdrawal to consolidate their forces behind newly completed and strengthened trenches called by the Allies the Hindenburg Line.

In an effort to make the land between the old and new line impossible for the Allies to traverse, the Germans systematically burned villages, felled trees, poisoned wells, and scattered mines. Towns like Briecourt would have been entirely demolished. Any remaining citizens (like Ori) would have been allowed to take what they could carry then sent to refugee camps like those in the Ardennes Forest.

Greece officially joined the Allies in the First World War on June 29, 1917, for reasons far more complicated than intimated within the pages of this work of fiction.

Even after Greece's entry, the war raged on for another year, an armistice not signed until the eleventh hour of the eleventh day of the eleventh month in 1918.

About the Author

Maureen Lang has always had a passion for writing. She wrote her first novel longhand around the age of ten, put the pages into a notebook she had covered with soft deerskin (nothing but the best!), then passed it around the neighborhood to rave reviews. It was so much fun she's been writing ever since.

Eventually Maureen became the recipient of a Golden Heart Award from Romance Writers of America, followed by the publication of three secular romance novels. Life took some turns after that, and she gave up writing for fifteen years, until the Lord claimed her to write for Him. Soon she won a Noble Theme Award from American Christian Fiction Writers and has since published several novels, including *Pieces of Silver* (a 2007 Christy Award finalist), *Remember Me*, *The Oak Leaves*, *On Sparrow Hill*, and *My Sister Dilly*.

Maureen lives in the Midwest with her husband, her two sons, and their much-loved dog, Susie. Visit her Web site at www.maureenlang.com.

Discussion Questions

1. The villagers of Briecourt are separated by a long-standing feud, the origin of which no one recalls. Have you known anyone who held a grudge against someone for so long that they can't recall what broke the relationship?

2. When Julitte is unable to help Victor, she feels as though she's failed. She seems angry with God for not giving her a gift that would benefit others. Have you ever felt dissatisfied with the gifts God has given you?

3. Both Ori and Julitte long to get married, but they handle the pursuit of that goal in different ways. What factor do you think played the biggest role in the way each woman allowed herself to fall in love?

4. Though Julitte and Ori have a strong friendship at the beginning of the story, Ori's actions—specifically her relationship with Hauptmann Basedow—build a barrier between the two. How did you feel about the way Julitte handled this? Have you ever witnessed a friend make the wrong decisions? What advice would you have given Julitte?

5. How did you see Charles change as the story progressed? What made him go from self-admitted cowardice during the battle he witnesses to being able to jump from an airplane (albeit terrified to do so)?

6. Toward the end of the story Julitte no longer receives her visions of heaven. Like any relationship, things between her and God seem to change. Do you think this was a

change for better or for worse? How have you seen your own relationship with God change over time?

7. The villagers were eager to attribute a miracle to Julitte when her brother survived the near-drowning. What about her made it so easy for them to label her a miracle worker?

8. Misplaced faith is one of the themes throughout this story. The villagers placed their faith in Julitte instead of God as the author of miracles. Ori placed her faith in a man's love to make her happy. And before Charles was tested by this war, he'd placed his faith in himself. How often do you see yourself or others misplacing your faith? What do you place it on instead of God?

9. Read 2 Kings chapter 7. In this passage, you'll notice the starving lepers were overjoyed to find bread left behind by the soldiers who had deserted the encampment. Has anything in your life reminded you of how God worked in the lives of the people in the Bible? Do you ever see a parallel in Biblical stories to things that happen today?

10. Julitte doesn't chafe against the poverty of her circumstances, but she does hint at being familiar with the allure of wealth. However, her upbringing and the examples set by both biological and adoptive parents suggested humble lifestyles were the better choice. Do you believe, as Narcisse reminded Julitte, that it's easier for a camel to go through the eye of a needle than for a rich man to be saved? Why or why not? What struggles do you think Julitte will face because of the life of wealth that's offered to her through both Charles and her biological grandfather?

Turn the page
for an exciting preview
of book 2 in
THE GREAT WAR
series.

Travel to Belgium, where an
underground newspaper
keeps the hopes and spirit
of the occupied country alive
but puts the lives
of those who run it at risk.

Available summer 2010.

1

On the Border of Holland and Belgium

"Oh, God," Isa Lassone whispered, "you've seen me this far; don't let me start doubting now."

A few cool raindrops fell on her upturned face, blending with warm tears on her cheeks. Where was her new guide? The one on the Holland side of the border had said she needed only to crawl through a culvert, worm her way ten feet to the left, and there he would be.

Crickets chirped and from behind her she heard water trickle from that foul-smelling culvert through which she'd just crept. Some of the smell clung to her shoes and the bottom of her peasant's skirt, but it was Belgian dirt, so she wouldn't complain. Yet despite her certainty that she was exactly where God wanted her, she wished at the moment she were away from here, anywhere but here so long as she was still inside Belgium. She wished she were already with Genny . . . and Edward, especially Edward.

But the prayer and the contents of her satchel reminded her why she was here. For over a year she had plotted, saved, worked, and defied everyone she knew—all to get to this very spot.

Then she heard it. The sound was newly familiar, taught to her by the priest who'd arranged this meeting despite her brother Charles's plea otherwise. The priest had whistled the chirrup himself just yesterday, until it was a cadence Isa could pick out among others.

She leaned upward to see better, still hidden in the tall grass of the meadow. The misty rain splashed on her cheeks, joining the oil and ash she'd been given to camouflage the whiteness of her skin. She must have grown used to its unpleasant odor, coupled with the scent she had picked up in the culvert, because now she could smell only grass. Twigs and dirt clung to her hands and clothes, but she didn't care. She, Isabelle Lassone, who'd once bedecked the cover of the Ladies Home Journal with a group of other young American socialites, now crawled like a snake across a remote, soggy Belgian field. She must reach that sound.

Uneven ground and the things she'd hidden under her cloak and skirt slowed her crawl. Her wrist twisted inside a hole—no doubt the entrance to a home belonging to one creature or another, and she nearly fell flat before scuttling onward again. Nothing would stop her now, not after all she'd been through to get this far, all she'd given up. She doubted Charles would ever speak to her again, after sneaking away from him just yesterday.

Then her frantic belly-dash ended. The tall grass hid everything but the path she left behind, and suddenly she hit something—or rather, someone.

"Say nothing." She barely heard the words from the broad-shouldered figure. He was dressed as she was, in simple, dark clothing, to escape notice of the few guards left to enforce the job their wire fencing now did along the border. Isa could not see his face, and his hair was covered with a cap and his skin, like hers, was smeared with ash.

Keeping low, the guide scurried ahead, and Isa had all she could do to follow. Sweat seeped from pores suffocated beneath her clothes. She ignored rocks that poked her hands and knees, spiky grass slapping her face, blinked away dust kicked up from beneath the toe of her guide's boot.

He stopped without warning and her face nearly hit his sole.

In the darkness she could not see far ahead, but they'd come to a fence of barbed wire. A moment ago she had been sweating, but now she shivered. The electric fences her brother Charles had warned her about, where bodies were sometimes trapped, left for the vultures and as a grim warning to those like her. She didn't want to look but forced herself to scan the horizon. No bodies. Thank God.

The route she'd taken was supposed to have spared her of this. The priest back in Holland had taken her to a tunnel, dug out of the backside of a cave whose mouth led to the awful culvert on the Belgian side. Wires, she'd been told, were above that. Where was this guide taking her? Back to Holland?

She pulled on his ankle but he raised a hand to silence whatever words she might have uttered. Then he reached for something— a canvas—hidden by the grass, pulling it away from what lay beneath. Isa could barely make out the round shape of a motor tire. Her guide took a cloth from under his shirt and slipped it beneath the fence where the ground dipped. With deft quickness he hoisted the wire up with the tire, only rubber touching the fencing. Then he motioned for her to go through.

Isa hesitated. Not long ago she would have thought anyone crazy for telling tales of the things she'd found herself doing lately, things she'd nearly convinced Charles she was capable of handling against his urgent warnings.

She took the precious satchel from her back and tossed it through the opening. She followed with ease, even plump as she was with more secret goods padded beneath her rough clothing. Her guide's touch startled her. Looking back, she saw him hold the bottom of her soiled cotton skirt so it would touch nothing but rubber. Then he passed too, and strapped the tire along with its canvas to his back while she slipped her satchel in place.

Clouds that had barely sprinkled earlier suddenly released a steady rainfall. Isa's heart soared heavenward even as countless droplets fell to earth. She'd made it! Surely it would've been impossible to pass those electrified wires in this sort of rain, but God had held it off. It was just one more blessing, one more confirmation she'd done the right thing, no matter what Charles and everyone else thought.

Soon her guide stopped again and pulled the tire from his back, stuffing it deep within the cover of a bush. Then he continued, still pulling himself along like a frog with two broken legs. And Isa followed even as the journey went on farther and took longer than she'd expected.

She heard no sound other than her own uneven breathing. She should welcome the silence—surely it was better than the sound of marching, booted feet or a motorcar beaming its headlamps over the terrain. Despite the triumph she'd felt just moments ago, her fear returned. They hid with good reason. Somewhere out there German soldiers carried guns they wouldn't hesitate to use—for no better reason than being caught on the border. Where citizens were verboten.

She hadn't realized she would have to crawl through half of Belgium to get to the nearest village. Tension and fatigue soon stiffened her limbs, adding weight to the packets she carried.

"Let me have your satchel," her guide whispered from over his shoulder.

She pulled it from her back, keeping her eye on it all the while. He flipped it open. She knew what he would find: a single change of clothes, a purse with exactly fifty francs inside, a small loaf of bread — dark bread, the kind she was told they made this side of the blockades, plus two books: her small New Testament and a journal. And her flute. Most especially, her flute.

"What is this book?" His voice was hushed, raspy.

"A Bible."

"No, the other one. What is it?"

"It's mine."

"What is it doing in this satchel?"

"I—I wanted to bring it."

"What have you written in here?"

Instantly heated with embarrassment, she was glad for the cover of darkness and that he couldn't see her face any better than she could see his. No one would ever read the words written in that journal, not even the person to whom she'd written each and every word. Well, perhaps one day he might, if they grew old together. If he let her grow old at his side.

"It's personal."

He thrust it toward her. "Get rid of it."

"I will not!"

"Then I will." He bolted from belly to knees, hurling the little book far beyond reach. It was gone in the night, lost in the deep grassland from which they'd just emerged.

Isa rose to her knees, the object of her gaze vanished in the blackness. The pages that securely held each intimate thought, each dream, each hope for her future—gone. Every page a visit with the man she loved, now forever lost.

"How dare you! You had no right."

He ignored her as he resumed the scuttle forward.

Fury pushed Isa now. That journal had meant more to her than this dark figure could know. When at last he stopped and stood beneath the low branches of a forest to brush the wild heath off his clothes, Isa circled to confront him.

At that moment the clouds parted enough to allow a bit of moonlight to illuminate them. And there he was, in all the glorious detail—the black brows, perfectly straight nose, square jaw and the eyes that with a single look could toss aside every sensible thought she might have. The very man about whom—and to whom—that journal had been written.

Her heart skipped wildly, rage abandoned. "Edward!"

More great fiction from
Maureen Lang

A legacy she never expected.
A love that knows no bounds.

A legacy she never wanted.
A love she'd only hoped for.

Two sisters. One committed the unthinkable.
The other will never forgive herself.

Engaging the mind.
Renewing the soul.

www.maureenlang.com

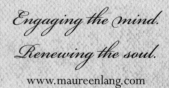